FINDING HOPE

FINDING SERIES #5

SLOANE KENNEDY

CONTENTS

Copyright — v
Finding Hope — vii
Trademark Acknowledgements — ix
Acknowledgments — xi
Series Reading Order — xiii
Series Crossover Chart — xvii
Trigger Warning — xix

Prologue — 1
Chapter 1 — 15
Chapter 2 — 28
Chapter 3 — 38
Chapter 4 — 47
Chapter 5 — 63
Chapter 6 — 75
Chapter 7 — 86
Chapter 8 — 99
Chapter 9 — 109
Chapter 10 — 114
Chapter 11 — 123
Chapter 12 — 131
Chapter 13 — 145
Chapter 14 — 161
Chapter 15 — 170
Chapter 16 — 178
Chapter 17 — 188
Chapter 18 — 203
Chapter 19 — 218
Chapter 20 — 226
Chapter 21 — 233
Chapter 22 — 238

Chapter 23	245
Chapter 24	255
Epilogue	262
Sneak Peek	273
Prologue	275
About the Author	283
Also by Sloane Kennedy	285

Finding Hope is a work of fiction. Names, characters, businesses, places, events and incidents are either the products of the author's imagination or used in a fictitious manner. Any resemblance to actual persons, living or dead, or actual events is purely coincidental.

Copyright © 2017 by Sloane Kennedy

Published in the United States by Sloane Kennedy
All rights reserved. This book or any portion thereof may not be reproduced or used in any manner whatsoever without the express written permission of the publisher except for the use of brief quotations in a book review.

Cover Images: © Wander Aguiar

Cover Design: © Jay Aheer, Simply Defined Art

ISBN-13:
978-1544058375

ISBN-10:
1544058373

FINDING HOPE

Sloane Kennedy

TRADEMARK ACKNOWLEDGEMENTS

The author acknowledges the trademarked status and trademark owners of the following trademarks mentioned in this work of fiction:

Grindr
Mack Trucks
Matchbox

ACKNOWLEDGMENTS

A big thank you to my amazing beta readers who continue to help me make sure my books are the best they can be.

Claudia and Kylee, not sure what I'd do without you and hopefully I'll never have to find out!!

SERIES READING ORDER

All of my series cross over with one another so I've provided a couple of recommended reading orders for you. If you want to start with the Protectors books, use the first list. If you want to follow the books according to timing, use the second list. Note that you can skip any of the books (including M/F) as each was written to be a standalone story.

Note that some books may not be readily available on all retail sites

Recommended Reading Order (Use this list if you want to start with "The Protectors" series)
1. Absolution (m/m/m) (The Protectors, #1)
2. Salvation (m/m) (The Protectors, #2)
3. Retribution (m/m) (The Protectors, #3)
4. Gabriel's Rule (m/f) (The Escort Series, #1)
5. Shane's Fall (m/f) (The Escort Series, #2)
6. Logan's Need (m/m) (The Escort Series, #3)
7. Finding Home (m/m/m) (Finding Series, #1)
8. Finding Trust (m/m) (Finding Series, #2)

9. Loving Vin (m/f) (Barretti Security Series, #1)
10. Redeeming Rafe (m/m) (Barretti Security Series, #2)
11. Saving Ren (m/m/m) (Barretti Security Series, #3)
12. Freeing Zane (m/m) (Barretti Security Series, #4)
13. Finding Peace (m/m) (Finding Series, #3)
14. Finding Forgiveness (m/m) (Finding Series, #4)
15. Forsaken (m/m) (The Protectors, #4)
16. Vengeance (m/m/m) (The Protectors, #5)
17. A Protectors Family Christmas (The Protectors, #5.5)
18. Atonement (m/m) (The Protectors, #6)
19. Revelation (m/m) (The Protectors, #7)
20. Redemption (m/m) (The Protectors, #8)
21. Finding Hope (m/m/m) (Finding Series, #5)
22. Defiance (m/m) (The Protectors #9)

Recommended Reading Order *(Use this list if you want to follow according to timing)*
1. Gabriel's Rule (m/f) (The Escort Series, #1)
2. Shane's Fall (m/f) (The Escort Series, #2)
3. Logan's Need (m/m) (The Escort Series, #3)
4. Finding Home (m/m/m) (Finding Series, #1)
5. Finding Trust (m/m) (Finding Series, #2)
6. Loving Vin (m/f) (Barretti Security Series, #1)
7. Redeeming Rafe (m/m) (Barretti Security Series, #2)
8. Saving Ren (m/m/m) (Barretti Security Series, #3)
9. Freeing Zane (m/m) (Barretti Security Series, #4)
10. Finding Peace (m/m) (Finding Series, #3)
11. Finding Forgiveness (m/m) (Finding Series, #4)
12. Absolution (m/m/m) (The Protectors, #1)
13. Salvation (m/m) (The Protectors, #2)
14. Retribution (m/m) (The Protectors, #3)
15. Forsaken (m/m) (The Protectors, #4)
16. Vengeance (m/m/m) (The Protectors, #5)
17. A Protectors Family Christmas (The Protectors, #5.5)

18. Atonement (m/m) (The Protectors, #6)
19. Revelation (m/m) (The Protectors, #7)
20. Redemption (m/m) (The Protectors, #8)
21. Finding Hope (m/m/m) (Finding Series, #5)
22. Defiance (m/m) (The Protectors #9)

SERIES CROSSOVER CHART

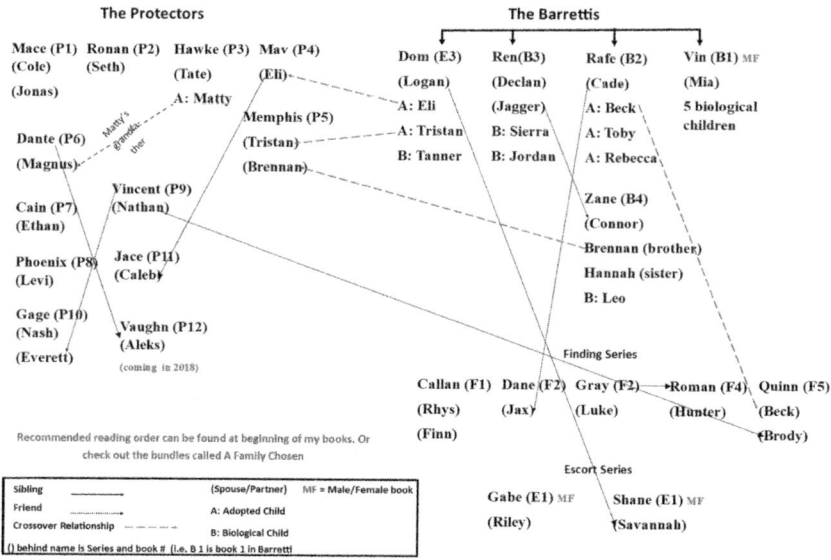

TRIGGER WARNING

Listed below are the trigger warnings for this book. Reading them may cause spoilers:

This book contains references to suicide as well as sexual abuse of a child and rape.

PROLOGUE

QUINN

The kid definitely didn't belong here. No question about it.

My eyes tracked his every move as he shifted past a couple of big bears who'd been loitering near the front door in hopes of snagging the freshest meat. And the kid was as close to fresh meat as you could find in a club like *The Blue Door*. Not only was there absolutely no chance he was over twenty-one, he barely looked like he was even legal. But he was trying his damnedest to play the game as he calmly made his way to the bar, ignoring the countless eyes on him.

He settled on one of two empty barstools and pushed his shaggy brown hair out of his face as the bartender sauntered to a stop in front of him. Davey eyed the kid and I could tell he was on the same page as me when it came to the kid's age. But that didn't stop him from sliding a shot glass in front of him and filling it with what looked like the cheapest vodka Davey kept on the shelf. Only one of the barstools around the kid was empty, but I knew it wouldn't last long. And sure enough, within a matter of seconds, a tall, scrawny-looking guy with jeans that might as well have been painted on settled on the stool, only to skulk off when one of the bears from the front door ambled over and motioned to him with a jerk of his thick neck.

Once the guy was gone, the bear leaned against the bar so his beefy body was practically brushing up against the kid's.

For his part, the kid seemed unconcerned as he glanced at his new neighbor just before he downed the shot. He tapped the bar and Davey was right there to refill the glass. He started putting the bottle away when the bear grabbed it and took a swig as he watched the young man swallow his second shot. I watched as the bear filled the shot glass yet again, but I didn't see if the kid drank it because I felt a hand stroking up my arm. I glanced to my right and saw a skinny little blond number sizing me up. I was standing near the doorway leading to the back of the club, a clear signal of what I was looking for. I'd already been there for a few minutes and been approached by no fewer than three guys, but none had been my type and I'd dismissed them without a second thought. I didn't come to the city that often to scratch my itch, so I was damn well going to make it worth my time and shop around for exactly what I wanted.

Like the cute little blond twink who had, by now, sidled up to me. I ignored the need to shift my gaze back to the bar to check on the kid and focused on the small hand that was sliding over my abdomen.

"Never seen you here before," the guy said, his voice a well-practiced purr.

I didn't respond because there was no point. I hadn't come here for conversation and I certainly wasn't going to entertain the guy with useless foreplay.

I was about to tell him to follow me when I felt a shiver snake down my spine. I lifted my eyes and saw the kid's gaze on me. The bear was still with him, but he seemed irritated that he hadn't managed to hold the kid's attention.

Fuck, he was gorgeous. Even from across the room, I could make out his lithe body and striking features. I couldn't see the color of his eyes, but they sat beneath full, perfectly shaped eyebrows that peeked out from the guy's hair. A slight five o'clock shadow covered a square jawline, but it was his lips that were holding my attention…and making my cock finally wake up. They were full and wide with the bottom one just a little plumper than the top.

I heard the twink next to me hum appreciatively and I had no doubt it was because he could see my cock thickening in my jeans. Too bad it had nothing to do with him and everything to do with the young man who was watching me hungrily from the bar.

Too fucking young, I reminded myself even as I fought the urge to shove the hand away that was now pressing against my crotch, grazing my hardness. I needed to just grab the little shit and take him in back and fuck him until it was his face I finally saw, not the jailbait still watching me from the bar. I saw the bear lean down to say something to him, but if the kid heard him, he didn't acknowledge it. Instead, he rose to his feet and started towards me, his gaze holding mine.

The rest of the occupants of the club disappeared as he reached me and I finally got to see that his eyes were a stunning combination of green and gold. He was shorter than me by a few inches and I knew that his age wasn't the only thing about him that didn't fit in the place. He was a city boy through and through, but not a city like Missoula. Because in Missoula, the city kids still looked like the country bumpkins they were. This kid belonged in a big place like New York with his skinny jeans, designer shirt, fancy sneakers that probably cost more than my piece of shit truck and a leather jacket that hung carelessly from his narrow shoulders.

The kid didn't speak when he reached me and I waited to see what he'd do. My twink was still feeling me up, but the kid didn't seem bothered by that fact. His eyes traveled the length of my body and I knew he liked what he saw. I suspected I fit the bill in terms of what he'd been hoping to find in an off-the-wall gay club in Montana. I hadn't bothered changing from my work clothes before heading to Missoula, so I more than likely had horse shit on my boots and my hair was probably still showing the circular ring from where my cowboy hat had been pressing it down all day, despite my efforts to get rid of it by running my fingers through my dark locks. The only reason I hadn't kept the hat on was because I liked being able to see the guy I was fucking and hadn't wanted to worry about it shifting on my head and obscuring my view.

Several long moments passed before the kid reached for my hand...the one that wasn't holding my beer. He began to pull me towards the entrance leading to the back of the club, but I tugged him to a stop, not giving too much thought to how he knew where to go for all the real action.

"How old are you?" I asked, my voice sounding heavy with lust. God, he was beautiful. I could already feel my dick sinking into his tight heat.

No...no fucking way. I didn't fuck kids. At thirty-three, I knew better. Even knowing we were all in this shithole on a Thursday night for one reason, I still made sure there wasn't more than a ten-year age gap between me and whatever toy I chose to play with for the night. The twink, who was now hanging onto my other arm, was a safer bet.

Only problem was, I'd already forgotten what he looked like and I certainly didn't care what sounds he'd make as I fucked into him.

"You're not gonna be looking at my face when you're fucking me, so what does it matter?"

I knew he'd meant the comment as a come-on, but the way he said it wasn't quite right. I willed myself to release his hand even as the electricity fired up the limb, through my body and centered all its energy in my rock-hard dick.

"Come on, cowboy," the twink murmured as his hand closed over my cock and gripped me hard. "I'll take care of you."

I ignored him as I watched the kid's reaction which was pretty easy to read.

He didn't give a shit. He was looking for a body...nothing more.

Which meant he was in exactly the right place.

He sighed and dropped my hand and turned away from me and I saw the bear at the bar straighten. Just like that, he was off his chair and heading towards us and my only thought was, *No fucking way*. The kid wanted to get fucked, he'd get fucked. But it wasn't going to be by that fat prick. I snagged his hand and yanked him back towards me when the bear reached us. I thrust my beer at the twink and then swung around and led my new fuck buddy through the doorway leading to the back. Now that the kid's lack of innocence had freed me, I couldn't shake my rabid lust as I searched for the perfect place to lose myself in his tight little body.

"You got a name?" I asked, though I wasn't sure why I cared. I sure as hell wasn't planning on telling him mine.

"The last guy seemed partial to 'Cockslut' but whatever makes you fuck me hardest is fine by me."

The dispassionate way he said it had me pausing, but the young man didn't seem to notice as his eyes fell on the various couples we passed who hadn't made it to any of the private rooms. I was ready to call the whole thing off when he tugged me to a stop. I saw his eyes skim over two big guys working a third over between them. He was being fucked from behind by one guy while a massive cock was jammed down his throat. The sight in itself was erotic enough, but the mewls of pleasure falling from the guy's mouth as he took it from both ends were enough that the few guys watching the show were going to get off without needing to take a turn. The kid's hand tightened in mine and for the first time, I saw his eyes darken with need. His excitement sent me to a whole new level and I leaned down to run my tongue along the shell of his ear before saying, "Next time... tonight, you're all mine." I knew very well there wouldn't be a next time, but my words had the effect I'd intended. The kid shivered and then he was turning his attention on me. He gave me the slightest of nods and then his mouth parted. I was tempted to lean down and take his mouth, but I remembered where we were and pulled him forward instead.

I'd come here to fuck, not explore. The kid could get that mushy shit from his cute little skater boyfriend or whatever guy hadn't been able to satisfy him enough to keep him from seeking out the likes of me.

I gave up on searching out one of the several curtained-off areas the club had set aside for private encounters and kicked open the door to the bathroom instead. There were two stalls and I could see one was occupied, but the other one wasn't. My eyes lit on two guys in the corner of the bathroom near the sink. I barely noticed the guy on his knees doing the servicing because my eyes locked on the stunning blond getting his cock sucked. His gaze connected with mine before going to the young man behind me. A current of sexual awareness blanketed the air around us and I felt like I was going to come in my pants. The blond wasn't my typical type either, but I knew without a shadow of a doubt that if I'd seen him in the main area of the club, I would have likely been the man sucking him down right now...before I turned him and bent him over the sink.

It was just too fucking much. I herded the young man into the empty stall and slammed the door shut. My body shook with excitement as I finally found myself alone with my prey and I immediately turned him so he was facing the wall. As much as I wanted to enjoy playing with him, I was too lost in a haze of lust. I stripped off his jacket and dropped it on the floor and then jerked his shirt up and tucked it under his armpits, revealing the soft, pale skin of his back. I sighed as I skimmed my hands over him, reveling in the gentle slope of his back. I dropped my mouth to the back of his neck as I pressed my groin against his ass. The young man was quiet, but I could feel the tension running through his lean body.

My conscience kicked in and I forced back my need to rip the rest of his clothes off and plunge into his hot body. "You sure you want this?" I asked softly as I gently teased his nipples.

"No," he said, and then his hands were pushing mine away. I was shocked by the turnaround, but I stepped back immediately. But instead of pulling his shirt down and turning around to leave, he worked his pants loose and pushed them down, along with his underwear. He plastered his hands against the wall and bit out, "What I want is for you to get on with it and fuck me."

God, the kid was an irritating little shit. I should just get the fuck out of there and leave him to whatever asshole that came along. But one look at his tight, muscled ass and I knew I wasn't going anywhere. My mouth filled with saliva at the prospect of exploring his milky white flesh, but I doubted he was interested in anything beyond my dick shoved up his ass. I searched out my wallet for a condom and packet of lube and then jerked my pants down enough to release my dick which was slick with pre-cum.

I rolled the condom on in record time and then opened the lube. I slathered my dick with it and then stepped forward and stuck a well-lubed finger between the globes of his ass. I dropped the packet of lube to the ground and used my free hand to separate his cheeks. His pretty hole greeted me with a flutter of anticipation and I gently brushed the cool liquid over it. The guy deserved the least amount of preparation necessary, but I couldn't force myself to follow through on the silent thought.

I liked a rough fuck as much as the next guy, but I wasn't into hurting my partners.

The young man was rigid as I began toying with his hole. I heard a soft sigh escape him as I massaged him and then he stiffened and speared a sharp look over his shoulder. "Just do it already."

Whatever was left of my patience disintegrated and I pressed forward until my body was pinning his to the wall. "Be careful what you ask for, little boy," I said calmly as I nipped at his ear. I grabbed both his hands and lifted them above his head, pinning them to the wall with one hand, rendering him immobile. I pressed my other hand between the globes of his ass and pushed a finger into him. Once I was in as deep as I could go, I whispered, "You wanna top from the bottom, you're gonna have to go out there and find another cock to fill you up, 'cause it ain't gonna be mine." I pulled my finger out before shoving it back into him, causing him to groan, no doubt from a mix of pain and pleasure. I did it again as I licked a path up the side of his neck. His pulse was going crazy beneath my tongue.

"Now let's try this again," I offered huskily as I pressed a gentle kiss to his jawline. "What is it that you want?"

The young man was dragging in breath after breath, his forehead pressed hard against the wall. "I want you to fuck me...please," he whispered, his voice husky with need now, instead of dispassion.

Finally...a response that worked for me.

"You want my cock inside this beautiful body of yours?" I asked as I slipped another finger into him.

"Yes...yes," he breathed as he shifted his ass back on my still fingers. I didn't move them until he was squirming against me, his ass brushing my cock. When I finally slid them out and pushed them back in, I pressed them against his prostate. He let out a startled cry and then looked over his shoulder at me, his eyes wide and unsure.

What the hell?

I shook my head in disbelief. Certainly someone who was as cock-hungry as he was had been pleasured this way before.

But I could tell by the way he was staring at me with a mix of confusion and need that he had no idea what had just happened.

A cold feeling went through me and I went stock still. "Is this your first time?" I asked.

He shook his head without hesitation.

"Tell me the truth!" I demanded.

"I swear it, it's not," he said quickly even as he clamped his ass down on my fingers. "Please," he begged as he tried to shift his body against mine. I knew what he wanted and gave it to him, watching him with eagle eyes as I pushed against his gland again. He closed his eyes and moaned. I watched in fascination as he pressed his mouth to his upper arm as if trying to stifle the sound.

"No," I said harshly as I released his hands long enough to force his head back. "Let them hear you," I ordered and then I nailed him again. The keening sound that fell from his lips was beautiful and my already-leaking cock demanded more. I pulled my fingers free of his body and began pushing my cock into him. I made sure to slide over his prostate as I buried myself inside him and he gasped.

"Oh God!"

I was dimly aware of the silence in the bathroom and I doubted it was because all the other occupants had miraculously finished what they were doing and left. I, myself, was lost in the sound of the young man's pleasure as I bottomed out inside him.

Never in the nearly ten-some odd years I'd been having sex had I ever been as turned on as I was in this very moment. I'd come in here to fuck this kid, but what was happening was nowhere near fucking. I had no clue how to even start attaching a label to it.

"What's your name?" I demanded as I pulled out of him and pushed back in, hitting his gland again.

A harsh sob escaped his lips as he said, "Beck."

"Beck," I repeated and then I fucked into him again, his unbearably tight ass gripping my cock like it had been made just for me. I muttered his name again as I turned his head and then I did what I'd promised myself I'd never do in a place like this.

I kissed him.

Hard.

Deep.

Completely.

Another warning bell went off in my head when I recognized that he had no clue what to do with the tongue I'd plunged into his mouth.

Fuck, what the hell had I gotten myself into?

I kept sliding my dick in and out of him even as I gentled my invasion of his mouth and let my tongue slide over his. Several long seconds passed before he tentatively kissed me back. When his tongue finally followed mine and slipped between my lips, I let out a guttural groan and began hammering into him. When I had to come up for air, I pressed my forehead against his and began fucking him in earnest, his sleek body meeting my every thrust. I looked down over his shoulder and saw his weeping cock standing tall from a thatch of brown hair. I was about to reach for it when I spied a couple of fingers tapping against one of several glory holes that had been punched into the wall at some point. My mind rebelled at the idea of sharing even a small part of Beck with someone else, but then I remembered his excitement at seeing the three men together in the hallway.

I let my lips slide along Beck's jaw and said, "Look down, baby."

I felt his head drop and heard him gasp when he saw the waiting fingers. "He wants to suck you," I murmured as I slowed my glides. Whereas I'd been eager to nail him and be done with it, now I was reluctant to end the encounter, despite my blinding need to come.

"Do you want that?" I asked as I kissed the corner of his mouth. He turned his head and looked at me, his eyes bright with lust and awe. And God, a look of innocence that had me wrapping my arms around him. His own hand came up to cling to my arms. "Do you want to feel it all tonight, Beck?" I asked.

Beck closed his eyes for the briefest of moments and then nodded. Another harsh sob escaped his lips and I felt an overwhelming protective streak surge through me. How the fuck had I ever thought he knew what he was getting himself into? He was a fucking lamb among wolves.

But I knew it was far too late to stop. I wanted him too badly. And I could tell he was too far gone in his need for anything but release.

"Please," he whispered and then his eyes fell to the waiting fingers again. I maneuvered us until his dick was right next to the hole and then I carefully worked his stiff flesh through the opening. I watched a condom being rolled onto his length and felt him tense in my arms. I didn't even need to be looking down to know when his dick was sucked into a strange, hot, wet mouth because Beck cried out in ecstasy and slammed his hips forward, hitting the wall hard. I lowered one arm to protect his lower body as he began fucking the hole and I used my other arm to brace myself against the wall. I began sliding in and out of Beck again, pushing him forward with each thrust.

"Fuck, yes! Please!" he pleaded as he began to come apart in my arms. I knew he was overwhelmed by the sensations bombarding his body and as much as I wanted to draw out the encounter, I knew he wouldn't last. I began ramming into him hard, striking his prostate on each pass and he wailed, his fingernails digging into my arm. One of his hands came up to cover mine where it was pressed against the wall and I immediately let him link our fingers. I captured his next scream of pleasure with my mouth as his ass clamped down on my dick and he came. He cried out into my mouth over and over again as the orgasm tore through him with crippling force. His knees began to buckle and I had to brace his lower body with my arm to keep him upright as my own climax ripped into me.

I shouted in relief as I came deep inside of him and I couldn't stop myself from continuing to fuck into him as the orgasm crashed through me in cascading waves that seemed to go on forever. When the tension in my body finally began to relax, I slumped against Beck, pressing him against the wall. His breath came out in ragged wisps. I looked down to see the condom being pulled off his flushed dick. I saw a pair of brown work boots beneath the wall of the stall for a brief moment as the stranger on the other side climbed to his feet. I pulled Beck back enough so I could gently pull his dick back into the stall. I didn't miss the fact that there was a pool of semen on the floor beneath the wall.

I kissed the side of Beck's neck as I straightened, taking him with me. His breathing was far from normal, but he kissed me back as best he could. I carefully withdrew from him, grabbing the edge of the condom as I did and then sliding it off my sensitized flesh. I tied it off and tossed it into the garbage can next to the toilet. I pulled my own pants up before working Beck's up and then gently rolling his shirt down. I turned him around so I could button his pants because he was still too dazed to do much.

His lips were flushed and full from my kisses and his cheeks were red from the exertion of what we'd just done. His eyes were glassy as he rode what remained of the natural high. I pulled him forward and kissed him languidly and only separated when there was a knock on the stall door. Beck jumped in my hold. "Just a second," I snapped, but before I could kiss him again, there was another knock. I was about to tear into the asshole for the interruption when I glanced down and saw the same work boots standing on the other side of the door. And in my gut, I knew who it was. I didn't even consider the ramifications of what I was doing when I flicked the latch to unlock the door. It immediately swung open and, sure enough, the blond I'd noticed when we'd first come into the bathroom stood there, his own lips shiny with spit and swollen from his efforts.

The blond was a big guy. His broad chest practically filled the doorway as he stepped into the stall, as much as the small space would allow. He was wearing a pair of butter-soft jeans that encased thick thighs and a narrow waist. His black T-shirt clung to a well-defined six-pack and prominent pecs. If my cock hadn't been completely spent, it would have been standing to attention for sure.

The man's gaze settled on me for a moment before they shifted to Beck who tensed. Embarrassment swept over his features as he realized who the guy was, but he didn't have time to dwell on it because the man dropped his head and sealed his mouth over Beck's in one swift move. Beck gasped in surprise and then began kissing him back. I should have been pissed.

I wasn't.

And I had no idea why.

They were fucking gorgeous together. The man consumed Beck's pretty mouth at first, then gentled his kiss, probably because he was realizing just like I had that Beck was new to kissing. The man's amber colored eyes skimmed over Beck as he pulled back and then shifted to me. I wasn't sure what to expect, but it certainly wasn't him pulling me forward so he could kiss me in the exact same way.

The fucker kissed like a dream. His mouth expertly took over pleasuring mine and I was leaning into the kiss, Beck pressed between us, when he slowly eased back. He nipped at my lips for a brief moment before giving me another gentle kiss and then he put a fraction of space between us. "Let's find someplace a little more private," he suggested. His eyes went back to Beck. "Just the three of us."

I'd never been in a threesome before because I'd simply never been interested. I didn't share the guys I was with, period. But it was on the tip of my tongue to agree when Beck shifted between us, his hands pushing at both of us. We immediately stepped back to give him as much space as we could.

"No!" he shouted, his voice high and uneven as his panicked eyes drifted around the stall as if seeing it for the first time. "No, it wasn't…"

Whatever pleasure Beck had gotten out of what had happened was obliterated as he went into a complete and full-on panic mode. He scrambled out of the stall and his eyes darted around the bathroom, taking in the few men lingering around. I hoped like hell he didn't realize they'd probably all gotten off on the sounds of him getting off. But my hopes were dashed when color flooded his face.

"Beck," I said as I stepped out of the stall.

"No!" he yelled again, putting out his hand as if to stop me from reaching for him, which I'd actually been planning on doing. "It wasn't supposed to be like that!" he whispered in despair.

"Beck," the man beside me began, but Beck was beyond consolation.

"I have to go," he said quickly and then he was shoving past a couple of guys near the door. Shame and confusion tore through me.

He'd wanted it, damn it.

Hadn't he?

I went through everything in my head and wracked my brain for any sign I'd forced him in some way…or that I'd missed some kind of warning that he hadn't been into what had been happening between us. But there was nothing. He'd pleaded with me. *He'd* made the choice to allow the blond to help get him off. I could understand his embarrassment that others had been listening to us, but even that seemed inconsequential considering the entire situation. He'd come here to get fucked by a stranger. *He'd* pursued *me*.

"Hey," the blond said as he gave me a gentle tap. "You didn't do anything wrong."

I managed a nod. Whatever sexual energy there'd been between us was gone and even if it hadn't been, I was too blindsided to even consider acting on it. I leaned down to scoop Beck's forgotten jacket off the floor. I searched the pockets, but they were empty.

So he probably wouldn't be back for it. I could leave it with the bartender in case Beck returned on another night for it.

But I wouldn't.

Nor did I dwell on the jealously that went through me at the prospect of Beck coming back to this place in the future. Even if he did, I wouldn't know it because there was no way I could ever come back to this club. Not after what had happened in that shitty little bathroom stall.

I nodded at the gorgeous blond, but didn't speak to him as I left the bathroom. I doubted he cared because he seemed just as confused as me. And I had no doubt he was asking himself the same question that was now playing on a loop in my head.

What the hell just happened?

CHAPTER 1

BECK

It was childish, but I couldn't stop myself from closing my eyes when I heard the bedroom door snick open. I had my back to the door, so whoever had entered wouldn't have seen me resort to feigning sleep, but I still held myself perfectly still and tried to keep my breathing even as I waited for them to leave. It wasn't the first time since I'd arrived that someone had popped their head in to check on me and it wasn't the first time I'd ignored them either. Several long moments passed, but I didn't hear the door close. What I did hear was just the slightest creak of the floorboard near the foot of the bed.

I'm not ready yet.

The thought was fleeting because it didn't matter. I'd managed to put off my hosts all day yesterday with the excuse that I was wiped out from the drive, but I doubted they'd bought my story. After all, it only took eight hours to drive from Seattle to the tiny town of Dare, Montana, and I'd left the city two days earlier. My fathers had expected me to make it to Dare by late Thursday afternoon, but I'd called them from the road and explained that I'd been caught in traffic in Spokane and then again just outside Missoula and had decided to spend the night in the city so I wouldn't have to make my hosts wait up for me.

My fathers had been reluctant about the whole thing of course, but I'd gotten used to the inherent fear they went through anytime I was left alone for any extended period of time. At nineteen years old, it should have bothered me that I was on such a short leash that I was literally calling or texting my parents every couple of hours, but it was a lack of trust I'd rightfully earned. I considered it a small miracle that they'd even let me make the drive to Dare on my own at all.

Lying to my fathers should have been harder than it was...or, at the least, should have left a bitter taste in my mouth. But I'd become an expert at hiding the truth from the men who'd given me and my younger brother and sister a future.

It wasn't that I didn't love or respect Cade and Rafe Barretti. No, it was the exact opposite, actually. In the seven years since they'd saved me and my siblings from a dire home life, I'd learned what real love was...and what being part of a family truly meant.

But none of that was strong enough to change who I was...who I'd always be. And it hadn't been enough to keep me from shattering their lives with one selfish act.

And mine.

"I know you're awake."

The soft, very feminine voice was unexpected and I opened my eyes, not bothering to pretend I was just waking up. "How?" I asked as I took in the little girl standing just a few feet from my bed. She had long dark hair that was currently in pigtail braids and she was wearing a pair of pink cutoff overalls with white flowers on the legs and a frilly white shirt. She had two tiny kittens snuggled up against her chest that couldn't have been more than six weeks old.

She shrugged and I dismissed her observation as one of the mysteries that came with being a pre-tween girl. My own sister had gotten that shrug down to an art form when she'd been this girl's age.

"You're Emma, right?" I asked, not bothering to sit up. If she'd been one of her fathers, I would have made more of an effort, but I'd take a few more minutes of not having to play the role of well-adjusted guest if I could get it.

Emma nodded and sat on the edge of my bed. "Here," she said as she handed me one of the kittens. "You can help me feed them."

While my only real interest was in closing my eyes and losing myself in sleep for as long as I possibly could, I took the kitten and put it on the bed next to my chest as I levered myself up on my arm. Emma handed me a small bottle full of milk. I watched as she offered the nipple to the kitten she was holding lovingly in her lap. The kitten instantly latched onto the bottle so I did the same with mine and was satisfied when the kitten began hungrily sucking on the bottle.

"What are their names?" I asked.

"Daddy says their new moms and dads should get to name them," Emma said easily and then she leaned over to adjust the way I was holding the bottle.

"They're not yours?"

She shook her head. "God just brought them to us to watch over for a while."

I nodded in understanding. I knew one of her fathers was a veterinarian so it didn't surprise me that the family would end up with a slew of unwanted animals.

"I get sad sometimes," Emma said as she looked up at me with her pretty blue eyes. "But Dad says every time we say goodbye to one, it's like telling God we're ready for another one."

"Makes sense," I said.

From what I'd seen the day before when I'd stepped over the threshold of the small Victorian house, they'd been saving a lot of animals because I'd counted at least four cats and three dogs. I'd also heard some kind of parrot, though I hadn't seen it. There'd been various livestock in pens out by the barn too, though I wasn't sure how many were permanent residents versus guests of the attached veterinary practice that was housed on the same property.

We sat in silence as the kittens nursed. I sensed motion to my left and glanced over my shoulder to see a little boy, no more than two, come into the room and head for a box of toys in the corner.

"That's Swirl," Emma said as she nodded to the boy. "This is his room."

I'd guessed as much based on the zoo animals painted on the wall and endless supply of toys and books taking up one side of the room and spilling over into the closet. The twin bed I was sleeping in was likely the child's as well, though the bedding was a neutral color like you'd find in any guest room.

"Swirl?" I asked, lifting a brow.

"His name's really Ben, but I heard Daddy and Dad telling Uncle Finn that he was a swirl baby, so…"

I chuckled at that because I suspected what the little girl was talking about, though I doubted she did. My own fathers had recently welcomed twins via surrogacy and they'd been the product of both my fathers' sperm being mixed – or swirled – during the in-vitro process so that the only way to truly know who was the biological father was to test the child's DNA.

Ben came over to the bed, his arms full of toys and stopped in front of his sister. He didn't say anything, just looked at her expectantly. She gave him a baleful look and sighed. I was surprised when she placed the other kitten next to the one I was feeding. "If I don't play with him, he gets cranky," she explained in an exasperated voice. But it was all for show because I saw her take the little boy's hand in hers as she led him from the room, closing the door behind her.

"What should I do with these guys?" I called as I motioned to the kittens.

But Emma must not have heard me because she didn't respond. The kitten she'd been feeding had fallen asleep and the one I was feeding seemed to be on the verge of doing the same even as its mouth remained curled around the nipple. I gently pulled the bottle free and set it on the nightstand and watched as the kitten pressed against its sibling. I rested my head on my hand as I used my other to test the softness of the kittens' fur.

They were so small and helpless.

I felt unexpected tears sting the backs of my eyes. I couldn't really explain the wayward emotion, but it wasn't an unheard-of occurrence for me. Yeah, most days I was just numb, but every once in a while, there'd be something deep inside of me that would break free...like a sliver of sunlight during a violent thunderstorm.

Like two nights before.

The tears dried up even before they could fall as the humiliation crashed over me. I lowered myself back down to the bed and settled my eyes on the window, mindful of the kittens next to me. I wasn't sure who'd opened the curtains, but I distinctly remembered closing them after I'd stumbled into the room twenty-four hours ago, my ass sore and my insides burning with shame.

I'd been planning the stop at the *The Blue Door* club from the moment I'd left Seattle and I'd spent the first several hours of my trip coming up with the lies I would need to tell my fathers to explain why I wasn't driving straight through to Dare as planned. I'd spent the rest of the drive in excited anticipation. I'd found the club online and had even managed to find a few comments on the site from satisfied customers who'd unabashedly shared stories about their experiences. It was how I'd known that the place was so much more than just a place to hook up. And that it would meet my needs perfectly.

From the moment I'd walked through the front door, I'd been like a hunter seeking out his prey, though I'd known most of the patrons, like the bear who'd sought me out at the bar, would have seen it as being the other way around. He'd told me as much with all the things he'd said he wanted to do to me...to show me what it was like to be with a real man.

I'd nearly laughed at that. He'd pegged me as some naïve little innocent who was looking for an exciting and forbidden encounter.

He'd had no fucking clue why I was there.

And nothing about him had fit the bill.

But the dark-haired, steely-eyed cowboy had.

Until he hadn't.

I shook off the reminder of how everything had gone so terribly wrong in that bathroom stall and focused on how I was going to get through the next three months. Coming to Dare hadn't been my idea, but I'd welcomed the opportunity. Not the part where I would be spending the summer working at a nearby ranch, but most certainly the part where I got to get out of Seattle for a while. My father, Cade, had made the suggestion that I spend some time with his former army buddy and the man's husband and two kids. Although he'd posed it as an opportunity for me to have a change of scenery, I couldn't help but wonder if he was the one who needed a break.

I definitely had no grounds to blame him if that was the case. He'd never really recovered from that cold, wet March day fifteen months earlier when I'd destroyed our happy, perfect family with one selfish decision. It wasn't something we spoke a lot about, mostly because I wanted to forget the whole thing.

But there was no forgetting. My father would never forget the scene he'd walked in on when he'd come to my room to let me know he was home early from work and I'd never forget the feeling of peace that had come over me the moment I'd taken that final step.

I'd known I wasn't like other kids long before Cade and Rafe came into my life and offered to be the family my siblings and I'd never really had. As a child, I'd struggled to fit in with kids my own age and I'd often preferred to keep to myself. My chaotic home life would have been explanation enough for my behavior, but there'd always been this sense of distance between me and the people around me, my family included. After my father's death when I was ten and my mother's fatal drug overdose just a year later, I was forced to interact with the world in a whole new way when I was left as the sole provider for my little brother and sister. We'd been sent to live with our maternal grandmother, but she'd been unable to do more than keep a roof over our head with her meager social security check, and her declining health had made her practically an invalid. While my new life hadn't exactly been ideal, in a strange way it had helped ground me by forcing me to focus on one thing and one thing only.

Surviving.

There'd been no time to dwell on the darkness that so often took control of my thoughts. Sleep hadn't been a luxury I could afford.

Even the moments of silence I'd sought out in my head to calm my raging anxiety hadn't been available to me anymore. Every moment had been about finding a way to get food on the table and hiding the truth of our situation from children's services during their rare, but random, check-ins.

I'd managed it for less than four months before it had all come crashing down around me. A few suggestive words to an off-duty cop – that was all it had taken to change things yet again. And while that one encounter had led me to Cade and Rafe Barretti, it had taken away the one thing keeping me from giving in to the darkness of my mind. I'd been stripped of my base need to survive day after day and been given a new, perfect life with two men who were offering me the world.

Except it hadn't been perfect.

Because I wasn't perfect.

I'd literally been handed a fairy-tale life and I hadn't been able to make it work. I'd been lavished with love, kindness, respect, money, opportunity – and I'd still had nothing.

It had taken three years and several doctors to finally acknowledge what I'd known all along…that I wasn't normal and never would be.

I closed my eyes when I heard a knock at the door. Fuck, I really wasn't ready for this. "Come in," I called. I sucked in a deep breath and pasted a smile on my face as I looked over my shoulder at my visitor.

"Morning."

"Morning," I responded as my eyes settled on the man who was one of my father's oldest and closest friends.

Jaxon Reid was so much like my father that it was scary. From his imposing size to his assessing gaze, he could have been Cade Barretti's twin. Which meant I was going to need to be on my game this summer because if anyone would be able to see right through me, it would be this man.

"Breakfast is almost ready. You up for joining us?"

No.

"Sure," I said as brightly as I could. I carefully sat up and collected the kittens.

Jax chuckled. "I see you had a visitor this morning."

I nodded. "She's in high demand," I observed.

"That she is," Jax said, a broad smile spreading across his mouth as he headed towards me. I fought back the violent surge of nausea that went through me as he neared the bed and handed him the kittens.

"Come on down whenever you're ready," Jax said as he cuddled the now-squirming kittens against his wide chest. I nodded and waited until he'd left the room before I pushed the blanket back and swung my legs over the side of the bed. I struggled to catch my breath as the rolling in my gut started to ease.

He's your father's friend.

I nodded as if the voice in my head had been real.

Fuck, I needed to get a grip. Forcing myself to my feet, I searched out the clothes I'd need for the day and went to the bathroom that was just outside the bedroom. I could hear voices coming from downstairs so I quickly skimmed off my sweats and T-shirt and got the shower going. I was just about to step into the stall when my eyes caught on several dark smudges on my left hip.

It took several long seconds to register what it was that I was seeing and when I finally did, I stifled a gasp as my already morning wood thickened with excitement.

He left his mark on me.

Shame flooded my veins as I ran my fingers over the small bruises where the stranger had been holding onto me as he'd pounded into me…as yet another stranger had sucked me to the back of his throat.

My ass actually clenched in anticipation as my hand went unbidden to my cock. I jerked it away and wrapped it around the edge of the shower door instead, willing my body to settle.

"No," I whispered as my cock hungrily jerked and more images sprang into my head.

Firm lips skimming mine.

A hot, wet tongue sliding between my lips.

That deep, sexy voice whispering things in my ear as my hands were pinned to the wall.

"No!" I cried out softly even as I reached for my dick and began frantically stroking it.

I'm sorry, my beautiful boy...

A whimper escaped my throat. I couldn't do this. It was wrong.

But I did. I fucked my hand, pretending it was the blond guy's perfect mouth. I stuck my finger in my mouth to wet it and then searched out my hole with my free hand. I shook my head even as I pushed the wet digit into my body as far as I could. I pressed my mouth against my shoulder to stifle my cry of relief as I came.

Tears flooded my eyes as I collapsed on the floor just outside the shower, my cum mixing with the water that was hitting the back wall before disappearing down the drain. My despair turned to fear as I snatched a towel from the towel rack, not even caring whose it was, and frantically wiped up the few spots of cum that had hit the floor outside the shower. I staggered to my feet and jammed the towel into the laundry hamper in the corner and then stumbled to the shower and stepped under the spray. My body felt ice cold despite the hot water and I eagerly searched out the soap and began scrubbing my body as hard as I could, ignoring the bruises on my hip.

"It didn't happen," I muttered to myself.

A sense of calm settled over me as I repeated the words to myself again and again. I managed to ease off on the need to scrub my skin raw and used the rest of my shower to get control of myself. I felt the familiar mask of contentment surround me in warmth as I finished up and then turned off the water. I deliberately kept my eyes off the marks on my hip and searched out a clean towel to wrap around my lower half. I took my time getting dressed, leaving the towel on for as long as I could and only felt a complete sense of calmness return when the fabric of my pants did what I couldn't.

Hide the truth about what I'd let happen…

"You have my number if you need anything, right?" Jax said as he came around his police cruiser to my car. Even though I'd been okay with driving myself the short distance to the CB Bar Ranch, Jax had insisted on accompanying me before he headed to work.

"Yeah," I responded.

"Rhys was telling me that Callan had to go to Great Falls this morning to pick up a horse and Finn's got an appointment in town so their foreman, Jerry, will be showing you around and getting you started on things."

I nodded. "Sounds good."

It didn't, but I kept that to myself. I wanted nothing more in that moment than to crawl back into bed and will away the events of the morning.

I'd managed to keep control of my emotions throughout breakfast with Jax, his husband Dane and their two little ones, but it had been pretty easy because both men had been preoccupied with dealing with the inherent chaos that came with trying to get a fussy toddler to eat his cereal instead of throw it on the floor for the four-legged members of the family to clean up. Emma, for her part, had been arguing with Jax about not needing to wear her life vest for when she, Ben and their babysitter went to the nearby pond to go swimming. I'd enjoyed watching the byplay between the pair as Emma laid out all the points of her argument which were far more succinct than any eight-year-old's should be, but I'd ended up silently siding with Jax when the kids' babysitter, Harriet Greene, a woman I guessed to be in her early eighties, waltzed in wearing a bright yellow pants suit and sparkly sneakers.

I didn't know much about the CB Bar Ranch other than it had both horses and cattle and that I'd be working with the horses. I'd never been around a horse in my entire life, but welcomed any kind of distraction that would make this summer go by faster. Although there was a certain relief that came with getting out of Seattle for a while, I couldn't say that rural Montana held a lot of appeal for me.

It was just one more place I wouldn't fit.

"So Rhys, Callan and Finn are all together?" I asked as we began walking towards the smaller of the two barns.

"Yeah, they've been together as long as me and Dane, but they didn't get married until a few years ago."

Since I was no stranger to threesomes in my own family, I knew he probably meant the men had committed themselves to each other in every way other than the legal one, since I doubted not even a backwoods place like Montana allowed polygamy. My uncles had done the same thing, each taking the Barretti name in a commitment ceremony, unwilling to even choose between one another for the purpose of two of them getting legally married. I didn't know all the intricacies that went with being committed to two people at the same time, but I knew my uncles had managed to make it work. And the simple fact that Jax referred to his friends as married told me they were making it work too.

"Callan manages the horses and Finn runs the cattle side of the business."

"And Rhys is a deputy like you," I finished for him.

Jax nodded. We both fell silent for a moment, but I knew Jax wasn't done talking because he kept sending me quick looks.

The same looks my fathers always sent me when they thought I wasn't looking.

I didn't need him to voice the worries running through his head because I knew what they were.

Is he okay?

What if I say the wrong thing to him?

Is he going to try it again?

But Jax surprised me when, instead of offering the standard 'I'm here if you need to talk' line, he simply said, "We're glad you're here, Beck."

The words should have made me feel good. But all they did was add more weight on my very tired shoulders. It was exhausting to have to convince others I was okay, even if I wasn't, and now it looked like I had a whole new group of people I'd need to play the game with.

"Thanks, me too," I managed to say.

I focused my attention on my surroundings as we made our way into the smaller barn which was one of those old-fashioned red barns. There was a larger barn next to it and I'd noticed as we'd driven up that the two were connected with some kind of walkway. I'd seen numerous pastures behind the barns along with what I thought might be an indoor riding arena attached to the larger barn. A few small cottage-style houses were just north of the barns and on the top of the hill was a large, two-story farmhouse.

The place was quiet as we walked through the small barn. As we neared the doorway that led to the walkway attaching the two barns, my eyes caught on a horse at the end of the aisle. It was in its stall, but a small door in the upper part of the stall had been left open so the animal could stick its head through. The horse was huge and had nearly an all-white face. I moved a little closer towards the animal to see it actually had a combination of large splotches of black and white color all over its big body.

"Hey, I'll be right back," Jax said as he noticed me eyeing the animal and I nodded as he made his way to the other barn. I moved closer to the horse as it craned its neck out to try and reach me. It made these odd little snuffling sounds as I neared it and when I was just shy of it being able to make contact with me, it began flapping its lips. I smiled at the odd behavior and then carefully reached out my hand to stroke its face. The animal's mouth skimmed over my palm, but it didn't bare its teeth so I figured it was just looking for food. I stepped a little closer and slid my hand down the horse's sleek neck. I nearly jumped out of my skin when it let out a sharp whinny and began stomping its foot impatiently.

"Hold your horses," I heard a humor-laced voice say and I automatically froze at the familiar register.

No, it couldn't be.

Religion was something I'd given up a long time ago, but I still found myself praying to anyone who would listen that it wasn't *that* voice I'd just heard.

But I knew before I forced myself to turn that it was him. Despite spending just a handful of minutes with the man, his voice was burned into my memory and I suspected it would be for the rest of my life.

Bile rose in my throat at the sight of him and if I hadn't been so horrified, I would have been amused by the look of disbelief on his face as he recognized me.

"Beck," he whispered and I felt my legs threaten to give out as the sound of my name on his beautiful lips brought me right back to that bathroom stall when he'd done to me what no other man ever had.

He'd kissed me.

CHAPTER 2

QUINN

I could honestly say I wasn't someone who surprised easily, but in the span of less than 48 hours, I'd met my quota and then some. Five minutes ago, I'd been greeting my horse before remembering I'd left the new bit I'd wanted to try out on my kitchen table, and now here I was face to face with the young man who'd been playing a starring role in my dreams for the last two nights.

"Oh God," Beck ground out and I saw him reach out and grab onto the edge of the stall for support. For a second, I thought he might actually throw up then and there.

"Hey, I didn't find him so-" I heard a voice say behind me and I forced myself to look over my shoulder to see one of the local sheriff's deputies rounding the corner from the other barn. Beck instantly dropped his eyes, probably to hide the turmoil swimming in them.

While I was still trying to process how I was feeling about seeing him again, he'd clearly already come out on the other side, if his look of horror was anything to go by.

"Oh, hey, Quinn," Jax said as he turned his attention to me and held out his hand. I saw Beck glance at me over Jax's shoulder.

"Deputy Reid," I murmured distractedly as I watched Beck shake his head at me slightly, the desperate, unspoken plea as obvious to me as if he'd shouted it.

I was dimly aware of Jax saying, "I was looking for Jerry."

It felt like it took much longer than it should have to find the strength to respond, but I finally managed to say, "Jerry had to head out to check on the herd with some of the other guys. One of them spotted signs of a bear near the river so he wanted to check it out…"

Jax nodded in understanding. "Oh, let me introduce you," Jax said suddenly and then he was turning towards Beck who'd managed to recover enough to let a mask of indifference slip over his features. It wasn't the same look he'd had at the club, but it was disturbing all the same.

I couldn't help but wonder how many masks he had in his repertoire.

"Quinn, this is Beck Barretti. He's visiting with us for the summer from Seattle. Beck, this is Quinn Donavan. He's Callan's assistant horse trainer."

Beck didn't say anything, but he managed to extend his hand. It was cold and clammy to the touch and he released my hand a split second after he took it.

"It's nice to meet you, Beck," I said as casually as I could. I wasn't one for lying, but even if Beck hadn't cared about Jax finding out we already knew each other, I sure as hell did. I still wasn't one hundred percent sure the kid was legal and now that I knew he was a friend of the hulking deputy, I had no interest in finding out what non-legal steps the man would take if he found out what I'd done to Beck in that bathroom.

Jesus, what a clusterfuck.

"So, Jerry was going to show Beck around…he's going to be working here for the summer."

I nodded because I knew that already. Not that it was Beck who'd been hired on as the newest employee of the CB Bar, of course. I'd only been told that the son of Jax and Dane's friends from Seattle would be spending the summer helping out at the ranch.

More specifically, he'd be helping *me* out.

"Yeah, Jerry told me. He asked me to get him started since he'll be primarily working with me."

At that, Beck stiffened and I saw a brief flash of despair in his pretty eyes – the same look he'd shot me and our blond companion in the bathroom before he'd taken off.

"Oh, great," Jax said and then he turned to give Beck a smile. Beck managed to school his features so well that if I hadn't already known how upset he was, I wouldn't have had a clue that he was even remotely bothered. "I'll see you at home tonight?" Jax said and I didn't miss the hint of concern in his voice.

"Definitely," Beck said as he sent Jax a smile.

A smile that looked so unnatural and wrong on the young man that I wanted to order him not to ever do it again.

Jax reached out to shake my hand again and then he was heading out of the barn. Beck and I stood there in complete and utter silence as we heard Jax's cruiser start up and head down the driveway. It wasn't until the sound of the engine faded away that Beck's stance changed and he took several steps away from me. My horse bumped Beck's arm, but he didn't seem to notice.

"I can't believe this is happening," he whispered as he shook his head.

He wasn't the only one. But while I was more shocked than upset, he was clearly on the verge of a complete breakdown because he began muttering to himself as he turned away from me and just started walking. He ended up exiting through the back door of the barn which led towards the pastures, so I suspected he was less interested in his destination and more interested in getting away from me.

"Beck," I called as I hurried after him. I grabbed his arm to stop his forward movement, but predictably, he tore free of my hold.

"Don't!" he bit out.

I put my hands up and said, "I just want to talk. That's it."

Beck looked frantically around us and seemed to finally realize he'd gone the wrong direction. "It…it was a mistake," he whispered.

Even though I wholeheartedly agreed with the young man in front of me, the comment still hurt.

Though I had no idea why.

Beck quieted and while he was still restless, he didn't appear to be on the verge of running for the moment.

"Beck, I have to know," I began as even thinking about what I was going to say caused bile to creep up the back of my throat. "Did...did I do something that night that...that you didn't want?" The idea that I'd somehow forced Beck had been haunting me every second of every day for the last two days. I'd run through the details of that night over and over in my head trying to find an explanation for Beck's reaction just before he'd run out of the bathroom, but I hadn't been able to make sense of any of it.

"What?" he asked in surprise and then shook his head. "No...no, of course not."

A huge weight was lifted off my shoulders, but it didn't go very far. The fact that it had been consensual didn't change the outcome. "You...you were so upset afterwards. You said it wasn't supposed to be like that."

"No, I..."

His voice dropped off and then he shook his head frantically.

"If it was your first time-" I began.

"It wasn't!" he nearly shouted and then seemed to remember himself. "I can't do this," he bit out with another shake of his head. He tried to step past me, but I grabbed his arm. He immediately fought my hold so I grabbed his other arm as well.

"Let me go!" he demanded, though he sounded more scared than angry.

"Beck, I just need to understand what happened-"

"No!"

His efforts to escape me were nearly inconsequential and I was reminded how much stronger and bigger I was than him, even though he wasn't a small man by any means. There just seemed to be no strength in him. Lots of fight, but not the physical prowess to back it up.

"Was I too rough?" I asked. "Or was it the other guy-"

"It wasn't supposed to feel good!" Beck cut in, his voice cracking in anguish.

"What?" I asked stupidly. I was so unprepared for his response that I loosened my hold on him and he took advantage and pulled free of my hands. He was past me like a shot and I had to run to catch up with him. I managed to reach him as he was pulling his car door open and I was stunned to see tears sliding down his face.

"I don't understand," I admitted as I tried to stop him from getting in the car, but he tore free of my grip. "Beck, wait, you're too upset to drive," I said, but he yanked the door shut as the engine of the small sedan roared to life. The car lurched backwards briefly and then forward and I barely managed to step back as the rear tires spun on the gravel. My heart caught in my throat as the car picked up speed as it headed down the driveway and I felt my gut clench as it fishtailed violently.

"Slow down," I said to myself even as I watched the car speed up even more. And then everything did slow down as I watched in disbelief as Beck lost control of the car and it swerved to the left. I could only watch helplessly as it struck a large tree head-on and then I was running.

"Beck!" I screamed as panic tore through me. It felt like it took me hours to reach the car which had smoke coming out of the engine, but I knew it only took seconds. I tore at the driver's side door when I reached the sedan and swallowed hard at the sight of the deployed airbag. Beck was leaning back against the seat, a large gash on his forehead where it looked like he'd hit the window.

"Beck," I said as I carefully put my hands around his neck to keep him from moving his head. Dismay tore through me when I realized he hadn't been wearing his seatbelt.

"Quinn?" Beck whispered, his voice heavy with confusion. I watched his eyes slowly open.

"Don't move, okay?" I said desperately as I held his neck steady with one hand while I searched out my phone with the other. I dialed 911 and gave the information to the operator before hanging up. "Tell me where it hurts, Beck," I said softly.

He was quiet for a moment before saying, "My head I guess."

"Just stay real still. Help's coming."

A few tears slipped down Beck's face and I flinched when they collected against my hand where I was still supporting his neck. "You're going to be okay," I murmured.

"Tell them I didn't do it on purpose."

I froze at the odd statement. "Tell who?" I finally managed to ask.

"My fathers…please, I promised them I wouldn't try again…it was an accident, Quinn, I swear it. Please make sure they know that."

His panic was starting to build and I gently rubbed my thumb back and forth over the pulse point in his neck in the hopes I could calm him down. "You're going to be okay, Beck. I'll tell them, but you'll be able to tell them yourself."

"It was an accident…" he said as a sob tore free from his throat.

"I know it was," I said reassuringly, though in truth, I was completely clueless as to what the hell was going on. I watched as Beck's eyes drifted shut and the sheer panic of what that might mean had me saying, "Did you like my horse?"

I had to repeat the question before Beck's eyes opened again. "Your horse?" he asked, confused.

"The black and white Paint," I clarified.

"Paint?" he asked tiredly.

I chuckled and said, "Sorry, forgot I was talking to a genuine city slicker." I was glad when a tiny smile flitted across Beck's mouth. "He's an American Paint Horse. A Paint is a breed of horse that usually has pinto coloring."

"Only pinto I've ever seen is the kind with four wheels."

I laughed. "I have a lot to teach you, I guess."

Beck's green eyes shifted to mine and I realized how my words must have sounded. I saw a flash of emotion go through his gaze before he lowered his lids. "What's your horse's name?"

"Koda," I said. "It's short for Dakota, which means friend."

"Is that what he is?" Beck asked.

I felt my throat clog with emotion. "Yeah, he is."

Beck opened his eyes and studied me. His gaze was surprisingly sharp considering how much pain he must have been in. "He's special to you."

I nodded. "My...my husband gave him to me as an engagement present six years ago."

"You're married?" Beck whispered, and I didn't miss the hint of disappointment in his voice, though I wasn't sure if he was bothered by the fact that he thought I was married or that I'd cheated on my husband with him.

I sucked in a deep breath. "Not anymore. He died two years ago."

"What was his name?"

"Griff...Griffin." Pain lanced through my heart, but I forced it away.

"I'm sorry," Beck said softly as his eyes held mine and I knew his words were genuine. I managed a nod, but that was as much as I could get out. I could hear sirens in the distance and from the way Beck tensed up in my hold, I knew he could hear them too.

"Please," he said unevenly. "Please don't tell anyone what happened back there," he said as he shifted his eyes over his shoulder.

Between his strange request to tell his fathers he hadn't run his car into the tree on purpose and his behavior back at the barn, I didn't have even the slightest clue what was going on, but I knew I couldn't deny the request. "I'll tell them you were heading home to pick up something you forgot, but that I didn't see the accident."

Beck started to nod, but I tightened my hold on his neck. "Don't move," I reminded him.

He didn't say anything else as the ambulance rolled up. I heard another siren off in the distance and suspected it was likely Jax or Rhys responding to the call.

I held my position as the first paramedic showed up at my side. I recognized him instantly as a friend of my bosses. His eyes skimmed me briefly and then settled on my hands. "Hi," the man said to Beck as he made eye contact with him. "My name's Luke. What's yours?"

"Beck," Beck said tiredly.

"Beck, how are you feeling?"

"My head hurts."

"Okay, we're going to take care of you. I just need you to stay real still, okay?"

"Yeah," Beck murmured.

Luke's gaze shifted to me. "You called it in, Quinn?" he asked.

I nodded. "I heard the accident from the barn," I said, ignoring the bitter taste that flooded my mouth along with the lie.

Luke put his hands over mine. Once he had a firm hold on Beck's neck, he gave me a nod and I dropped my hands and then moved out of his way.

"Quinn," Beck said hesitantly and I leaned down to settle my hand on his shoulder as Luke took over the spot where I'd been sitting on the bottom part of the door frame.

"I'm right here, Beck."

"Brody, grab the C-Collar," Luke calmly called to his partner.

"Already got it!"

I glanced behind me at the ambulance and went still at the sight of the man who had his back to me.

No fucking way.

But I knew even before the man turned around what he'd look like. Blond and built...and a fucking fantastic kisser.

The man Luke had referred to as Brody turned and froze when he saw me, his eyes going wide. He managed to collect himself pretty quickly, but I knew it would only last the few seconds it would take for him to see who the patient was.

Brody hurried past me and, sure enough, he came to a dead stop at the sight of Beck. His eyes jumped to mine and I shook my head.

How the fuck was I supposed to explain any of this?

"Brody," Luke called, but it wasn't until he said the man's name again that Brody finally snapped out of his daze.

"Sorry," he muttered and then he was bending down to secure the collar around Beck's neck. Luckily, Beck seemed too out of it to recognize Brody.

Luke and Brody were still stabilizing Beck when two police cars rolled up.

"What the hell happened?" Jax yelled as he rushed past me. He didn't wait for an answer so I stepped back to give the men some more room. Rhys flashed me a quick glance as he hurried by.

"You okay?" he asked.

I nodded. Fuck, I hated having to lie to this man, but I knew that was what I was going to have to do. Once they got Beck out of here, Rhys would need some answers. Brody moved past me as he went back to the ambulance and he motioned to me. I followed and watched as he pulled a backboard from the ambulance. "What the hell is going on?" he asked.

I knew he didn't have time for all the answers he undoubtedly wanted, so I said, "Try not to let him see you." I motioned to the car. "He might panic."

Brody nodded in understanding and I had no doubt he was remembering Beck's reaction at the club. "My shift ends at 10 tonight. Can you meet me at 10:30 at the hospital in Cedar River?"

"Is that where you're taking him?" I asked.

He nodded. "Doctors will keep him overnight for observation for sure."

"I'll be there," I said, though that was the last thing I wanted. What I wanted was to go back to that night in the club and take that damn twink up on his offer and pretend I'd never set eyes on Beck Barretti.

Except that wasn't the complete truth and I knew it.

Brody hurried past me with the backboard and I stood off to the side as they got Beck out of the car and loaded into the ambulance. I was glad to see that Brody was the one who got in the driver's seat of the ambulance, meaning it would be Luke who rode in the back with Beck. But as much as I wanted to get in my truck and follow them, I knew it would look strange since I'd supposedly only known the kid for a few minutes.

As the ambulance took off, Jax dug out his phone. "I've got to go with them," he said to Rhys. "I'll call his parents on the way."

Rhys nodded. "Go, I'll cover for you."

"Deputy Reid," I said before the man could get in his cruiser. I flinched when his dark eyes shifted to me. "He wanted me to tell his fathers it was an accident." I hesitated and said, "I don't know why he said that, but he was adamant that they know he didn't do it on purpose."

Jax was quiet for a moment and I saw a flash of sadness in his gaze. "Thanks, I'll tell them."

I hated that I couldn't tell the man I'd seen the whole thing and believed it was what Beck had said it was – an accident – but then I'd have to explain what had led to Beck taking off like he had and I wasn't about to break my promise to him. And as I watched Jax drive off in a cloud of dust, I prepared myself to keep that very promise.

Lying was something I hated with a passion, but I'd do it because I knew in my gut it was what Beck needed.

I didn't know why it mattered so damn much to me to give him that, but it mattered.

More than I wanted to admit.

CHAPTER 3

BRODY

"He said it wasn't supposed to feel good?" I asked, not sure I'd heard the man across from me correctly.

Quinn nodded, but didn't say anything else.

We were sitting in the quiet hospital cafeteria. Neither of us had felt like eating so we'd each just grabbed a cup of coffee and selected a booth in the back of the large room, so we would have the privacy we needed.

"What happened after that?"

"He took off. Ran to his car, got in and drove off like a bat out of hell. He lost control of the car and hit the tree…"

Quinn's voice dropped off. I could tell he was haunted by what he'd seen, and I didn't blame him. While the accident wasn't even close to the worst I'd been called to, it was different when it was someone you knew behind the wheel.

I still couldn't wrap my head around the events of the day or that I was sitting across from one of the men who'd fucked with my senses two nights earlier. While I hadn't been to that particular gay club before since I'd only moved to Missoula a few months earlier, I'd been visiting similar establishments for years and knew the score of what went down in places like that. I'd been there for just a few minutes when I'd found what I was looking for – a well-built muscle head who'd been trying to climb his dance partner like a tree on the dance floor. It hadn't taken much to lure him away – all I'd really needed to do was get into his line of sight and let him know with my eyes what I wanted. I was lucky that way – I'd been born with good genes and took care of myself and that got me pretty much whoever I wanted when it came to partners.

I'd led the guy to the bathroom, not wanting to deal with the hassle of trying to find a less public spot. I wasn't an exhibitionist, but I had to admit, there'd been a certain thrill in being watched. My guy had been sucking me voraciously for several minutes when everything had changed.

I'd wanted both men the second they'd entered the bathroom and the sexual electricity that had hung in the air between us as our eyes had connected had been unlike anything I'd ever known before. I was no stranger to lust or the darker side of sex, but that night was the first time I'd ever *needed*.

And when the younger man had started making those sounds...

Hell, I'd been so turned on that I'd actually grabbed the man at my feet and shoved him to all fours with the intent of fucking him right there and then. But those mewls and whimpers coming from the bathroom stall along with the other man's rough orders had had me stepping past the man at my feet and going to my own knees outside the bathroom stall. Never in a million years would I have thought I'd rather suck a dick and get myself off with my own hand instead of sinking my cock into a tight, hot ass, but that was exactly what I'd done. I'd managed to retain enough sense to put a condom on the long, slightly curved dick that had been worked through the glory hole, but I certainly hadn't wanted to. I'd known the second I'd taken that pulsing flesh in my mouth that it wouldn't take much to finish the young man off and I'd quickly worked over my own rock hard dick. I'd come at nearly the same time as the dick in my mouth and then I'd listened to the other man shout his own completion.

At that point, the only common sense thing to do would have been to zip up and walk away. But that need had continued to course through me, despite my body being sexually sated.

The older man knew how to kiss and I'd been hard pressed not to shove him back against the wall and get on my knees for him too. The younger man had had no clue how to kiss.

And I'd fucking loved it.

I hadn't just wanted more...I'd needed more. Never once since I'd been frequenting sleazy clubs had I ever invited a guy to continue the night's activities. I went to those places for one thing and one thing only. And once I got it, I was done.

Always.

But I would have done anything to get both men to a hotel or hell, even my own apartment.

And then the younger man had lost it completely.

I'd passed the whole evening off as one of those once in a blue moon events and accepted the only time I'd get to relive those few minutes of pleasure would be in my dreams. Forty-eight hours later and I was back with both of them, but there was nothing erotic about how we'd come together again.

I was lucky my training was so thoroughly ingrained or I would have made a fool of myself in front of my partner this afternoon. It was bad enough that I'd hesitated for even a moment at the sight of Beck sitting hurt in that car. And while the case was one I normally would have handled while Luke drove the ambulance to the hospital, the fact that Luke indirectly knew the young man had made it so I didn't even need to ask to drive. Which was good since Quinn had warned me how Beck might react to seeing me.

And from what Luke had told me about him, as well as the disturbing byproduct of Beck and Quinn encountering each other again, I was glad Beck had been too out of it to recognize me.

"You're sure it was an accident?" I asked.

Quinn stiffened and lifted his eyes to mine. "Yes, why?" When I didn't answer right away, he said, "I saw him try to stop the car just before it hit the tree. It *was* an accident."

I nodded.

"What aren't you telling me?" Quinn asked.

I was on shaky ground because what Luke had told me was in confidence. But I couldn't help but think Quinn and I were somehow partially responsible for what had happened to Beck today.

"My partner Luke and his husband are friends with the men Beck is staying with."

Quinn nodded. "I know. I've met Luke and Gray. Roman and Hunter too…they come to the ranch all the time for dinner."

I knew he was talking about Luke's brother-in-law, Roman Blackwell and his husband, Hunter. I'd met the pair on a few occasions when Luke had invited me to dinner at his and Gray's cabin. The introduction had actually benefited me in more ways than one since Roman had offered me some work after he'd discovered I owned my own construction business.

"Luke told me Beck came out here from Seattle to spend the summer with Jax and Dane."

"Right," Quinn responded. "He's going to be working on the ranch…with me. Helping out with the horses."

Beck's freak out moment made more sense now. He clearly hadn't planned to ever see either of us again. Working around Quinn all day every day would certainly make it harder to forget the events of that night in the club and whatever trauma it had set off inside the young man.

Jesus, this was a mess. I ran my fingers through my hair and took a sip of my coffee to try and get control of myself. "Luke told me some stuff about Beck after we got him to the ER."

"What stuff?" Quinn asked warily.

"For starters, he's only nineteen."

Quinn paled and then swallowed hard. He managed a nod, but I knew the revelation bothered him. I'd been in the same boat. I didn't have a problem fucking younger guys, but *that* young?

I just wished that was the worst of it.

"Beck has a history of depression," I continued. "Medication has helped stabilize him, but fifteen months ago he…"

Fuck, I didn't even want to say it.

"He what?" Quinn asked, though I could tell by the tone of his voice that he already knew what I was going to say.

"He tried to hang himself."

Quinn's eyes slid closed and he covered them with his hand for a moment as he sucked in a deep breath. "Fuck," he whispered.

I let Quinn have the moment he needed to absorb what I'd told him and I watched the emotions play out on his face when he dropped his hand. I could see that despite that night in the bathroom being a one-night stand thing, like me, it had been more for Quinn too.

"That's why he kept saying…"

"What?" I asked when Quinn didn't continue on his own.

Quinn shook his head and rested his forearms heavily on the table. "He kept asking me to tell his fathers it was an accident – that he didn't do it on purpose."

"I guess one of his fathers was the one who found Beck that day. He'd come home from work early. If he'd been even a minute later…"

"Jesus fucking Christ!" Quinn ground out as he slammed his hand onto the table, rattling our mugs enough so that coffee spilled over the side of mine. "Sorry," he muttered when he saw the mess. He reached for a napkin from the dispenser on the table and started cleaning up, but I gently grabbed his hand when I saw how badly it was shaking.

"I got it," I said quietly.

Quinn didn't pull his hand free of mine right away and I had the strangest urge to link our fingers. His hand was warm against mine and the rough callouses felt good against my skin. I actually felt the loss when he pulled it back. I turned my attention to cleaning up the mess even as I subtly watched the other man. He looked the part of a cowboy with his black hair, rugged, work-hardened body and tanned skin. His chiseled jaw was covered with the perfect amount of stubble and his gray eyes reminded me of a coming storm. While the encounter in the bathroom had clearly pegged him as an alpha type, the vulnerability I could see in his eyes was intriguing.

"Is he okay?" Quinn asked. "He had a cut on his head."

I nodded. "He's fine. He's got a concussion so he'll spend the night here for observation. I checked on him before I met you in the lobby. I made sure he didn't see me," I added when Quinn shot me a questioning look. "A nurse told me one of his fathers arrived a few hours ago."

We both sat in silence for a moment before I worked up the nerve to ask, "Do you think maybe he was trying to convince himself he wasn't gay?"

"What do you mean?" Quinn asked.

"Why else wouldn't he have wanted the sex to feel good?"

Quinn shook his head. "He walked into that club knowing exactly what he wanted. No hesitation. Someone who was still questioning wouldn't do that, would they?" Quinn was quiet for a moment. "I thought maybe he got off on the pain, but when I touched him…" He dropped his eyes and shook his head. "Guys who like pain still feel pleasure…he seemed surprised by it…like he'd never even gotten off during sex before."

I nodded, even though nothing made sense.

Quinn shifted in his seat and then he was picking up the cowboy hat he'd put on the bench next to him when we'd first sat down. "I never should have touched him."

"Quinn-" I began, but he shook his head.

"I need to go."

"You're not going to go see him?" I asked.

"I don't think that's a good idea." Quinn stood and hesitated. "I guess we might be running into each other since we know some of the same people…I just…"

I waited patiently for him to find the words he wanted to say.

"I'm not looking to start anything up," he finally said. "I go to clubs like that to scratch an itch, nothing more."

Even though I was of a similar mind when it came to my feelings on sex and relationships, his declaration still bothered me more than I wanted to admit.

"Understood," I said simply and watched him go, my eyes falling to the sway of his trim hips and tight ass. He really was a good-looking guy, but there was something about him that tugged at something deeper inside of me. He had a certain sadness about him that seemed to be too ingrained to have been caused by the events of the day.

I watched him leave the cafeteria and then sat back against the booth and studied my cooling coffee. If my family could see me now, they'd be absolutely horrified. But everything they'd hate about my new life, I fucking loved.

Not just the fact that I was finally free of that damn closet I'd been forced to hide in for most of my life. No, it was so much more than that. I had a career I loved, a side business I was growing that was all mine and friends who didn't know, or even care, what being a Wilder really meant.

Yes, I'd lost some things along the way, but I'd gained more.

I'd known I was screwed the first time I'd realized boys were what did it for me, not girls.

Because Brody Wilder, member of one of the most influential and very conservative political families in the country, couldn't be gay.

I'd fought my needs for years and had even managed to fool myself into thinking the whole thing was some crazy phase fueled by the stress that came with living a very public life…until the night I'd had sex for the first time with my girlfriend, the daughter of my parents' closest friends. On paper, we'd been the perfect couple and our families had already started mapping out our future together. But as soon as I'd dropped her off at home after an awkward and humiliating encounter after a clichéd prom night when I was eighteen years old, I'd gone home and cried. Then I'd done something that had shattered any illusions I'd had left that I could have a normal life.

I came out to my twin brother, Nathan.

It was the first time since we'd shared a womb that he hadn't had my back.

And he'd never had it again after that.

After telling me I was a sick pervert, he'd gone directly to my father and I'd been ushered right back into the closet. Countless sessions with our family's Baptist minister followed until I was deemed "cured" of my depraved urges and I was welcomed back into my church and family because I'd repented.

But my definition of repented had been very different than my family's. I'd spent my days excelling in my classes at Yale Law School and my evenings shuttling my longtime, respectable socialite girlfriend around to various events, and making love to her on the rare occasions when I hadn't been able to put her off with the standard excuse of being busy with studying. But nights…nights had been all mine and I'd taken full advantage of that fact.

Gay clubs had become my salvation because they'd offered me the anonymity I'd needed so I could explore every facet of my sexuality. Fucking, getting fucked, group sex, bondage and pain…I'd tried just about all of it. And soon I'd been caught up in a revolving door of needing more and more forbidden sex to balance out the constant fear of discovery and shame of who I'd become. It wasn't until I'd gotten sucked into the dangerous world of breath play with a guy who had no clue what he was doing that I'd come to my senses and stuck to the things I knew were a sure thing for me.

Living a lie became second nature to me after graduating law school and planning my upcoming nuptials to the young woman who'd been selected for me like some broodmare. But the guilt of what I'd become had weighed heavily on me, to the point that I'd finally broken down and told my fiancée the truth, though I'd left out the part about it being men I'd been cheating on her with. I'd expected histrionics, anger, despair, betrayal…what I'd gotten was a lecture on being discreet and a stern warning to keep my baser needs out of our marriage bed. Her response should have freed me, but all it had done was spill more water into the already waterlogged glass box I'd been living in my whole life.

Until the night I'd finally woken up.

"Hey, Brody."

The feminine voice distracted me from my thoughts of the past and I nodded at the young nurse I recognized from the ER. "Hey, Jill," I responded politely as she walked by. I could tell she was looking for me to invite her to sit with me, but I was too distracted to deal with her. She'd flirted with me the last few times Luke and I had brought patients to the rural community hospital and I hadn't yet had a chance to tell her she wasn't anywhere near my type. I stood up quickly so she wouldn't invite herself to sit down and said, "Have a good night."

My thoughts drifted back to Beck and Quinn. I was at a loss as to what to do next, but I couldn't shake the need to do something. Even though my role in the encounter between the two men at the club had been minimal, I still felt responsible for fixing it.

Only problem was, I still didn't have a clue how the hell to fix something I wasn't even sure how had gotten so broken in the first place.

CHAPTER 4

BECK

I'd seen a lot of things I shouldn't have early on in my life, but the sight I woke up to would surely haunt me for the rest of my days.

I'd felt light pricking at the backs of my eyes and had initially thought it was yet another doctor shining his light into my eyes looking for what, God only knew. But it had actually been a little bit of sunlight streaming in through the gaps on the vertical blinds covering the window. My first thought was that my body shouldn't hurt so bad considering I hadn't been going very fast when I hit that tree. At the least, it should have just been my head that hurt from where I'd hit the window, but just about every part of me felt some twinge of pain, though I knew it wasn't nearly as bad as it could have been.

But none of it held a candle to the fiery stab of agony I felt as I opened my eyes and saw my father sitting next to my bed, his elbows on his legs and his hands holding his head. His face was downcast and his fingers were buried in his dark hair. I felt tears sting the backs of my eyes at the sight of Cade Barretti looking so broken. The man was larger than life itself, but I'd managed to reduce him to this.

"Dad," I managed to rasp out, despite the dryness of my throat.

My father quickly lifted his eyes and I was dismayed to see they were red and swollen. "Hey," he said as he dashed at his eyes and then stood so he could lean over me, one hand taking mine where it was resting on the bed, the other settling on my head as he stroked over my hair. "How are you feeling?"

I nodded but stopped abruptly at the pain. "Good," I said. "Water?"

My father snatched up a cup from a table next to the bed and filled it with water from a pitcher and then grabbed a straw. He held the straw to my lips and let me drink my fill before setting it down again.

"I'm sorry-"

"Don't," my father immediately said and then he shook his head and leaned down to kiss my forehead. He seemed to be struggling to speak so I just focused on holding his hand until he pulled back a little so I could see his face.

"I didn't do it on purpose," I whispered.

"I know that," he said as he reached out to cup my cheek.

I didn't believe him, but I kept that to myself. My actions fifteen months ago had ensured he'd never trust anything I ever said again.

"Sorry about the car," I murmured.

"Fuck, Beck, your father and I don't give a shit about the car," he said, his voice as close to angry as I suspected he was going to let it get. It was something else that had changed in the last year and a half – both my parents walked on eggshells around me, even if they were upset about something I'd done like when I'd been caught drinking at school earlier this year. Neither of them had ever been the type to yell and scream when they were angry, but they'd always been firm and made sure the discipline fit the crime. Now when they were displeased with my behavior, there was always a thread of uncertainty in their voices as they spoke…like they were afraid they were going to somehow set me off. After I'd been caught drinking, they'd taken away my car and put a ban on electronics for a week which had left me with little to do but help around the house and spend time in my room working on homework or reading. None of that had really been an issue for me. What had bothered me was the fact that they'd changed their schedules for that entire week so that one of them was home with me the whole time when I wasn't at school...and not because they wanted to make sure I didn't break the rules of their punishment.

No, they'd been afraid that I'd try to kill myself again simply because they'd grounded me. They'd been subtle about the whole thing as they'd knocked on my door every twenty minutes, but a guy only needed to be asked if he was hungry or thirsty or needed anything so many times before the motives behind the endless interruptions became clear.

"When can I get out of here?" I asked as I glanced at the IV in my arm and the device on my finger that tracked my heart beat.

"They'll discharge you this afternoon. We'll stay with Jax and Dane for a few days so you can rest and then we'll fly home. Jax said he'd bring your car out to Seattle when it's fixed."

"Wait, what? Home?" I tried to sit up, but my father held me down by the shoulder and instead used the controls on the bed to lift the head of it. "I thought I was staying for the summer."

"Your father and I think it might be a good idea for you to spend the summer at home."

Frustration went through me. It wasn't that I wanted to stay in Dare – the exact opposite actually, considering staying meant I'd likely be working with Quinn on a daily basis. No, I was motivated by a whole other set of reasons, only one of which I could give voice to.

"You said you believed me," I said softly.

My father's eyes shifted to me briefly and then he sat back down in the chair. His big hand settled on my outer wrist. "That call, Beck," he whispered. "That fucking call you get that your kid is hurt..."

His voice dropped off and I had to look away from him. He was the strongest man I'd ever met and yet I'd shattered him with one selfish decision.

"So this is what it's going to be like?" I asked. "You're going to try to keep me in some bubble for the rest of my life?"

Fuck, what would he do if he found out that I was no safer in that bubble than I'd been in the years I'd lived with two drug addicts who'd also happened to call themselves my parents or when I'd resorted to selling my body for enough money to keep food on the table for what was left of my family?

My father didn't answer me and I guessed it was because he didn't really have a good answer. "I need this," I said softly. I waited until he looked up at me before saying, "*You* need this."

"No," he said, but there was uncertainty in his voice. He didn't *want* to need a break from me, but he did all the same. Between the inherent worry both my fathers would always have when it came to me, whether I was physically with them or not, along with the challenges that came with the arrival of newborn twins, both men were stretched thin. It was why I hadn't fought the suggestion to spend the summer in Dare. It was an escape for me and it gave my fathers a chance to focus on something besides their burdensome oldest son for once.

"It really was an accident," I said softly. I debated telling him the lie I'd come up with about me being distracted by my phone as the cause of the accident, but I found that, for once, I didn't want to tell him something that wasn't true. The fact was that it had been an accident.

And I wanted my word to be enough for him.

I held my breath as my father studied me for a long moment and then he finally nodded. "If you want to stay…"

"I do."

"Okay." He reached for his phone and said, "I'm going to talk to your father first about the change of plans and then I'll let you talk to him, okay?"

I nodded.

"I'll be right outside," he said as he nodded towards the door.

"Okay, I'll be right here."

My father smiled at that, but it didn't quite reach his eyes. God, what I wouldn't give to be the reason he smiled for real. Like he did when my little sister won some academic prize or when my brother, Toby, scored goal after goal during a soccer game.

But it was a lofty dream. Because the truth was, if he had any idea of all the things I'd done in my life, of the things I'd let happen, he'd never be able to look at me again, let alone smile.

My nerves were stretched so tight I was sure my entire body would shatter any second now. It had been exactly one week since the accident and I was right back where I'd been, except this time there was no Jax to pave the way for me. He'd wanted to come with me to make sure I made it to the ranch okay, but like with my father who'd finally agreed to leave two days after I'd gotten out of the hospital, I'd been insistent that I was okay on my own. I'd spent the entire week at Dane and Jax's house resting, either in bed or, on the occasions I could find the energy to force myself out of my safe haven, interacting with Emma and Ben and their babysitter, Mrs. Greene. Of course, interacting meant I had to sit quietly wherever we happened to be, whether it was while the kids played in the living room or went swimming in the pond. That had been Mrs. Greene's condition and I'd learned very quickly that you didn't mess with a woman who had the confidence to wear bedazzled sneakers with fancy dresses and gray-blue hair styled in a way that I'd only ever seen in pictures of Hollywood starlets from the sixties.

I climbed out of the car and headed for the barn, but stopped when I saw a man walking down the driveway with two small boys. Each child had ahold of one of his hands and I could tell he was having trouble with one of the kids because the little boy's face was scrunched up in an unhappy frown. And sure enough, within a few seconds, the kid started crying and the young man knelt to pick him up. Which immediately set off the second little boy. I smiled to myself as I trotted up the driveway.

"Do you need some help?" I asked as I neared the man who was trying to figure out how to pick up the second boy while the first was clinging to him.

He chuckled and said, "I was sure we were going to make it the whole way this time."

I reached down to pick up the second child and the man shifted the first to take him. "Do you want me to carry him?" I asked as the little boy quieted in my arms. The man looked surprised.

"Wow, yeah, that would be great. He usually doesn't take to strangers so quickly." He maneuvered the boy in his arms to a more comfortable position and then held out his hand. "I'm Finn," he said as he shook my hand. "This is Charlie" – he pointed to the child in his arms – "and this is Rowan." He tugged on the pant leg of the little boy I was holding. I guessed the boys to be around a year old or so and they were clearly identical twins with their dark hair and blue eyes. They were wearing matching outfits all the way down to adorable little cowboy boots.

"Hi, I'm Beck," I said and I watched Finn's eyes widen just a bit. I knew it would have been stupid to think he might not know about the accident, but I'd held out hope that I wouldn't be the talk of the ranch. I wondered absently if he knew about my suicide attempt too. I'd figured my fathers had told Jax and Dane about it, but I wasn't sure who else knew. I kind of didn't want to know at this point because I didn't need more eyes watching my every move for any sign that I was looking to try and hurt myself again.

"Welcome to the CB Bar," Finn said as we began walking towards the barn. "We're so excited to have you helping us out for the summer."

"I'm excited to be here," I said politely. It wasn't like I could say what I was really feeling.

Thanks for giving me a place to hide out from my fucked-up life, but where I'd really like to be right now is asleep in my bed because it's the only place I can ever find any kind of fucking peace. And oh, by the way, I let one of your employees fuck me in a dirty bathroom without even knowing his name while another complete stranger sucked my dick.

"Have you ever worked around horses before?"

I shook my head. "Never actually even been around one," I admitted.

Finn laughed. "My husband, Rhys, was pretty much in the same boat when he arrived and he did okay." The man's smile was huge as he talked about one of his husbands. I ignored the pang of envy that went through me.

"You'll be fine. Quinn's a great teacher. He's as good with the horses as Cal, but don't tell Cal I said that."

"Cal?"

"Oh, yeah, sorry. I meant Callan, my other husband. I've been calling him Cal since we were kids…well, since I was a kid."

"You and Callan grew up together?" I asked.

"Sort of. My father worked for his and Cal and I hung out. Well, hung out is probably the wrong word. I kind of latched onto Cal when I was thirteen and never gave it a second thought. He was a good sport about it, especially since he was so much older than me."

"You guys are married, so I guess he was more than just a good sport about it, huh?"

Finn smiled. "Yeah, he was." He glanced at me and said, "Usually the first thing out of people's mouths when they find out I have two husbands is some kind of question asking how that's even possible."

I chuckled. "Jax must not have told you much about my family," I said. "My father's brother has been married to two men for nine years now and my cousin, Tristan, is in a relationship with his best friend and another man."

"Really?" Finn said with a smile. "Sounds like an amazing family."

"It is," I murmured.

It was too bad I didn't feel like I was a part of it.

All too quickly we reached the barn and I felt my anxiety start to creep back up. The aisle was empty when we entered, but as soon as an older man entered the barn from the other side, Rowan began flapping his arms and excitedly saying something that sounded like "Papa." I tensed when I saw the man, who I suspected was Callan Bale based on both kids' excited reactions, wasn't alone. Quinn was walking next to him and behind them was a white horse.

Callan's eyes lifted to see his husband and children and his whole face lit up. He began walking towards us and I quickly lowered Rowan to the ground when I saw Finn do the same with Charlie. I steadied the little boy before releasing him so he could waddle towards his father. Quinn stayed back with the horse, presumably so the large animal wouldn't inadvertently injure one of the kids.

I felt my heart clench at the sight of Callan scooping up his kids and holding them against his chest. Even though I'd never had that particular experience, I'd still felt that love every time my fathers held me. The fact that I wasn't their biological child hadn't ever seemed to register with them or affect the level of affection they'd shown me and my younger siblings.

I couldn't stop myself from taking a step back as Callan neared us and I inwardly cursed myself. I felt a tingling along the back of my neck and saw Quinn watching me.

Fuck, had he seen my reaction to Callan's approach?

Callan, for his part, seemed not to notice my reaction, especially since he only had eyes for his husband.

"Hey," the man murmured as he leaned down to brush his lips over Finn's.

Callan Bale was a big guy – well over 6' and heavily muscled, though he wasn't a tank. While the man's physical appearance caused my insides to flutter nervously, it was the way he carried himself that had me on edge. Just like Jax, I instinctively knew he was the kind of man who knew what he wanted and went after it. And just like with Jax, I was ashamed of my reaction to him.

But it wasn't something I could control anymore…well, that wasn't quite true. I had ways of controlling it, but that wouldn't help me here in this moment.

My eyes shifted to Quinn again and saw him studying me intently.

Jesus, I needed to get a grip.

"Hey," Finn murmured softly. "The boys wanted to come down to visit their Papa."

As soon as Finn said the word, one of the twins began babbling "Papa" over and over again and then the second boy chimed in.

"Rhys is going to be so pissed," Callan said with a chuckle.

Finn laughed and said to me, "They've managed to figure out 'Dada' for me and just recently 'Papa' for Cal, but they can't manage to say just 'Da' for Rhys."

"He's feeling a little left out," Callan added. "You must be Beck."

I swallowed hard and nodded.

He's not a threat to you, you idiot.

"I am."

"Callan Bale." The man looked like he was going to try to shake my hand, but then abandoned the thought since he didn't seem willing to relinquish either of his sons. "It's nice to meet you."

"You too," I murmured.

"Is Aunt Dolly here yet?" Callan asked as one of the boys began playing with the man's dark brown cowboy hat.

"She's on her way." Finn turned his attention to me and said, "Aunt Dolly is Cal's aunt. She moved to Boca years ago, but she came back last year after..." – Finn's eyes shifted to his husband briefly – "After Cal's dad passed."

I nodded in understanding and watched as Finn stroked his husband's back as if to comfort him. They shared a silent look between them, but I didn't need to hear the words to know what these two men meant to one another.

Callan seemed to remember himself because he tore his eyes from Finn and said, "How are you feeling?"

"Good," I said. "Ready to get to work," I added because I figured it would sound good.

"Great," he responded. "Quinn will get you started, but make sure to take breaks if you need to and if you need to end things early today, that's absolutely fine."

"Thank you, I appreciate that."

Callan nodded and then he glanced at his husband. "I'll walk up to the house with you before I head over to the Halsteads' farm to take a look at their new mare."

Finn nodded and then put his arm around his husband's waist. "See you later, Beck."

"Bye," I murmured as I watched them walk out of the barn, their voices low as they spoke.

I forced my attention to Quinn and saw that he was no longer looking at me. Instead, he was stroking his big hand over the white horse's neck, murmuring softly to the animal. The horse's ears flicked back as if he were actually listening to the man. I made myself walk towards the pair and ignored the tingling in my body as I got closer.

Once I reached them, Quinn quit talking and shifted his eyes to me, but he didn't speak. Instead, he handed me the reins and as soon as I took them, he began working on loosening the animal's saddle.

The silence had me on edge. I'd expected an interrogation after the events of last time, but he remained quiet as he worked. The fact that he didn't seem interested in interacting with me hurt, though I didn't know why since men like him nearly always only wanted one thing from me.

Except that wasn't quite true. I'd honed in on Quinn that night in the club because I'd known he would be like all the others…until he hadn't been.

Until he'd kissed me…until he'd made me feel something I'd spent a lifetime not feeling.

Alive.

I forced back the uncertainty that came with being around this man and turned my attention to the horse. The animal was beautiful despite numerous spots all over his body where the hair didn't seem to lay right. I ran my fingers over one such mark on his neck and stilled at the raised flesh.

Scars.

"What happened to him?" I automatically asked as my eyes flicked over the rest of the horse's body.

"His former owner took exception to being thrown off whenever King here got spooked. Took a weighted whip to him."

"Wow," I murmured softly as I ran my hand down the horse's face. "After all that and he still trusts people…"

Quinn approached the horse's head and I struggled not to move back like I was tempted to.

"Took years to earn his trust," Quinn said softly as he slipped the animal's bridle off and replaced it with a halter. His eyes pinned mine as he said, "It takes just seconds to destroy trust, but a lifetime to get it back."

I flinched at that.

I couldn't help but think he wasn't just talking about the horse.

Fuck, I really didn't want him to know the truth about me...

"Here," Quinn said as he handed me the lead rope. "Time for your first lesson." Quinn started to reach for me, but then seemed to rethink the move because he took a step back. "You lead a horse on his left side."

I got into what I could only hope was the right position and glanced over my shoulder at Quinn.

"Okay, take him a few steps forward and then turn him around – we're going out this door," he said as he motioned behind him.

I took a few steps forward and was glad when King followed me. I wasn't sure about the turning around part, but the horse again followed my lead and I easily got him facing the right direction. I followed Quinn out the back door of the barn and towards a small space with three cement walls and a cement floor with a drain in it.

"Bring him in here," Quinn said and I led the horse to where he was waiting. "This is a wash stall," he explained as he took the lead from me. "You can tie him up here so you'll have both hands free to wash him down."

I nodded in understanding and watched as Quinn explained how to secure the lead to the small metal ring affixed to the wall. "This is a release knot," he explained. "It will let you release the lead quickly if the horse starts to spook." He showed me how pulling hard on one end of the lead caused the whole knot to unravel. He demonstrated once more before handing me the lead and saying, "You try."

I forced myself not to focus on his strong fingers as I took the lead from him and went through the motions. It wasn't until I drew the knot tight that I felt my insides clench. The lead rope was made of nylon, but all I felt was smooth fibers of rope as it rested lightly in my hand.

"Beck."

Quinn's voice sounded far away, but I made myself turn to look at him, mostly because he sounded kind of scared which was a quality I couldn't associate with him.

"Beck," he said again softly and then I felt warmth surrounding my hand and I glanced down to see his fingers resting on my hand...the hand I currently had curled around the knot on the lead rope and whose knuckles had gone white with the tight hold I had on the material.

Blue nylon...*not* white rope.

Awareness slowly returned as Quinn's warmth seeped into my skin and I remembered how good it had felt to have his calloused fingers linking with mine against the wall as he'd held me impossibly close to him.

I hadn't just felt indescribable pleasure that night – I'd felt protected and safe.

I'd *felt*.

"Beck," Quinn said for a third time and the cobwebs in my brain finally disintegrated and I remembered where I was. I looked at my hand in disbelief as I realized I'd practically been fondling the knot on the lead rope like it was a lover. I shot a glance at Quinn and felt my stomach drop out when I saw the pity in his gaze.

He knows.

I wanted to curl up into a ball as I realized he knew what I'd been thinking which meant he knew what I'd done fifteen months ago.

Even how I'd done it.

Humiliation swamped my entire body and I struggled to remain upright. I tugged my hand free of his and managed to say, "What's next?"

"Beck-"

"What's next?" I repeated as I stepped away from Quinn and escaped to the other side of King's neck.

It took everything I had not to take off like I wanted to. Instead, I focused on the quiet rumble of Quinn's voice as he explained to me how to wash King down and I ignored his watchful eye as I worked.

It was easy work and I found myself getting lost in the task of rubbing a rubber brush into the horse's coat to loosen some of the dirt and sweat. By the time I was done, my shoes were sopping wet and my pants were damp, but oddly enough, it felt good...like I'd accomplished something. I followed Quinn's instructions to lead King to one of the many pastures surrounding the barn and smiled when the animal began whinnying in excitement at the sight of another horse standing near the gate.

"That's Pilot," Quinn said as he motioned to the horse covered in brown and white spots. "He and King are pretty much inseparable these days." Quinn opened the gate and used his body to keep Pilot back as I led King inside. I unclipped the lead from the horse's halter and he immediately took off at a trot, Pilot right behind him. I chuckled when the very first thing King did was drop to the ground and began rolling in the dirt. Pilot pawed at the ground until King was up and then they both took off at a dead run towards the far end of the pasture. "He's come a long way," Quinn said as he closed the gate and secured it. "King used to attack any other horse we'd put with him so we had to keep him by himself."

"But he likes Pilot," I said as we began walking towards the barn.

"Pilot's another rescue. A few nights after he got here, he got out of his stall and we found him and King in the same stall the next morning. Turns out Pilot is somewhat of an escape artist and not only did he let himself out of his stall, he managed to open King's too. Could have been a disaster, but for whatever reason, King was okay with him."

"Guess he was lonely," I mused as we reached the barn and Quinn took the lead rope from me.

When Quinn didn't say anything, I glanced up at him and saw him watching me. "I guess we're lucky Pilot is such a pushy bastard or King would have spent the rest of his life by himself."

Quinn's words made me shiver…or maybe it was the way he said them. I shifted uneasily and was reminded of my soaked shoes and socks.

"Yeah, those aren't going to cut it," Quinn said as he looked down at my sneakers. "You have some boots at home?"

I shook my head. "Not really my thing," I said.

"Come on," Quinn said. "I think I have a pair that might fit you."

I couldn't help but glance at Quinn's feet which I instantly regretted because it reminded me of how much bigger than me he was all over. But I followed him anyway and felt my pulse ratchet up as I realized our destination was one of the small cottages just beyond the barn. I really didn't want to be confined with the man in any kind of enclosed space, but I knew I'd look foolish if I told him I wanted to stay outside, so I followed him up the couple of porch steps and into the house.

The outside of the house was a soft gray color with white trim. Inside was small but clean and surprisingly cozy. The furniture was simple, but looked comfortable and welcoming. There were a few pictures on the walls depicting horses and landscapes and there was a small flat screen TV hanging on the wall across from the single couch. The kitchen had modern appliances and a small table with two chairs.

"Have a seat," Quinn said as he motioned to one of the chairs. "I'll be right back."

I watched him head down the hallway and disappear into a door to the left, a bedroom presumably. I used the alone time to pull out my phone and send my obligatory morning text to my parents and waited for the response I knew would be forthcoming. I hated the fact that my fathers' days revolved around my texts, but I couldn't argue the point. I just wondered if there would ever come a day when they'd be able to go more than a couple of hours without worrying I'd offed myself.

"Here, try these on," Quinn said as he came back out of the room, a pair of boots in one hand and a cowboy hat in the other.

He handed me a dry pair of socks which I was supremely grateful for. He leaned back against the wall and watched me swap out my footwear for the well-worn brown boots that looked like they belonged in a western movie. They were a little big, but it felt so good to have dry feet, I didn't care. "No way these are yours," I mused as I glanced at Quinn's feet.

"No, they were my husband's."

I stilled at that and shifted my eyes up to Quinn's. I remembered him telling me his husband had died. The fact that he still had the man's boots after a couple of years was telling. "Fuck, Quinn, I'm sorry," I said as I immediately started to take them back off. "I shouldn't-"

"Leave them on," Quinn said softly and I froze. His words could have been an order, but they weren't. His gaze was on the boots. "They look good on you," he murmured. He seemed to lose himself for a moment before he straightened. "Besides, Griff would have turned over in his grave knowing a city slicker like yourself was working around horses with sneakers *and* no hat," he said as he handed me the hat.

I smiled. "City slicker, huh?" I tested the texture of the hat before I tried it on. It felt awkward so I only left it on for a second before removing it. "I guess I am a little out of my element out here," I said. I stood up to get a feel for the boots and then looked up to see Quinn staring at me.

And just like that, the air in the room changed as it came alive with energy.

"I don't know," Quinn murmured. "I think you fit in just fine."

His words struck a chord deep inside of me and I momentarily forgot my insane need to step forward until our bodies were touching.

How many times in my life had I felt like I fit anywhere?

The answer was both simple and pathetic. I didn't even need a single finger to count that high.

Quinn's eyes held mine for the longest time, but, for once, the need to take control of the situation didn't rear its ugly head. Nor did the need to escape and we both just hung there for several beats until Quinn finally tore his gaze free of mine. "You want something to drink before we head back out?"

"Um, sure," I managed as I watched Quinn grab a couple of bottled waters from the fridge. "I'll talk to Jax about taking me someplace this afternoon to get some boots," I offered.

"No rush," Quinn said as he handed me one of the bottles which felt good against my heated skin. "We actually need to head down to Clear Creek this afternoon so we can stop on the way if you want."

"Clear Creek?" I asked as I followed him out of the house.

"Yeah. Clear Creek Ranch. It's a resort about thirty miles south of here. Have you met Roman and Hunter Blackwell yet?"

I shook my head. "No, but Dane and Jax have mentioned them. Roman, he builds luxury resorts, right?"

"Yeah. He's been building one in a valley near the Bitterroot National Forest. Very high end. It's set to open in about a month. Anyway, Callan and I have been finding him the best horses for the place so you and I are going to head down there to see how things are coming with the stables. Callan wants to get the horses moved within the next week so they have plenty of time to get used to the place."

Quinn cast a glance at me. "That's where you and I will be spending most of our time for the next month. Roman's still hiring the staff so I'll be helping him interview people when you and I aren't taking care of the horses."

I nodded. I didn't really care where I'd be working or even what kind of work I'd be doing. As long as it kept me busy enough that I didn't seek out the comfort of my bed, I was good.

Though, admittedly, I'd enjoyed interacting with King today, so maybe things wouldn't be so bad. And Quinn seemed to be keeping things between us professional, so maybe I'd make it through the summer after all. I'd prove to my fathers I wasn't a complete and total mess.

And that they could start trusting me again.

"So, why don't I give you a tour?" Quinn said as we reached the barn. "Then the real work starts."

"Bring it on," I said, feeling encouraged for the first time in a long time.

Yeah, I could do this.

Piece of cake.

CHAPTER 5

QUINN

"Beck," I said softly as I gave his arm a gentle pat. "Wake up."

Beck mumbled something into his shoulder that sounded suspiciously like "Piece of cake, my ass" as he sank deeper into the seat of the truck. I smiled to myself as I gave him a little shake. "Time to get up, city slicker," I said a little more loudly.

"Huh, what?" Beck said as he startled and then straightened. He looked around, his bleary eyes shifting back and forth between me and our surroundings. I loved how rumpled and cute he looked with his hair sticking up all over the place. He'd adamantly refused to wear the hat I'd given him this morning, but I knew it was just a matter of time before he caved. He hadn't needed the protection while working in the barn, but once he spent a few hours beneath the hot Montana sun, he'd be begging me to return it to him. I'd urged him to buy one he liked when we'd stopped to get him his own boots, but he'd muttered something about not being caught dead in a cowboy hat and I'd left it alone. He'd managed to find a pair of boots that fit and had put them on in the truck just moments before he'd fallen asleep.

It had been hard to give him Griff's boots and hat, even for a short amount of time. I'd purposefully kept both the hat and boots at the back of my closet and hadn't pulled them out even once in the two years since I'd arrived at the CB Bar. They were the only things I'd kept besides pictures and Griff's wedding ring to remind me of my husband, though I certainly didn't need any of those things to remember the man I'd loved and lost. And sadly, the hat and boots hadn't even been Griff's favorites. Like the ring, I'd initially gotten his favorite hat and boots back after his death, but one look at them in the police issued plastic bag and I'd quickly handed the bag back to the cops after removing just the ring and asked them to destroy everything in it.

"Wow, sorry," Beck said as he rubbed at his eyes.

"No problem," I responded as I watched Beck try to pull himself together. "You cleaned twelve stalls this morning…that's bound to wear you out if you aren't used to that kind of work. That reminds me," I said as I reached past Beck to the glovebox. The young man flinched and shifted away from me as my hand neared his body. I ignored the fleeting pain that went through me at knowing he wanted nothing to do with my touch and flipped the latch on the glove compartment. "Here," I said as I pulled out the small bottle of generic ibuprofen. "Take a couple now or you'll really be feeling it later."

Beck hesitated and then took the bottle from me. "Sorry," he murmured as his gaze settled on my hand as I closed the glove compartment.

"No worries," I managed to get out. I went to open my door but stopped when I felt fingers on my arm.

"Quinn," Beck said softly and I forced myself to turn and look at him. Sensation flared to life where his fingers were resting against my forearm. I'd rolled up my sleeves earlier in the day so he was touching my skin. "That wasn't about you," Beck whispered as he motioned to the glove compartment.

I desperately wanted to ask him what it *was* about, but I already had a good idea of the answer. If Beck's reaction to our sexual encounter hadn't been enough to tell me the young man had some serious trauma in his past, his reaction to Callan would have been. I doubted Callan or Finn had noticed Beck putting space between himself and Callan when the older man had approached him, but the move was all I'd been able to think about after the men had left the barn, leaving me to deal with Beck. That was why I hadn't touched Beck when I'd explained to him how to lead King to the wash stall or properly wash the horse down.

"You don't owe me any explanations, Beck," I offered as Beck withdrew his hand. "Not about that night in the club, not about this," I said as I motioned between us. "Not about anything, okay?"

Beck nodded. I knew I should just leave it at that and get out of the truck, but I couldn't force myself to open the door. I turned to look at Beck and held his gaze before saying, "But if you ever want to talk, I'm here. I may not have all the answers, but I know how to keep my ears open and my mouth shut." I chuckled and added, "Griff used to say it was one of the qualities that used to drive him craziest about me...and one of the first things he fell in love with."

A small smile drifted over Beck's lips. "What about you?" he asked.

"What about me?"

"What was the quality you fell in love with?"

I chuckled. "The fact that he could love someone who also drove him nuts," I admitted. "He was really good at loving me," I murmured, more to myself than anything else. It took me a moment to remember where I was and I shook my head. "Let's go check things out."

Beck nodded, his knowing eyes holding mine for a moment. We finally got out of the truck and headed towards the huge barn. There was a second pickup truck sitting closer to the entrance and I absently noted the name *Wilder Construction* stenciled on the side of the door. Roman had told me the main barn was mostly done in terms of construction but there were a couple of stalls that needed to be finished. There'd apparently been some kind of problem with the original contractor and a new company had been brought in to complete the job. Since there were already enough completed stalls for the horses we'd be bringing to the resort, it wouldn't have any kind of impact on the work Beck and I would be doing over the next several weeks.

While Callan's barn was modern and had some great amenities, this barn was top of the line and I could tell no expense had been spared in designing the place. Which made sense since the clients would expect nothing but the best. The horses would be well cared for which would hopefully make up for having to be handled by inexperienced riders. Callan and I had been very careful to select only the most docile of horses with the temperament to deal with all manner of riders and I was pleased that Roman was letting me help in the hiring of the staff who would ensure the animals were well cared for.

While Roman catered to a very exclusive clientele, he'd made it clear that no amount of money would excuse rough treatment of his horses and he really did see them that way - as *his* horses. The guy gave off the impression of being a ruthless businessman, but I'd interacted with him and his young husband enough to know that while he could probably hold his own in the business world, he was a softie when it came to his man and his little menagerie of animals that lived on the land surrounding the house he and Hunter had built in a valley just outside of Dare.

As soon as we entered the barn, we could hear the sound of a hammer striking wood so I led Beck towards the stalls at the end of the aisle so we could introduce ourselves. A bunch of tools were sitting outside one of the stalls. The man inside had his back turned to us as he finished pounding a nail into the wall, but it didn't matter because I instantly recognized his broad shoulders and blond hair and I felt my gut clench. Beck stood completely unaware next to me and I debated whether I should try to get him out of there, but I was too slow because the man turned around and Beck instantly gasped when their eyes met.

"Beck," Brody said in surprise and then his eyes shifted to me. "Quinn," he acknowledged, his voice quiet, but clearly caught off guard.

"What...what are you doing here?" Beck whispered in disbelief and then his gaze shot to me. "What is he doing here?" This time his question was much more high-pitched and I could tell he was close to losing it. "You...you know each other?"

Fuck, I had no clue how to handle this.

Brody stepped out of the stall, his hammer loose in his hand. Beck instantly stepped back and I could tell he was getting ready to flee so I stepped in his path. "Beck, this is Brody." I cast a glance over my shoulder at Brody before returning my attention to Beck whose eyes were wide. I could see the pulse point in his neck thrumming frantically. "I didn't know he'd be here," I added, though I wasn't sure why since it was irrelevant and Beck was too far gone to actually give a shit.

"Did you set me up that night?" Beck nearly shouted. "Was it some kind of game you play-"

"No," Brody cut in and then he was moving closer to me so that we were effectively caging Beck in. He too must have sensed the young man was ready to run. "We'd never met before." I felt Brody's eyes on me but kept my gaze on Beck. My anxiety was sky-high because he was experiencing the same level of panic he'd been feeling the day of the accident. And now that I knew what he was capable of...

"I met Quinn the day of your accident."

"What?" Beck asked in confusion.

"I'm a paramedic. My partner and I responded to Quinn's call to 911 that day."

Beck shot me a quick look, the betrayal clear. "I didn't see you!"

"I told him not to let you see him," I finally said when Brody didn't say anything. "I knew it would upset you and you needed to stay calm so you wouldn't hurt yourself further..."

My voice dropped off when I saw Beck's jaw tighten with my last words. Fuck, I hadn't meant it like it sounded, but before I could say anything, Beck tried to move past us. "Just hang on, Beck," Brody implored as he stepped in Beck's path but kept his hands out so Beck would see he wasn't trying to touch him.

"No, get out of my way!"

"Quinn and I hadn't met before that night in the club," Brody cut in as he continued to block Beck who'd retreated until his back hit the wall behind him. "After your accident, we met at the hospital where you were being treated. He told me what happened at the ranch and I told him..."

When Brody's voice fell away, I glanced at him. He actually looked flushed and he momentarily dropped his eyes.

"You told him I tried to kill myself," Beck murmured.

Brody nodded. "When we brought you in, my partner, Luke, told the ER doctors about your history. I guess he knew from talking to Jax and Dane."

"Yeah, everyone fucking knows," Beck snapped. "Gotta all band together to keep an eye on the suicidal kid so he doesn't off himself on your watch."

Brody ignored the comment. "I asked Luke about you when we were headed back to the firehouse where we're stationed."

"And you told *him*," Beck said bitterly as he cast me a glance before returning his attention to Brody. "Did you tell your partner that you sucked my dick while he" – his eyes shot to me briefly – "was fucking me in a dirty bathroom stall while everyone and his brother got off listening to us…me?"

"No," Brody said softly. "No one knows what happened that night but the three of us."

Beck's eyes landed on me. "Would you take me back to the ranch now? I want to go home."

"Beck, we need to figure this out-" I began.

"No, we don't," he interjected. "This was a mistake," he bit out. "This place, that night – it was all one big fucking mistake," he muttered. "I'm going back to Seattle."

"Beck," Brody started to say, but I cut him off, my temper flaring.

"And then what?" I asked. "You go back to the way things were? You go back to a life where you'd rather-" I stopped myself before I could finish the thought because it was just too damn disturbing. "You came to Dare to get away, right?" I asked when I'd managed to calm myself. Beck didn't answer me, but he didn't need to. "You think I don't know what that's like?" I managed to get out. "To want to start over…to get away from a place that only reminds you of everything you've lost…that was taken from you?!"

It wasn't until Brody's hand brushed mine that I realized I'd started to yell. The spark of electricity caught my attention and I glanced at the man next to me. He was looking at me with a mix of pity and understanding and I knew he knew exactly what I was talking about. I sucked in a breath and turned my attention back to Beck. "You want the truth, Beck?" I finally asked.

He didn't respond, but I knew I had his complete attention.

"I don't regret that night. Being with you...with him," – I shot Brody a quick look – "was..."

I struggled to find the right words, but realized there weren't any. I'd come alive that night and that was something I hadn't felt in any of the 762 days since I'd lost Griff. I finally shook my head because there were no words. "I understand it wasn't the same for you and I'm truly sorry if we hurt you...either that night or with how we reacted after your accident. But it doesn't need to change what this place can be for you. A place to start over, clear your head...whatever." I held Beck's gaze as I whispered, "Just tell us what you need, Beck. We'll give it to you." I risked a glance at Brody and saw him nod at Beck.

Beck didn't respond. He barely even reacted to what I'd said and I finally stepped back from Brody so there was a clear gap between us that Beck could walk through. Resigned, I dug my car keys out of my pocket.

"I need two things," Beck said softly, his eyes shifting back and forth between me and Brody. "I don't want to talk about that night."

"Okay," Brody responded and I nodded my head.

"What's the other thing?" I asked eagerly, too eagerly. I had no idea why it was so goddamn important that Beck not run again.

"I need you to not be waiting..."

When he didn't continue, Brody prodded, "Waiting?"

Beck sucked in a breath. "I need you to not be waiting for me to try it again."

I knew he was talking about his suicide attempt. The request made sense, but I also knew how tough it would be. From the moment Brody had told me Beck's secret, I'd looked and thought of the young man differently...which was exactly what he didn't want.

He wanted to be normal.

The realization struck me hard. He *had* come here to start over yet that was nearly impossible now that practically everyone knew about his past. And while I could appreciate his family's need to know that the people he was spending the summer with were watching out for Beck, the knowledge of what he'd done would always color the way they saw him.

He'd never just be Beck, the young man visiting from Seattle for the summer.

He'd be Beck, the young man who'd made the decision to tie a rope around his neck and take that one step that would ensure he'd never feel even another moment of pain.

"We..." Brody began and then I felt his questioning eyes on me. I nodded. "We can do that," Brody said as he held Beck's gaze.

Some of the tension seemed to drain from Beck's body as we all hung there wondering what to do or say next. The awkward silence grew, but I was more aware of something else growing between us. It was the same thing that had flared to life from the moment Beck and I had walked into that bathroom and spotted Brody. My body came alive as I remembered how tight Beck's lithe body had been around my flesh and the feel of Brody's firm lips owning mine. I risked looking at Brody and saw that he wasn't faring much better than me. I was close enough to him to hear his breathing tick up and there was absolutely nothing he could have done to hide the hunger in his whiskey-colored eyes. We both shifted our gazes to Beck at the same exact time and my dick shot to full attention at the sight of the young man with his back now pressed against the wall. But he didn't look like he was trying to escape us anymore...more like he needed the support because his lips were parted and his skin was flushed. The air crackled around us with electricity and I was actually taking a step towards him when the sound of footsteps behind me registered.

"Quinn," a man's voice called and I both cursed him and sent him a volley of silent thanks for the interruption. Embarrassment swamped me as I pulled my hat off my head and held it over my groin to cover my erection. To the man, it would look like I was just being polite, but I suspected Brody knew what was happening because he seemed to be doing the same thing with the hammer in his hand. It was utterly ridiculous that two grown men were behaving like pubescent teens sporting their first boners.

"Mr. Blackwell," I said as I held out my right hand to shake his as he reached me. The man tilted his head at me and I realized my mistake. "Roman," I said sheepishly. I'd met the man many times in non-business settings, but still failed to see him as anything other than my quasi boss, even though he really wasn't. My goal when I'd come to Dare had been to keep things professional with the men I worked with, but it was a challenge when they were all so open and insistent about pursuing friendships outside that relationship.

"How are you?" Roman asked as he gave my hand a firm shake. Luckily, he didn't notice anything off with me or the situation because he nodded briefly at Brody before shaking his hand as well.

"I'm fine," I murmured. "The place is looking amazing," I added.

Roman smiled brightly as he nodded. "Thank you. It's really coming along." He turned his attention to Brody. "Are you finding everything you need?"

"Yes, thank you." Brody glanced at the stall behind him. "I should have these finished within a week and then I'll start on the tack room."

Another nod from Roman. "You're a lifesaver, Brody. Luke tells me you actually took some vacation time to help me finish this job."

A smattering of color brightened Brody's cheeks and I felt my slightly softened dick threaten to fill again. God, the man was beautiful.

"It's not a big deal...one of the other paramedics had asked me to cover for her this fall when she and her husband head to Europe for their ten-year anniversary so we just did a swap."

"Still, I'll be adding to the price we agreed upon. Luke also told me you haven't been there long enough to earn paid time off."

"No, Mr. Blackwell," – Brody hesitated at Roman's brief frown – "Roman," he corrected. "That isn't necessary."

"You should know better than to argue with my husband by now, Brody." I looked up to see Roman's young husband, Hunter, enter the barn, a big white dog and three little scrappy-looking terrier mixes at his heels.

Roman's whole face lit up as his eyes fell on Hunter and there was no hesitation between them when Hunter reached his side. They kissed for several long seconds, seemingly oblivious to the world around them.

Griff and I had kissed like that.

It seemed like a lifetime ago.

"Hey," Roman murmured against Hunter's lips.

"Hey yourself."

I busied myself with greeting the dogs as they surrounded me and began sniffing my legs. I cast a glance over my shoulder to see Beck watching us all nervously. The biggest dog, Champ, left me to go check Beck out and I bit back a smile when Beck visibly relaxed as the giant animal began nuzzling his hands.

God bless the power of animals.

"You must be Beck," I heard Roman say and since my eyes were still on Beck, I saw all the tension and then some return the moment Roman said his name. Roman stepped between me and Brody to walk towards Beck and I didn't miss the way the younger man's back straightened and his hands fisted. It was the same reaction he'd had to Callan in the barn back at the ranch.

Was he actually afraid of men?

I thought on it and remembered how relaxed he'd seemed around Finn.

"Um, yeah," Beck said. One of his hands actually closed around Champ's collar as if he were trying to prevent the dog from leaving his side. He managed to shake Roman's hand, but he dropped his eyes when he did it. "It's nice to meet you."

Roman seemed to notice Beck's tension, because he stepped back as soon as he'd shaken Beck's hand. "Beck, this is my husband, Hunter."

Hunter wasn't quite as tall or heavily built as his dark-haired husband and while they both were friendly and open, Hunter had a lightness to him that Roman couldn't pull off. Whereas Roman was naturally assertive, the impression I'd always gotten of Hunter was that he was the more soft-hearted of the pair. I'd seen him volunteer at the ranch with some of the abused horses that came through and his kind-hearted nature made him a valuable asset for those animals that struggled to trust humans.

"Hi, Beck, welcome to Dare. We've been looking forward to meeting you," Hunter said as he strode up to Beck and shook his hand. Beck seemed a little less tense as he thanked the man. With Roman he'd looked like he'd wanted to run away. With Hunter he was more wary than anything else.

I cast a glance at Brody to see if he'd noticed the behavior and I could see from the concern in his eyes that he had.

For whatever reason, Beck seemed to have an issue with more dominant, naturally confident men. If I hadn't seen his reaction to Brody, I would have thought the physical aspect of the man being dark-haired to be a factor, but Brody was blond just like Hunter and Finn. The common denominator between me, Brody and the other men who seemed to make Beck more uncomfortable was that we were physically larger than him and had personalities that were assertive rather than submissive.

The idea that Beck had been hurt in the past by someone matching our characteristics was disturbing, but I didn't have time to dwell on it because Roman turned to me and said, "Quinn, I've got that list of applicants in the office. Do you have time to go over the interview schedule with me?"

"Of course," I said, though I didn't really want to leave Beck alone since he was looking like he was going to fly off the handle at any moment.

"How about I show Beck and Brody around?" Hunter offered. "You haven't seen the entire place yet, right, Brody?"

"No, I haven't," Brody said. "If it's okay with Mr. Blackwell... Roman, I'd love to see it."

"Sounds like a plan," Roman said. He looked over his shoulder at Beck. "You okay with that, Beck?"

Beck merely nodded, averting his eyes from Roman's almost immediately. I saw a small frown creep over Roman's mouth and he furrowed his brow before he shot me a questioning look. I suspected he'd be asking me about the young man's behavior the second he got me alone.

"Okay, great," Hunter said. "We can drive over to the lodge and grab a golf cart."

Roman nodded and then took Hunter's hand in his. They began walking towards the barn door as the passel of little dogs followed at their heels. Champ stayed with Beck even though he wasn't clinging to the dog's collar anymore. Beck finally pushed off the wall and moved past me and Brody. I gently grabbed his arm, ignoring his gasp as sparks flared between us. "Are you okay with this? I can come on the tour with you. Roman will understand."

A part of me was worried Beck would be irritated by the question, but he shook his head and cast a quick glance at Brody. "I'll be fine. Thanks."

I nodded and released him.

Brody and I exchanged a silent, but very charged look between us and I knew we were thinking the same thing.

How the hell were we going to get through the next few weeks together?

CHAPTER 6

BRODY

What were the fucking odds?

Twenty minutes ago I'd been bent over in a stall hammering some nails in place while my thoughts were dominated by the same two men who'd been invading my every waking moment, not to mention starring in some very raunchy dreams, and now I was about to spend nearly every day of the next few weeks in their company…was in the company of one even now.

After leaving the barn, I'd driven with Hunter and Roman in one of their cars to the lodge where Roman's office was located and where I'd assumed we'd be starting our tour as Roman and Quinn talked. Quinn and Beck had followed in their truck. I'd hoped Beck's stress level would ease a bit once we got out of the barn, but he'd seemed just as tense as before as he and Quinn had gotten out of the truck and he'd watched Quinn follow Roman into the lodge. Hunter and I had waited near a golf cart sitting in front of the lodge for Beck, but it had taken him several long moments to seem to garner up the courage to join us. In the end, the big white Great Dane had seemed to pull Beck from his funk and he'd finally walked towards us. Though he'd looked more like a lamb heading for slaughter.

And I had no doubt it was because of me, not Hunter.

I hadn't missed how tense Beck had been around Roman, myself and Quinn, but less so with Hunter. Quinn hadn't missed it either, if the look we'd exchanged was anything to go by. The whole thing was confusing as fuck. If Beck was afraid of a certain type of man, why had he gone to that club that night? Why had he hooked up with someone like Quinn when there'd been plenty of different types of guys to choose from, some even what one might consider docile. Even if he'd wanted to be topped, he could have found an unintimidating guy to give him what he needed.

My mind raced with possibilities until I felt like it was going to explode. I'd never been one for accepting something at face value. I liked having the answers to questions because it made it easier to react. I knew it probably went back to my days as a kid when I didn't understand why I couldn't be like I was supposed to when it came to wanting to be with girls or when I was trying to make sense of a God who supposedly loved me, but not the real me.

I focused my attention on Beck as he sat stiffly in the front passenger seat of the golf cart. Hunter was driving, so that left me sitting in the back seat. The Great Dane, which Hunter had introduced as Champ, was running next to the slow-moving golf cart while his three little counterparts were all crowded onto Beck's lap. I liked how the animals seemed to help relax Beck, though he was still a far cry from enjoying himself.

"What are their names?" Beck finally asked as he protectively held on to the little dogs which I was thinking were some kind of Yorkshire Terrier/Dachshund mixes.

To Hunter's credit, he hadn't acknowledged the tension wafting off of Beck and when all three dogs had initially climbed on his lap, he hadn't offered to rescue Beck from them, presumably because he too could see they had a calming effect on the young man.

"That's Larry," Hunter said as he pointed to one dog. "This is Curly," he said as he settled his hand on the second dog's head. "And this little girl is Moe."

I smiled at that and was pleased to see Beck's mouth pulling into a grin. "Larry, Curly and Moe?" he repeated. "The Three Stooges?"

Hunter chuckled. "My grandmother named them. She has a thing for old sitcoms."

"Your grandmother is Mrs. Greene, right? She takes care of Dane and Jax's kids."

"Yep, that's her," Hunter said with a smile, like he knew what was coming next.

"She's…she's…" Beck began.

Hunter laughed. "Yes, she is." He looked over his shoulder at me. "Have you met my Gran yet, Brody?"

"I have," I said. "Luke and I responded to a call when one of her friends fell and twisted her ankle. She rode in the ambulance with us to the hospital."

Another laugh from Hunter. "Why do I feel the need to apologize?"

I ignored the flutter in my belly as Beck cast me a look and kept watching me as I spoke.

"Your grandmother kept telling me to give her friend the "good drugs" and then started asking me if I was single or married. She seemed quite pleased to hear I was gay."

"She would," Hunter responded. "Gran's made it her personal mission to make Dare a mecca for homosexuals. She got the school to sponsor a PFLAG chapter and she's arranged the annual Dare Pride Day every year for the past four years. Don't be surprised if she starts an account for you on a dating website…you have to put your foot down with her."

I smiled at that. I guessed the woman didn't weigh more than eighty pounds sopping wet, but she intimidated the hell out of me.

My eyes met Beck's and I became lost in the humor I saw there as I murmured, "I'll keep it in mind."

I had absolutely no interest in dating anyone and the only site I occasionally checked out was Grindr because *dating* was the last thing on my mind these days.

But I couldn't help but wonder what it would be like to do all the "date" things with someone like the young man currently studying me with open curiosity.

Not someone *like* him…*him*.

Or maybe with a certain gorgeous cowboy.

What about both?

The unbidden image of the three of us lying in a tangle of limbs in bed had me sucking in a breath. Another one of us sitting around a table eating and chatting was even more disturbing…and unexpected.

"The ad she posted for Quinn was called, Save A Horse, Ride A Hunky Cowboy Instead," Hunter said.

Beck and I held each other's gazes for several seconds until it hit us both at the same time what Hunter had just said. Then we both burst out into laughter.

"Oh my God, what did Quinn say when he found out?" Beck asked.

Hunter shot him a grin. "He had no idea it was even happening until Gran showed up at the ranch with one of the guys who'd responded to the ad. Gran spent almost a week chatting with the guy online before she told him she wasn't Quinn."

"She *catfished* him?" I managed to get out.

Hunter nodded. "The guy was a good sport about it. I guess after seeing Quinn's picture, he was all in, if you know what I mean."

I did know what he meant and some of my humor fled and was replaced with a shot of jealousy. I'd just assumed Quinn was single, but in actuality, I had no idea if he was or wasn't. A glance at Beck showed he didn't seem as carefree as he had a moment ago. He shot me a glance and just like that my laughter was snuffed out and all I could think was one thing as Hunter continued his story.

Ours.

Jesus, what the hell was wrong with me? Quinn didn't belong to me and Beck. Hell, I had no claim to either man.

But I couldn't shake the dark thread of possessiveness that was weaving through my body.

"What happened when they met?" Beck asked, though his voice sounded more worried than curious.

Hunter didn't seem to notice the change in either of us because he barreled on. "Quinn finally agreed to have coffee with the guy if Gran promised to take the ad down and never pimp him out again. Gran was so sure she'd found his future husband that she agreed and reminded them she was still certified to perform marriages."

I laughed, but it was forced.

"She was quite put out when Quinn told her it was a no go. But she kept her word and stopped playing matchmaker for him. But you two might want to keep an eye out...if she starts sneaking pictures of you..."

Hunter ended the statement with a chuckle. We'd reached the area of the resort where most of the lodging was located and I only half-listened as Hunter began the tour. The site Roman had picked for his resort was beautiful and he'd clearly spared no expense if the extravagant lodgings were anything to go by. There was also a golf course, a large lake with an array of watercraft for guests to use and a waterfront restaurant. And while we didn't see it, Hunter explained there would be several ski slopes available to guests in the winter along with things like snowmobiling and cross-country skiing.

The stables were surrounded by dozens of paddocks and next to the barn was a building for the barn staff. We didn't actually stop to go inside, but I'd already seen it when Roman had offered me the option of living onsite for the next few weeks instead of commuting from my apartment near Missoula. The building was in the shape of a U with a large courtyard. Each unit was equivalent to a small studio apartment with its own bathroom and a separate, private entrance. There was a second door in each residence that led to a hallway that allowed the residents to access an open area where there was a full kitchen and entertainment space. Even though they were staff quarters, they were extremely spacious and well designed.

Once we got back to the lodge, Hunter parked the golf cart and took us on a foot tour of the massive building which offered countless amenities to guests including two indoor pools, a gym, another restaurant, a salon and spa and a coffee shop. The list of services was endless and left me wondering how anyone could afford such luxury. My own family had been considered wealthy, but coming from "old money" in Charleston, South Carolina might as well have been the wrong side of the tracks compared to the money that would grace the resort's coffers.

After the tour, Beck and I managed to say all the right things about how nice the place was, though I suspected we were both equally intimidated by what we'd seen. We were following Hunter back to the driveway where the golf cart was located when Hunter's cell phone rang.

His face went pale as he checked the Caller ID and he quickly looked at us and said, "I have to take this. Do you mind?"

"No, go ahead," I said and Beck nodded. "We'll wait by the golf cart."

Hunter answered the phone and took a few steps away from us so his voice wouldn't carry. Beck and I made our way to the golf cart, the little dogs trailing us. Champ had stayed with Hunter and I could see the big dog sitting quietly at his master's feet as Hunter talked on the phone. Concern went through me that it was bad news, but I forced myself not to watch the man since it felt like an invasion of his privacy, even though I couldn't hear anything.

I was very aware of the fact that Beck and I were alone for the first time since the blow-up in the barn…hell, since ever actually.

And predictably, Beck's tension returned as he stood next to me, his eyes on Hunter.

"He's sweet, huh?" I asked as I motioned to Hunter.

Beck glanced at me and then nodded. "He is."

"If you think this place is beautiful," I said as I scanned our surroundings. "You should see where they live." When Beck kept his gaze on me, I continued. "It's this amazing valley just outside Dare. I guess that's how they met…Roman originally came to Dare to buy the land so he could develop the resort there, but then he met Hunter whose grandparents owned the property…"

"And the rest is history," Beck finished, his mouth pulling into a smile. "Do you know what he does for a living?" Beck asked as he motioned his head towards Hunter.

"He's some kind of environmental engineer. Something to do with designing alternative energy sources. I think Roman actually used Hunter's company to make this place greener," I said.

"And Roman's brother, he's married to your partner, Luke, right? He's a famous author or something?"

I nodded. "Gray Hawthorne." I shot Beck a smile. "And if things weren't complicated enough already, Luke and Rhys were foster brothers when they were kids. It's a very busy family tree."

Beck snorted.

"What?" I asked when he shook his head at me.

"You should see my family. They make this one look like a straight line."

I chuckled, but my humor fled as my eyes connected with Beck's and we got stuck in time. "I'd like that," I finally said and I realized it was the truth. I'd give my right arm to learn even a little bit of what made the young man tick. "You have pictures?" I asked softly.

Beck was quiet for a moment as he seemed to consider me. Finally, he nodded and reached for his phone and a tremor of excitement shifted through me. But before he could unlock the phone, we heard Champ let out a short bark. I looked up and saw the dog nudging at Hunter's hands as Hunter stood frozen, his phone hanging loosely in his fingers.

"Hunter," I said as I hurried towards him, concerned about how pale he looked. "Everything okay?" I asked. Beck went around to Hunter's other side and carefully pulled the phone free of his lax fingers.

Hunter looked up at me and I saw a shimmer of tears in his eyes. "What?" he asked. It took him a moment to return to the present and then he let out a little laugh. "I'm sorry," he said. "I'm fine...really." He swiped at his tears and shook his head. "Happy tears," he whispered as he pointed to the wet tracks on his face.

"So, everything is okay?" I asked.

He nodded. "Better than okay," he murmured softly and I finally saw his eyes brighten and color began to return to his skin. "Um, that was the adoption agency Roman and I have been working with."

"You're adopting?" Beck asked gently.

Another nod from Hunter who finally sucked in a deep breath. "Last fall Roman and I went to Mississippi to meet a young woman who was considering putting her child up for adoption. She picked us, but when we went down there when the baby was born, she changed her mind. We...we were heartbroken."

I nodded in understanding and I saw Beck put his hand on Hunter's arm.

"We weren't sure we wanted to go through all of that again," Hunter explained.

"Understandable," Beck said. "You lost a child."

Hunter nodded. "Yeah...I mean, the baby was never technically ours, but..."

"But you still grieved the loss," I finished for him.

"We did. The agency called us the night before we were supposed to go home and asked us if we were interested in maybe adopting an older child. They told us about a little girl in Texas. The agency had handled her adoption when she'd been a baby, but her parents split up. The adoptive father took off and the adoptive mother was having mental problems so she contacted the agency to help her find the girl a new family. We decided to go meet her...Allie...her name is Allie. She's three."

I nodded and cast a glance at Beck who was still gently stroking Hunter's upper arm.

"We knew she was meant to be ours the second we met her. Since it's an out-of-state adoption, it's been a lengthy legal process," Hunter explained. "But..."

He looked at the phone in Beck's hand and stared at it for a long moment. "She's ours."

I sighed in relief and I saw Beck's arm go around Hunter as he handed him his phone.

"Congratulations, Daddy," I said with a smile and Hunter's eyes widened.

He nodded and then laughed. "I need to tell Roman."

"Go," Beck said.

Hunter smiled and then wiped at his eyes one last time. "You guys will be okay getting back to the barn?"

"We'll be fine," I said quickly. "Go find your husband."

At that exact moment, the sliding doors to the lodge opened and Roman and Quinn exited the building, deep in conversation. But as soon as Roman's eyes met Hunter's, the conversation ceased and Roman was striding towards us.

"Hunter," he said with concern and I realized he'd seen his husband wiping at the remnants of his tears.

Hunter didn't say anything as he closed the distance between him and his husband and then they were wrapped around each other.

"Hunter, baby, what is it?" Roman whispered as a sob tore free of Hunter. "You're scaring me."

Hunter pulled back enough so his husband could grip his face. He let out a wet laugh and whispered, "She's ours, Roman. We have a daughter."

Roman stood frozen for several long beats until he managed to get out, "We're fathers?"

Hunter nodded and then they were both laughing and embracing. Quinn gave them a wide berth as he made his way towards us, presumably so he wouldn't interrupt the intimate moment. He motioned to us and Beck and I quietly followed him to his truck. No words were spoken as we got into the truck, me in the passenger seat and Beck in the back seat. Quinn was silent as he started up the vehicle, but he didn't put it in drive and I finally realized he was still watching the two men where they continued to hold on to each other as they talked.

I cast a glance at Beck who was watching Quinn with concern and he briefly shrugged at my questioning look.

"Quinn," I said softly.

Quinn didn't respond so I put my hand on his forearm. The move got his attention and he glanced first at my hand and then at me. "You okay?" I asked.

His pained eyes snapped back to the happy couple and then he nodded. "Yeah, of course." Quinn jerked the gears and put the truck in reverse. I removed my hand from his arm and felt the loss almost immediately. Not a word was spoken during the short drive back to the barn. Quinn's mouth was pulled into a tight frown the entire time. As soon as he put the truck in park once we reached the barn, he started to reach for the door handle, but I grabbed his arm once again. The pain was rolling off of him in waves and the idea of just letting him walk away was unacceptable to me.

"Talk to us, Quinn."

Quinn stilled, but didn't jerk his arm free like I thought he would. But he also didn't say anything.

"You're happy for them, right?" I asked, hoping to prod him into speaking. I moved my hand to his leg so it was resting just above his knee.

"Of course I am," he said, his eyes connecting with mine for a brief moment. "I know how long they've been waiting for this moment…"

He fell silent again and I willed him to say something…anything that would explain his behavior. But when he remained mute, I knew he was done talking and I began to remove my hand from his leg so he could escape us like he so clearly wanted.

But to my surprise, Beck shifted in the backseat until he was almost directly behind Quinn's seat. Quinn had removed his hat once we were in the truck and put it on the dash and the older model truck had no headrests so I had an unobstructed view of Beck's fingers skimming over the back of Quinn's neck. The move surprised me, but I was even more surprised by Quinn's reaction to it. He actually closed his eyes and leaned his head back, seemingly into the touch. Beck obliged him by letting his fingers slide into the short hairs at the nape of Quinn's neck. My whole body lit up as if Beck were touching me that way.

"You and Griff wanted that," Beck said gently. A statement, not a question.

I had no idea who Griff was, but Quinn eventually nodded.

"I'm sorry, Quinn," Beck murmured and then he slid his arm around Quinn's neck so it was lying gently over his collarbone. Quinn's left hand came up to hold onto Beck's arm. Even with the car seat separating most of their bodies, the embrace was incredibly intimate and I almost felt like an intruder.

Until Quinn's other hand closed over mine where it was still resting on his leg and gently squeezed.

We held there like that for what seemed like hours, but was really only seconds. I'd never been a part of such an intense moment that had absolutely nothing to do with sex.

And all I could think was one thing.

More.

CHAPTER 7

BECK

I had no idea what had possessed me to reach for Quinn, but I couldn't make myself regret it as I felt his fingers curl over my arm. I was reminded of how Quinn had held me in a similar manner in that bathroom stall and how safe I'd felt in that moment.

I'd meant to offer that same kind of comfort, but hadn't known how.

I wasn't sure it worked until Quinn sighed softly and leaned into my touch just a little bit more. His skin was warm and soft, his hair silky between my fingers. I fought the urge to press my nose against the crook of his neck so I could inhale more of his unique scent which was a combination of horses, leather and man. I settled for lowering my chin to the top of his shoulder, but a need inside me that I couldn't explain had me pressing my lips to that same spot. I cursed the layer of fabric preventing me from feeling his skin, but the thought was fleeting as I settled my gaze on where Quinn's hand was resting on top of Brody's on Quinn's leg. At some point they'd linked their fingers.

Just as images of those hands stroking over my body began to loop through my head, I felt Quinn stiffen. "We should get to work," he said quietly and then he was straightening, forcing me to release my grip on him. The loss was striking and confusing.

I'd never had a problem showing physical affection with my family, but it wasn't something I'd ever shown a sexual partner or even a friend, though admittedly there hadn't been that many friends to share that kind of connection with.

Sadly, I couldn't say the same about the number of sexual partners I'd had.

I sat back in the seat for a moment as Quinn exited the vehicle. I could sense Brody's gaze on me, but I was feeling a little too raw to look at him. Less than an hour ago I'd been ready to run for the hills when I'd recognized Brody, but now...now, I didn't know what I wanted. They'd agreed to my demands without hesitation, but just because they weren't going to talk about that night at the club or pretend that they didn't know I'd tried to take my own life, didn't mean those things wouldn't be front and center in their minds whenever they looked at me.

Hell, I wanted to forget that night in the bathroom stall myself, yet from the moment Brody had been shoved back into my existence, I'd been thinking of little else.

Not to mention a whole slew of new fantasies that had taken up residence in my brain, starring both men.

At the same time.

I climbed out of the truck and followed Quinn into the barn. He'd stopped by the first stall and was examining the door latch like it was the most interesting thing in the world. Brody stopped near Quinn, but when Quinn failed to notice him, murmured, "I should get back to it," and then headed towards the other end of the aisle, presumably to continue working on the stall he'd been in when we'd arrived.

I waited by Quinn for several long moments while he entered the stall and looked around. When he seemed satisfied with whatever it was he'd been looking for, he finally focused his attention on me. Whatever emotion he'd been feeling was shuttered behind an indifferent expression. "Come on, I'll show you around," he said.

I nodded and followed. Quinn explained things about the barn's layout that didn't really mean much to me so I nodded occasionally. I understood the gist of what he said, though. Basically, we'd be moving the horses to their new home within the coming few days and then it would be several weeks of letting them get adjusted. My job would be to clean stalls and help care for the horses until the new staff started. He also mentioned something about taking the horses out to explore their new surroundings, but I had no idea what he meant by that and I didn't ask. His standoffishness bothered me more than I wanted to admit and I didn't like the emotions rolling through me because of it. These days I typically moved at two speeds. I was either numb and exhausted or I was anxious and seeking escape. Those emotions took up most of my energy so they were kind of a blessing and a curse. Being numb meant I didn't have to care about the things happening around me and being wired meant I couldn't even focus long enough to even worry about it.

But now...now all I could think about was how hard it had been for Quinn to witness the joy Hunter and Roman had been experiencing as they faced the prospect of starting their family. And instead of wanting to avoid the topic, I wanted to ask Quinn to share his story with me.

"Any questions?" Quinn asked and I tuned in long enough to see that we'd left the barn and walked past the paddocks so that we'd looped around to the front of the stables where the trucks were parked. My gaze fell on Brody's truck and then my eyes moved on their own to the dim interior of the barn to see if I could see him.

I couldn't.

"Beck?"

"Huh?" I said, automatically. When there was just silence, I snapped out of the headspace I'd been in and realized Quinn was studying me, his face impassive and unreadable. Hell, I liked it better when he was looking at me with concern.

Which made no fucking sense whatsoever.

"Do you have any questions for me?" Quinn repeated.

Yes.

"No," I murmured.

Quinn glanced at his watch and then said, "Let's head back to the ranch. We just need to bring the horses in and feed them dinner, then we'll call it a day."

I nodded and followed Quinn to the truck. The ride to the ranch was quiet which I should have liked but didn't, which only served to confuse me more. Once we reached the CB Bar, Quinn was mechanical as he showed me how to use a laminated chart to determine how much feed to place in each horse's stall while he went out and brought the animals into the barn from the pastures. I couldn't help but feel like he was eager to get rid of me at that point and that actually stung a little.

Once the last horse was fed, I watched Quinn give Koda an affectionate pat before closing the partition on his stall that allowed the horse to stick his head out. It was barely five o'clock and still light out, but exhaustion started to settle in my limbs as I followed Quinn towards the front of the barn where my car was parked. But it wasn't the same kind of empty exhaustion I was used to…no, my body actually ached and my muscles burned, but in a pleasant way. While I suspected Quinn had taken it easy on me today in terms of actual physical labor, I still felt like I'd done more in a handful of hours than I'd done in a year. Back home, I hadn't been stable enough to have a job so most of my free time had been spent in my room reading… when I wasn't sleeping, that is.

"Same time tomorrow?" I asked as I watched Quinn reach into his truck to retrieve the hat and boots he'd lent me earlier in the day…his dead husband's hat and boots.

Quinn nodded. As I turned to go, he called my name and I felt my belly flutter in anticipation.

This was it…this was the part where the Quinn from this morning would show up…the kind, concerned Quinn who hadn't wanted me to be too uncomfortable in wet socks and sneakers.

"Yeah?" I said as I turned to face him.

"Roman offered to let us stay at the resort over the next few weeks. In the staff quarters near the barn."

I remembered the U-shaped building Hunter had pointed out.

"I'll probably take him up on it to save on the commute each way, but it's up to you if you want to stay there as well. Dane and Jax might miss having you stay with them…" Quinn began, but then his voice faltered.

It didn't matter. I knew what he meant. If I stayed at the resort, I'd have a room to myself with minimal supervision. A dream come true for me, but a nightmare for my keepers for the summer. And even if my hosts didn't object, my parents surely would.

"I'll talk to them about it," I said.

While the commute didn't bother me overly much, the prospect of being able to have my own space, even just for a few weeks, appealed to me more than I wanted to admit. Not because I hoped to get away with anything or because I didn't like being around Jax, Dane and their kids. No, my reasons were much more simplistic…boring even.

I wanted the chance to act like a fucking adult.

I was the first to acknowledge how much I got away with just because of the labels I'd earned. And there were times when I'd taken advantage of it. But something about the idea of being accountable – of me having to hold myself accountable – appealed to me like nothing had in a really long time. It was more than just about being a grown-up. It was a chance to see what being normal was like…even if it was a title I'd never truly hold.

"You should know that Roman told me Brody's going to be staying there too."

Whereas my belly was fluttering before, now it was doing somersaults. The idea of sharing even a fraction of living space with both men should have scared the shit out of me (and it did). But it also excited me. Even though I couldn't let anything happen with either or both men…

A violent shiver snaked down my spine as the word 'both' got stuck in my head. Jesus, what was wrong with me?

"Okay," I said, hoping my voice didn't sound as shaky as I felt.

I turned to my car and opened the door.

"Hey, Beck."

Fuck, at this rate my insides were going to be twisted so tight I wouldn't be able to remain upright much longer.

"Yeah," I said, not turning around this time.

There was a long pause. "Thanks," Quinn said softly. "For this afternoon."

I nodded because I knew he wasn't thanking me for a job well done. My dick stirred as I remembered the feel of his hair against my skin and the warmth of his flesh. I basically ripped my car door open and climbed inside, refusing to look over my shoulder at Quinn like I was tempted. My phone beeped, but since I knew it was one of my fathers doing their regular check-in, I ignored it since I'd be at Dane and Jax's place in a few minutes. The car sputtered once before starting up and only when I put it in reverse did I look up at Quinn.

Except he was gone already, though his truck was still in the same spot. It wasn't until I backed my car up so that Quinn's truck wasn't blocking my view anymore that I saw him heading towards his little cottage. I sat there watching him as he reached his porch and saw him hesitate at the door. He looked so small and broken as he clutched his husband's boots in one hand and his hat in the other. I willed him to look at me, but he didn't. It wasn't until he'd finally crossed the threshold of his house and closed the door that I snapped out of my daze and focused on getting the car moving.

I resolutely ignored the scarred tree that I'd slammed into a week earlier as I drove down the driveway. It took less than five minutes to get to Dane and Jax's house. I saw Jax's police cruiser and their SUV in the driveway so I knew both men were home. Mrs. Greene's spiffy little red sedan was nowhere to be found as I parked my car.

"Hey, you're just in time," Dane said as he came walking out of the house just as I was heading up the stairs.

"For what?" I asked.

He held up the cooler in his hand. His other hand had what looked like several towels in it and there was a bag slung over his shoulder. An older yellow lab named Millie was standing next to him.

"Picnic down by the pond. It's such a nice afternoon that we decided to skip cooking and just do sandwiches and snacks. I left you a note on the fridge, but if you want to go change, I'll wait for you."

My first reaction was to say no because as much as I liked these men and their kids, I still couldn't get past the insecurities that went through me whenever I was around them. Logically, I knew that when they looked at me, they didn't *only* see a kid who'd tried to kill himself, but I felt like it was a big neon sign that I would always be wearing in their presence and would be hard to ignore. But then I remembered my plan to talk to them about staying at the resort. If I could get them on board, I'd probably have an easier time with getting my fathers to sign off.

"Um, I'm good like this," I said as I motioned to my clothes.

"You don't want to put some shorts on so you can go swimming?"

I shook my head. "Kind of beat," I said. "Wouldn't mind just relaxing."

"Fair enough," Dane said.

"Can I help you with something?" I asked as I reached for the cooler.

"Yeah, thanks."

Dane handed me the cooler and I followed him towards the path that led to the pond. Millie trotted ahead of us, but I didn't miss how she would stop and wait for us to catch up before going too far.

"So how was your first day?" Dane asked.

"It was good," I said. "Harder than I thought," I admitted.

"That means you did a good job," Dane responded. "If it doesn't hurt at first, it's probably because you're not doing it right."

I smiled at that.

"Quinn took me to the resort today."

"It's beautiful, isn't it?" Dane asked.

I nodded. "I met Hunter and Roman too."

Dane slowed. "So, you must have been there when they got the news," he said.

I nodded. "Yeah, we were. They...they were really happy," I said, though the word seemed too inconsequential to describe the emotions I'd seen.

"Losing out on that baby last year hit them pretty hard. And then having to wait to see if this adoption would go through…"

"They didn't want to try surrogacy like you guys did?" I asked.

Dane shot me a questioning look.

"Emma told me Ben is biologically yours."

Dane chuckled. "She called him Swirl, didn't she?"

I hedged and Dane just laughed harder. "If Ben didn't love her so much, I'd be worried he'd someday get a complex." Dane quieted and said, "Roman and Hunter both had pretty bad childhoods. I think they wanted to give what they didn't have to a kid who needed it."

I nodded because that made sense to me.

Perfect sense.

We both fell silent as we walked and I grew more on edge the closer to the pond we got. I could already hear the kids laughing and dogs barking.

I was surprised when Dane slowed to a stop. I did the same and cast him a questioning glance.

"What's bothering you, Beck?"

"Nothing," I said as I shook my head.

Dane tilted his head. "Try again," he said softly.

"I want to ask you and Jax something, but I guess I'm worried how you'll react," I admitted.

Dane considered me for a moment and finally said, "I can't pretend to know everything you're going through, Beck. But I know how hard it can be to try and be different things to different people."

I stilled at that because his words were just a little too close to the truth for my liking.

"We're hoping someday you'll feel safe enough to just be yourself with us," he added.

Fuck, if it were only that easy. I managed to not say the words aloud, though. Dane didn't say anything else, but he didn't seem eager to start moving forward again, either.

"I was thinking about talking to my dads about me staying at the resort for a few weeks while we're working there."

I waited for the question, prepared myself for it.

Do you think that's a good idea, Beck?

So, when Dane said, "Sounds like a smart idea," I wasn't sure I'd heard him correctly.

"We'll miss you of course, but knowing Emma, you'll be here for dinner more often than not."

That's it? That was all he had to say about it?

I realized it was when Dane started walking again.

"I can text you each night after work…mornings too," I offered.

"You can text us whenever you want, Beck. But do it because you want to, not because you have to."

It couldn't be this easy.

I waited, but there were no additional comments about calling if I was feeling down or sideline comments about them coming to "visit" me on the spur of the moment. We walked in silence for several beats before Dane finally spoke again, but it still wasn't what I was expecting. "Do you want me to let Jax know?"

Since I was considerably more intimidated by Jax than I was Dane, I wanted to say yes.

"No, I'll talk to him tonight. Thank you."

"Don't thank me," Dane said with a chuckle. "Because I'm going to make sure Jax and I are nowhere to be found when you tell Emma."

I laughed at that and damn, it felt good. I knew it wouldn't last, but I felt like riding the high. "Hey," I said to Dane and he stopped to look at me. "I'm going to run back to the house to get my shorts. A swim actually does sound like a really good idea."

Dane nodded and took the cooler from me and before I could give it too much thought, I turned and hurried back towards the house.

One battle down, an entire war to go.

~

"Shit…son of a bitch!"

Those were the first words I heard when I walked into the barn after taking the last horse out to the paddock. My eyes quickly adjusted to the dim interior of the barn and I saw Brody at the end of the aisle. It looked like he was leaning against something.

"You okay?" I called as I hung the lead rope I was carrying over a hook on one of the stall doors.

"Can you give me a hand?" I heard him ask and I quickly made my way to him.

It had been almost a week since Quinn and I had gotten all fifteen horses moved from the CB Bar to the resort in Clear Creek. It had been nearly the same amount of time since I'd moved my stuff from Jax and Dane's house to my new, albeit temporary, digs in the staff residence building.

My conversation with Jax about moving had gone much better than expected, but I couldn't say the same for the talk I'd had with my fathers about the move. They hadn't expressly forbidden me, but by the time we'd gotten done talking, I'd found myself agreeing with them that maybe it wasn't for the best. When I'd gone to bed that night, all the sense of accomplishment I'd felt, along with the excitement that had come with my newfound independence, had disappeared and I'd felt the black cloud that had haunted so many of my days threaten to return. But the next morning when I'd gotten up, there'd been a text from my dads to video call them when I was up. I'd waited until a reasonable hour since they were an hour behind me and had called them from the CB Bar during my first break. Both of my fathers had looked terrible and I'd instantly known they'd gotten no sleep.

But before the guilt could even settle in, they'd told me they'd changed their minds and that if I wanted to live at the resort, it was my decision. I'd known how hard it had been for them to come to that decision and I'd been half-tempted just to forget the whole thing so they wouldn't have to suffer any more sleepless nights, but the need to experience the sliver of independence had been just too great and I'd found myself promising them everything would be okay instead.

Moving into the staff building had gone off without a hitch and my new home away from home was far more comfortable than I would have expected. Of course, it wasn't like I had a lot of time to enjoy my newfound freedom since I was so physically exhausted from work each night that I barely managed a shower before collapsing on the wonderfully soft queen-size bed. I was finally at a point where my muscles didn't scream in protest anymore when I woke up and I'd become comfortable enough around the horses that Quinn didn't need to stick around to supervise me when I was handling them.

Which I was sure Quinn appreciated since he made himself pretty scarce whenever he could. We'd meet up every morning at exactly eight o'clock so he could give me my instructions for the day, then he'd saddle up one of the horses and disappear. I'd see him throughout the day interchanging one horse for another, but we barely spoke beyond him asking me to wash down the horse he'd been riding while he saddled up the next horse.

The minimal contact with him should have been ideal.

It wasn't.

And then there was Brody.

I saw him every morning too and while he was always polite and friendly, he too was keeping his distance.

It was what I should have wanted.

But just because I wasn't interacting with either man very much, didn't mean I didn't notice every little thing about them. Or that my body didn't violently react when I was around them. I was in a perpetual state of being half-hard all day as I was tormented with memories of the night in the club and all it took was the sound of their voices or one of them saying my name a certain way for my cock to stand at full attention. I'd resorted to jacking off every night in the shower as I imagined their big bodies surrounding me, our slick, heated flesh pressed together, their mouths on me, their cocks filling me. But inevitably, the moment I spurted all over the shower wall, my fantasy lovers disappeared and the memories of the past assailed me until I found myself curled up on the shower floor, overwhelmed with guilt and shame for giving in to my baser needs once again.

As I neared Brody, I pushed away the disturbing reminder that despite the fact that I was doing okay with Adulting 101, deep down I was still the same person and that a temporary respite from my normal life didn't make me normal.

"What can I do?" I asked Brody as I took in the situation. It looked like the stall door had come partially off its rails because Brody was holding the door in a way that only the top portion of the door was correctly attached.

"Can you stand on this side of me," – Brody motioned to his right – "and guide the rollers into the rail on the bottom?"

"Yeah, sure," I said, as I moved around to his right side. I used my hand to position the door as Brody moved it and when it was lined up I said, "You've got it." Brody slid the door all the way onto the rails. My gaze fell to the muscles of his arms which flexed deliciously as he moved. He was wearing a T-shirt so I could see the definition of his huge biceps. A light sheen of sweat clung to him and I found myself licking my lips as I wondered what it would taste like if I were to run my tongue over those muscles.

Jesus, what the hell was wrong with me?

"Thanks," Brody said.

"No problem," I murmured. I hated the fact that it felt like I was being dismissed with the simple response. I needed to just turn around and get back to work. Brody and Quinn had made it clear that we were just three guys who happened to occupy the same space for a certain number of hours a day. Yeah, we'd had one mutual fucking session and there'd been that weird moment in Quinn's truck last week where it seemed like we'd been connected or something, but none of that meant anything.

The reminder that I'd once again been nothing more than a good fuck caused a dead weight to settle in my stomach.

My skin itched as the need to escape warred with my need to take control. But one look at Brody and I knew that just like with Quinn, I wouldn't have control. It would just be an illusion and in the end, I'd feel that same forbidden pleasure.

I'm sorry my beautiful boy...

Bile crept up the back of my throat and I turned away from Brody, intent on finding someplace I could hide out for a few minutes.

"Beck."

I stilled and forced myself to remain calm. "Yeah?" I managed to get out before I made myself turn around. Brody seemed to study me for a moment and I willed myself to relax.

"Do you want to grab some lunch?" he asked. "I've got plenty of stuff for sandwiches."

Five minutes ago, I would have jumped at the offer. But now…

"Um, I've got a lot of work to do."

Brody dropped his gaze, but not before I saw something flash in his eyes. Holy shit, was he actually disappointed?

"Sure. Another time maybe," he said as he turned back to fiddle with the stall door.

Except I knew there wouldn't be another time. Emotions warred within me.

Was he just looking for an in so he could fuck me? Or did he want to be friends? Maybe he just wanted to thank me for helping with the door?

God, why the fuck was I so clueless when it came to shit like this?

"Okay," I blurted before I could think too much about it.

It seemed like hours before Body responded. "Great. Are you ready now or do you need to finish something up?"

"Now."

Jesus, why couldn't I talk like a normal person instead of practically yelling one word answers at him?

"Okay, let's go then."

I nodded stiffly and stepped away from him. I managed to stay at his side instead of walking behind him like I was half-tempted to do. But for the life of me, I couldn't keep my eyes off the ground.

What the hell had I just done?

CHAPTER 8

BRODY

"Oh, hey, you're bleeding."

They were the first words out of Beck's mouth since we'd left the barn and entered the communal kitchen in the staff residence.

"It's just a scratch," I said as I glanced at my palm. "I'll take care of it in a second."

Beck didn't respond. He had the same deer in the headlights look he'd had the first day in the barn when we'd encountered one another again. I had no clue why he was so on edge since I'd spent the better part of a week ignoring him in the hopes he'd see I was no threat to him. Apparently, my efforts hadn't worked.

"Do you want to start getting stuff out of the fridge?" I said to Beck. He nodded and after washing his hands in the sink, he began rifling through the refrigerator while I searched out the first aid kit from under the sink and then washed my hands. The cut was deep, but not so deep that it needed stiches. I gingerly dried off my palm and then took the first aid kit to the nearest table and sat down. The cut was on my right hand which made it awkward to clean.

"Here, let me," Beck said as he approached the table. He pulled out a chair and sat down so he was facing me, our legs nearly touching.

"Thanks," I murmured. "Clean it with this," I instructed as I handed him a prepackaged antiseptic wipe.

I flinched as the antiseptic came into contact with the wound, but the pain disintegrated when Beck's left hand slid beneath my outstretched hand to support it while he dabbed at the cut with his right hand. I wondered if he'd felt the jolt of electricity too. I knew he had when his eyes flashed to mine for a moment.

"Use the topical cream next," I said, my voice sounding husky even to my own ears.

Beck shot me a slightly annoyed look. "Sorry," I said, as I realized my instructions probably weren't necessary. "Not used to being the patient."

A smile flitted across his face. "I guess I should consider myself lucky that I don't have to sing to you to distract you."

I chuckled. "I didn't know that was an option. I definitely would have asked for that level of service."

Beck's smile grew as he searched out the cream and took the cap off. "I only offer it when the patient passes out at the sight of blood." His eyes shifted to mine for a brief moment before he squirted some of the cream into my palm. "Since that would make you the worst paramedic ever, I'm going to assume you don't have that problem."

Beck began gently rubbing the cream over the injury.

"So, who was the recipient of your excellent bedside manner?" I asked, more to distract myself from how badly I wanted to reach out and run my fingers through Beck's shaggy hair as he bent over my hand. It would be so easy to tug his head up and seal my mouth over his.

"My little sister. She was constantly scraping her knees and hands when she was little…always in such a hurry to get places."

"How old is she now?" I asked.

"Almost twelve."

"Do you have any other siblings?"

"Toby. He just turned fifteen. My fathers are freaking out because he's getting his learner's permit soon."

"Fathers?" I asked. "With an s?"

I remembered Luke and Quinn both mentioning Beck had two fathers, but I hadn't asked for details at the time.

Beck nodded. "My parents are gay. I guess technically I have three fathers, but I don't think much about my real dad anymore."

"You're adopted?"

Another nod. Only this time Beck seemed a little tenser. "Rafe and Cade Barretti adopted me and my brother and sister when I was thirteen. We were their foster kids before that."

"They sound like amazing men," I said. "I still want to see those pictures of your family."

Beck paused and looked up at me before finally saying, "Okay. But it'll need to wait till we have more time since my hour lunch break won't even get us halfway through the pictures."

Beck smirked and I felt my insides light up. I wanted to touch him so badly that I shook with it. Luckily, Beck didn't seem to notice as he searched out a gauze pad.

"What about your family?" Beck asked.

While I preferred to talk about his, I knew I needed to give something if I wanted to get something back. "It's big, but mostly because there are lots of cousins. My uncles and aunts have been busy over the years."

"What about your parents? Do you have any brothers or sister?"

I felt pain bloom in my chest. "A brother," I finally managed to get out.

"Older or younger?" Beck asked as he tore the packaging open and pulled the gauze out.

"Older…by five minutes."

Beck's eyes lifted to mine. "You're a twin?"

I nodded.

"Identical or fraternal?"

"Identical."

Beck smiled. "Wow…two of you. That's…"

His cheeks colored as his voice dropped off and some of the tightness in my chest eased. "That's what?" I asked.

Beck avoided my eyes as he pretended to focus on getting the gauze pad in the perfect position over my injury. "That's…interesting," he finally said.

"Liar," I whispered and Beck's eyes shifted to mine. He smiled shyly and then went to work wrapping my hand with a bandage.

"What's his name?"

"Nathan."

"Does he live around here?" Beck asked.

"No."

Something in my voice must have clued him in that it wasn't a great topic for me because he paused in what he was doing and looked up at me. "Brody, wow, I'm sorry. I didn't realize-" he began.

"It's okay," I said with a shake of my head. "I'm not used to talking about it. I keep trying to tell myself that that part of my life is over, but I guess when it comes to family, it's not so easy."

"No, it isn't," Beck agreed as he began wrapping my hand again. We were both silent a moment before Beck said, "Why construction? Are you thinking about quitting your paramedic job?"

"No, definitely not," I said. "I've always liked working with my hands so I wanted a business I could start in my spare time where I could be my own boss and earn a few extra bucks at the same time."

"How long have you been doing it?"

"The construction work or being a paramedic?"

"Both, I guess."

"I worked in construction when I was younger…during summers off from college. I finished my paramedic training about six months ago, and took the job out here a few months ago."

"So you didn't initially want to be a paramedic when you were a kid?"

It was another sticky area for me, but I was enjoying the fact that Beck was even talking to me too much to risk shutting down the conversation.

"I always wanted to be a paramedic, but my parents had other ideas."

Beck's pretty green eyes held mine. "What did they want you to be?"

"A lawyer. Like my dad. Like his dad. Like his dad before him…you get the picture."

Beck nodded. "What made you decide not to follow in their footsteps?"

I debated how much to say and finally settled on, "I met someone who showed me what I was in for."

Beck seemed to know I was nearing the end of my rope when it came to taking a walk down memory lane because he didn't ask me any more questions. "What about you?" I asked as he began tearing off strips of tape to secure the bandage.

"What about me?" he asked in confusion.

"You must be heading off to college in the fall." I inwardly flinched at the reminder of how young Beck truly was.

Beck stilled and I saw the easy expression on his face disappear only to be replaced with lines of tension that seemed to age him instantly.

"Beck, I'm sorry…"

"No," Beck said. "It's okay. I'm just…I guess this is the stuff *I'm* not used to talking about," he murmured, reminding me I'd made the same statement about talking about my family. Beck began carefully putting the tape on the bandage as he said, "I kind of missed the window on applying to schools last year. My parents mentioned taking a few classes at a community college this fall, but I'm not really sure I can take any more school right now." Beck's gaze shifted to me for a brief moment. "It's hard to focus sometimes."

I nodded in understanding. "What about just entering the workforce?"

Beck secured the last piece of tape and then began repacking the first aid kit. "That's probably what will happen. A couple of my uncles have each offered me jobs in their businesses, but…"

"But?" I prodded.

Beck stopped packing up the kit and surprised me by making direct eye contact with me. "I don't want to let them down too."

The raw honesty behind his words was so unexpected, that I was momentarily left speechless. Which gave Beck time to snap the first aid kid closed and get to his feet. "You're all set," he said.

I hated the way his voice had turned cold and dismissive so I did what I'd promised myself I wouldn't and grabbed his wrist before he could walk away. He tensed in my hold, but didn't try to pull free. I took that as a good sign and gently urged him to sit back down. I began absently stroking his wrist as I said, "I don't know much about you, Beck, but everything I've seen, I like. A lot."

Beck stiffened, but luckily, he didn't pull away.

"I don't know what your life is like back home, but I've spent a week watching you work your ass off. Even with Quinn gone most of the day, you're throwing yourself into your work. A lot of guys your age would take advantage and slack off. They'd treat this as some summer job that doesn't matter. But not you..."

I paused as I tried to get control of my lust which was beginning to ratchet up as Beck's body subtly leaned in towards mine. My injured hand had a mind of its own when it settled on Beck's elbow. In my mind, I could see how easy it would be to pull him forward just enough so our lips would meet.

I forced the thought away, though I couldn't make myself release him as I continued.

"I don't look at you and see someone who tried to end his life and I'm not sitting around wondering if you're going to do it again. What I see is a kind-hearted young man just trying to figure out who he is." I sucked in a breath and said, "And I know the way we met was messed up, but I'm up for trying to be friends if you are. God knows I could use more of those."

Beck was quiet for so long that I was sure he was going to tell me to fuck off, but he just held there as he nodded and said, "Okay."

It wasn't the most exuberant agreement I'd ever heard, but he'd said yes so that was all I really cared about.

Since being friends meant I couldn't drag him onto my lap and kiss the shit out of him, I said, "I guess we should eat."

Beck seemed to be in some kind of daze because he murmured, "Yeah," absentmindedly and then his eyes fell to my mouth. My heart seized in my chest as he hung there. Even though my brain was telling me a kiss would fuck up everything I'd just managed to build, I didn't move away from him like I should have. And I didn't release him like I should have.

I had no idea how long we hung there for before Beck finally leaned forward. His mouth was just scant inches from mine when a familiar voice shattered the silence around us.

"Beck."

Beck scrambled back so fast at the sound of Quinn's voice that he lost his balance and it was only my hand on his elbow that kept him from hitting the floor. I ignored the sting of pain in my hand as I gripped him hard and steadied him until he could clamber to his feet.

I cast a glance over my shoulder and saw Quinn standing in the doorway that led from the communal space to the back hallway where the individual suites were located. His mouth was drawn into a hard line. His steely eyes shifted between us before settling on Beck. "When you're finished with lunch, meet me in the barn."

Fury tore through me as Beck's body drew up tight with anxiety.

He nodded vigorously and said, "Be right there."

Quinn didn't respond as he turned to go down the hallway. Beck grabbed the first aid kit from the table and took it over to the kitchen counter. I watched as he gripped the edge of the granite countertop as if trying to get control of himself. I got up and went to stand next to him, but as soon as I neared him, he said, "I should go."

"Eat lunch first."

He shook his head. "No, I should-" – his eyes darted to the doorway as if he half expected Quinn to still be standing there – "I should go."

Beck started to move past me, but I snagged him around the waist with my left arm to stop his forward movement. "Eat something, Beck. You have time."

He shook his head again, but before he could speak I said, "Then make yourself a sandwich to go."

Beck hesitated and then nodded. I forced myself to release him and stepped back as I watched him hurriedly slap some meat between two slices of bread. He snatched the sandwich off the counter. "Sorry," he murmured to me as he rushed past me.

I waited until he was out of sight before I headed towards the hallway. Once I reached Quinn's room, I slammed my fist against the door and waited. It was practically ripped off the hinges in response.

"What?" Quinn snapped as he pushed past me and yanked his door shut behind him. His shirt sleeves were rolled up and I could smell the lingering scent of soap.

"That was a dick move," I bit out as I followed Quinn back towards the kitchen.

"Not any more dickish than preying on a vulnerable kid."

That pissed me off but mainly because I was afraid there might be a kernel of truth in his words. I grabbed Quinn's arm and yanked him to a halt.

"That's not what you saw-"

"What I saw was you taking advantage of a guy you know is too messed up to know any better."

"Fuck you, Quinn," I snapped. "You don't know shit." I refused to release him when he tried to tug his arm free. "You've been ignoring him all week and now you've got your dick in a twist because of something you think you saw."

"He asked us for two things, Brody! One of which was not to talk about that night! Do you really think he wants a repeat?" Quinn nearly shouted. His body crowded me back until my body hit the wall of glass that faced the courtyard.

"I wasn't making a move on him. But hell if I'm gonna tell him no if he decides he wants more." My body was wired with energy as the heat and electricity from Quinn's body burned through me. "I'm sorry if that's hard for you to watch-"

That was all I got out before Quinn's mouth suddenly smashed down on mine. The force of his kiss knocked my head backwards against the glass, but I was too surprised to even notice the momentary flash of pain. My body lit up like a brushfire as Quinn's mouth stole over mine and his tongue sought entry. I gave it to him instantly and moaned when his hot flesh stroked over mine.

His big hands closed over my wrists, pinning my hands next to my head and his groin brushed mine as he pressed me against the glass.

When I'd first started exploring my sexuality, I'd let other men dominate me, but after a few too many overly aggressive experiences, I'd begun taking on the dominant role and had started only picking partners who were naturally submissive. There was nothing submissive about Quinn or the way he was owning me in that moment. And for once, I had no desire to turn the tables.

He kissed me for what seemed like hours, but was probably only seconds, before he tore his mouth free of mine. We were both panting heavily and he seemed just as surprised as me at what had happened. "I'm not jealous, you asshole," he muttered. "I would give almost anything to see the two of you together again."

What?

"Then why-" I began.

"I interrupted you because it scares the ever-loving shit out of me what might happen if he freaks out like he did the last time." Quinn paused briefly before saying, "You weren't the one who saw his car hit that tree, Brody. I know it was an accident, but what if the next time he loses it, it isn't?"

Quinn still had me pinned, but I made no move to free myself. His dark eyes were heavy with worry and his brow was drawn tight. If my hands had been free, I would have used one to try to smooth the worry lines away.

"He asked us not to see him that way, Quinn," I reminded him.

"And I'm trying really hard not to."

"Is that why you've been ignoring him this week?" I asked softly.

"I haven't," he said with a shake of his head, but when his eyes met mine, he fell silent for a moment. "That's part of it," he finally said. "Things were getting too heavy," he murmured. "After that day in my truck."

I knew he was talking about the day when Beck had offered him comfort after Hunter and Roman had learned their daughter's adoption had come through.

"I'm not sure I can stay away from him," I admitted. Quinn released me and I instantly missed the sensation of his skin on mine.

"I know," was all he said.

"And you just made it really fucking hard to keep my promise to stay away from you," I said softly.

Quinn raised his eyes again briefly before they fell to my mouth. I held still as he brought his thumb up to trace my lower lip. I shivered at the sensation.

"I know," he said again. "But I meant what I said…I'm not looking to start up something."

"Why not?" I asked. "Are you in a relationship or something? Is this Griff guy-"

"He's dead," Quinn interjected. "He was my husband and I buried him two years ago, after a bunch of homophobic, sick fucks beat him to death because he refused to hide who he was."

"Quinn-"

"I had my shot at happiness, Brody. It's gone and I have no interest in trying to get it back."

Quinn stepped back from me, his eyes going hard. "Be careful with him," he said and then he was moving past me.

My mind raced as my body struggled to recover from the moment. Was Quinn right? Would pursuing something with Beck, even if he instigated it, do more harm than good? I'd been honest when I'd told Beck I didn't look at him and only see someone who'd tried to end his life. But the fact was that he had, and I had no idea why or if it was something that was still on his radar. The mere fact that he had been so upset at finding pleasure in sex was a big red flag that he probably had some pretty messed up views about sex. Was I really willing to risk sending him over that edge again just so I could see if there was something between us?

I had my answer before I even finished the question.

Quinn was right. I needed to be careful. And I needed to start by keeping my hands off the young man and be what I'd said I'd be.

A friend.

CHAPTER 9

QUINN

Another round of guilt went through me when I spotted Beck hovering near the barn doorway. I absently noticed Beck stop fidgeting only long enough to feed what looked like a sandwich in his hand to a small mixed breed dog I didn't recognize. I held back as Beck squatted low to the ground and held out pieces of the food. The mangy-looking animal took forever to crane its neck out to reach the food and didn't bother chewing it. It jerked back as Beck tore off more of the food, but this time it was faster to reach for it. The back and forth went on that way until the sandwich was nearly gone, but the dog bolted when it finally noticed me. Beck stiffened as his gaze fell on me and then he was jumping to his own feet.

"New friend?" I asked as I motioned to the dog who'd taken refuge near the tractor which was parked outside one of the storage barns.

Beck shook his head. "She showed up this morning," he murmured. "Figured she lived here."

I shook my head. "Don't think Roman and Hunter would let any dog live on its own, even here."

Beck nodded. "I won't feed her again. Sorry."

The young man was shifting back and forth on his feet and he refused to look at me.

Fuck, I'd really messed this up.

"Did you want me to do something?" Beck asked as he tossed what was left of the sandwich in one of the garbage cans outside the barn.

I debated taking a hold of him then and there so I could try and explain myself, but I held back and said, "Saddle Dusty up and meet me in the outdoor arena."

Beck was a natural when it came to horses and he picked up things quickly. So I didn't stick around to help him with getting the horse tacked up since I knew he'd done it enough times that he wouldn't need assistance. I used the time to return to the kitchen and searched out two plastic containers from the cupboard. I stacked one high with what was left of Brody's deli meat and filled the other one with water. I searched out a pen and pad of paper and left Brody a note since he wasn't around.

Took what was left of your lunch meat...tell you about it later. I'm cooking dinner tonight. 6pm. -Q

I took both containers back to the barn and set them down near the wheel of the tractor where they'd be out of the sun. I didn't see the dog, but I doubted she'd run very far. By the time I was done, Beck was leading Dusty, a small gray mare, into the arena. He was still hesitant around me as I checked the saddle to make sure it was tight enough, but when he handed me the reins, I said, "Keep 'em. Mount up."

Beck stiffened and finally raised his eyes. "Me?" he asked, his voice heavy with worry.

"I'm going to need some help getting the horses used to the trails as groups since they'll be going out together more often than not." I walked around the horse and said, "Put your left foot here, hang on to the mane with this hand, and pull yourself up and over," I explained as I demonstrated each move.

I stepped back and watched silently as Beck considered the horse for a moment and then finally did as I asked. It took him only two tries to get himself on the horse who stood patiently. My fingers tingled as I maneuvered Beck's leg out of the stirrup long enough to adjust it so it fit his leg. I did the same to the other side and then proceeded to show him to hold the reins. I watched with pride as Beck's instincts took over and he adjusted his body in the saddle.

Definitely a natural.

"Go ahead and move her to the rail," I said. I gave instructions as Beck began walking the horse around the arena. His hands were naturally soft on the horse's mouth and his body automatically adjusted to the animal's short, stocky gait. I limited the lesson to having him walk and trot as well as steer the horse through certain patterns and then told him I'd be back. It took me only a few minutes to get another horse saddled up. I bit back the disappointment that Brody hadn't returned from lunch, but was pleased to see that at some point the dog had reappeared and eaten the lunch meat I'd left her.

By the time I reached the arena, Beck had stopped Dusty and was stroking her sleek neck as he spoke softly to her. I couldn't hear what he was saying, but I liked that he was showing her that level of attention. It spoke volumes in itself.

I mounted up and motioned for Beck to follow me. The gelding I was riding was pretty laid back and was a natural leader, so I didn't have to do much besides point him towards the trail head. Once the trail widened, I called for Beck to move his mount up next to mine.

"You're a natural at this," I said to him despite the fact that he wouldn't look at me.

"At what?" Beck asked.

I motioned to Dusty. "They're taught to behave with all kinds of riders on them, but only they can decide if they want to trust that rider. Every horse I've seen you with trusts you almost immediately. That's not something that can be taught."

Beck finally shot me a sidelong glance. "I'm not doing anything special," he finally said.

"Yeah, Beck, you are," I said softly. His eyes held mine for a moment before he shifted them away. We walked in silence for a few minutes before I said, "I've been working with the lodge director in Roman's absence to get the barn staff hired. We found someone to take care of the horses day-to-day. She'll be starting next week. After we transition your work to her, I'd like for you to be more hands-on with the horses. You okay with that?"

Beck nodded. "Sure, whatever."

His lack of enthusiasm bothered me, but I had only myself to blame.

"I wasn't prepared for you, Beck," I finally admitted. I didn't have to look at him to know his eyes were on me now. "I guess running seemed like an easier way to go than admitting it."

"Running?" Beck asked in confusion.

I glanced at him and saw that he was indeed now looking at me. I tilted my head at him rather than say anything because I knew he knew what I was talking about. He eyed me a moment before pulling his gaze away.

"I didn't know what to think," he finally said. "People either talk to me too much after they find out the truth about me," – his eyes shifted back to me – "or they don't know what to say. I guess I figured you were in that category."

My horse shifted beneath me and I realized it was because I'd stiffened in the saddle and the sensitive animal had sensed the change. I willed myself to relax as I said, "It wasn't about you…not about *that* anyway," I said. "I kept my distance because I'm not used to someone seeing so much of me and that day in the truck-"

"I'm sorry about that," Beck interjected. "I didn't mean to embarrass you by bringing it up."

"You didn't," I said softly. "Just listen for a second, okay?"

Beck flushed, but then nodded.

"I liked it," I whispered. "Too much. You, Brody…not having to get through that moment alone. Griff was the only other person who knew how to ground me…I wasn't expecting to ever feel that again and then you touched me and Brody…"

I sighed as the words I was trying to say continued to escape me. "I ignored you this week because I didn't want to be tempted to take you up on what you were offering that day in the truck."

Beck didn't say anything. I cast him a quick glance and saw that he was staring straight ahead, but he didn't really seem aware of his surroundings. Suspecting I'd made him uncomfortable with the direction of the conversation, I said, "We've got an entire summer of working together ahead of us, Beck. But I don't want it to be like this past week so I'm hoping we can start over."

"Um, yeah, okay," Beck mumbled, but he still seemed lost in thought.

The awkwardness of the situation wasn't lost on me and since I wasn't sure what to say next, I kept my mouth shut and turned our horses onto a side trail that I knew would require us to ride single file. With Beck behind me, some of the tension inside of me eased. Neither of us spoke again until we reached the barn. We took turns washing our horses off and turning them out in their paddocks. I met up with Beck near the entrance of the barn and noticed the stray dog was watching the young man from beneath the tractor.

"I've got another interview at the lodge," I said as I motioned in that direction. "You mind washing out water buckets?"

Beck nodded. "No problem."

I started to go, but then forced myself to turn back to him. "Um, I'm cooking dinner tonight. I'd love it if you joined me."

Beck tensed, but before he could speak, I said, "I asked Brody too. I'm not a great cook or anything, but I promise not to give you food poisoning or some shit like that."

Jesus, could I be any more fucking awkward?

"Anyway, I figure it's the least I can do for shortchanging you on your lunch. Even if it did make you a new friend," I murmured as I motioned to the dog who'd come out of her hiding spot so she could watch Beck expectantly.

"Okay, thanks," Beck murmured and I nodded. Not the most enthusiastic response, but it was the best I was going to get. Obviously, I'd upset Beck with my honesty about why I'd spent the better part of a week ignoring him. I guessed I'd be lucky if he even showed up for dinner tonight. Hell, between my awkward conversation with Beck and that bone-melting kiss with Brody, I'd very likely be cooking for one tonight.

CHAPTER 10

BECK

"Okay, all set."

I jumped at the sound of Brody's voice and turned to see him and Quinn walking towards me. I'd been pacing the small living area where the TV and two couches and several oversized chairs were located as I waited for Brody and Quinn to finish up with washing the dishes. It was the deal we'd come up with in the three nights we'd been eating together. Whoever cooked got out of clean-up duty. I'd made my dad's semi-famous chicken casserole so after the last noodle had been eaten, I'd gotten to sit back and watch my dinner companions begin the process of cleaning up. Only, it had been impossible to sit there and watch the two men joke and laugh as they argued over who was washing and who was drying, so I'd left the kitchen to hide out in the TV room. I'd finally agreed to show both men pictures of my family so I couldn't escape to my room like I had the past two nights.

And escape was exactly what I needed.

But for all the wrong reasons.

Because being around Brody and Quinn was driving me insane with need. I couldn't understand the insatiable desire that held me in its grip every time I was around them. Neither had made a move on me in the three nights since we'd somehow formed a silent truce to be friends or colleagues or whatever the hell it was we were now. But that was all I fucking wanted one of them to do – to give me the excuse I needed to explore what was happening to me.

The first night after my ride with Quinn had been tense when we'd all arrived in the kitchen for dinner. Quinn had seemed nervous as he'd explained that all he'd made for us was macaroni and cheese, but that it had been his mother's secret recipe and he hoped we liked it. We hadn't spoken much as we'd eaten the surprisingly delicious meal, but then Brody had made a comment about how many more responses Quinn would have gotten on his dating ad if Mrs. Greene had mentioned his mama's secret mac 'n cheese dish. There'd been this long moment of awkward silence as Quinn had absorbed what Brody had said and then he'd laughed long and hard and the blanket of tension that had clung to us wafted away. We'd stuck to safe conversation topics the rest of the night. Afterwards, we'd stumbled through saying our good nights to one another, but the relief had been instantaneous when Brody had offered to cook the following night.

After Brody's coma-inducing fettuccini alfredo, we'd sat around the table long after the food had been consumed and chatted some more, but we'd steered clear of any topics that would threaten the laid-back atmosphere. Brody had suggested watching a movie, but I'd been too wrapped up in my emotions to agree. Not to mention the dull, throbbing ache in my body that never seemed to go away at this point. I'd given up on trying to avoid jerking off to the image of both men in my shower...in fact, I was doing it twice a day now.

"The couch okay?"

I jolted to awareness as I said, "What?" a little bit too loudly.

Quinn's dark eyes settled on me as he carefully repeated, "Is the couch okay?"

"Um, yeah," I said. I needed to get a fucking grip.

My skin tingled and a wave of heat went through me as I watched Brody and Quinn each take up position on the couch, leaving me a spot in the middle. I forced myself to sit down between them. My phone was already in my hand, but I was dismayed to see moisture on the screen. Why the hell were my palms so sweaty?

I wiped the phone on my jeans, trying desperately to ignore the sight of Brody's thigh muscles bunching beneath his jeans as he shifted closer to me. Neither man was touching me, but all I'd have to do was move my legs just an inch or two and I'd be able to feel their hot bodies against mine.

I fumbled with my phone for several seconds and finally found the batch of pictures I was looking for. A fleeting pain went through me at the sight of the first picture and that helped dull some of the anxiety rolling through my body.

"Is that them?" Brody asked as he leaned in to get a better look.

"Yeah," I said. "We took this just before I left. These are my dads," I murmured as I let my fingers skim over my fathers' faces. "And this is my sister Rebecca and my brother Toby. And these are the newest members of the family, Lincoln and Lily."

I only half-listened as Brody and Quinn remarked how cute the babies were and what a great-looking family I had. It wasn't until I felt a big hand stroking my back that I realized I'd gotten lost in myself.

"You okay?" I heard Quinn ask and I realized it was his hand on my back.

I nodded. "Sorry, a little homesick I guess."

Quinn nodded in understanding. I flipped the screen to the next image which was a shot of the entire family at our last family dinner. I smiled as both men stared in shock at the huge group of people around the table. I lost track of time as I began going through all the pictures, but I didn't lose track of my body's growing desire as the heat from Quinn and Brody washed over me. Every once in a while, they would brush up against me, but they didn't seem to be going out of their way to touch me which should have been a relief.

It wasn't.

It frustrated the ever-loving hell out of me.

I tried to remind myself that I couldn't want this…them. That it was wrong.

But the argument did nothing to calm the sensations that kept building in my body.

I had no idea how I managed to explain who was who in the pictures, but I must have been able to because neither Quinn nor Brody sensed my internal struggle. They asked all the right questions in all the right places and their voices were so damn even-keeled that I wanted to scream at them and ask how they couldn't feel it.

This thing that was between us.

It wasn't until Quinn and Brody both pointed to one of the pictures at the same time, their bodies leaning into me simultaneously, that I lost it and sprang to my feet, my phone clattering to the floor. My dick felt like a spike in my pants, but I had no means to hide my condition. Not that it mattered anyway because I felt like it had to be written across my forehead.

"Beck?" Brody asked in concern. I turned and saw both men had remained seated, but were now leaning forward. Quinn had picked up my discarded phone.

"Do you really not feel it?" I asked desperately.

I didn't wait for an answer because I couldn't. My body was beyond my control and my mind was strangely glad. I went for Brody only because he was closer. It took just two strides to reach him and my mouth was on his before he could even register what was happening. I slid onto his lap, straddling him, as I threaded my fingers through his hair and held him in place for my kiss. A moan of relief tore through me as his tongue met mine and then he was blessedly kissing me back and the arms he'd been holding open in surprise wrapped around me like steel bands.

I felt tears sting my eyes at how good it felt. I knew my kiss was sloppy and unpracticed, but that didn't seem to bother Brody in the least because he kissed me back without hesitation. I let him take over the kiss and just sank into him, my body boneless. His hands palmed my ass as he began grinding our lower bodies together and I was pleased to feel he was already hard.

So maybe he hadn't been as unaffected as I'd thought.

As my need for oxygen forced me to tear my lips from his, I

continued to hold onto his hair in what was sure to be a painful grip. I was terrified that he'd try to get away from me if I let him go for even a moment. With my free hand, I began searching out Quinn even before my eyes locked on him. He was too far away for me to actually grab hold of him without letting Brody go and the space between us suddenly seemed like a chasm as wide as the Grand Canyon. It would be so easy for him to get up and walk away.

I could see the open lust in his eyes, but the fact that he was hesitating spoke volumes.

Shit, did I want this moment if I couldn't have it with both of them?

Luckily it was a question I didn't have to answer because the whimper that escaped my throat as I even pondered the thought seemed to spur Quinn on and he suddenly shifted his body so that it was pressed up against mine and Brody's. His lips claimed mine in a searing kiss and I felt his big hand cupping the back of my head as he held me in place. Brody's hands were roaming up and down my sides causing delicious friction between my skin and the fabric of my T-shirt. When Quinn's lips left mine so I could suck in a much-needed breath, he immediately latched onto Brody's mouth and I felt what was left of my sanity disappear at the sight of the two men kissing.

I could have come just from watching them go at one another, each seeking to claim ownership of the other. I was still straddling Brody's lap, but Quinn's right hand was gripping my ass. Quinn finally won control of the kiss and then he was pulling me forward and I didn't know how it was possible, but somehow all three of us managed to kiss each other at the same time, our lips and tongues doing a perfect dance as we writhed against one another. When the kiss broke, Brody's fingers were pushing up the fabric of my shirt and I got the silent message. I reached down to grab the hem when Quinn's hand closed over one of mine.

The move was like ice water being dumped over us at the same time and we all stilled.

"Beck," Quinn said huskily as his eyes met mine. "You need to be sure about this."

I began nodding because in that moment all I cared about was getting his and Brody's mouths and hands back on me. But Quinn kissed me hard and then pressed his forehead to mine.

"It can't end like last time," Quinn whispered.

Meaning I couldn't panic and run away. I couldn't pretend nothing had happened. I couldn't ask them to do the same.

Panic welled inside of me. I knew what he was asking, yet I couldn't promise him anything. But I needed him and Brody so badly...

"Please, Quinn," I begged. "I'll try, okay?"

It had to be enough. It just had to.

"Please," I whispered one more time. I didn't even recognize my own voice, it was so heavy with desperation.

"Come here," Quinn said roughly and then he was dragging me forward into his arms. I cried out in relief as his mouth sought out mine. I felt cool air feather over my heated skin as my T-shirt was worked off my body, presumably by Brody since Quinn's arms were wrapped around me like a vise. Firm, warm lips ghosted kisses over my shoulder as hot, calloused hands explored my skin. I began grinding my hips against Quinn's in the hopes I could make myself come, but two large hands settled on my hips.

"Not yet, baby. Hold on just a little longer."

Brody.

"Can't," I managed to get out.

"You can," Quinn assured me. His kisses turned soft and gentle, forcing my own passion to cool enough so I could keep up with his soft lips moving perfectly over mine. He turned me so I was facing Brody who was half kneeling on the couch. His kisses too had lost their fervor, but they were no less intense. The out of control need I'd been feeling shifted to a simmering burn that kept washing over me in building waves.

Quinn's hot body brushed my back and I moaned when I realized he'd taken his shirt off at some point. His lips were exploring the side of my neck and would leave my skin only long enough to exchange kisses with Brody over my shoulder.

I felt Brody's fingers working the button on my pants free. The sound of my zipper in the silence had my lust spiking up again. The idea that one or both of these men would be fucking me in a matter of minutes should have caused a whole host of feelings to go through me, none of which should have been excitement. But that was the only thing I felt. I'd tried to pass off the encounter in the bathroom as a fluke, but I knew it wasn't. The only thing these men would make me feel was pleasure. Anything that came afterwards would be all on me.

I turned my head to give Quinn access to my mouth as Brody pushed my pants and boxers down. Quinn swallowed down my moan of pleasure as Brody took me in hand and began stroking me. I was caught in a vortex of pleasure as they worked me between them, each taking turns kissing me and gripping my leaking dick. Another hand was rubbing my ass and I shivered when a finger sought out my hole.

"Oh God," I bit out as the finger began massaging me and another finger began playing with the ridge beneath my crown. Electricity shot up my spine and I arched my back in response to the nearly painful sensation. "Please," I begged, knowing I couldn't last much longer so strung out, but also terrified that I wouldn't be able to make it to that place where I'd finally be free.

"Lie back," I heard Quinn urge and I felt his arm come around my chest as he pulled me backwards. I ended up sprawled across his broad chest, his lap cradling my ass as he maneuvered me into the position he wanted. I could feel his rock-hard dick against my lower back. I'd somehow missed the point when he'd worked it free. My head was resting on Quinn's shoulder as he kissed me and let his hand skim over my chest. I turned my head enough so I could see Brody settling on the floor between my legs as well as Quinn's. His big hand was still gripping my cock which was glistening with pre-cum.

"Beck," Quinn said softly.

I couldn't manage a response, but I was able to turn my head to look at him.

"Are you negative?"

It took me several precious seconds to grasp what he was asking me and I quickly nodded. The second I did, my cock was engulfed in white-hot wetness and I screamed out in pleasure. Quinn's arms clamped around me to hold me in place as Brody began sucking me intently, giving me no time to adjust. I grabbed ahold of Quinn's arm where it was crossing my upper body and held on for dear life as I began bucking my hips upwards, fucking Brody's mouth. I expected him to stop me, but instead, he put his hands on my hips and urged me on as he hollowed out his cheeks and sucked hard. Quinn was grinding his dick against my back. I desperately wanted to feel him inside of me again, but I was too far gone to ask. Keening cries began to fall from my lips as Brody took me to the back of his throat over and over again.

I knew I should have warned Brody how close I was, but I wasn't capable of anything but trying to get myself deeper and deeper inside of his body. Quinn's breath was hot against my ear as he whispered words of encouragement to me. The contrast between his naked chest and jeans-clad lower half scraping over my skin as he humped against me sent me higher. White light suddenly snapped to life behind my closed eyelids as the pressure inside of me exploded. Relief shredded my entire body as my orgasm crashed over me in a violent starburst of pleasure.

"Yes!" I screamed as my climax rolled through me in wave after violent wave. Quinn shouted in my ear and a moment later I felt the hot proof of his release hitting my lower back.

My body went lax as the pleasure continued to ricochet through me. Brody finally released me and I looked down just in time to see his semen-covered lips open wide with pleasure as he came, presumably in his hand. His stubble-covered cheek rested on my thigh as he rode out his orgasm. Quinn had quieted beneath me, but his hold on me had lessened only a little bit. I could feel his cum dripping down the crack of my ass.

Brody rose enough so he could lean over my shoulder to kiss Quinn. Quinn moaned as he cleaned what was left of my release off Brody's mouth before they kissed deeply. Then Brody's mouth was on mine and I could taste myself on him. I told myself I needed to move my sated body, but Quinn had yet to release me and Brody's weight was now pressing me farther into the cradle of the hard body beneath mine. In truth, I could have lain there between them like that for hours, but the cold reality of what I'd just done started to come back. I tried to will the impending shame away, but it wouldn't be ignored. Brody or Quinn or both must have sensed my tension because they both stiffened and the little circles Brody had been rubbing into my chest with his thumb stopped.

"You okay?" Brody asked softly. His voice said he already knew the answer.

No, I wasn't.

I really wasn't.

"Can you let me up, please?" I managed to get out, though my voice was so hoarse I barely recognized it myself.

"Beck-" Brody began.

"Let me up!" I demanded as all the heat fled my body.

Brody immediately moved off of me and Quinn released his hold on my body. I scrambled to my feet, yanking my boxers and pants up as I stood. The sight of Quinn's glistening half-hard dick and Brody's wet hand were enough to drive me over the edge and I did exactly what they'd asked me not to.

I ran.

CHAPTER 11

BRODY

"Fuck," Quinn bit out as he rose to his feet and yanked his pants up and buttoned them. I hurriedly wiped my hand on my T-shirt which had ended up tossed over the back of the couch. Ignoring the sensation of my own cooling cum against my skin, I did up my pants.

"We need to check on him," I said even as disappointment cascaded over me. Thirty seconds ago, I'd been on top of the world. Now...

"Yeah," Quinn said as he snagged his shirt off the floor and hurried towards the hallway that led to the bedrooms. He stopped at Beck's door and knocked.

My body was struggling to deal with the combination of the lingering high from my orgasm and the adrenaline that had started flooding my veins as soon as Beck had ordered me to get off of him. I sent Quinn a worried look when there was no answer at Beck's door. He tried the knob but it didn't open.

"Beck, open up or we're going to break it down," Quinn said without hesitation. I could tell he was both worried and angry and I couldn't blame him. He'd been the only one out of the three of us who'd made sure Beck had wanted this.

Until he hadn't.

Fuck, why had I let this happen? We'd been making progress with Beck. Yeah, it had been slow, but it had been genuine. At least I thought it had. Besides dinner these past three nights, Beck and I had exchanged pleasantries here and there over the past few days. It wasn't much, but it had been more than we'd had before. And I'd noticed that Quinn and Beck had been working more closely with one another as well so I'd figured they'd hashed out whatever was between them.

And dinner...

I'd been thrilled when Quinn had invited us to join him for dinner the first night and after the initial awkwardness had passed, we'd gotten along well. Sure, the topics we'd discussed had been safe ones, but we'd started to see some commonalities that we shared as well as some differences. By the end of the first night, it had almost felt natural being around both men. So it had been easy to offer to cook dinner the next night. Tonight when Beck had cooked, I couldn't have planned it any better myself. And when Beck had mentioned the meal was a family favorite, I hadn't even thought twice about reminding him he had promised to show us pictures of his family.

Had he thought it had all been some kind of come on?

That we'd planned the whole thing?

Relief went through me when the door was unlocked, but it was short-lived when it was yanked open. Beck was standing there, his eyes wild as he shoved something at Quinn.

"Here!" Beck shouted. "Will you leave me alone now?"

Quinn and I both stared at the pair of sneakers and singular belt that Beck had thrust at him. It was Quinn's fast action that had him sliding his foot into the doorjamb to keep Beck from closing it again.

The move seemed to make Beck even angrier because as he stepped back into the room he threw his arms out wide and yelled, "What?" He didn't wait for an answer before striding towards the bathroom. He returned a moment later with a razor, a bottle of aspirin and several prescription bottles and threw them at our feet. "What else?" he muttered as he looked around the bedroom. It didn't finally hit me what he was doing until he started tearing the bed sheets from the bed.

"Beck, stop it!" Quinn snapped and he moved past me to grab Beck by the arm.

"That's why you're here, isn't it?" Beck shouted as he motioned to the discarded items on the floor. "To make sure the dumb kid doesn't try offing himself again, especially not while he's on your watch!"

"We're here because we're worried about you," Quinn returned just as loudly. "Not because we think you're going to hurt yourself!"

"Beck, talk to us," I urged as I moved closer to him. Quinn still had ahold of his arm. "You said you wanted what happened-"

"I know that! It's my fault, okay?"

"It's no one's fault!" I snapped, unable to contain my own frustrations. "We didn't do anything wrong!"

"Is that what you think?" Quinn asked. "That what happened between us was wrong?"

When Beck remained stubbornly mute, Quinn softened his voice as he asked, "Are you ashamed of being gay, Beck?"

Beck shook his head and my heart broke for him when tears welled in his eyes and began slipping down his face. I gave in to my need to touch him and wrapped my arm around his shoulders. Dropping a kiss to the top of his head, I glanced at Quinn and briefly shook my head. He seemed to understand my silent message that we weren't going to get anything else out of the young man tonight because he nodded.

"Beck," I said softly. "Do you mind if Quinn and I stay here with you tonight?"

I expected an argument, but Beck surprised me when he slowly shook his head. "How about you and I get cleaned up while Quinn straightens up out here?" I asked even as I began steering Beck to the bathroom. He didn't protest as I led him into the bathroom and my eyes met Quinn's to make sure we were on the same page. He'd already started getting the bed back in order so I had to take that as a sign that we were.

I closed the bathroom door behind us and reached into the shower to turn the water on. Beck's eyes were still wet from his tears, but all the emotion seemed to have been sucked out of him because he didn't react in any kind of way as I began working his pants off his body. The boxers were next and then I gently urged him into the shower. When he did nothing but stand stiffly beneath the spray of hot water, I shucked my own clothes and climbed in with him. The shower was big enough for two people, but Beck made no move to either step away from me or get closer and when I poured some body wash into my hands and began running it over his body, he barely reacted. Under any other circumstances, I would have enjoyed the opportunity to explore his body, but his continued silence had me on edge. Once I got him clean, I made quick work of cleaning myself and then tugged him out of the shower and got him dried off. Spying a pair of sweats sitting on a small shelf near the toilet, I grabbed them and worked them up his legs. I didn't relish the idea of putting my damp briefs back on so I wrapped a towel around my hips and tied it off as best I could.

Quinn was in the bedroom when I opened the bathroom door, but I could tell from his damp skin that he must have rushed through a shower in his own room. Beck's room had been straightened and the bedding fixed and Quinn was wearing what looked like pajama bottoms. He was on the opposite side of the bed and had turned on a small light on the nightstand. I could see Beck's phone sitting there as well and I realized Quinn must have gone back to the TV room to grab it since Beck had left it behind earlier.

I urged Beck under the covers. Quinn climbed in at the same time and drew Beck forward into his arms. Beck didn't protest at all, but I didn't necessarily take that as a good sign. I crawled in after Beck and positioned myself at his back. I ended up extending my arm over Quinn's where it was resting on Beck's waist. My eyes met Quinn's over Beck's shoulder and I saw the same question in his eyes I was sure was in mine.

Now what?

"How do you know?" Beck whispered, his voice sounding raspy and dry. I immediately reached over to the nightstand on my side of the bed and grabbed the bottle of water Quinn had left there earlier. Beck was lying quietly against my chest and though I was reluctant to disturb him, I handed him the water. I was pleased when he took a few sips, handed it back and then lay right back down in the same position he'd been in for the better part of an hour.

"How do I know what?" I asked as I let my fingers trail up and down his spine.

It had been almost 24 hours since Beck's meltdown. Quinn and I had stayed with him the whole night and had been privy to the nightmares that had plagued the young man all night long. He'd always ended up only half waking up as he cried and told someone he was sorry over and over. By morning when the alarm on his phone had gone off, Quinn had turned it off and told me to stay with him while he went and took care of the horses. We'd spent the day taking turns staying with Beck as he'd slept, waking him long enough to eat or take the medicine as outlined on the prescription bottles and to text his fathers after I'd read one early morning text expressing concern for Beck's whereabouts.

Beck, for his part, had continued to function on auto-pilot, but the fact that he snuggled up to me and Quinn was promising.

Or at least I liked to think so.

It was a sure sign that my emotions were getting more and more entrenched with these men each day. And that wasn't necessarily a good thing. While I hadn't been seeking out any kind of relationship, I wasn't completely opposed to it either. Though the idea of being with two men at the same time had never even entered my orbit, at least not outside the bounds of sex anyway, now it was all I could think about.

I knew Luke's childhood friend was in a threesome with two other men, though I'd only briefly met Rhys and his partners a couple of times.

"How do you know what we did wasn't wrong?" Beck asked softly.

The door to the bedroom opened at that moment and I looked over my shoulder to see Quinn entering the room. I wasn't sure if he'd heard Beck's question or not so I sent him what I hoped was a silent message not to say anything. If this was our only chance to get Beck talking, we needed to make sure we didn't waste it.

"Because I don't believe sex between people, no matter their sexuality, is wrong. As long as they're able to consent to it, it's between them and only them." As I spoke, I watched Quinn get undressed until he was just in his underwear. He slipped into the bed quietly and pressed up against Beck's back. I bit back a smile when Beck immediately sought out Quinn's arm and pulled it up and over his body like it had been so many times over the past 24 hours.

"Did you always like it?"

"What? Sex?" I asked. My gut tightened because I knew we were treading on dangerous ground. As much as I wanted to understand what was going through Beck's head when it came to sex, I didn't want to say something that would skew his perception even more than it already was.

"Yeah...did it always feel good?" Beck asked.

I glanced at Quinn who was watching me with a mix of pity and confusion.

"No, it didn't," I admitted. "My first time was with a girl and even though I was able to go through with it, I didn't enjoy it."

I felt Beck shift in my arms a little and I looked down to see him looking at me in confusion. "So you...you..."

"Came?" I supplied for him.

He nodded. "But you didn't really want it?"

I pushed aside the awkwardness of the conversation along with the painful memories it brought up for me and said, "Yeah, something like that. She was my high school girlfriend and we'd been together for a while. I'd been in denial that I was gay and I thought I could prove I was straight if I was with her like that. But it was like my body was responding even though my mind wasn't. Afterwards it felt like..."

"Like what?" Quinn asked softly when I'd been quiet for too long.

I was surprised to feel the sting of tears at the backs of my eyes. "Like I'd lost something special." I reached up to discreetly wipe at my eyes, but when I felt Quinn's fingers on my forearm, I knew I hadn't succeeded. I shook off the darkness that had threatened to settle over me and said, "It was different when I was with a guy for the first time. The sex wasn't even all that great, but I didn't walk away feeling like I'd lied to myself."

"Because you weren't," Beck murmured.

I nodded.

"I'm not going to lie and say I've been a saint in the years since I was honest with myself about who I was, but every encounter was my choice and while I might regret one or two, I've never looked at them and thought of them as having been wrong in any kind of way."

Beck was quiet for a while before he said, "Quinn?"

Quinn's fingers were still resting on my arm and I felt them tighten just a little bit before relaxing again. I knew what Beck was asking us was extremely personal, but I hoped like hell Quinn would answer him. I couldn't say why it mattered so much, just that it did.

"Griff was my first," Quinn finally said. "I grew up in a small town in Nevada so I didn't have a lot of options when it came to exploring my sexuality. I knew my dad would lose it if he found out I was gay so I didn't risk hooking up with other guys until I was out of the house. I'd found a job with this guy who toured the rodeo circuit. He was a pretty big deal at the time. I went on the road with him and met Griff about a year later. Griff was a bull rider who was very much out and proud. The first time we were together..." Quinn quieted for a moment and I had no doubt he was lost in his own memory.

"It was unlike anything I'd ever known. But I wasn't ready to be out and Griff wasn't looking for someone who was still comfortable hiding in the closet. I kept running into him from time to time on the circuit over the following few years, but it wasn't until I started competing myself that I knew it was time to admit who I really was. It took me another couple of years to convince Griff to give me another chance, especially since I wanted us to keep a low profile – rodeos aren't exactly the most tolerant of communities. We started traveling together, but we kept our relationship a secret. Some people suspected, but as long as we didn't advertise it, they seemed happy enough to leave us in peace." Quinn sighed and shifted and I looked down to see him leaning over Beck so he could brush a stray hair off his face.

"So no, I never felt like it was wrong being with him or the few hookups who came after I lost him…the only thing that ever felt wrong was hiding who I was."

Quinn ran his finger up and down Beck's cheek as he whispered, "Did being with us really feel so wrong, Beck?"

It seemed to take forever for Beck to shake his head. The relief I felt was palpable because with that singular movement, I knew maybe we still had a chance at figuring out what this thing between us was.

"But it's made me see that all the other times were wrong," Beck murmured. And just before he tucked his face against my chest, he whispered, "And what does that say about me?"

CHAPTER 12

QUINN

I came awake to the sound of a door opening and turned my head just in time to see Beck coming out of the bathroom. His eyes connected with mine just before he turned the light off in the bathroom and shut the door. I watched as he grabbed his boots and came around to my side of the bed. Brody was snoring softly on the other side and I glanced over to see him lying on his stomach, his arm flung out over Beck's pillow as if searching for him.

"What time is it?" I asked as Beck sat down on the bed next to me and began pulling on his boots. There was no light filtering in through the curtains so I had to guess it was pretty early still.

"It's early," Beck confirmed softly as he quietly pressed his feet into his boots. I started to sit up, but he put a hand on my shoulder. "Sleep a little longer," he urged. "I'll take care of the horses."

As tired as I was, I doubted I could get back to sleep. Brody and I had spent another night with Beck and whatever nightmares were plaguing him. Even though he rarely woke all the way up while in the midst of one, I had to assume they left him feeling drained. I was also worried about him being alone since we really hadn't resolved anything since his breakdown two nights earlier. He hadn't said anything about his cryptic statement about the sexual encounters he'd had in the past being wrong and Brody and I hadn't pressed him.

"Are you sure?" I asked.

Beck hovered over me and then, to my surprise, he leaned down and kissed me. He kept the kiss light and simple, but it still made something deep inside of me unfurl.

"Thank you," he whispered.

I nodded because I didn't need to ask what he was talking about. I brought up my hand to caress his face, damning the fact that there was no light to see his eyes. He sounded stronger, but I needed to *see* it too.

Beck held there a moment, pressing his face into my hand, and then he brushed his mouth over mine once more before standing. He left the room, leaving me with Brody who hadn't woken up. I turned over so I could see the other man more easily and watched the rise and fall of his body as he breathed. We'd kept Beck between us in the 36 hours we'd spent with him, so I hadn't had a chance to touch Brody. I let my hand trail up his muscular back and reveled in how warm his skin felt.

I hadn't shared a bed with another person in the two years since I'd lost Griff and I was surprised to acknowledge how much I'd missed it. It had felt so natural and easy to share the too-small bed with Beck and Brody.

"Mmmm, feels good," Brody said with a sigh and I watched as he turned his head so he was facing me. His voice sounded sleepy and content. "Beck?" he asked.

"Went to take care of the horses."

Brody was silent for a moment and even though he was awake, I didn't stop caressing him.

"How did he seem?" Brody asked.

"He seemed okay," I responded. "Good, actually."

"That's good," Brody murmured and then he was shifting his body so that not only was he on his back, he'd closed the space between us. I ended up dropping my hand to his chest. He was perfectly built with just the smallest smattering of chest hair.

"Morning," I said softly as I let my fingers skim over one of his nipples.

Brody let out a breathy sigh and said, "Morning."

I levered up on an elbow and watched him, though I couldn't make out as much as I wanted since it was too dark. I was tempted to turn on a light but figured maybe it wasn't such a great idea to see certain things.

Because I couldn't get too comfortable with all of this.

Whatever *this* was.

Brody's hand came up to capture the one I was stroking over his chest. He pulled it up to his mouth and kissed each fingertip before placing it on his muscled abdomen. "What are we doing, Quinn?" he asked softly.

I shook my head because I didn't have an answer. I'd been trying to keep my distance from both men for the better part of a week now, but here I was in bed with one while wishing I'd woken up just a little bit sooner so I'd been able to catch the other one before he'd gotten up.

"I have no fucking clue," I admitted just before I leaned down to kiss Brody.

Unlike my kiss with Beck, this one went from early morning greeting to full-on inferno in a matter of seconds. I was shaking with need by the time Brody released me. But I was glad he had, because as turned on as I was, it wasn't the same without Beck between us. I couldn't explain why, but the fact that Brody didn't try to kiss me again or pull me closer had me thinking he felt the same way.

"If I can talk Beck into dinner tonight, will you join us?" Brody asked. "I'll cook."

I needed to say no. Clearly the three of us couldn't be in a room together and not nearly set it on fire with whatever this thing between us was. But I found myself nodding just before I brushed my mouth gently over his. And then I did something I hadn't thought I'd ever do again. I sought out the safety of Brody's arms. He didn't hesitate to envelop me in his warm grasp and I felt his lips press against the top of my head as I settled on his chest. How many times had I wrapped myself around Griff's pillow in the days and months after his death dreaming it was his strong body cradling mine? That it was his raspy voice soothing me?

I didn't expect to fall asleep like that, but the next time I came to awareness, I was alone and daylight was seeping into the room. A glance at the clock showed I'd slept through my alarm or I'd forgotten to set it all together because it was well past my normal time to get up. I went to my own room to shower and dress and then went out to the barn to find Beck. The barn was spotless and all the horses had been turned out. I found Beck helping Brody in the tack room. They were installing a piece of wood that I suspected would act as a support for the saddle racks. I held back as I listened to them laughing about something.

It took several minutes before Beck noticed me and while his smile didn't exactly fade, there was a moment of uncertainty in his gaze as he greeted me.

"I've got a couple of interviews over at the lodge in a few minutes," I said as I entered the tack room and looked around. It would likely be done within a week at the most. Which made me wonder if Brody would be moving on at that point.

"I was thinking we'd go for a ride after lunch. You good with that?" I asked Beck.

He nodded, but didn't say anything. My eyes shifted to Brody. "How about you?"

"Me?" Brody asked.

"Can you spare an hour with all this and help me and Beck out? We need to take the horses out in larger groups. You up for it?"

"I've never ridden before," Brody said.

"Even better," I responded with a smirk. To Beck I said, "Tack up Ladybug for him."

Beck smiled. "Will do."

"Be ready to go by 1," I said as I left the tack room.

"You got it, boss," I heard Beck say and then I heard the two of them chuckling. That put a smile on my face that didn't disappear even after I entered the lodge and made my way to the director's office.

Gabriella Phelps was considerably younger than I would have thought someone in such an important position should be, but I'd known pretty quickly after meeting her that Roman had picked wisely when it came to the person who would run the day-to-day operations of the resort. In her late twenties at the most, Gabriella was a no-nonsense type, but she was also very easy going and kind-hearted. I'd been a little nervous about her stepping in to participate in the interviews after Roman had taken time off to be with his husband and their new daughter, but Gabriella had proven me wrong. She'd looked to me to assess each candidate's skill when it came to working with the horses, but she'd also spied some potential problem candidates based on their past work history or things they'd said that I hadn't picked up on. All in all, we made a good team, but I would be glad when the interviews were done.

What I wouldn't be glad about was finishing up at the resort and transitioning the work to other people. I had no doubt the horses would be well cared for, but going back to our regular work at the CB Bar meant I wouldn't be seeing Brody and my interactions with Beck would be limited to the day-to-day work stuff and nothing more.

Was that what I wanted?

Something more?

"Morning, Quinn," Gabriella said as she greeted me just outside her office door with a cup of coffee in hand.

"Morning," I said as I took in her crisp business suit and perfectly styled hair. I half-listened as she began talking about the first candidate we were interviewing, but my mind was already on this afternoon's trail ride.

Because I had a little surprise in store for my men.

My men?

I shook my head at the slip of the mind and then forced all my attention on Gabriella.

Beck and Brody weren't my anything.

No matter how badly I might have wanted them to be.

∼

"Cannonball!"

The warning came just as Beck jumped on the thick rope, his momentum carrying him out over the water. He let go at just the right time so that when he hit the water, he fell between me and Brody, soaking us both.

The second his head broke the surface, Brody grabbed him and dunked him under the water again. They took turns splashing and dunking each other as they wrestled in the crystal-clear water. I used the time to check on the horses tied to a nearby tree.

I'd decided to take the trail leading to the small, natural pool this morning when I'd realized how hot it would get this afternoon. It would surely be a popular spot for the resort's guests not only because of the privacy, but because of the small waterfall that filled the pool with mountain runoff.

Beck and Brody hadn't hesitated to strip down to their underwear when I'd told them we had time to go for a swim and I'd watched as they'd raced each other to the water and jumped in without any kind of hesitation. I hadn't intended to join them at first, but when they'd both gotten out of the water and each grabbed one of my arms, threatening to force me in the water fully clothed, I'd relented and started stripping. The atmosphere had turned heated as both men had returned to the water and watched me get undressed, but a well-placed leap into the water that had left them both sputtering had broken up the tension.

I watched Brody and Beck wrestle for a few more minutes before they both cried "Uncle" at nearly the exact same time. As the humor drifted away, the familiar heated energy returned and I watched as Brody and Beck stared at each other, as if each was waiting for the other to make the next move. I found myself not caring who did what first...hell, I was seriously considering grabbing whoever was closest to me and getting things started myself.

"Can we check out the waterfall?" Beck finally asked. I nodded and followed him and Brody towards the small cascade of water on the far side of the small pool. Beck tested the waterfall with his hand first before taking the plunge and swimming to the other side. Brody and I followed and found ourselves in small cocoon of darkness and light. Beck's eyes shifted back and forth between us as the wall of water closed off behind us. There was barely enough room for the three of us, but none of us seemed to notice. Beck had a hold of the wall of rocks behind him that offered natural outcroppings to hang on to. I glanced at Brody and saw the unfettered lust in his eyes…a mirror to my own desire that had spiked up the second I'd breached the waterfall.

I was the first to move. Beck didn't hesitate to open to me as I reached him and slammed my mouth down on his. I took over holding onto the rocks as his arms came around me. I groaned when his legs wrapped around my waist and his hands fisted my hair. Somehow in the time since I'd first kissed him in that bathroom, he'd turned into an expert at kissing. He quickly took control of my mouth and then Brody was there, his firm lips taking over. I felt a hand close around my dick through my underwear, but it wasn't enough so I grabbed Beck's wrist, forcing him to release his hold on me. "Let's go," was all I said to both of them, and then I was dragging Beck behind me as I swam back through the waterfall.

Excitement flooded my nerve endings as we reached the shore and before Beck could even climb to his feet, I dragged him back to me and kissed him hard. He did what I'd hoped and wrapped himself around me once again, soft whimpers falling from his throat as he clung to me and I took ownership of his mouth. I didn't even clear the water before I was lowering him to his back. With one sweep of my hand, I pushed his wet boxers down to reveal his dick. My own underwear cleared my ass thanks to Brody who was at my back. I settled my weight on Beck, our cocks sliding together as Brody's solid form pressed against my back, his lips at my neck. I turned to kiss him even as I began humping against Beck, our dicks sliding together. I groaned at the feeling of Brody's cock between my ass cheeks. His shaft slid back and forth over my hole and for the first time ever, I felt the need to be filled.

But there wasn't even time to consider the newfound moment because I was already unbearably close to coming. I hadn't even touched Beck's dick, or even my own, with my hand – it was just our wet bodies sliding together and Brody's hot shaft urging me on. I couldn't even imagine the sight we must have made, the three of us grinding against each other desperately, our bodies half in, half out of the cool water. Beck's arms were wrapped around my shoulders and Brody's were braced alongside of my body. Pleas for relief kept falling from Beck's mouth in between kisses and that only spurred me to grind against him harder, our slick dicks burning as we sought our release. I cried out in relief when my orgasm finally slammed into me and I felt Beck's fingers digging into me when my hot cum hit his skin. He shouted my name as he bucked his hips against mine one final time and I felt his semen mix with mine between us. Brody's cry of completion shattered the air around us before the proof of his release slickened my ass and burned over my hole.

My muscles felt like noodles as I collapsed all of my weight on Beck and I was dimly aware of Brody and him kissing over my shoulder. We lay there for long minutes in a tangle of limbs and broken breaths. Brody was the first to move and I instantly missed the feel of his heavy cock nestled in the crease of my ass and his muscled body pinning mine. I forced myself to climb off of Beck and I steeled myself for what I knew would come next – Beck's panic. But to my surprise, Beck merely sat up, eyed the mess our mixed semen had made on his softening dick and belly and then he kissed me. He got up and returned to the water to wash off. He and Brody kissed languidly before both looking at me expectantly. I bit back my smile and got back in the water. I quickly rinsed the proof of what had just happened from my body and then we all got out of the water and laid on our backs on the rocks as we let the sun dry us.

∽

"What did you compete in when you were in the rodeo?"

The question came from Beck which was a surprise since he'd been pretty quiet since we'd returned to the barn this afternoon. Of course, after the events at the small reservoir, none of us had been particularly chatty. I had no doubt we were each thinking about what the whole thing had meant. For my part, I was at a complete loss. I'd had no intention of pursuing a relationship with either man, yet I was doing things I knew would bring us together rather than keep us apart.

Like our little swim this afternoon.

And what had happened behind that waterfall.

I had no one but myself to blame for that.

And here I was having dinner with both men again, despite how things had ended after the last meal we'd shared.

"Roping mostly," I said. "My parents owned a ranch in Nevada so I learned early on how to ride and work cattle."

"And you said Griff rode bulls?" Brody said.

I nodded. "He was fearless and a big-time adrenaline junkie. He didn't always know when it was time to quit."

"What do you mean?" Brody asked.

"He would put proving himself above his safety sometimes. He once rode in the championship with a fractured hand because no one believed he could win. He did, of course, but he fucked his hand up so bad he needed surgery and spent six months in PT trying to regain normal use of it. The day after he finished PT, he was on a bull."

Brody shook his head solemnly. "That must have been hard to watch."

I nodded and swallowed hard, debating how much to say. I glanced at Beck and saw him watching me with a mix of pity and concern. "It was hard to accept that some things just meant more to Griff than us and our future together. Winning, for one," I murmured.

"But you got married," Beck said. "You were planning a family."

"Yeah, it took a while to get Griff to agree to leave the rodeo circuit, but once that need to always be number one was gone, things got better. We bought a small piece of property in Wyoming and got jobs at a nearby cattle ranch so we could save up enough money to get our own place going. It took a few years, but we finally managed it. We were looking into options for adoption and surrogacy when he died."

"What happened to him?" Beck asked softly.

"I was supposed to meet him at our favorite restaurant for our anniversary – we'd been together for five years. He didn't show. I got a call from the cops that his body was found behind a bar he used to frequent. Witnesses said he'd gotten into an altercation with a couple of guys earlier in the evening…they'd been hassling a waitress and he'd stepped in. He was never one to hide his sexuality so when one of the guys called him a fag, he made some snide comment that he'd known would piss them off. The bartender broke up the fight and kicked the guys out but they caught up to Griff when he left."

I felt Beck's hand close over my forearm where it was resting on the table. I liked that neither he or Brody told me how sorry they were – they were words I'd heard often enough yet somehow, they always managed to make me feel even emptier.

"What about you?" I asked Brody, hoping to get the attention off of me. I eyed him and said, "My guess is you were the quarterback on your football team and you led your team to the championship four years running."

Brody smiled. "Not quite. That would be my brother, Nathan. Along with valedictorian, prom king, captain of the debate team, class president..." Brody's voice dropped off as he picked at his food and I instantly regretted bringing up the topic.

"What about you?" Beck asked.

"Me..." Brody seemed to mull over the word for a moment. "Just like the night we were born, I was always late to the party." He smiled half-heartedly. "I held my own, I guess. I idolized Nathan, so it wasn't bad living in his shadow. As we got older, I was kind of grateful…took the spotlight off me."

"What do you mean?" I asked.

Brody was quiet for a moment before saying, "Either of you heard of Chandler Wilder?"

I shook my head, but Beck said, "He's that governor who ignored the Supreme Court's ruling on gay marriage. He tried to block gay marriages in his state even after the court handed down its ruling."

Brody nodded, but before he could say anything else, Beck said, "Wait, is he your father?"

"Yep, dear old dad," Brody murmured.

"Chandler Wilder is your dad?" Beck said softly. "He did all that knowing his own son…"

"I'm not his son anymore," Brody responded. "Haven't been since I told him no amount of prayer was going to make me not want dick anymore."

"When was that?" I asked. The food I'd eaten felt like a lead weight in my belly so I put my fork down and pushed the plate away.

"Three years ago. About a month before I was set to graduate from law school and two months before I was supposed to marry my fiancée."

"What about your brother?" Beck asked.

"Last time I saw him was the night he came to my apartment to try and stop me. He told me I was a sick fuck and that we weren't brothers anymore."

"Fuck, Brody," I began, but Brody cut me off with a shake of his head.

"It was for the best. I felt like I was drowning in that life. When we were kids, Nathan got most of the attention, but not enough that I could have the life I wanted. My dad had high hopes for both of us to walk in his footsteps…law school and then political office. After I had sex with my girlfriend for the first time, I told Nathan the truth. He told our father and all hell broke loose. I stood to lose everything so I convinced myself it was a phase and I could be cured. I wasn't, of course, but I knew better than to tell anyone that. I thought maybe I could have both worlds…be the prodigal son my family expected me to be while using gay clubs and random hookups to feed that darker part of me that I just couldn't get rid of. I did it for years…" Brody said quietly, his eyes on the plate of untouched food in front of him. At some point, Beck had taken his hand in his, but I wasn't sure Brody had noticed.

"I finally realized how fucked-up my life had gotten when I got a glimpse of my future. I was in this club that was well known for some of its seedier offerings and I actually ran into someone I knew."

Brody's eyes shifted to me and Beck before saying, "He was my father's general counsel and close friend of my family since before I was even born. Happily married with four kids…or so I thought."

Brody dropped his eyes again. "The things he was letting those men do to him…" Brody shook his head. "When he saw me, he panicked and begged me not to tell my father. Said it was just something he needed to do once in a while. That he wasn't actually gay. It was so fucking pathetic but I knew," - Brody's hand tightened on Beck's – "I knew that would be me someday. That was it. I went home that night and told my fiancée we were through and I told my family I was gay the next day. I left South Carolina and moved to Florida. I'd worked construction when I was younger so I got a job hanging drywall and as soon as I had enough money saved up, I enrolled in a training course to become a paramedic. When I saw the job opening in this area a few months ago, I jumped at the chance and here I am."

Beck and I both sat in stunned silence for several long minutes. I didn't miss how Brody began playing with Beck's fingers, linking and unlinking them with his own.

"Your family didn't look for you? Try to make contact?" I asked.

Brody shook his head. "Some reporters showed up after the Supreme Court ruling to get my reaction and to ask if I was gay, but I ignored them. I didn't want to become a part of his story, if that makes any sense."

I nodded. The reporters would have had a field day exposing the truth about Brody.

"My family painted me as a black sheep and I was fine with that," Brody said. "The reporters eventually lost interest once my dad was forced to concede that he couldn't fight the ruling. He lost his re-election bid last year, but it looks like Nathan is making waves as the new poster boy for the far-right wing. I read that he's considering a run for senate next year."

An awkward silence fell over the room and lasted until Brody pushed back his chair and collected his plate. He took it over to the kitchen and began scraping the leftovers into a plastic container, presumably for the stray dog Beck was still trying to befriend. Beck and I exchanged glances and then he got up and went to Brody. My insides tripped over themselves as I watched Beck wrap his arms around Brody from behind and rest his head against his back. Neither spoke, but I could see some of the tension ease from Brody's body. When he turned around, Beck didn't hesitate to embrace him and when they kissed softly, I smiled.

I didn't know what we had, but somehow it was working for us. I could either spend the rest of the summer fighting it, or just enjoy it until the time Beck had to go home. Hell, it likely wouldn't last beyond the couple of weeks we had left together until we left the resort to go back to our normal lives.

With that thought in mind, I said yes when Brody suggested we watch a movie. Surprisingly, Beck agreed and when we settled on the couch, there was no awkwardness as he settled between us.

Less than an hour later, Beck had nodded off and I was nearing the point of no return myself so I sent Brody a quick look. He got the message and turned off the TV and gently shook Beck awake.

"Beck, it's late," he said softly.

Beck made a noncommittal grunt before climbing to his feet. As we neared the hallway leading to the bedrooms, Beck paused at the entrance and then turned to face both of us. He looked like he wanted to say something.

"Everything okay?" I asked.

He nodded, but didn't move. I was about to reach for him when he finally turned around and began walking again. We were almost at his door when he stopped and turned again, his face drawn into a mask of worry. It took him a long moment to lift his eyes. "Do you…do you guys wanna sleep in here again?" he asked as he motioned to his door. "Just sleep."

Brody didn't even hesitate. He simply took Beck's hand and led him to his door and waited for Beck to open it. Once it was open, both men looked at me expectantly. I ignored the part of me that was warning me it was a bad idea and said, "Only if you promise to kick Brody when he starts snoring."

Brody let out a snort, but smiled. Beck laughed and said, "Deal" and then disappeared into the room.

CHAPTER 13

BECK

"She looks good," Dane said as he ran his hands along the length of the dog's back one final time. "She just needs to gain some weight and she'll be good as new."

The dog was shaking in my hold, but she hadn't snapped or growled at Dane which was encouraging. It had taken me nearly a week to get the little dog to finally trust me enough to allow me to touch her, and once I did, that was it – she refused to leave my side. I'd even taken to sneaking her into my room at night, though with Brody and Quinn both still sleeping with me each night, my secret hadn't lasted very long. Neither man had said anything, of course, and I often caught both of them sneaking her food from their dinner plates when they thought I wasn't looking. Quinn had repeatedly assured me he doubted Roman would have a problem with the dog staying in my room, but I'd gotten so attached to her that I'd been too afraid to risk asking permission.

"You name her yet?" Dane asked as he began preparing the vaccines he'd said the dog would need.

"I figured I shouldn't. She might belong to someone and even if she doesn't, I need to find her a new home so those people should get to name her…"

Dane glanced at me, but didn't say anything at first. The dog barely noticed when he injected the first vaccine. "I can ask around if anyone is missing her, but based on her condition and demeanor, I'm guessing she wasn't loved enough to be missed." He gave her another injection and said, "And seems like she's already found herself a new home."

My heart clenched at that because I'd grown far more attached to the dog than I'd intended.

"Maybe…maybe you can find her a good family," I suggested.

Dane studied me for a moment. Finally, he said, "Tell you what…if you still feel that way when it's time for you to go home, she can stay with us."

The relief was so overwhelming that I couldn't find the words to respond so I merely nodded.

"Now, with that in mind, she needs a name," Dane said gently. He began applying some kind of medicine along the skin on the back of her neck.

"Harley," I said.

Dane smiled at the quick response. "Harley it is," he said as he gave the dog a quick pat. "So how are things going at the resort?"

"Good," I responded, though I could feel the heat creeping into my cheeks at the lie.

Because things were way better than good.

Even when they were confusing as hell.

My relationship with Brody and Quinn had intensified in some ways, but stalled in others. After the first night I'd asked them if they wanted to sleep in my room, they'd hadn't needed to be asked again – we just all naturally ended up there after we were done with whatever movie we ended up watching after dinner. In the mornings, I usually got up first, though admittedly, it was a challenge to force myself to climb out of the warm cocoon the two bodies around me created. As soon as I left the bed, Quinn and Brody would migrate to each other until they were wrapped in each other's arms. Sometimes one or both would wake up and I'd kiss them and tell them to go back to sleep, but on most occasions, I'd get a few minutes where I could just watch them holding onto each other, their faces relaxed in sleep.

Quinn almost always was up within a half an hour of me and would join me in the barn and help me feed and turn out the horses before we went back to the residence for breakfast that Brody would have ready for us. We'd go our separate ways for most of the morning, but after lunch we'd reconvene and go for a ride, though we hadn't stopped at the natural pool again like that first time.

Much to my disappointment.

That was the part where our relationship had stalled. While Brody and Quinn were touchy-feely with me, neither had instigated any more sexual encounters and I'd still been too embarrassed by my breakdown after the episode on the couch that first night to try and encourage another one.

I'd had a lot of time that night to think about things, though I doubted my thoughts on the subject would have been the same if Quinn and Brody hadn't insisted on staying with me after I'd panicked. When they'd arrived at my door, I'd thought it had only been because they were worried I was so weak that I'd actually hurt myself. But the fact that they stayed with me long after they'd needed to had started to make me question things.

A lot of things.

But I had no answers for any of those questions. All I had were dueling feelings about wanting to be with both men. I craved their touch and yet my mind still couldn't process what it meant that I did. And the shame was still there, like a living thing beneath my skin. Only it had been amplified because now I feared what Brody and Quinn would think of me if they found out the truth about everything I'd done in my past...what my mind still tried to get me to do whenever it felt threatened. While I'd managed to tamp those emotions down during the day, I knew I hadn't escaped them completely because Brody and Quinn were waking me up night after night when the nightmares became too much.

Surprisingly, the physical exhaustion hadn't been as crippling as I thought it'd be. It had only been a few weeks since I'd arrived in Dare and yet that urge to stay in bed and hide away from the world wasn't there. Even with the poor quality of my sleep, I still felt more energized than I ever had after sleeping twenty hours a day, day after day, during my dark times. I'd also found that the need to steer clear of others had diminished too. I'd spent a couple nights in the past week at Dane and Jax's house for dinner and while I hadn't exactly been an expert conversationalist, I'd held my own and it hadn't felt awkward or forced. I'd actually enjoyed telling Dane and Jax about the work I was doing with the horses. My nerves still got the best of me whenever I was alone with Jax for any extended period of time, but I'd managed to get through those times without having to make an excuse to escape his company.

I'd spoken with my fathers several times via video chat and even they'd commented that country life seemed to be agreeing with me. I hadn't told them about my relationship with Quinn and Brody, of course, but I'd given them a virtual tour of the barn and the horses and they'd asked me lots of questions about my work with the large animals.

And not one question about how I was doing…at least not in the way they'd so often asked before. In the past, that question had always been asked with a certain level of fear and hesitation…like they didn't really want to know. Now the question was a benign one…a conversation starter and nothing more.

But the biggest change I was dealing with was my burgeoning feelings for Quinn and Brody. At some point, and I couldn't pinpoint precisely when it had happened, I'd started to want something more from both men besides the promise of pleasure they'd both given me. I loved watching them interact and I'd found myself waiting in anticipation for any time either one smiled or laughed or looked at me in that way that warmed my insides.

Like maybe I was more than just some pathetic kid who needed special handling.

I wasn't sure what I'd do if everything between us was based on pity. I tried not to think about it much because whenever I did, I could feel the darkness threaten to consume me and I was enjoying the light too much to let that happen.

Which was why I hadn't pressed the lack of sex issue. The last time we'd been intimate which had been at the mountain pool more than a week earlier, I'd managed to not have a freak out moment, but I wasn't sure what would happen if things went any further.

"Okay, she's all set," Dane said, ripping me back to the present.

I loosened my hold on Harley and she immediately snuggled her little body against my chest.

"Thank you," I said as I ran my hand soothingly over the dog's back.

"You're welcome," Dane said as he began cleaning up his supplies. "You're really good with her," he continued. "You have the touch."

"The touch?" I asked.

"Animals seem to instinctively trust you. You ever thought about turning that into a career?"

Surprise shot through me.

And to be honest, a shard of pride too, because Quinn had told me something similar.

"What, like do what I'm doing at the ranch full-time?" I asked in confusion.

"That," Dane said. "Or you could go to vet school. Or if the idea of that much school doesn't appeal to you, quality vet techs are in high demand."

Speech escaped me as his words washed through me. "Um, my grades weren't great in high school…" I murmured, even as Dane's words took root deep inside of me. I hadn't ever been around animals as a kid, but I'd always enjoyed interacting with my extended family's menagerie of animals. But I'd never thought it was something I could build a life around.

Which wasn't a surprise since most of my energy went to just getting through each day.

"Did you like your science classes? Biology, anatomy?"

I nodded. After my doctor had gotten me on the right dosage of anti-depressants this past year, I'd managed to focus a bit better in class. I hadn't liked the more creative classes like art and English, but I'd done okay in science and math.

"If you can get strong grades in those kinds of classes in your undergraduate program, vet school isn't an impossibility. And vet tech courses aren't as stringent. You could even do the vet tech courses first and work in the field while taking part-time college classes and then decide if you want to pursue vet school."

The ember of hope Dane had sparked to life grew with every word he said and I had to force myself to loosen my grip on Harley when she squirmed in my hold.

Was something like that really possible?

I blinked back tears at the prospect.

"I'll…I'll think about it," I managed to get out.

If Dane noticed the tremor in my voice, he was kind enough not to point it out. "Great," he simply said. "If you have any questions, I'm glad to answer them."

My throat was so tight all I could do was nod. I used the excuse of setting Harley on the ground to cover my shaking hands and then followed Dane to the front office. His receptionist had left for the day so I watched him go to the computer to type something into it.

"Okay, we'll need to see Harley again in about a month for boosters."

I nodded. My eyes caught on a display in the corner of the waiting room. A rack with several leashes and collars sat next to a shelf with all sorts of toys and pet supplies. I went over to it and fingered a pretty red leather collar and while I was tempted, the price was more than I could afford. I'd gotten my first paycheck earlier in the week but I was saving most of it to put towards paying my fathers back for the damage to my car after the accident. Insurance had covered most of the cost, but I wanted to pay the deductible myself, despite my parents' insistence that it wasn't necessary. And with the cost of Harley's care today, it was going to be tight.

I settled for a cheaper red nylon collar and matching leash along with a plush dog toy that got Harley's attention when I squeaked it. I would have liked to get her some nice bowls for her food and water, but the plastic containers I'd borrowed from the kitchen would do for now.

I took the items to the counter and dug out my wallet. Dane eyed me for a moment and then walked around the counter to the display of leashes. He snagged the red leather collar I'd been eyeing along with a matching leash, several toys, a few bags of treats and two ceramic bowls with paw prints painted on them and headed back to the counter. He remained on my side of the counter as he deposited everything on it and began removing the price tag from the collar.

"You've got a classy girl there, Beck," he said as he glanced at Harley. "She deserves a classy collar."

Embarrassment went through me as I murmured, "It's beautiful, but I can't afford it. Or any of this." I motioned to all the supplies.

Dane cocked his head at me and then crouched down, collar in hand. "Come here, sweetheart," he said softly. Harley hesitated, but Dane was undaunted and eventually she pressed up against him. He fitted the collar around her neck and smiled. "Perfect," he said. He gave her a pat and then stood. As he collected all the supplies in his arms, I resigned myself to the inevitable and dug out my wallet.

"How much do I owe you?"

"One night of your services. That's what you owe me," he said with a smirk as he started walking towards the door.

Heat flooded my system and bile crept up the back of my throat.

No...

The word kept repeating on a loop in my head, but I couldn't make any sound come out. I reached out to grab the counter to keep myself upright.

"Beck."

I shook my head violently. I needed to tell him to fuck off, but the words wouldn't come. Tears of frustration welled in my eyes, but I furiously blinked them back. I wouldn't let him see me like this...

"Beck, take a deep breath."

His voice sounded far away, but I felt his touch everywhere and the need to vomit overwhelmed me.

Tell him to back the fuck off!

But the words eluded me. Pain exploded in my chest as my lungs stopped working.

"Dane?"

"Jax, something's wrong with him," I heard Dane say frantically.

"Beck?" I knew who the deeper voice belonged to and I immediately backed up, but between the counter and the wall behind me, there was nowhere to go.

"Beck, you need to slow your breathing," I heard Jax say calmly, but my mind refused to obey. They were going to do it. I wasn't going to be able to stop them. I'd let my guard down and now I would lose the only thing keeping me from once again taking that final step. Only this time there might not be someone just on the other side of the door.

I wanted to scream and rage, but a familiar emptiness settled over me. I wanted to cry at its return, but I also welcomed it.

"What happened?" I heard Jax ask.

"Nothing!" Dane said, his voice filled with worry. "We were talking and I made a joke about having him babysit for us Friday night as payment for this stuff…"

The rest of Dane's words fell away as my mind frantically settled on just one.

Babysit…

Disbelief coursed through me as my brain and body finally began to catch up to one another. I felt air blessedly flow through my lungs.

Babysit.

Dane was going to ask me to babysit in exchange for what I owed for Harley's care and supplies. The relief was immediate, as was the humiliation. Awareness returned and I managed to lift my eyes to see Jax and Dane looking at me, their faces tight with concern. The word ambulance caught my attention and I quickly said, "I'm okay." My mind scrambled for an explanation. "Sorry, I was just suddenly feeling sick and was afraid I was going to throw up."

Both men looked at me like I was crazy and I couldn't blame them because it was a completely ridiculous explanation. "I think I just spent too much time out in the sun today…Quinn's been on me to buy a hat or borrow one from him…"

The verbal diarrhea continued until I finally saw both men relax a little bit.

"Why don't you come inside and lie down for a while?" Dane said. I hadn't noticed until now that he'd put all the stuff back on the counter.

I shook my head. "I'm fine, really. I need to get back...the new girl is stopping by tonight and I wanted to be there to show her around and help her get her stuff moved in."

"Beck," Jax began.

"I promise," I interjected. "I feel better already. I'll grab some water when I gas up my car and I'll be good as new. I'm sorry I scared you." I settled my eyes on Dane. "I'd be happy to babysit Friday."

My acting was once again up to par because both men finally stepped back, the tension easing out of their bodies.

"You're sure?" Dane asked.

I nodded. "I can text you to let you know I made it safely back to the resort," I offered.

"We'd appreciate that, Beck," Jax said. His voice sounded even and calm, but I could see the lingering suspicion in his gaze.

"Let me get this for you," Dane began, but I quickly grabbed the supplies off the counter before he could reach for them.

"It's okay, I've got it," I said brightly. "Thank you so much for this. I really appreciate it."

Dane nodded, but didn't say anything. He clearly wasn't one hundred percent convinced about the situation either.

I squeezed past them and hurried towards the door, my arms full. Harley darted ahead of me and was waiting by the door before I reached it.

"Beck."

I stiffened, but forced myself to stop and turn around. It took everything in my being to make my eyes meet Jax's.

"You sure you're okay?" he asked.

"Definitely," I said, nodding for good measure. I could see the lingering doubt so I scrambled for a distraction. "Oh, did Quinn call you about coming to the resort on Sunday for a group trail ride?"

Quinn had told me a couple days ago, that he wanted to put the horses through a dress rehearsal of sorts which meant we needed more people to join us on a large group trail ride. He'd arranged for Callan and his husbands and Luke, Gray and their young son to join us as well as Dane and Jax and their kids. I already knew Dane and Jax had agreed because Quinn had told me they had, but I kept that to myself.

My question did the trick and right after the men confirmed they were coming on Sunday, I got out of there and hurried to my car. Harley beat me to the driver's side door and she automatically took her spot on the passenger seat when I opened it. I saw Dane and Jax exit the building and I quickly waved at them as I put my car in reverse and got it turned around. It took everything I had not to squeal the tires in an effort to get out of there faster.

Please don't let them call my fathers.

While Dane and Jax didn't seem to know about my past as a prostitute, or they hadn't yet made that connection between Dane's comment and my over-the-top reaction to it, if they spoke to my fathers, chances were they'd all figure it out.

It was another humiliation I just couldn't bear.

Not to mention the fact that my fathers were under the impression I'd left that part of my life behind me. Well, as much as one could, anyway.

The drive back to the resort calmed me, as did the sight of Quinn and Brody's trucks parked next to each other. It was nearing the end of the work day, so I suspected both men would be in the barn finishing up. My need to see them was intense and I completely missed the fact that another car was parked next to the trucks. It wasn't until I was halfway down the aisle, Harley at my side, that I realized Gabriella, the resort's director, was there. I barely noticed the young woman standing next to her because my eyes were on Gabriella whose eyes were on Harley.

Fuck.

My gaze flashed to Quinn and Brody, but I forced myself to return my attention to Gabriella. I wanted nothing more than to feel Quinn and Brody's arms around me, but I didn't have that luxury.

"Gabriella, I'm sorry," I stammered. "She showed up a couple weeks ago, and I was trying to befriend her so I could try to find her a new home-"

I stuttered to a stop when Gabriella stooped down, her attention on Harley. "Hi sweetie, aren't you a cutie?" she cooed. She put her hand out, but Harley stayed by my side. Luckily, the young woman didn't seem to be fazed because she merely smiled and rose.

"I'm so glad you were able to make friends with her, Beck. If you need anything for her, just let me know, okay?"

What?

That was it?

I was dumbfounded as Gabriella returned her attention back to Quinn and said, "I'll leave you guys to it then."

Quinn nodded. "We'll take good care of her," he said as his eyes shifted to the girl standing next to Gabriella. I finally managed to take notice of her myself and my first thought was that she looked really young, younger than me even. I guessed her to be barely over the five-foot mark. Her long, dark blonde hair was pulled into a neat braid and she was wearing loose-fitting jeans, worn sneakers, and an oversized T-shirt with what looked like a sports team logo on it. A sweatshirt was wrapped around her waist and her hand was protectively clutching a tattered duffle bag that looked like it could fall apart at any moment.

I managed to nod at Gabriella as she walked past me. My feet were frozen in place as my eyes returned to Quinn and Brody and I saw them both send me worried looks.

The fact that they could both read me so well made something inside of me twist in a way that wasn't at all painful. I forced a smile to my lips and walked towards them.

"Beck, this is Delilah-" Quinn began.

"Lilah," the girl interjected and then blushed. "No one calls me Delilah," she murmured. I didn't miss the way the girl's eyes shifted to Gabriella as she left the barn.

"Lilah," Quinn corrected. "Lilah, this is Beck. He'll be showing you the ropes."

I put out my hand. The girl hesitated before taking it and I didn't miss the wariness that crept into her gaze as her eyes met mine and then shifted back to Quinn and Brody. It was a feeling I was all too familiar with and my automatic instinct was to try and put her at ease.

"Hi," I said. "It's nice to meet you."

"You too." Her voice was barely a whisper. Quinn glanced at me and I saw the silent question and nodded. I knew all too well how intimidating being around two big guys like Quinn and Brody could be.

"Brody and I are just going to finish up out here and then get started on dinner," Quinn said, his focus on Lilah. "Lilah, you're welcome to join us. We're having lasagna."

She shook her head before he even stopped speaking. "Um, no… I'm really tired. And I ate at the center before Gabriella…Miss Phelps picked me up."

Quinn nodded. "Okay, well, if you get hungry, the leftovers will be in the fridge. Help yourself. And if you need any help moving your stuff in, let us know."

Another shake of her head, but this time she remained silent. Brody and Quinn didn't linger. Quinn moved past me, his body brushing mine in the briefest of touches. Brody was next and I had to keep from smiling as his fingers touched mine for just a split second.

I couldn't help but watch them both head out of the barn, Brody grabbing his toolbox as he went. I forced myself to return my attention to Lilah and noticed her watching me curiously. I cleared my throat and smiled briefly. "How about a tour?" I said.

She nodded and slung her bag over her shoulder.

"You can leave that here," I offered.

"It's okay, I can carry it," she responded, her tone firm.

"Okay," I said awkwardly. I began the tour, introducing her to each horse as we went and explaining what I knew about their individual personalities. Her coolness evaporated as she began interacting with the animals so I began opening each stall door as we went so she could touch the horses.

"Have you worked with horses before?" I asked about halfway through.

"No…but I'm a quick learner," she said defensively.

I wasn't sure how to put her at ease. A full minute passed before I said, "I'd never even touched a horse until three weeks ago when I got here."

Her eyes shifted to me. "Gab…Miss Phelps said you're just here for the summer and that you're going back to working on a ranch when the resort opens?"

I nodded. "The CB Bar…it's about half an hour from here."

"Where are you from?"

"Seattle."

When she didn't respond, I asked, "Have you ever been there?"

She shook her head. "Never been outside of Montana." Her voice was low and slightly pained.

"There's still time," I said.

I'd meant the comment to be a way to lighten the mood, but she kept her eyes downcast.

"You said Gabriella picked you up from a center? Like a job center?" I asked.

Lilah slowed her pace marginally and then stopped all together. "It's…it's a youth center."

I wasn't sure why that was cause for such hesitation, but before I could respond, she said, "For LGBT kids."

Understanding dawned. She was sending me a very clear message. I couldn't help the smile that spread across my face. "Good, more men for me," I joked.

She stilled for a moment and then a small smile graced her lips. She didn't say anything, but she seemed less tense as we continued meeting the remaining horses. It wasn't until we started walking towards the residence that I asked, "How old are you?"

"I turn eighteen in a couple of weeks," she murmured. It took several long seconds for her to say, "You?"

"Nineteen." As we neared the living quarters, I asked, "So is this going to be a summer job before you start college?"

She shook her head. "I'm here to stay…hopefully."

The last part was said with a hint of sadness. "Do you have family nearby?"

I knew I was prying, but something about her tugged at my heartstrings. She seemed so…lost.

Another shake. "No…my Mom, um, she kicked me out a few months ago. My dad left when I was seven – not sure where he is."

"I'm sorry," I murmured. I was definitely curious to know more, but I didn't pry. *I* certainly wasn't an open book. "Do you know which room you're in?" I asked.

Lilah pulled a key out of her pocket. "Miss Phelps said it was room 10…on the end." I nodded and veered us towards the right side of the building.

"I think she's okay with people calling her Gabriella," I noted and was surprised when Lilah's cheeks went bright with color. I smiled inwardly at that. I didn't blame the girl. Gabriella was a beautiful woman. I wasn't sure what the exact age difference was, but I suspected it was less than the gap between me and Brody and Quinn.

Once we reached room 10, I waited for Lilah to unlock the door. I didn't cross over the threshold until she waved me and Harley into the room. I gave her a quick tour of her suite and then motioned to the door leading to the communal areas. "If you have a few minutes, I can show you the kitchen and stuff," I offered.

"I'd like that," Lilah said softly. I liked that she seemed more comfortable around me.

I explained the layout of the building as we walked towards the main living space and let her know that Brody's, Quinn's and my rooms were on the other side of the building. I didn't mention the fact that both men shared my bed each night.

Once we reached the kitchen, we ran into Quinn and Brody as they cooked. They had their backs to us so they weren't aware of our presence. My body heated as Brody turned his head and smiled at something Quinn said and then he leaned in and brushed his mouth over Quinn's. The kiss was sweet and brief, but the way the men looked at each other…

I wasn't exactly jealous, but a twinge of fear went through me as I began to wonder if whatever was between them wasn't the same as what I'd thought we had between us.

Except I didn't even know what that was.

It wasn't until Harley let out a little bark to get my attention that Quinn and Brody turned around. Their eyes remained heated as they met mine, but their expressions quickly changed to something unreadable the longer we watched one another. The whole thing lasted less than a handful of seconds, but it was enough to have a knot of despair growing inside of me.

Maybe everything they'd said and done in the last couple of weeks had been about pity and nothing more. Besides, there could be no relationship because I was only in town for a couple more months.

"Hey, did you decide to join us?" Brody asked Lilah.

"No, thank you. Beck was just showing me around."

Brody nodded and then I felt his eyes on me. *Felt* because I'd dropped my eyes.

"The TV room is back here," I murmured as I led Lilah to the seating area. I was on autopilot as I explained the rest of the layout of the building. As we began to leave the kitchen, I could still feel Quinn and Brody's eyes on me.

"Dinner will be ready in about ten," Quinn offered.

"Okay," I managed to say.

I led Lilah out the door leading to the courtyard and showed her the grill that was there for everyone to use, as well as the seating area. Instead of going back to her room using the kitchen door, I used the door at the end of the courtyard which was right across from the door to her room.

"You okay?" she asked softly.

I lifted my eyes and gave her a quick nod. "Yeah, I'm good."

I saw the pity in her gaze and knew what she was likely thinking. That I was crushing on either Brody or Quinn, but that they were a couple, leaving me out in the cold. I could have told her the truth, but I didn't because I'd finally begun to realize that just like most everything else in my life, my version of the truth didn't exist.

Just cold, hard reality.

And I'd had enough of that to last a fucking lifetime.

CHAPTER 14

BRODY

Beck was a no-show for dinner. He'd made the excuse that he had a headache when I'd gone to knock on his door to check up on him, but since he'd said it through his locked door, I hadn't believed him.

Neither did Quinn.

And we both knew the cause.

We'd seen it in his gaze as he'd watched us together while we were cooking. I hadn't even given much thought to kissing Quinn…it had just felt so natural that I'd done it instinctively after he'd made a joke about me being up next on Mrs. Greene's matchmaking list. I hadn't cared that Lilah had seen the move because I knew she wouldn't have a problem with it. Quinn had told me that Roman had found her through an outreach program he was participating in with an LGBT center for kids in Missoula that helped find homeless kids jobs. So I doubted the young woman would be upset by the sight of two men kissing.

No, Beck had been my concern.

Because I'd seen almost instantly the look of pain that had flashed in his eyes before he'd dropped them to the floor. From that moment on, he'd been a mile away. Quinn and I had held dinner for a while in the hopes that he'd join us, but when he hadn't, we'd both ended up pushing our untouched plates away and packing the leftovers in the fridge for later.

It was a familiar scene as we reached Beck's door, only this time I was the one to knock.

"Beck, can you open the door please?" I asked.

We were greeted with silence. Since the kitchen had a window with a view of the barn, we'd been able to see that his car was still here so I wasn't concerned that he'd left. I'd also heard the smallest of barks coming from within the room. Since Beck and his new pet were practically tied at the hip these days, I highly doubted he'd left without her. A shimmer of worry went through me that his silence was because of a darker reason than him just being angry or upset, but I refused to dwell on it simply because I couldn't.

He wasn't the same young man he'd been in that bathroom at the club. No, he hadn't done a complete one-eighty, but I'd seen enough changes to know he was doing relatively well. Quinn and I often talked after Beck left us in bed so he could go feed the horses in the morning and we'd come to the conclusion that we needed to table the sexual activity so we could show Beck that he meant so much more to us than that. Although Quinn and I had often had some kind of physical contact those mornings, it never went beyond a few soft touches and the occasional gentle kiss. Until we were at a point where we all understood what exactly our relationship was, we'd decided to keep it platonic.

Until I'd fucked things up with an innocent kiss.

Quinn knocked on the door and then tried the knob. "Beck-" he began, but before he could say anything else, the door swung open. But we weren't greeted by an angry Beck like last time. No, before we even entered the room, Beck had retreated to the bed and sat down. The dog jumped up next to him, licked his lax hands and then lay down next to him.

I closed the door behind me and watched as Quinn settled next to Beck, the dog separating their bodies. I held off on sitting on his other side because I didn't want to crowd him.

"Beck, what is it that you think you saw earlier in the kitchen?" Quinn asked. I watched as he brushed some unruly hair behind Beck's ear. My gut tightened when Beck leaned away from his touch instead of towards it.

Damn it, how had I managed to fuck this up?

"I get it," Beck whispered. "It's okay. I understand."

"What do you understand?" I asked.

"You two...you want to be together but you didn't want to hurt my feelings-"

"God, I want to kick the ass of whoever did this to you," Quinn interjected, his voice rising in anger.

The comment surprised me as well as Beck. The young man turned to look at Quinn, his eyes wide.

"Whoever the fucker is who made you believe you weren't worth anything doesn't deserve to hold that kind of power over you, Beck. Brody and I have spent the last ten nights in this bed with you. Do you really think we only did that because we feel sorry for you? Or out of some sense of obligation? Do you think we wait until you leave the room each morning and then fuck each other's brains out?" Quinn snapped.

Beck lowered his head. A clear sign he *had* been thinking that.

"What about the rest of it, Beck?" he asked. "The way Brody massages your shoulders at night while we're watching a movie? The fact that we all crowd onto that tiny fucking couch in front of the TV despite there being plenty of other places to sit? Do you think I just go around touching any guy the way I touch you every single day?"

Beck gnawed at his upper lip, but remained silent.

"Beck," I said softly. I was glad when he looked up at me. "I kissed Quinn because it's become natural for me to do that. If you'd been in that kitchen, believe me, I would have done the same to you. Only, it wouldn't have ended there."

There was enough light in the room to see a flush of color light up Beck's pale skin. His fingers began stroking through the dog's fur.

"We never do more than kiss," he finally said. "That last time at the water...I thought..."

When his voice dropped off, Quinn said, "What did you think?"

"I thought it meant something," he admitted. My heart clenched.

"That's the problem, Beck," I whispered. "It *did* mean something. It meant whatever this thing between us is, it's too important to mess up with just sex. There needs to be more than that. Quinn and I were just trying to give you and ourselves the space and the time to figure that stuff out."

"It's not because I keep messing things up afterwards? Running away?" Beck asked.

Quinn reached out and used his hand to force Beck to look at him. I loved the contrast of his tanned skin on Beck's pale flesh. He continued to hold onto Beck's cheek, his thumb rubbing softly back and forth as he said, "You haven't messed anything up. Brody and I want you to be ready if and when we take the next step. Sex might be something that's a little harder for you to deal with, but Brody and I are struggling just as much."

"How so?" Beck asked, his eyes shifting to me, though he didn't pull free of Quinn's hold.

"I've never been in a relationship that wasn't based on a lie, Beck. I've had sex with countless men, but I don't know the first thing about what comes after."

Beck held my gaze for a moment before he looked at Quinn.

"I lost the only person I've ever loved and who loved me back," Quinn whispered. "I never expected…" His voice dropped off momentarily before he finally said, "I never expected *this*." His eyes shifted between Beck and me.

My gut clenched because I hadn't been sure about Quinn's feelings. He'd insisted early on that he wasn't interested in pursuing a relationship, but these two weeks he hadn't repeated that comment and he hadn't shied away from all the little things that made what was happening between us so much more than physical. For my own part, my emotions were so tightly wrapped up in both men, I was both freaked out and as excited as hell. It had been a long time since I'd dreamed of the perfect life with the man I was supposed to be with.

Those dreams had returned and that perfect life didn't seem so far off now.

And the fact that it was two men who now had starring roles in those dreams didn't bother me in the least.

Beck dropped his eyes again, forcing Quinn to release him. His hand stroked back and forth over the dog's tan fur as silence engulfed the room. His next words were spoken so quietly, I barely heard them.

"It was a lot of fuckers."

Pain slashed through me as I realized he was responding to Quinn's earlier comment about the fucker who'd made Beck believe he wasn't worth anything.

"Do you want to tell us about them?" Quinn asked.

Beck shook his head.

"How about dinner?" I offered.

"Don't want to eat," he answered simply.

Quinn and I exchanged a frustrated glance.

"Do you want to go to sleep?" Quinn asked.

Beck raised his eyes. "I've been asleep my whole life," he whispered.

"Then what do you want, Beck?" I asked gently.

"I want more. More of you," he said, looking at me. "More of you," he said softly when he turned his gaze on Quinn. "More of us."

Excitement flared deep in my belly as the meaning of his words sank in. But I tethered the runaway emotion and met Quinn's eyes when he shifted them in my direction. I could see the open hunger burning there, mirrors to what was in my own eyes.

I expected Quinn to ask Beck if he was sure or to suggest we wait a little longer, but he surprised me when he leaned in and kissed Beck, his mouth moving softly over our young lover's. Beck kissed him back. When they broke the kiss, Quinn whispered, "Tell us what you want."

Beck didn't answer right away. Instead, he climbed to his feet, jarring the dog who immediately trotted to a pillow that Beck had placed in the corner of the room for her as her sleeping area. Beck reached out his hand and Quinn immediately took it. My eyes locked with Beck's as he walked to me, not stopping until his body was pressed against mine. I automatically settled my hands on his hips. He tugged Quinn to him until Quinn was tucked up against his back.

"This," Beck murmured. "Whatever we do, I want it to be me between you both just like this."

And then his hand was cupping the back of my head and he was gently pulling me down to meet his waiting lips.

I groaned as his tongue swept over mine. I could feel Quinn's chest pressed against my arms which were resting on Beck's back. I moved them so I could wrap them around Quinn too. His mouth was on mine next as he leaned over Beck's shoulder to reach me. It felt so right in that moment that I felt all my emotions rise to the surface. The struggle to tamp them down was more than I could take and I had to momentarily press my face into the crook of Beck's neck. Hands were running up and down my back in a soothing gesture so I knew my men had noticed my reaction. I stood there for several long seconds and just reveled in the sensation of being surrounded…of being wanted. I was on the precipice of something great and I knew it. This would be nothing like what had happened in that bathroom at the club. Yes, the sex would be phenomenal, but it would be so much more than that. Because it wasn't my body that was most invested in this encounter.

It was most definitely my heart.

Only by the time this was over, I knew it wouldn't be mine anymore.

I felt Beck's lips skim over my neck as he continued to let me cling to him. "You okay?" he whispered.

I managed a nod, but nothing more. I pulled back so he could see my face, but I couldn't manage a smile to reassure him. But I didn't have to because as he studied me, he nodded.

Yeah, he knew.

I kissed him softly, let my eyes slide over Quinn who was watching me intently, and then sealed my lips firmly over Beck's and took control of his mouth. He moaned and pressed his fingers into my back before Quinn and I took turns kissing him. The sight of them consuming each other had my dick spiking in my pants. I turned Beck so he was facing Quinn and then I went to work lavishing attention on the rest of his body as I worked his shirt off. When Quinn turned Beck back to me, I sucked on his neck and then slid my mouth down to his chest and laved his nipples with attention. Whimpers fell from Beck's throat as he began bumping his groin against mine.

I heard the jingle of a button and then a zipper being drawn down, but wasn't sure if it was Beck's or Quinn's. I had my answer a moment later when Beck's bare dick brushed my seeking hand. I wrapped my fingers around his straining cock and squeezed and was rewarded with a harsh grunt. Beck tore his lips from mine and looked down to watch me playing with him. The sound of another zipper breached the silence and Beck suddenly moaned, "Oh God." His hands went behind him to seek out Quinn's thighs. While Quinn was still wearing his jeans, I had no doubt he'd released his dick and was currently pressing it against Beck. Based on the young man's reaction, I was guessing that thickness was being slid through the length of his crease. I kept up my stroking as I stepped even closer to Beck so I could see around him. Sure enough, Quinn's beautiful cock was tucked up between those tight globes and he was bucking his hips just enough to give Beck some stimulation.

I gave Quinn a searing kiss and stepped back to put some space between me and Beck so I could get to my own zipper. But before I could even contemplate doing just that, Beck suddenly dropped to his knees between us, forcing me to release my hold on him. His right hand immediately sought out Quinn's dick as his left hand rubbed over my groin before going to work on the button. One-handed, it took him a while to get my dick free and I used all of that time to watch Quinn's face as Beck stroked him. His eyes were closed and one hand was on Beck's shoulder while the other hand was on my waist. I was just about to lean in and steal a kiss when I was blindsided with exquisite pleasure. I hadn't expected Beck to suck me down so quickly, but that was exactly what he did, taking me expertly to the back of his throat in just a few quick swallows.

"Fuck," I snarled and since I needed an outlet for the lust that slammed into me like a Mack truck, I snagged Quinn by the back of the neck and dragged him to me for a brutal kiss. He returned it without hesitation, but didn't try to take control. As the suction on my dick increased, I was forced to release Quinn's mouth. I pressed my forehead to his and looked down and watched Beck work me over. His other hand was still on Quinn's cock and while most of his attention seemed to be centered on me, he was still giving Quinn's leaking shaft long, slow tugs. It went on like that for several long moments and I was on the verge of telling Beck he needed to stop because I was sure I was going to come when he suddenly popped off of my dick and in one swift move, swallowed Quinn's cock down. Like me, Quinn snarled in pleasure. His fingers snagged Beck by the hair as he began fucking the young man's mouth and I nearly came when Beck looked up at Quinn with his big, beautiful green eyes. The sight of his plump lips stretched wide around Quinn's flesh was something to behold and it took everything in me not to grab my dick and pump it until my cum was drenching that beautiful mouth and cock.

Beck went back and forth between us, sucking us each only long enough to keep us riding the edge. Quinn and I used the time to strip our shirts off and play with each other's chests. When we weren't watching Beck working us, we were consuming each other's mouths.

It was Quinn who finally growled and reached down to snag Beck's arm and drag him to his feet, forcing his dick to slide free of Beck's mouth. He slammed his mouth down on Beck's and ate at him ferociously, then turned him to me so I could have my turn. The taste of Quinn lingered in Beck's mouth and I eagerly drank down what I could as Quinn knelt and jerked Beck's pants and underwear off. As soon as he was naked, Beck turned back into me and I grabbed his ass so I could grind our dicks together. Within seconds, Quinn's pants were completely gone and he bit out, "Bed, now!"

He didn't give Beck time to actually follow through on the order. Instead, he whirled Beck around and lifted him by the backs of his thighs even as their mouths met. The sight of Beck's pale, lithe body wrapped around Quinn's was driving me to distraction as I tried to get my pants past my ankles. Quinn carried Beck to the bed and followed him down, his bare ass grinding as he humped against Beck. Grunts and groans fell from both men's mouths. I managed to get the rest of my clothes off and had enough sense to snag a condom from my wallet along with a packet of lube. I took a flyer and checked Quinn's wallet and found he was similarly prepared. With both condoms in hand and two packets of lube, I hurried to the bed. But the sight of Quinn's ass was too beautiful to resist and I quickly dropped to my knees behind him. The height of the bed gave me the perfect angle and I gave Quinn no warning whatsoever as I split him open with my hands and then dove in with my mouth.

CHAPTER 15

BECK

When Quinn suddenly stiffened in my arms and shouted, "Fuck, yes!" in my ear, I thought maybe he'd come, but there was no accompanying warmth of his release against my body where his dick was grinding against mine. His thrusting slowed, but he remained tight in my arms and his dick was still rock hard. It took me several long seconds to realize what Brody was doing behind Quinn and though I couldn't get a good view, watching Quinn's reactions was almost better. The abandon on his face and the way the muscles in his neck were flexing as Brody ate at his hole was a bombardment on my own senses. My body was wracked with the need to find my release, but my mind didn't want any of this to ever end. Not only because I feared what would happen when it did, but because I'd never felt more safe and wanted...and *free* than I ever had in that moment.

Nothing in the world existed but my men.

Nothing...not my past, not my future.

Nothing.

Quinn's mouth sought mine out again as his arms wrapped around me, drawing me up so I was pressed against him from head to toe. I'd wrapped my legs around his lower back when he'd put me on the bed, but now I crossed my ankles to lock them. I didn't want him to put any more space between us than was necessary, not even for a second. Whimpers of pleasure spilled into my mouth as Quinn tried to keep up the passionate kisses, but he finally gave up as whatever Brody was doing to him took over. He buried his face in my neck and just clung to me as moan after moan left his body. I felt so fucking hot that I was sure I'd burst into flames any moment, but it wasn't enough. His sweat-slickened body against mine wasn't enough. I needed to be filled.

By him.

By Brody.

Hell, if I had my way, it would be both of them at the same time.

The thought of both of them filling me up, surrounding me in heat, had me grabbing Quinn's ass so I could force him to start grinding on me again. I needed to get off and I needed it now. Fingers closed over mine where I was holding onto Quinn and I cursed the fact that I couldn't see what Brody was doing.

Next time I would make sure I had a front row seat to that particular show.

"Quinn," I whispered as the need began to grow until it was crashing over me in uncomfortable waves that kept building and building.

I wasn't sure if he'd heard me or Brody had or both, but suddenly things shifted and I was exactly where I was supposed to be, pressed between Brody and Quinn's bodies. Brody was beneath me, our chests touching and Quinn was at my back, his dick once again pressed against my hole.

"Brody," I murmured in happiness as I covered his mouth with mine. The musky flavor on his tongue just drove me higher. I'd never rimmed a guy, but it was definitely moving to the top of my to-do list with my men.

And they were mine.

In that moment.

Forever.

Even after I left, they would still be mine.

I didn't realize I'd even whispered the word "mine" until Brody stilled and his hands came up to clasp my face. "Yes," he murmured. He kissed me softly and then whispered, "Make love to me, Beck."

Quinn had stilled at my back, but his hands were soothing circles into the skin just above my ass.

Had I heard Brody right? Did he really want me to...?

"I...I've never been with a guy like that," I whispered. "I don't know what to do."

Brody smiled and kissed me again. "I could come from just your voice alone, Beck. So I can guarantee I'll love anything you do to me."

His words warmed me and I kissed him, letting my tongue play with his.

"Quinn," I called softly when I forced myself to release Brody's mouth.

"Yeah, baby?" Quinn whispered as he leaned over my back, pushing me down even farther onto Brody's hard body.

"I need you too," I said. I had no idea how the mechanics of it all would work, but I knew that even as much as I wanted to feel Brody's body clenched around me, I needed Quinn to be there too.

It had to be all three of us.

"I'll take care of you, Beck," Quinn said softly. His lips skimmed my shoulder. "I'll take care of both of you."

Relief coursed through me and I turned my head enough so he could kiss me. Then I plastered myself to Brody and let my instincts take over. Brody's powerful hands skimmed so gently over my back as he held me that I wanted to cry. I'd seen his strength firsthand as he'd been working, so I knew very well what those hands were capable of.

But with me, they would only deliver pleasure.

There wasn't a doubt in my mind.

I felt Quinn shift behind me, but before I could protest, I felt his hand sneak between mine and Brody's bodies. "Lift up a little," he said gently. I forced myself to separate long enough from Brody to do as Quinn asked and was rewarded with a condom being rolled down my length. I was close to blowing as Quinn's big hand coated my cock with lube. Once his hand was gone, I felt bereft and didn't give much thought to the lube as I dropped my hips again and began rubbing my dick against Brody's. Brody moaned and kissed me hard. But a moment later, he hissed beneath me. I thought maybe I'd hurt him, but I realized it was Quinn he was reacting to.

I glanced over my shoulder to see Quinn behind me once again. His lust-filled eyes were on Brody and Brody's were on his. I stilled my own body as it finally occurred to me that Quinn was preparing Brody's body for me. I was tempted to shift off of Brody so I could watch, but the idea of leaving the warmth of his skin even just for a few moments left me cold and I stayed where I was and, like with Quinn, I just watched Brody's reactions. I remembered the feel of Quinn's calloused fingers working me open back in that bathroom and my dick jumped in anticipation.

I dropped my lips to Brody's and murmured, "He feels so good, doesn't he?"

Brody sucked in a breath and I felt some of the tension drain out of him as his eyes shifted to me. He managed a nod, but nothing else. I kissed him softly over and over again as Quinn worked. When Quinn once again leaned over my back, his hot, damp skin making me feel like I was inside a furnace, he whispered in my ear, "Make him yours, Beck."

"Ours," I automatically responded. I reached between our bodies to grab my dick. Quinn levered off of me so I could lift my hips and maneuver myself into place. I moaned when his thick fingers wrapped around me and helped guide me to Brody's slick opening. I pressed forward, but when nothing happened, my nerves kicked up.

What if I fucked this up?

What if I hurt Brody?

My eyes fell to Brody's and he immediately reached his hand up to cradle my cheek. "It's okay, keep going," he whispered.

I nodded and tried again, but the panic started to build. Quinn's body once again pressed down on mine, his weight automatically forcing me forward. The pressure had my crown finally piercing Brody's body. Brody's eyes slid shut as his face contorted.

"Quinn," I whispered, terrified I was hurting my lover.

"It's okay, just give him a minute," Quinn said in my ear. I could feel his dick pressed against my ass and I tried to remind myself what it had felt like when he'd entered me in that bathroom. Pain at first, then burning, then…

Even the reminder of how good it had felt when his shaft had filled me had me turning my head to kiss him. He kept the kiss brief and when we both returned our gazes to Brody, Quinn used his body to drive mine deeper into Brody's. Another hiss escaped Brody's mouth, but before I could even consider stopping, Quinn kept up the forward movement. He didn't stop until Brody's body finally gave in and his outer muscles relaxed. At that point, the heat and pressure surrounding my dick took over and I fought the urge for more. I managed to quell my instincts to slam into him.

"That's it, baby," Quinn murmured in my ear. Quinn pushed me forward a little more so nearly half my dick was buried in Brody's tight body. Brody's eyes were back on me and I was relieved to see that the worst of the pain seemed to have passed for him. I felt Quinn lift off me a little and then his hand was at my hip, guiding me backwards just a little before pushing me forward. Another inch disappeared and Brody sighed.

"So good," he said on a groan.

I pulled back and then gently thrust into him, making sure not to go too fast or too hard. I was rewarded with another grunt. I could still feel Quinn at my back, but he wasn't controlling my moves any more.

I kept up the gentle strokes until my balls finally pressed up against Brody's ass. I moaned at how good it felt and then leaned down to kiss him and then closed my hands over his where they were lying on the bed. His legs wrapped around my body as he returned the deep kiss. I would have been happy to just lie there like that and explore his mouth, but my body had other ideas and my hips began moving. I kept the pace slow as I worked myself in and out of him, using the sounds he made and the way he kissed me to gauge his reactions.

"More," Brody whispered against my lips and I increased my pace.

"You feel so good," I said and then immediately felt foolish for the simplistic statement. He felt so much better than good.

"It's so perfect, Beck," he murmured. "Knew it would be," he said softly and then he was kissing me again.

I began driving into him harder as our hips slapped together. But I stilled when I felt Quinn's fingers dip between the globes of my ass and brush over my hole. The cool lube felt good against my hot skin and the reminder of what was still to come had me sucking in deep mouthfuls of air in the hopes of staving off my orgasm. Quinn leaned over me as he began pushing his finger inside of me. When he glanced over that spot inside me that had nearly driven me insane with pleasure that night in the bathroom I said, "Don't prep me too much – I'm not going to last."

Quinn nuzzled my neck. "Just a little more," he murmured. "You two are so fucking beautiful together," he added and then his lips sealed over mine. I groaned as his finger slid all the way in. He leaned past me to kiss Brody. His finger fucked into me over and over even as his tongue drove into Brody's mouth. I couldn't help but think it was like he was fucking us both at the same time.

"Quinn, please," I managed to get out. Between the erotic sight of the two men going at each other, Quinn's thick finger thrusting in and out of me and the way Brody's inner muscles were clenched around my cock, I was so close to the edge that I couldn't even be sure I'd last once Quinn got inside of me.

Quinn took pity on me and reared back long enough to replace his finger with his cock. He held my hips as he began to push into me, preventing me from trying to thrust even deeper into Brody's pliant body. It wasn't until I felt his heavy balls brush against my ass that I felt like I could breathe.

Tears threatened to fall as I realized they'd both given me exactly what I'd asked for. Me between them, surrounded. It wasn't until Brody released one of his hands from mine to brush over my cheek that I realized I hadn't managed to stem the tears after all. But he didn't call me on it. Instead, he pulled me down for the gentlest of kisses and then pressed my head against his chest. "We've got you, Beck."

I nodded, but that was all I could do as Quinn began to fuck into me with even, smooth glides. There was no pain, no burn. Just a feeling of rightness. Within moments, Quinn was releasing his death grip on my hips and then he was shoving me flat against Brody as his entire weight came down on my back. His hands closed over my shoulders and his mouth pressed against the back of my neck as he increased the pace. Since he wasn't holding my hips anymore, every time he drove forward, he sent me deeper into Brody's body. I began matching his moves as he pulled back, but I allowed him to control how quick and how hard I fucked Brody. I clung to Brody with every powerful surge of our bodies coming together and I reveled in the sensation of Quinn's strong fingers digging into my skin, his hot breath near my ear. I couldn't see his face, but I could hear the grunts falling from his lips as his passion grew. My own orgasm was so very close, but I fought it. Not because I was afraid of it. But because I never wanted this moment to end.

I never wanted another moment where they weren't a part of it.

We became a mass of limbs, wet, hot skin sliding over skin, moans, whispers and unspoken promises as we moved in perfect unison.

As one.

I felt Brody's inner muscles begin to ripple around my cock and I knew that would send me over, so I slipped my hand between our bodies and closed it around his shaft. I'd ended up smearing enough lube on him earlier when I'd pressed my wet cock against his before entering him, so my strokes were smooth. I matched my rhythm to Quinn's brutal thrusts and within seconds, Brody's eyes closed and his mouth opened on an agonized cry. A strangled moan tore free of my own throat when he yelled mine and Quinn's names and then everything went dark as nerve-shattering pleasure ripped through my entire body at once. I spilled into the condom over and over as Quinn fucked into me with jerky strokes. He shouted in my ear as his release hit him and despite that latex barrier separating us, I felt his heat scorch my insides.

I had no idea how much time passed as we lay there together like that. Quinn was heavy on my back, but I loved it. And I loved the feeling of Brody's semen stuck between us. I felt lips ghosting over my temple – Quinn's lips. Fingers were playing with my hair – Brody's fingers.

The sex was over, but they were still with me.

Even as it confused me, it thrilled me. In my heart, I'd known it wouldn't be over once they'd gotten off, but my mind was slow to catch up. So there was no surprise when we were finally forced to move that one of them stayed in bed with me and peppered me with soft kisses and touches as the other went to get a washcloth to clean us up. And as my tired eyes gave up the fight and drifted closed, I had no doubt that both men would be at my side in the morning when I woke up.

And that they'd also be there when the nightmares inevitably returned.

CHAPTER 16

QUINN

I kept one eye on Beck as the guests for our dress rehearsal trail ride started arriving and that was only because, despite the fact that he hadn't panicked after our sexual encounter a few nights earlier or any of the others that had followed, I knew in my heart Brody and I hadn't "fixed" whatever was broken inside of him. I couldn't put my finger on how I knew that, I just did. Maybe it was how quiet he got after we had sex. If he didn't fall asleep right away, then he'd lay between me and Brody and literally cling to us, but he wouldn't say anything. And no amount of kissing, touching or reassurances that we weren't going anywhere relaxed him. It wasn't until he fell asleep that he ever finally looked at peace.

But the biggest clue was the continuing nightmares. They'd become more frequent and more violent. Not towards me and Brody, but towards himself. He'd thrash and cry out the same damn two words over and over and we'd stopped him more than once as his fisted hands had begun striking his own body.

I'm sorry.

Those were the words Beck would repeat on a loop until we woke him up and I'd come to dread hearing them fall from his lips. Because I knew in my heart that he had nothing to be sorry about. Whatever had happened to him, had been done to him. But those words proved his mind didn't see it that way.

Worrying about Beck left me little time to dwell on my own feelings, which was a good thing, because I was more confused than I'd ever been in my entire life. After losing Griff, I'd promised myself I'd never let myself become so attached to another person that my life didn't exist separate from theirs. But deep down I knew that was what was happening. My every waking moment was caught up in Brody and Beck and I'd gotten to the point that I couldn't go more than a few minutes without wondering what they were up to and looking forward to the moment I'd see them again. Even when we were doing something as benign as cooking dinner or watching TV, I found myself needing their touches or their laughs or their smiles. Those things became fuel for me. They were as necessary as breathing.

I hadn't even had that level of need with Griff.

And that was exactly what I was struggling with the most.

Losing Griff had nearly destroyed me. What would losing Beck and Brody do to me?

And I would lose them. It was inevitable. We had less than a week left at the resort and then we'd go our separate ways. Yes, I'd still see Beck at the ranch, but it wouldn't be the same.

I wouldn't be the same.

How would I ever go back to sleeping in my big bed by myself? Cooking for one person? Not sharing a shower or being woken up with a soft kiss and whispered words?

Once we got back to the ranch, Beck would be here for only six more weeks and then he'd be returning home and to whatever the future held for him. There was a possibility of continuing to see Brody, but without Beck, it wouldn't be the same. In my heart, I knew I would take what I could get even if that meant one third of us was missing, but I wasn't sure Brody would feel the same way.

The sound of a diesel engine and creaking metal distracted me from watching as Beck interacted with Luke, Gray and their young son, Oliver. The couple had arrived a few minutes earlier and Luke had introduced Gray and their little boy to Beck. I'd seen Beck's reaction even though he'd tried to hide it. He'd been nervous around both men, though he'd managed to school his reaction in front of them by keeping busy with the horse he'd been tacking up as well as using Lilah as a shield by making the introductions between her and the two men.

I glanced at the driveway and recognized the CB Bar ranch truck heading towards the barn. All three men, Callan, Rhys and Finn, were joining us along with their two sons and Callan's aunt. The boys were too small to go riding, but Callan's aunt had agreed to babysit the toddlers while their fathers joined us and Gabriella had suggested the kids make use of the swimming pool that had a special play area for small children. Jax and Dane's son would be joining them along with Mrs. Greene.

I walked towards the truck, surprised to see the horse trailer attached to it since we had enough horses for the ride.

"Hey," I said to Callan as he got out of the truck. The big man smiled and shook my hand. I watched as his husbands got out and pulled their children from their car seats. Callan went to the back seat to help his aunt climb out of the tall truck.

"Hi honey, how are you?" Dolly asked as she gave me a hug. I wasn't surprised when she handed me a big plastic container.

"Chocolate oatmeal chip," she said with a wink and I smiled. One of the first questions the woman had asked me when she'd been introduced to me was what my favorite kind of cookie was and ever since then, I'd been getting a batch delivered to my little house every week.

"Thank you," I said and gave her a kiss on the cheek. I had to lean over quite a bit because the woman was so damn short. She gave me a pat on the cheek and then went around the truck to gather up the kids.

"What's this?" I asked Callan as I pointed at the horse trailer, but I had my answer when a familiar whinny sounded from inside it. A smile split my lips as I handed Callan the container and hurried to the trailer and opened the side door. Koda's face immediately thrust through the opening and pressed into my hands.

"He was missing you," Callan said with a smile. He patted me on the back and then went to the back of the trailer to open it up so I could unload my horse. The familiar comfort of being around the animal eased some of the tension that had been inside of me and I took just a moment to soak up the calmness he never failed to bring me.

I'd seen the horse for sale at one of the final rodeos Griff and I had attended before leaving the circuit to start our new life at the ranch in Wyoming. With his prized bloodlines and perfect conformation, he'd come with a high price tag that I hadn't been able to justify. Griff and I had saved up a little bit of money that we'd planned to add to over the years so we could someday start our own ranch. It had been enough to cover the cost of the three-year-old stallion, but I'd gone with logic instead of emotion. So I couldn't have been more surprised when I'd come home from work just two days after moving into our new place to find the beautiful horse in one of the stalls in the dilapidated barn that had come with the property. Griff had been grinning from ear to ear as he'd walked me to the barn telling me he needed to show me something. I'd argued with him that it was an expense that we couldn't afford, but he'd simply told me that our dream to run our own ranch could wait just a little bit longer.

I hurried into the trailer and unhooked Koda's halter from the tether and then led him out of the trailer. I followed Callan into the barn and put Koda into cross ties. My eyes connected with Beck who was tacking up another horse and I saw him smile as his eyes fell on my horse. I felt that smile everywhere.

It was chaotic as more and more people began to arrive and while I couldn't keep my eyes on Beck the whole time, I did notice that Brody stayed nearby as he helped get horses ready. The large number of people made it easier for Beck to stay busy and not linger with any one or two people and I think that helped settle him. When Dane and Jax arrived, their daughter immediately sought out Beck and I enjoyed the sight of him interacting with her as he showed her how to brush the horse he was getting ready. He seemed a little tense around Dane and more so Jax, but when they each gave him a brief hug, he held his own.

The last to arrive were Roman, Hunter and their daughter. I'd talked with Roman on the phone a few times in the past few weeks and while he'd taken the time off to be with his husband as they welcomed their daughter into their lives, he'd been working from home as much as he could.

"Quinn," Roman nodded as he entered the barn carrying his daughter with one arm and holding his husband's hand with the other. Allie was an adorable little girl with black hair and a darker skin tone, hinting at a mixed heritage. She was quiet in Roman's arms, but she didn't seem distressed. Her arms were around his neck and her face was resting against him as she took everything in.

"Hey, glad you could make it," I said. "Hey, Hunter."

Hunter nodded at me and then turned to look at Roman. "I'm going to go say hi to people."

Roman nodded and I wasn't surprised when they kissed softly. To Allie, Hunter said, "I'm going to go say hi to some friends. Do you want to come with me or stay with Papa?"

Allie was quiet for a moment before she said, "Papa."

Hunter smiled and then caressed her cheek with his finger. It was clear both men were completely in love with their new daughter.

Hunter wandered off to greet people as I continued to get Koda ready.

"How are things going?" Roman asked as he moved around to Koda's front so Allie could see the horse's face. Pride went through me as my horse gently nuzzled at her hand when she put it out towards him.

"Really good," I said. "Lilah started a few days ago." I motioned behind Roman to where Lilah was getting a horse saddled under Beck's watchful eye. Like Beck, the girl was a quick study and she got along well with the horses. Even better, she and Beck had struck up a friendship that I suspected was equally good for the both of them.

"And Dale is starting next week."

Dale was the new barn manager who would essentially take on the role I'd been playing the past few weeks, along with the business side of things like managing the staff and dealing with the vendors for all the things needed to care for the horses. Besides Dale and Lilah, there'd be another four stable hands to help with trail rides and such, but they weren't scheduled to start until a couple days before the resort actually opened.

"Great. Gabriella said he's got great experience."

I nodded. That was true enough. Dale came with an excellent résumé and references, but there was something about the guy that just rubbed me the wrong way. He was a cocky bastard, but lacking in charm so he just came off as an arrogant know-it-all. But I kept that piece of information to myself because he had a proven track record of working at dude ranches, which meant he knew how to handle the tricky combination of horses and guests of all different riding abilities.

Roman and I chatted a bit more about business before he wandered off to show his daughter the other horses and to catch up to Hunter. I felt my heart hurt a little bit at the sight of the big, happy, extended family. It wasn't something I'd ever had, so I'd never really missed it growing up. But after moving to Dare two years ago, I'd been around these folks enough to know that even though most of them weren't related by blood, they were as strong as any family could be.

It took another twenty minutes to get the riders and their mounts organized. Gabriella joined us just long enough to escort Mrs. Greene, Dolly and the younger children to the lodge. Since we had an extra horse now that I could ride Koda, we managed to convince Lilah to join us, though she'd never ridden before. Since I was leading the group, I couldn't spend as much time focusing on Beck and Brody as I would have liked, but it never failed that I could feel their eyes on me. I never ignored that shiver creeping up my spine and as soon as I felt it, I searched them both out. We hadn't talked about whether we wanted people to know what was happening between us, so I was always careful not to let my heated looks linger.

The trail ride went off without a hitch. The horses behaved perfectly and every single person was smiling by the time we returned. While the actual lodge guests wouldn't be required to help untack their horses if they didn't want to, most everyone stayed behind to get the horses settled. It had been Gabriella's idea to offer to let people swim in the resort's main pool after the trail ride so people began driving over to the lodge in small groups. When it was just me, Beck and Brody, I was the one who suggested we join everyone else. We stopped at the residence just long enough to grab some shorts and convince Lilah to come with us and then we were headed towards the lodge in my truck.

It turned out my men were fish because long after I'd gotten out of the pool, they were still at it. Dane and Jax's oldest child was playing with them, as was 7-year-old Oliver Hawthorne. We were sitting around the outside pool which happened to also extend inside through a glass wall that could apparently be opened and closed depending on the weather. Gabriella had surprised the group by having some food brought in for an early dinner so we'd ended up making a party of it. My own belly was pleasantly full and the ice-cold beer I was working on was refreshing in the early evening heat. But most of my attention was on Beck and Brody as they interacted with the kids. Beck was definitely more comfortable around them, but Brody was figuring it out pretty quickly and they'd gotten to the point where they were each throwing the kids in the air so that they'd land several feet away in the water with a huge splash. A sliver of pain went through me as I remembered how badly Griff and I had wanted exact moments like these, but it didn't ruin the moment for me.

I'd been so caught up in watching my guys that I didn't notice Callan had sat down on the lounger next to me until he clinked his cup of beer against mine.

"Nice job today, Quinn," he said as he sat back. "And not just today," he added.

"Thanks," I said. "The horses make my job pretty easy," I murmured. "You picked some damn good ones."

"We," was all Callan said. After a moment he said, "I'm sure you're looking forward to getting back to the ranch and your house."

"Yeah," I murmured noncommittally since it was a lie. I wasn't looking forward to it all. I was one of the lucky ones who worked for the CB Bar because I had a place all to myself. The other guys who worked cattle had to share the remaining two cottages on the property and the rest lived off-site.

"It's not as hard as you thought, is it?" Callan asked. The question confused me so I tore my eyes from Beck and Brody to look at him.

"What is?"

"Loving two men at the same time."

Fear skittered through me as my eyes darted to my men and then the rest of the other people around the pool.

"I'm not..." I began, but then I let my voice drop off because I knew the next words out of my mouth would be a lie and I just wasn't going to go there – not when Beck and Brody were involved, even indirectly.

Was that what I was? In love? I wasn't a stranger to love because I'd been there before. But I hadn't thought it possible. Griff had been my soulmate and you only got one soulmate.

Right?

So what? Did I just *like* Beck and Brody? I shook my head, not realizing how odd it would look. No, like wasn't enough. Not even close.

It was more than that...so much more. Even love didn't seem like enough sometimes to describe how being around them made me feel. Making love wasn't the right words to describe what it was like when our bodies were joined.

Guilt went through me as I realized some of the things I was describing to myself were things I hadn't even considered when I'd been with Griff. He'd made me happier than I'd ever been in my life, but now, in this moment, I couldn't find a memory with Griff that could quite match it. It wasn't that being with Beck and Brody was better, it was just...different.

"No, it's not," I finally admitted. I should have been more afraid of what I was admitting to, but if anything, it just brought me down.

Because while Beck and Brody were mine, there was a very fast time clock counting down the time we had left together. And even if by some miracle Brody wanted to try to build something with me, it would never be quite as perfect as when it was the three of us.

"How did you know?" I asked.

"You can't take your eyes off of them, for starters," Callan said. "And when you do, you don't relax again until they're back in your sights."

"I'm sorry," I said. "I know I shouldn't have started something up with them...Beck especially, since we work together."

Callan snorted and then shot me a glance. "The only reason I have the best fucking life imaginable was because both my men worked for me. We don't get to pick and choose the people our futures are with or the circumstances under which we meet them."

That was most certainly true.

"Beck's leaving in six weeks. Brody has a whole other life. This," – I motioned to the pool – "only happened because we were forced into such close proximity to one another. That shit doesn't happen in the real world."

"Yeah," Callan agreed. "The real world isn't going to make it easy for you. If it did, you'd still be in Wyoming with your husband and a passel of kids, right?"

I nodded. It was a bittersweet thought because I would have loved that life, but this moment...I couldn't deny this perfect moment either.

"I almost missed out on them," – Callan looked at where his husbands were drying off their little boys with huge bath towels – "because I was too afraid of what the real world would think about me...us. Or that things would be too hard." He looked at me and said, "Ask me now if I care that the real world tried to keep us apart."

I shook my head. "Don't need to."

I looked around at the other couples. I'd only heard snippets of their pasts, but I knew every single one of them had had to fight to be together.

So why was I so afraid to do the same?

I didn't have an answer for that and luckily, Callan didn't press me. I barely noticed when he got up to help his husbands start getting their kids packed up to go home. We'd agreed that Koda would stay at the resort for the last week and I'd bring him home with me when I left. Callan had already unhitched the trailer and left it by the barn so it would be easy to hook it up to my truck when it was time for me to go.

As the party wound down, Beck and Brody helped the kids out of the pool and then they were joining me. I hated that we didn't have the freedom to touch like all the other couples, but within the hour when everyone was on their way home, it would be just me and my men again and I'd make up for the time we'd been apart, even if we hadn't actually been.

At some point we'd need to talk about the future, because we had just days left in our little bubble, but I had some stuff I needed to work out in my head first. Despite what Callan had said, the real world sometimes was just too powerful and I knew that better than most.

After all, it had cost me the first love of my life.

Now it would likely cost me the other two.

CHAPTER 17

BRODY

"Fuck," I whispered when Quinn slid into me.

"Don't come," Quinn reminded me as he nipped at my lips. "Or you'll miss out," he added and I followed his gaze to where Beck was sitting in a side chair, one hand jammed down his pants, the other rubbing across his naked chest.

It wasn't my first time with Quinn's huge dick shoved up my ass, but it was the first time Beck hadn't joined us.

At his request.

He'd whispered his request to watch us together as soon as we'd entered his room, which I'd long ago started to think of as our room since Quinn and I continued to spend every waking moment there instead of back in our private rooms. We'd even started leaving some of our things in our new shared room. The fact that we were playing house wasn't lost on any of us, but we hadn't talked about what it actually meant.

We also hadn't stopped fucking since that night Beck had taken me and Quinn had taken him at the same time. That night had to have been one of the most intense moments of my entire life, and not just sexually speaking. I'd had plenty of great sex in the past, but it had never reached deep down inside of me like that encounter had.

Even the night in the bathroom at the club couldn't rival what we had now.

I wasn't sure anything could rival what we had.

Somehow, we'd just seemed to seamlessly fall into being one unit. We'd become so in tune with each other that it didn't take more than a look or a comment to know when one of us might be in more need than the other. The night of the trail ride, Quinn had been particularly quiet and while we hadn't forced him to tell us what was going on with him, we'd picked up on some of it during our lovemaking session. He'd been desperate to be with us both so he'd ended up fucking us each back and forth until he'd made us both come before finding his own release. Afterwards, he'd wrapped himself around us in such a way that he was holding on to us equally tight. And he hadn't let up even long enough for us to clean up properly and Beck and I hadn't pressed the issue. Quinn had been acting normally again the next morning, but I'd seen and felt enough to suspect what the issue was.

We were running out of time.

Quickly.

I had just three more days before I needed to return to my regular shifts at the firehouse. I'd actually finished the construction work I'd been charged with two days earlier, but I'd drawn it out by making little improvements here and there, which I had no plans to charge Roman for. I'd done it only so it wouldn't look odd that I was still at the resort, despite being finished with my work.

Beck and Quinn would be leaving the resort a couple days after me and while there was nothing saying we couldn't still keep seeing each other, it wouldn't be as easy with normal work schedules and distance keeping us apart for longer periods of time. And of course, there was the elephant in the room…

Beck.

He'd be back in Seattle in a little over a month.

While I'd managed to hide my distress over that fact, I wasn't sure how Beck was dealing with it because as each day passed, he seemed to work harder and harder to keep his emotions from showing. There wasn't anything specifically I could point to, it was more of a feeling I got. Like the night Beck had seen me kissing Quinn in the kitchen, he was terrible at hiding his emotions from us. But in recent days, he'd become quieter in a way.

I wanted to believe he was just as upset as me, and apparently Quinn, that our days together were numbered, but I couldn't be sure. Maybe he was just protecting himself by retreating now or maybe whatever feelings he might have had when we'd started this thing weren't as prevalent now.

"Tell him that," I moaned as Quinn's cock slid over my prostate.

"What?" Quinn asked.

"That he can't come yet."

Quinn glanced at Beck before looking back at me. "I think he's too far gone already." I shifted my eyes to Beck and saw that his skin was flushed and slickened with sweat and he was frantically stroking himself.

"Just imagine how much fun we'll have getting him ready for you," Quinn said loudly enough for Beck to hear as he began thrusting into me more steadily. I slid my hands down to his ass and held on to his hot flesh as he greedily fucked into me.

"I want to watch you eat his ass," I said.

Quinn grinned because he knew exactly what I was doing.

A whimper from the other side of the room proved it was working. I groaned as Quinn's tongue slid up the column of my neck.

"Imagine how pretty he'll look between us," Quinn said softly. "You behind him, buried to the hilt. Me in front, also buried."

Beck led out a loud moan and we both shifted our gazes to him. "Would you like that, baby?" I asked. "Me fucking that sweet ass and Quinn fucking your pretty little mouth?"

Beck vigorously nodded as his free hand slipped into his pants, presumably to grab his balls in the hopes of staving off his orgasm.

I was about to say something else, but suddenly Quinn was pulling free of me and changing our positions. He put me on my hands and knees so that I was facing Beck. I let out a guttural cry when Quinn slammed into me hard from behind. The new position let me see every emotion on Beck's face as he watched us. His eyes were wide and needy as his gaze flitted from Quinn to me and back.

I struggled to control my orgasm, but it took everything I had and luckily Quinn didn't torture me. But the man's dirty talk, meant for Beck, was nearly as effective in driving me over the edge as his hard cock burning up my insides.

"Lower your pants, baby," Quinn ordered, his voice husky as he continued to pound me hard, his motions nearly pushing me off the bed. Only his hands locked around my shoulders and my hands and knees digging into the mattress kept me from tumbling over with each brutal thrust.

Beck let out a little cry and quickly climbed to his feet. He ripped his pants and underwear off, but instead of sitting back down, he moved to the bed, his eyes wild and frantic.

He was definitely close.

"You want to fuck his mouth, baby?" Quinn asked. "Show me how you want me to fuck your mouth."

I opened eagerly as Beck reached me and shoved his dick into me. I struggled to stifle my gag reflex as he pushed down my throat. It was testament to how close he was. That and the fact that he grabbed my hair in both his hands and began fucking my mouth with hard snaps of his hips.

"Yeah, just like that," Quinn said as he increased his pace. I felt his hard palm crack against my ass before he fisted my globes between his fingers. Tears stung my eyes as Beck fucked my mouth, but the intense need to focus on not gagging helped stave off my own release. I could taste the sweetness of Beck's pre-cum as it leaked over my tongue and down my throat.

"I'm gonna come," Beck shouted. When he tried to pull out of my mouth, I used one hand to snag his ass and force him back down my throat. I hummed for good measure which caused him to curse and then he was shooting down my throat. The force of it caused me to gag and sputter and I instinctively pulled back. Beck's cum filled my mouth and then began to dribble down my chin as he filled me up. Quinn's cry from behind me and his brutal hold on my hips as he slammed into me signaled the end for him as well and I clamped my inner muscles down on him to add to his pleasure.

"Fuck!" he snarled and then he collapsed on my back and humped into me. Beck actually wrapped an arm around me to support me as Quinn continued to ruthlessly shove into me and I heard the slurp of their kiss as their mouths met over my shoulder. It wasn't until Quinn's movement slowed that Beck's mouth crashed down onto mine. He took control of my mouth as Quinn's aftershocks started to cause my own orgasm to build again and then Beck's tongue was sliding over my chin, collecting the cum that stuck to my skin. I turned my head just in time to see my men kissing again.

I hung there between them, both sated and not.

Because I needed to come like nobody's business. But I also didn't want to move because the moment was absolutely perfect.

My need ended up winning out and as soon as Quinn pulled free of me, I snagged Beck by the back of the neck and pulled him to me for a kiss. I tumbled him onto the bed beneath me and began exploring his body, leaving my mark all over him. Within moments, Quinn was joining me, helping me to get Beck worked up again. Our moves were frantic as we clung to one another, kissing and touching any part of each other we could. When Quinn swallowed Beck's dick, I pushed Beck's legs up, exposing his hole. He let out a strangled gasp as I licked over his fluttering opening and Quinn was actually forced to pin him to the bed with his arm to keep Beck from thrashing wildly as I sank my tongue into his body. Only when he was begging us to fuck him did we flip him over and pull him upright until he was on all fours. Quinn was gentle as he slid his hardening cock all over Beck's glistening lips before ordering Beck to suck him down. I used the time to prepare my own cock which was almost painful to touch and then I was shoving a well-lubed finger into Beck's ass. He moaned around Quinn's cock which caused Quinn to shut his eyes in ecstasy. By the time I slid into Beck, I was shaking badly. I should have given him more time to adjust, but I was too far gone. Luckily, Beck began pressing back to meet my thrusts so I knew I hadn't caused him too much discomfort.

I slid my hand up to hold onto Beck's shoulder as I slid in and out of him, desperately trying to keep the pace slow, but failing miserably. My consolation was that Quinn was fucking Beck's mouth hard and fast.

"Is this what you wanted, baby?" Quinn asked harshly.

Beck managed a nod, no easy feat considering how hard he had to work to get all of Quinn's thick length inside of him.

"To be loved this well by both your men?"

A gasp escaped Beck's lip as he nodded again.

Quinn suddenly pulled out and grabbed Beck by the chin, forcing him upright. The angle changed how I was fucking him and Beck shouted in surprise as I hit his prostate. Quinn forced Beck backwards so he was pressed against my chest and I immediately wrapped my arms around Beck to support him. Quinn and Beck kissed as Quinn fisted both their cocks and began jerking them off at the same time.

Moans unlike anything I'd ever heard fell from Beck's mouth despite Quinn's deep kiss and then Beck was shoving back onto my cock. I could feel his inner muscles pulsing in anticipation and I knew he'd go over in just a few thrusts. I managed to kiss Quinn when he leaned over Beck's shoulder to claim my mouth, but I reared back when I felt Quinn's finger from his free hand skim over my dick. I looked down to see him push his finger into Beck's hole just as I surged into him. The sensation of his calloused finger pressed against my sensitive flesh was only slightly diminished by the condom. But for Beck, it sent him to a whole other level. He became a wild man as he clung to Quinn and desperately fucked my dick and Quinn's finger. Quinn's finger followed my motions and when I shifted the angle just a little, he was right there. The move had me striking Beck's prostate with every pass and by the fourth glide over the bundle of nerves, Beck was screaming in relief. His ass closed around my dick like a vise, setting off my own orgasm and I leaned heavily against his back as I drove into him over and over. Quinn supported his weight because Beck had gone boneless as the orgasm continued to rock through him.

I couldn't stop from continuing to thrust into what had to be

Beck's pained ass by that point, but since he was still trying to press down on me, I knew he wasn't even cognizant of anything but pleasure. Quinn's loud groan shattered the air around us as he came and I managed to look over Beck's shoulder to see their cum mixing together over their dicks and Quinn's hand. The sight had an aftershock rolling through me and then we were falling onto the bed in a tangle of limbs. I somehow managed to stay inside of Beck as we went down and as soon as we were pressed up against each other, I felt Quinn's finger pull free of Beck's body and then his whole hand was grabbing my ass, holding me inside of Beck.

I knew we had to move, that I had to pull out and remove the condom, but I needed more time. More time inside of Beck's snug heat, more time with Quinn's big arm wrapped around me and holding me close.

But time was the one thing I didn't have enough of anymore.

None of us did.

~

"Spit it out," Quinn murmured as he handed me the bowl of vegetables he'd been chopping. I'd already gotten the meat on the skewers for the shish kabobs we were preparing to grill tonight for dinner. I glanced at the clock and saw that Beck would be a few more minutes in joining us since he was still feeding the horses and locking up the barn for the night with Lilah. The new barn manager, Dale, had taken off for the evening which I was glad for because I didn't particularly like the guy. We'd invited him to join us for dinner on his first day on the job a few days ago and that had been plenty. All he'd done was talk about himself and instead of lingering after dinner to watch a movie, Beck, Quinn and I had gone to our room to watch TV, despite the flat screen in the room being considerably smaller. Lilah had excused herself early so I got the impression she didn't much like her new boss either.

"Spit what out?" I asked.

"Whatever has you so quiet," he responded. I felt his gaze on me, but found it hard to look at him.

"It's not important," I murmured even as I railed at myself for being such a coward. Tomorrow was my last full day and night at the resort before I had to report to work the morning after that and I still had no idea where I stood with the men who'd become such a part of me that I didn't want to remember a time when we hadn't been together.

The men I'd finally come to accept I was completely in love with.

The revelation should have been a joyous one, but it wasn't. It broke my damn heart.

Because I'd finally found the place I was meant to be, but it wasn't real. It had been four of the best weeks of my life, but it was something we couldn't sustain outside the resort's boundaries.

Not with one of us leaving and the other adamant about not wanting to be in another relationship ever again.

I'd thought maybe I could still have something with Quinn after Beck left, but I kept hearing his words to me...the ones that it felt like had been spoken a lifetime ago...

I had my shot at happiness. It's gone and I have no interest in trying to get it back.

I knew Quinn cared about me and Beck, but there'd been no hint that he wanted us beyond these four walls.

And I couldn't bear to hear that truth again...not with just two nights left together.

Quinn bumped my shoulder. When I forced myself to look at him he gently said, "Talk to me."

God, I wanted him. I wanted them both so badly...

"I-"

That was as far as I got because I heard footsteps behind us. I tried to collect myself, but whatever progress I made was shot to hell when I turned around to smile at Beck and Lilah.

Only it wasn't just Beck and Lilah.

I stared in disbelief at the man standing next to my lover. "Nathan," I whispered.

My brother gave me the slightest of nods as he responded with a soft, "Brody."

I barely heard Lilah give her excuses as she left the room as the air around us grew thick with tension and the silence between us grew. I noticed Quinn taking the skewer I'd been working on from my hand and replacing it with a hand towel, and I went on auto-pilot as I wiped my hands clean.

"What are you doing here?" I finally managed to ask. I should have been happy to see him, but all I felt was cold.

You're a sick fuck, Brody! We're no longer brothers!

Nathan's final words were as clear to me now as they'd been the night he'd shouted them just before he'd walked out of my life forever.

"We'll leave you two to talk," I heard Quinn say. I snagged his arm before he could move and I shook my head.

"No, stay," I murmured. No way in hell I was going to hide my men. I reached down to link my fingers with Quinn's as I said, "He's leaving."

"Brody, I just need a few minutes of your time. It's important," Nathan said.

My brother looked like he'd aged a decade in the few years since I'd seen him. There were worry lines etched into his features and his eyes were devoid of the fire I'd always seen burning in them. Unlike me, Nathan had thrived on the standards my father had set and he'd had no reservations about becoming a part of our family's legacy.

"How did you find me?" I asked, my anger rising. I felt Quinn squeeze my hand, but it only marginally eased my fury.

"I hired a private investigator to track you down."

I shook my head in disbelief and laughed bitterly. "You're a piece of work," I muttered.

Nathan didn't react to the statement. Instead, he said, "Your landlady told me you've been working here. I ran into your friend in the barn-"

"Boyfriend," I cut in. "He's my boyfriend," I snapped. "They both are."

I felt a little guilty using Beck and Quinn to shock my brother, but I couldn't help myself.

To Nathan's credit, he barely reacted. I glanced at Beck and finally noticed he had his eyes downcast and his face was flushed. I dropped Quinn's hand and hurried to him. "Did he say something to you?" I asked Beck as I lifted his chin, forcing him to look at me. Rage shot through me as I put myself between Beck and Nathan. "What the fuck did you do to him?"

I had my hands on the lapels of Nathan's suit jacket before I even realized what I was doing.

"Brody, don't!" Beck said and I felt his hands closing around my upper arm as he tried to tug me back. But I wanted to draw blood. I wanted to wound my brother the way he'd wounded me when he'd cast me aside that very first night when I'd confided in him about who I really was.

I didn't get a chance to punch him like every cell in my body was urging me to do, because Quinn stepped between me and Nathan, forcing me to release my brother and step back. "He's not worth it," Quinn said calmly as he made me back up even farther and remained between us.

"Brody," Beck said. He grabbed my cheek and gently forced me to look at him. "He didn't say anything to me. When I saw him, I thought he was you…I thought the suit was some kind of joke so I made a comment…"

The way Beck's cheeks heated again, I had no doubt what kind of comment it had been and I could imagine my brother's reaction, considering what he thought of gay people.

"Did he touch you?" I asked.

Beck shook his head. "No. I even hugged him, not realizing he wasn't you. He didn't react at all…that's how I knew I'd messed up."

Relief went through me and I cupped Beck's cheek like he was cupping mine. I managed to take a deep breath as I nodded. I forced my eyes back to Nathan and said, "I'm not interested in hearing anything you have to say."

I turned away, but Nathan's next words stopped me cold.

"Someone's been threatening me...and you."

"What do you mean?" Quinn asked, his voice icy. I turned to see him stepping closer to Nathan. While my brother had a heavier build, I had no doubt Quinn could hold his own in a fight with him and likely do even more than that.

"Five minutes," Nathan said, but he wasn't talking to me. His eyes were on Quinn. "Five minutes and then I'm gone."

Quinn glanced at me and Beck was clutching my hand desperately.

"Talk," was all Quinn said.

Nathan shifted his attention back to me. "Have you been watching the news about me?"

"What makes you think I have any interest in knowing what's going on with you?" I snapped. "We're not brothers anymore, remember?"

It was the first time I saw a visual reaction from Nathan. He actually looked pained, but he quickly covered it with a mask of indifference.

"I've been getting emails," Nathan continued and I saw him remove a couple of pieces of folded paper from his suit jacket. "From an anonymous source," he added. He handed the pages to Quinn who opened them and began silently reading.

"The sender referenced you twice...the first time..."

Nathan hesitated and glanced at Quinn. Quinn's eyes hardened and then he was looking at my brother. He paused for a moment and then looked at me before dropping his eyes back to the paper and began reading out loud.

"If you continue on this course, you'll burn in hell just like your faggot brother," Quinn said quietly.

Beck's fingers clenched mine...hard.

Anger went through me, but something else was there too and I shifted my eyes to my brother who was watching Quinn as he read the second email. I wouldn't have thought it possible, but my lover's face went stone cold as he began reading the second page.

"Maybe if I go have a little talk with your fag brother, you'll start taking me seriously," Quinn murmured.

The words only served to anger me more and inside I was thinking, 'Bring it on' but with the way Beck was gripping my hand and Quinn's flinty eyes pinning mine, I kept that to myself and instead looked at my brother.

"Who is it?" I asked.

Nathan shook his head. "No idea. I had a computer savvy friend try to trace where they were coming from, but he says the user is covering his tracks by using different IP addresses."

"Are the threats only by email?" Quinn asked.

My brother didn't answer, but he didn't have to because I saw it in his eyes. "He's come after you?" I asked. When he didn't answer a tremor of unease went through me and I said, "Have you gone to the police?"

"There are some kinds of publicity you just don't want when you're about to announce a senate run," Nathan responded.

Of course. The job would always take precedence. He really was following in our father's footsteps.

"Is it just you or is he going after Dad too?" I asked.

Nathan hesitated before saying, "No…Dad's stepped away from things for a bit."

"What does that mean?" I asked.

A soft sigh escaped my brother's lips before he said, "He took an early retirement, Brody. He was diagnosed with dementia last year… it's progressing quickly."

The news shouldn't have bothered me since I'd written my family off long ago, but it did. And I hated that it did.

"He and Mom moved to Louisiana to be closer to Aunt Verona so she can help Mom with him."

I tried to digest that, but it was just too much. The idea that my father had gone from an unforgiving, driven, holier-than-thou political powerhouse to someone who couldn't remember his own name seemed impossible to me.

"I don't think you have anything to worry about, but I wanted you to know so you could watch your back," Nathan said quietly. "If there are any more, I'll have my assistant forward them to you."

I watched in disbelief as he turned to go. White hot rage went through me and I dropped Beck's hand. I was on my brother before Quinn could stop me. I shoved Nathan backwards until his back hit the wall. "You'll have your assistant contact me?" I yelled. "That's it? That's all you have to say to me?"

Nathan had a hold of my wrists where I was hanging onto his lapels, but he didn't try to break free of my grip.

"You walk out of my life like I'm nothing and then you waltz back in and drop this shit on me…"

I struggled to find my voice as the emotion took over. I shoved back from Nathan. "You were my big brother," I whispered, hating how my voice cracked.

For the first time, I saw my brother's face falter and he dropped his eyes. But he didn't say anything. He just stood there, locked in silence as my world fell apart all over again. It was like we were back in my apartment three years earlier, my brother's ugly vitriol ringing in my ears as I watched him walk away from me.

"You know what, go," I murmured. "I have all the family I need right here," I said as I glanced at Quinn and Beck. Quinn smiled at me and I didn't miss the brief nod he gave me. Beck came to my side instantly and wrapped his arms around me. I kissed him softly and said, "Let's go eat." Beck nodded, but as we turned away, I heard my brother's barely-there whisper.

"You were always so much braver than me."

He hadn't moved at all, not even to straighten his clothes from where I'd grabbed him. An uncomfortable sensation started in my chest and it took me a moment to realize what it was.

Yearning.

Despite it all, I wanted my brother back.

"I wasn't brave," I responded. "I was desperate."

"You always did sell yourself short," Nathan said softly. "You became my mirror, Brody," he whispered. "That night after prom and then again three years ago." He hesitated before he said, "Only, I didn't like what I saw and you paid the price."

His cryptic statement made no sense to me, but before I could respond, he straightened and fixed his clothes. "Take care of yourself."

Anxiety tore through me as I watched him head for the door that would lead to the parking area and I knew in that instant that I'd never see him again.

My eyes shifted to Quinn and then Beck. Neither man said anything, but they were both watching me with loving concern. That feeling fueled me. Beck dropped his arms, releasing me as he gave me the smallest of smiles. I wanted to kiss him, but I didn't have time. I caught up to Nathan just before he reached the doorknob and I stepped between him and the door.

"Stay for dinner, Nathan."

Nathan's hooded gaze lifted and I saw pain fill them. "I can't," he murmured. "My flight leaves in two hours."

"There will be other flights," I said. "Stay."

He seemed to hesitate for an inordinate amount of time before he shook his head. "I really can't. I have a meeting with my campaign manager in the morning."

Right. The job.

Disappointment flooded me.

"I'm really happy for you, Brody," Nathan said softly as he glanced over his shoulder at Beck and Quinn. "You've built something really amazing for yourself here. Don't…don't let that go, okay?"

Was he actually accepting my relationship?

The idea was so absurd to me that I forced myself to move as he reached for the doorknob. But in addition to my disbelief was the burning of ember of hope that lit up like a bonfire.

"Will you come back sometime?" I asked, hating how I sounded like a needy little kid. But in a lot of ways, that was what I was in that moment.

"I don't think that's a good idea," Nathan murmured. "At least not until things die down for me."

Fear ratcheted through me. "Nathan, don't go," I whispered desperately.

My brother sucked in a strangled breath. "I have to. I can't put you at risk."

Before I could respond, his arms were suddenly around me in a brutal hug. I automatically grabbed onto him.

"I'm sorry, little brother," Nathan said softly against my ear. "More than you'll ever know."

And then he was gone. Another set of arms went around me a moment later. Then a second set.

It wasn't the same, but it was enough.

CHAPTER 18

BECK

"I'm just going to go put Harley in my room and then I'll meet you in the car," I told Quinn and Brody as I gave them each a quick kiss. It was a risk to kiss them in the barn where anyone could see us, but I didn't care and from the way they each kissed me back, I suspected they didn't either.

"Do you know where Lilah is?" Quinn asked.

I shook my head. "Still changing maybe?" I said. "I'll check her room and let her know we're leaving in five."

"Sounds good," Quinn said. My insides warmed as both men's gazes lingered on me as I turned away and began walking out of the barn.

We'd gotten back from our final trail ride together a few minutes earlier and Brody and Quinn were just putting the last of the horses away before we went out to dinner. Although it was our last night together before Brody left tomorrow to go back to his regular job, we'd decided to go out to dinner to celebrate Lilah's eighteenth birthday when we'd found out she had no plans for the evening. On my way out of the barn, I greeted Gabriella as she was getting out of her car. She'd agreed to join us which I knew would make Lilah both happy and nervous. She was definitely crushing on the older woman big time.

My relationship with Lilah had grown quickly over the past couple of weeks and I'd learned a lot about her. She'd been kicked out of her house by her mother because she'd believed Lilah had been trying to seduce the woman's live-in boyfriend. And since there'd been no one to take the young girl in, she'd been forced to live on the streets. Luckily, she'd found refuge in a shelter that specialized in serving the needs of LGBT kids and they'd been the ones who'd gotten her set up with the job at Roman's resort, as well as helping her to get her GED. Fortunately, she hadn't been forced to earn money the way so many young people did when they were left homeless and alone…like I had. But she was still slow to warm up to other people, so I suspected she hadn't gotten out of her mother's house completely unscathed. Like me, she tended to shy away from men, though she'd grown more comfortable around Brody and Quinn in the days after she'd arrived and she often joined us for dinner and movie night. At least until Dale had started. After that, none of us had wanted to linger in any place he was.

Lilah had figured out my relationship with Brody and Quinn pretty quickly, but she hadn't judged the fact that I was with two men instead of just one. I'd told her a little bit about my past, but like with Quinn and Brody, I'd left out the worst of it.

Not because I thought she'd judge me.

No, I never brought it up because I wanted to pretend it didn't exist.

I knew I was in extreme denial about all the things I'd done, but the stakes were just too high to risk my men finding out the truth about me. Because I couldn't lose everything I'd gained these past few weeks.

I had no doubt I was in love for the first, and what I highly suspected would be the last time in my life, and it both scared me and set me free. Scared me because I didn't know if Brody and Quinn felt the same way and set me free because I finally felt like I belonged.

To a place.

To people.

To myself.

I wasn't foolish enough to think my depression had been miraculously cured since I hadn't had any episodes since my men and I had heated things up, but I couldn't deny that being around them had changed my life dramatically.

And not just them...the horses, Harley, my friendship with Lilah... they all helped to keep me grounded and moving forward. That need to hide away in bed day after day was non-existent at this point. If anything, I couldn't wait to wake up each morning, mainly because it meant I could be with Brody and Quinn outside of my dreams. Which was a surprise since my quality of sleep had worsened as I continued to be plagued with the same nightmare night after night. But I was convinced it was only because my relationship with Quinn and Brody continued to go undefined and that was what was causing the stress that was triggering my nightmares.

As good as I'd been feeling, I'd been careful about expressing my emotions with my guys. It was a form of self-preservation that had kicked in as I'd realized my feelings had turned into something beyond just liking each man and enjoying the pleasure they brought me. Because as my feelings grew, so did the knowledge that I was going to lose everything, and not because of something I said or did.

No, time was my enemy.

The countdown to my return to Seattle was like a living thing beneath my skin. It wasn't until the night before when I'd been lodged between Quinn and Brody's hard bodies as they'd slept that my mind had started to toy with an idea that I never would have had the strength to even consider if it hadn't been for the insight these past few weeks had given me.

What if I stayed?

That question had seemed impossible to answer at first because the idea of being away from my family and starting a new life in Montana seemed crazy to me. My fathers wouldn't go for it and I had nothing here besides my men.

But besides my family, I didn't have anything at home either.

If I wanted more, I needed to go after more.

That was when I'd remembered my conversation with Dane…the one before my freak out moment.

College, being a vet tech, going to vet school someday…they'd seemed like impossibilities when he'd mentioned them. But now… now that I was different, maybe it meant the future could be different too.

I hadn't slept a wink after that realization had hit me the night before. I'd merely lain there, Brody's face pressed against my neck and Quinn's strong arm wrapped around my body, and tried to work everything out in my mind.

What I'd be losing.

What I'd be gaining.

A normal life.

The thing I'd dreamed of from the moment I'd woken up in the hospital fifteen months ago, only to find that my plan to find eternal peace hadn't worked.

Something I was happy about now more than ever.

But my new future had one big sticking point…or two rather.

Quinn and Brody.

I had no idea if they wanted things to be the same once we left the resort. As well as I was doing, that old sense of self-doubt lingered and every time I wanted to ask my men if we could have something outside our perfect little bubble, that little voice in my head would remind me of who I really was and that no one would want the real me or the shitload of baggage I came with.

I shook off that feeling as it threatened to creep in on me again. I had one last night with my guys that was a certainty. I wasn't going to waste it.

As I entered the residence through the kitchen door, I was reminded about the previous night. The look on Brody's face after his brother had hugged him just before walking out the door…it had broken my heart.

For him.

For Nathan.

Brody's brother wasn't at all what I'd expected. When I'd seen him in the barn as I'd been locking up, it hadn't even occurred to me who he was. I'd laughed at the sight of my man dressed in a fancy suit and sporting carefully styled hair. And for some reason, as I'd gotten closer to him, I hadn't noticed what would be so obvious to me later on, after I'd realized my mistake.

There'd been no laughter in his eyes...no life.

Not like my Brody's beautiful, effervescent eyes that spoke volumes every time he looked at me.

No, the only thing Nathan's had said was that he was losing whatever battles he was fighting.

Since I'd thought he was Brody, I'd joked about how hot he looked, but that I still preferred him naked just before I'd pushed into his arms. I'd known almost instantly my mistake because his rock-hard body had been wrapped tight with tension and his arms hadn't come up to wrap around me. There'd been no rumble in his chest as he laughed, no smart comeback about me helping him to fix the problem.

I'd expected Nathan to rail at me after I'd scrambled away from him, but he hadn't spoken at all. He hadn't called me any names, hadn't looked at me with disgust. He'd merely watched me for several long seconds and then said he was there to see his brother.

The knowledge that Brody might be in danger was terrifying to me, but he had spent the evening promising me and Quinn he'd be careful and that there was nothing to worry about. I'd made him swear he'd talk to Jax about the threat to see if anything could be done and he'd readily agreed. It hadn't really eased my fears completely, but I was glad to know he was taking the threat seriously.

Dinner had been a quiet affair as Brody had been lost in thought, but once we'd gone to our room, Brody had pulled out his laptop and googled his brother's name. We'd been shocked to find that Nathan Wilder was not the same man he'd been three years earlier when he'd kicked his brother to the curb.

While he was still running for senate, he was doing it as a Democrat. There were countless articles outlining the man's change when it came to many issues, but the most glaring one was his sudden turnaround on gay marriage. While his and Brody's father had been a staunch critic, Nathan had somehow become one of its greatest supporters. When questioned by reporters what had prompted the change of heart, Nathan had actually made a sideline comment about someone close to him not being an abomination as the Bible suggested. And while he hadn't mentioned Brody by name, none of us had any doubt he had in fact been referring to his brother.

That had left Brody quietly devastated. He hadn't said so, but he didn't need to tell us for me and Quinn to know that was what he was feeling. We'd tried to draw Brody out so he could try to work through it all, but he'd asked us to give him some time. So Quinn and I had tried to show Brody with our bodies what we couldn't with our words.

Brody had seemed better this morning, but I knew it still weighed heavily on his mind. I was hopeful that he'd be more open tonight to discussing what his plans were, if any, in regards to reaching out to Nathan in the future.

Once I was inside the kitchen, I started walking towards the hallway leading to my room so I could drop off Harley before going to collect Lilah, but I stopped when I heard muffled voices.

One male, one female.

I couldn't make out what they were saying, but I knew it had to be Dale and Lilah. I veered off towards the opposite hall. Since the building was shaped in a U, I could actually see Lilah and Dale through the glass windows. From my position, I could look out into the courtyard to the end of the wing where Lilah's room was located. It was hard to make them out, but it looked like Lilah had her back to her door and Dale was standing close to her.

Too close.

Worry began to prick at me as I made my way to that part of the building. I lost sight of them momentarily as I rounded the corner, but I could hear them better.

"I'll show you what a real man feels like," Dale murmured, his voice thick and husky.

My insides lit up with apprehension at his tone. If Lilah

responded, I didn't hear it. But it didn't matter, because I didn't need to hear her voice to know what was happening.

Something happened to me in that moment as I neared them, my eyes going from where Dale was using one hand to hold onto the wrist of the hand Lilah had wrapped around her doorknob, his other hand between her legs. Lilah had her face turned away from him and I could see that her eyes were closed and tears were leaking out of them.

But she wasn't fighting him.

Because she couldn't…

I knew that look…she knew what was coming and she'd accepted it.

Just liked I'd accepted it…

I remembered nothing after that except a few brief words falling from Dale's lips right before my fist connected with his face.

She wanted it…

My body wasn't my own after that. I had no control and for once, I didn't want it. I didn't need it.

Reality returned to me in a haze as a pair of strong arms wrapped around me. Arms I knew very well.

Brody's arms.

"Beck, stop!" he said forcefully in my ear as he pinned my arms so I couldn't get free of him.

My vision cleared as I saw Dale lying at my feet, his face covered in blood. Blood that was smeared across my fists.

"You little shit," the man snarled as he tried to get up.

I looked around to see Lilah standing in the corner in Gabriella's arms. The older woman was talking soothingly to her. Quinn was standing over Dale. His eyes went from me to Lilah and then he jerked Dale to his feet.

"You stay the fuck away from her!" I shouted as Dale's beady eyes flitted to Lilah.

"She came on to me!" Dale snapped. "She wanted it!"

Dale's words set me off all over again and I tried to pull free of Brody's arms, but he refused to release me.

"No she didn't!" I yelled. "You think you can take whatever you want? That just because you're bigger and stronger you have that right? You have no right!" I screamed. Pain ripped through me in a violent wave as memories washed over me, one by one. I shook my head to try to stop it, but it was like a Pandora's Box and they all came flooding back at once. Every look, every suggestive word…every instance where what I'd wanted had been ignored.

"They had no right!" I shouted as something inside of me ripped wide open. "I didn't want it! I never wanted it!"

"Beck," Brody said softly in my ear, trying to calm me. But he'd also loosened his hold enough for me to shove away from him. I looked around the small group of people to see that they were all looking at me with various expressions. While Dale was looking like he wanted to rip my throat out, everyone else was staring at me with looks of pity, horror and disbelief.

Heat flooded my system as I heard my own words.

I.

I'd said *I.*

I shook my head as the truth hit me. I saw Quinn step forward as if to put his hands on me, but I instantly stepped back. My insides were rolling so violently that I felt like I was going to be ill.

Humiliation was what got me moving.

And fast.

By the time I hit the end of the hallway, I was running. I was dimly aware of Brody and Quinn calling my name, but all that did was spur me on. I crashed through the kitchen door and frantically darted for my car which, thankfully, was just a few steps away. My fingers slipped off the door handle the first time I grabbed it, but I managed to get the door open on the second try. I wasn't aware that Harley had followed me until I opened the door and she jumped inside. My keys were in the cup holder so as soon as I got in, I engaged the locks and scrambled for them. It seemed to take forever to get the engine going. I had just put it into reverse when Brody came running out the door. I ignored his shouts for me to stop and hit the gas, sending the car flying backwards. My tires gripped the gravel as I slammed the gearshift into drive and hit the gas again. It wasn't until I flew past Brody that I finally took a breath.

The tears didn't come until my car sped past the sign welcoming guests to the resort and I realized that the perfect little bubble I'd been living in had just burst.

~

No Beck, we can't. It's a sin...
I'm sorry my beautiful boy...

I jerked awake at the sensation of wetness on my cheek. My arms instinctively went around Harley as I straightened and as soon as I stopped moving, she resumed licking my face. I used my hand to wipe at the dampness and realized there was too much moisture on my skin to have just come from the dog.

It took me several long seconds to remember where I was. A glance outside showed darkness was just starting to fall. Which meant it had probably been a couple of hours since I'd left the resort.

As soon as I'd hit the main road, I'd automatically turned north since that was the way to Dare. But as I'd neared the town, I'd realized I had nowhere to go. I couldn't talk to Dane and Jax because they would insist on calling my fathers. So I'd kept driving and then I'd started taking random turns. It wasn't until the narrow road I'd been driving on had started to wind up a mountain that I'd started crying so hard that I couldn't see clearly anymore. I'd ended up pulling onto an access road and while there'd been a chain barrier preventing me from actually driving any distance down the secluded stretch of dirt road, I hadn't cared since I'd just needed to get off the main road so I could try to collect myself.

I hadn't intended to fall asleep, but that was exactly what had happened because it had still been light out when I'd fled the resort.

Which meant Quinn and Brody must be frantic by now. They were likely even out looking for me. They might have even called Dane and Jax to tell them what had happened. And that meant if my fathers didn't know what was going on, they would soon enough.

My thoughts drifted back to my lovers. Humiliation swamped me again, but even though I couldn't face them, I couldn't allow them to suffer through worrying about me. I reached into my pocket for my cell phone, but then remembered I'd left it in my room earlier in the day to re-charge since the battery had died.

I wiped at my face as I realized what the turn of events meant.

I had to go back.

I gently placed Harley back into the passenger seat and then got my car started. But when I put it into reverse and hit the gas, nothing happened. Concern turned to worry when the car didn't move and it hit me that one or more tires were spinning. I climbed out of the car and my feet immediately sank into heavy mud...the same mud that was now holding my car prisoner.

Despair consumed me as I sank back into my seat and closed the door. I tried several more times to free the car, but the back and forth motion of the wheels seemed to make the problem worse and I finally gave up and put the car in park. I was glad when Harley climbed back into my lap because the darkness settling around my car had me on edge. I could try walking down the mountain, but I hadn't noticed any houses on the way up it and I knew it had to be at least a dozen miles from the intersection leading up the mountain. There was no guarantee if I walked farther up the mountain that I'd find anyone either. I glanced in the rearview mirror and watched for traffic passing by, but there was nothing. I waited a good twenty minutes and not a single set of headlights went past.

I knew I was fucked as I realized how dangerous it would be to be out in the dead of night in rural Montana. Just this afternoon on our trail ride, Quinn had pointed out some bear scat. The world just outside my car window was an unforgiving one that I knew nothing about.

Which meant I'd be spending the night in my car.

And my men and my family would be in a full-on panic.

Guilt tore through me as I took stock of what I had. The gas tank was full so I left the car running and the lights on so I could see anything approaching me from the dirt road in front of me. I had no food or water, but since I could hike down the road in the morning when it was light out, I wasn't worried about it. Which meant it would just be a long night of watching and waiting since I doubted I'd be able to sleep. I patted my lap and Harley immediately climbed onto it and curled up into a ball. Her presence was comforting and I dropped my head back against the headrest. I let my eyes slide closed as the events of the evening began to replay in my head.

Never in my life had I struck out at another human being. The fact that I'd hit Dale repeatedly, if the amount of blood on his face had been anything to go by, was proof that the shit I'd been trying to pretend didn't exist anymore was alive and well inside of me. But instead of resorting to my usual tactics to deal with it, I'd gone a whole other way.

And my men had witnessed it all.

I closed my eyes as more tears threatened to fall, but before they could, Harley began growling and I quickly opened my eyes again. The inside of my car was lit up from the headlights of a car that had pulled onto the access road behind mine. Fear went through me as I saw a figure get out and approach my car. I'd been hoping help would come, but what if whoever it was wasn't here to help?

Harley was barking like crazy as the figure stopped outside my door and tapped on the window.

"Beck, it's me, Roman."

I let out a whimper of relief and couldn't stop the sob that tore from my throat. I managed to open the window, but my voice was stuck in my throat. I put my hand on Harley's muzzle to try and calm her.

"Are you okay?" he asked softly.

A nod was all I accomplished. It seemed to take forever for me to say, "It's stuck."

Luckily, Roman seemed to know what I was trying to say because he said, "Yeah, the runoff from the mountain causes the dirt to become like cement. We'll need to have it towed out of here."

I nodded, but couldn't make myself move. Logically, I knew this man meant me no harm, but my brain wasn't interested in logic. It was interested in the past and what men like Roman had wanted from me.

"Beck," Roman said softly and he actually crouched down so he was eye level with me through the car window. "Lots of people are worried about you. Let me get you out of here."

"Okay," I whispered, my voice sounding uneven and on the verge of tears. I closed my window and turned off the car. I held Harley in a tight grip against my chest as I got out. Roman didn't touch me despite the awkwardness of trying to get through the mud with the dog in my arms. He did, however, shut the door behind me. I went to his car which turned out to be a luxury SUV and climbed into the front seat. I knew Harley would be better off in the back seat, but I wasn't willing to release my death grip on her. She'd become the only barrier between me and the man who climbed into the driver's seat.

The car was warm and quiet. I watched as Roman picked up his phone and dialed a number.

"Jax, it's me," he said quietly. "I've got him." Roman appeared to wait for Jax to speak before he said, "His car is a few miles from Gray and Luke's…on that access road leading to the river trail. It's stuck in the mud."

Another pause and then Roman said, "I'll have him call you back in a few minutes, okay?"

Roman said his goodbyes and hung up. He put the car in reverse and got it out onto the road.

"Where do you want me to take you, Beck?" Roman asked. "I can take you to Dane and Jax's or the resort…or you can come to Hunter's and my house."

"Your house," I whispered. Despite my fear of the man, I wasn't ready to face anyone else.

"Okay," he said softly and then he was back on the phone with Jax. Once he told Jax where he was taking me, he handed me the phone.

"Beck, are you okay?" Jax asked gently.

I nodded and then remembered he couldn't see me. "I'm okay," I said. "I'm sorry if I worried you."

There was a brief pause before Jax said, "We're just glad you're okay. Would you do me a favor and call Brody and Quinn to let them know you're all right? They've been out looking for you for quite a while."

A fresh round of guilt went through me. "Yeah, I will."

"Okay…promise you'll call if you need anything," Jax said.

Emotion clogged my throat. This man and his husband had been nothing but kind to me, yet I'd put them in the same class as all the men from my past.

"I will," I responded. "Jax," I began after a moment. "Did you…did you call my fathers?"

The silence that loomed seemed to last forever. "No," he finally said.

The relief was instantaneous. It was bad enough I'd caused him, Dane and my men to worry…putting my fathers through that level of stress, especially when they were helpless to do anything about it, was just too much.

"Please don't call them," I said.

"Beck…"

"Please, Jax. I'll tell them what happened…I just need some time to figure things out."

After a beat, Jax said, "Okay."

"Thank you."

"Call me in the morning unless you need to talk before then. Roman and Hunter are good people."

I nodded as I dashed away the tears that were threatening to fall. "Thanks, Jax."

After we said our goodbyes, I glanced at Roman and said, "Can I call Quinn or Brody?"

Roman nodded. "They're both in my contacts."

I selected Brody's number only because his name was listed first.

"Roman, did you find him?" Brody asked before the first ring even finished.

"It's me," I said.

"Beck?" Brody said. "Thank fuck," he muttered and then I heard him shifting the phone.

"Beck, are you okay?" Quinn asked, his voice heavy with concern. I could tell Brody had placed me on speakerphone.

"I'm okay. I'm with Roman."

"Where are you? We'll come get you," Brody said.

Pain ratcheted through me as I whispered, "No…I'm not…I'm not ready to see you."

The silence on the other end of the phone broke my heart. My voice was strangled as I said, "I just need some time, okay? I promise I'll come home tomorrow."

Home.

That's what it was.

No, not it…Brody and Quinn. They were home for me.

When neither man responded, I whispered, "Brody? Quinn?"

"Tomorrow's fine, baby," Quinn finally responded, his voice sounding rusty.

"I'm sorry," I murmured. "I forgot my phone…I just needed some time. I didn't mean to scare you."

"We know, Beck," Brody said softly. "Just…just promise us you're okay."

"I'm okay, I swear," I said.

The words weren't exactly a lie, but I knew where Quinn and Brody's heads were. They were worried I was going to hurt myself. But as much as this shit was killing me, my mind wasn't going to that place.

"Okay, we'll see you tomorrow," Brody said. "If you need us, just call. Anytime."

"Okay," I said. "Bye." I hung up the phone without waiting for them to say their goodbyes because I was about to completely lose it. I felt Roman take the phone from my hand.

"Do you want to talk about it?" Roman asked gently.

I shook my head and bit back the sobs that were threatening. "Were you out looking for me?" I asked.

"Yes and no," he said. "I was up at my brother and Luke's cabin which is a few miles from where you were. I was helping Gray with some investment stuff. Jax called about twenty minutes ago to say you were missing so I left to help search. Luke was getting ready to go out too. I saw your taillights through the trees."

"Did they tell you what happened today?" I asked.

"They told me what Dale did to Lilah. Lilah has declined to press charges. Gabriella had Dale escorted off the property."

That was good news at least. But it didn't answer my question about whether or not Roman knew what I'd said in front of everyone. I didn't have the guts to ask him, so I fell silent.

Several minutes passed before Roman spoke again and I nearly jumped out of my skin at the sound of his voice.

"Beck, I need you to know that I would never hurt you."

I swallowed hard at that. It shouldn't have come as a surprise that the man could tell I was afraid of him. "I know that in here," I murmured as I pointed at my chest. "But here is another story," I said as I pointed to my head.

"Did I do or say something-"

"No," I interjected when I heard the dejection in his voice. "It's not just you. Certain types of men…"

I shook my head because I couldn't find the words to explain it to him. Not any words that would make any sense anyway. "It's me," I finally said. "I'm not right in the head."

I felt Roman's eyes on me even in the darkness of the interior of the car, but I didn't look at him.

"I don't believe that," he said softly.

"Believe it," I whispered as the shame crawled through me. "Because even though a part of me knows you're a good man and that you love your husband, the other part can't help but wonder if you're going to pull this car over and tell me to get in the back seat so you can fuck me. And the *really* sick, fucked-up part of me *wants* me to tell you to do it, to seduce you into doing it…even though it isn't what I want at all."

I glanced at him and wasn't surprised to see that my words had most definitely gotten his attention. "Now tell me again that I'm right in the head."

CHAPTER 19

QUINN

"Quinn, he's here," I heard Brody call from the barn door. I quickly put the horse I was working on in his stall and then rushed outside. My heart didn't cease its painful contractions until I spied Beck wrapped up in Brody's arms. They were standing next to Beck's open car door.

Emotion clogged my throat as I came to a stop and just stood there and watched them. Even though I'd known he'd been safe after last night's call, it felt like I'd been on a non-stop adrenaline rush from the moment he'd run off and I was just now starting to crash.

To say Brody and I had been in a near panic yesterday had been an understatement. From the moment we'd walked into the building and heard the muffled shouts, we'd been in overdrive. The sight of Beck on top of Dale, his fist slamming into the man's face over and over had shocked me to the point that I'd actually stopped moving forward. So Brody had reached them first and pulled Beck off of the man who'd been trying to defend himself by covering his face with his arms. Lilah had been plastered in the corner, sobbing hysterically. She'd calmed only after Gabriella had taken her into her arms.

The whole thing had been surreal. Seeing the blood on Dale's face, on Beck's hands. Hearing what had set Beck off. Finally getting confirmation that Beck had indeed suffered at the hands of men in his past.

They had no right...I didn't want it! I never wanted it!

He clearly hadn't meant to blurt the truth out that way, but in a way, I was glad it had happened.

I wasn't glad about what had happened next.

Watching Beck run again had been one of the worst moments in my life. It was confirmation that he still didn't trust us one hundred percent. Not to mention that I'd never seen him so upset...not even the day he'd run from the CB Bar and hit the tree with his car. That had been first and foremost in my mind as he'd fled and while I'd forced myself to remain behind so Dale wouldn't be alone with the two women, I'd been devastated when Brody had returned moments later without Beck.

We'd stayed at the resort long enough to contact the police. It was Jax who'd arrived to deal with things. We'd had no choice but to tell him everything, including what Beck had said. Dale had started spouting off some bullshit about how he wanted to press charges against Beck, but Jax had silenced him with a few choice words that a sworn officer probably shouldn't be saying and then he'd gotten Lilah's side of the story. Luckily, he'd believed the young woman one hundred percent and he'd put Dale in handcuffs. Since Lilah had refused to press charges, Jax hadn't been able to do more than escort Dale off the property. As frantic as Brody and I had been to go after Beck, we'd been more than happy to clean out Dale's few belongings so there'd be no reason for him to return to the resort.

We'd coordinated with Jax where we were going to search and then he'd taken off to get Dale out of there. Gabriella had taken a still shaken Lilah home with her and Brody and I had hit the road in search of our lover. We'd tried calling him repeatedly before we'd left, but there'd been no answer and it had been Brody who'd thought to check our room for Beck's cell phone. Sure enough, it had been sitting in the charger. That had raised our distress to a whole new level.

We hadn't talked much as we'd searched, but as each hour had passed, we'd started to reach for one another when the fear became too much. When Jax had called to let us know he'd called Roman, Callan and the rest of the extended family to help search, Brody and I had been even more terrified.

It had been another half an hour before we'd finally gotten the call that he was safe. And then Beck had torn our hearts out by telling us he wasn't ready to come home.

Brody and I had spent the night just holding onto one another in our too-empty bed. I'd been tempted to go to Roman's house on more than one occasion to try and talk to Beck, but holding on to Beck's words had helped.

I promise I'll come home tomorrow.

It wasn't the promise part so much as the home part that I'd clung to. It gave me hope that he really did feel that way. That Brody and I were home for him.

Brody and I hadn't made love, even though we could have since the three of us had talked about the "rules" of our relationship several weeks earlier, after the night Brody had kissed me in the kitchen, not knowing Beck was watching. It had been an awkward conversation, especially considering we hadn't actually defined our relationship, but we'd all agreed that two of us being with each other when the third wasn't around didn't stir any feelings of jealousy. And if it ever did, we'd discuss it. The talk had given us the freedom we'd needed to strengthen our individual bonds with each other. For my part, there was nothing hotter than walking in on my men when they were going at it. Wondering if they were when I wasn't with them ran a close second.

Neither of us had slept and Brody had helped me feed and take care of the horses this morning. He was supposed to have gone to work, but he'd managed to find a replacement so he could be here when Beck returned. We'd kept ourselves busy turning the horses out and cleaning stalls after I'd called Gabriella to tell her that Lilah didn't need to come back until she was ready.

And then the waiting game had begun as we'd watched and waited. I'd been half-tempted to call Roman after lunchtime came and went, but I'd forced myself not to. Because Beck had promised...

I watched as Brody released Beck. My young lover had trouble making eye contact as he approached me. Whether he was still embarrassed about what he'd admitted to the day before or because he hadn't come home when we'd ask him to, I wasn't sure, and it really didn't matter to me.

Nothing mattered except knowing he was here and unhurt.

We could figure the rest out.

"Quinn, I'm sorr-"

I kissed him before he could finish. He let out a cry of surprise and then he was in my arms, his body pressed flush against mine.

The relief was so instantaneous that my knees almost buckled. I tore my mouth free from his and just held onto him, needing to make sure he was real.

"I love you, Beck," I said softly, my mouth pressed to his ear. I felt him stiffen in my hold for the briefest of moments, and then a strangled sob tore free of his throat.

"I love you too," he choked out against my shoulder.

I'd known in my heart that my feelings would be returned, but his words still set me free. I grabbed Brody who was standing just behind Beck and dragged him forward into our embrace. "I love you," I said just before I kissed him softly.

"Me too," he said hoarsely as he nodded. He waited until Beck was looking at him before saying, "Both of you...so very much." I didn't hear Beck return the words as he wrapped an arm around Brody's neck, but the sigh of relief that escaped Brody's lips was proof enough that Beck had said those amazing three little words to him as well.

We just held on to each other after that. I wasn't sure how much time passed before Beck stepped back. He wiped at his eyes and I immediately noticed how swollen they looked.

I suspected, like us, he hadn't gotten much sleep the night before either.

"Where's Lilah?" he asked. "Is she okay?"

"She's with Gabriella," Brody said. "She's okay...she was worried about you."

Beck nodded and then his eyes fell to his bruised knuckles. "Am I...am I in trouble for what I did?"

"No," I said softly as I reached out to him and forced his eyes up. Never again did I want to see his head hung in shame. "Lilah told Jax what happened. Gabriella fired Dale and Jax escorted him off the property. Warned him to get out of Dare."

Beck nodded. "So Jax knows what I said?" he whispered.

"He does," Brody murmured.

Another nod. "I need to go see them...Jax had my car brought to Roman's this afternoon after the tow truck got it out of the mud, but I was asleep so I didn't see him."

"Do you want us to come with you?" I asked. I didn't tell him how I couldn't bear the thought of him leaving again, even if it was just for a little while.

"I'd like that," he responded. "Can we go now? I'd like to talk to you and them together."

"Absolutely," I said.

I put my arm around him and Brody moved to his other side to take his hand. Harley trailed after us as we went to my truck. I wasn't surprised when Brody climbed into the backseat with Beck and pulled him into his arms while Harley draped herself across his lap. None of us spoke as we drove to Dane and Jax's house beyond me calling Jax to let him know we were on our way. Beck held onto Brody throughout the drive and even nodded off for a few minutes. By the time we reached Dane and Jax's, he was stiff with tension, but he hadn't tried to move away from Brody at all.

It was a good sign.

Jax and Dane came out of their house as soon as we arrived. Beck was tense when both men hugged him. It took a few minutes to get settled in their living room with me and Brody on either side of Beck on the couch and Dane and Jax in the two side by side armchairs.

"Where are Emma and Ben?" Beck asked, his hands rubbing together nervously.

"Mrs. Greene took them down to the pond to go swimming for a bit," Dane said gently.

Beck nodded. "I owe you all an apology for making you worry last night. I just needed some time to calm down, but I forgot my phone and then my car got stuck in the mud...it wasn't intentional."

"We know that," Jax said. "No one believes you meant for things to happen like they did. We're just all glad Roman found you."

Beck nodded. "I lied to you," Beck said softly as his eyes shifted from Dane to Jax. "That day in the clinic after Harley's check-up. It wasn't the heat that made me act like that."

I had no idea what Beck was talking about, but remained silent.

Beck's eyes went to Dane. "When you made that joke about employing my services for the night, my mind...it took me someplace else...to the past."

I stiffened because it didn't take a rocket scientist to realize what Beck was talking about.

"Oh God, Beck, I didn't even think of that," Dane said, his eyes wide as he looked at his husband. Jax immediately reached out to take his hand. It was clear both men had some insight into Beck's past that Brody and I didn't.

"There was no reason for you to," Beck quickly said. "It happened so long ago and my life is so different now that it shouldn't matter..."

"It absolutely matters," Jax cut in. "But yes, we got the impression from your fathers that therapy helped you work through some of that stuff."

I saw tears fill Beck's eyes, but he dashed them away. "It didn't," he whispered. "But I let my fathers believe it did. I let them believe a lot of things."

I put my hand on Beck's knee and saw that Brody had taken hold of his hand. The fact that we were exposing our relationship with Beck to Jax and Dane didn't bother me in the least. Beck was ours and they needed to know that.

Beck took in a couple of deep breaths which seemed to calm him. "I've been keeping secrets," he said. "A lot of them." His eyes shifted between me and Brody and I squeezed his knee.

"It doesn't matter," I said softly. "Nothing you say will change anything."

Beck nodded. When he glanced at Brody, Brody lifted Beck's hand to his lips and kissed it. No words were needed to show he was on the same page as me.

His attention went back to Jax. "I was talking to Hunter this morning and he was telling me about the stuff he went through when he was my age. He gave me the name of his therapist...he said he used to see him while he was still in school and then again last year when he and Roman didn't get to adopt their baby. I called him and made an appointment for tomorrow."

Beck's gaze shifted to me. "I want to tell you and Brody everything, but I need to talk through it first with someone who doesn't mean anything to me. I'm afraid of what will happen if I don't."

I felt tears stinging the backs of my eyes, but managed a nod. "Whatever you need," I said. "Brody and I will wait for as long as you need."

My heart hurt for how much pain this young man must have had to live with over the years.

To Jax and Dane he said, "I'm going to tell my fathers about what happened and that I'm going to talk to someone about it. I'm going to ask them to stay in Seattle until I'm ready to tell them everything too."

Jax nodded. "I'll make sure your father knows this is what you need."

The comment seemed to ease a little bit of Beck's tension because he nodded.

"Quinn and I will be done with our work at the resort soon," Beck said softly. "When we are, I'm going to be staying with him and Brody instead of coming back here."

A mix of elation and relief went through me at his words and my eyes shifted to Brody's. We hadn't talked about what would happen once we left the resort, but then again, everything had changed in the last hour.

Because I'd finally had the courage to tell my men how I felt.

Brody sent me a small smile and I knew in that instant that we'd figure it out. It might not solve the long-term problem of Beck's impending return to Seattle, but his words had bought us at least another month together to figure it out.

Jax and Dane shared a look between them and I felt some of the tension return. Would they fight this?

"It's not that I don't love staying with you-" Beck began.

"You don't owe us any explanations, Beck," Dane said softly. "We've seen what being around them has done for you. You're a grown man and it's your decision."

I let out a breath I hadn't even realized I'd been holding.

"But we hope you'll still come to visit. And bring your men so we can get to know them better."

Beck smiled. "I'd like that." He glanced at me and Brody and said, "We'd like that."

We.

God, that sounded good. I brushed a kiss against Beck's temple and whispered, "Yes, we would."

CHAPTER 20

BRODY

"Fuck," Quinn hissed as his body opened up for me. He was lying over Beck's back, his tanned skin dark against our young lover's lighter complexion. His lips were pressed against Beck's shoulder and one arm was wrapped around his torso. The other arm was bracing some of his weight as he fucked into Beck from behind. He'd stopped his movements as soon as I'd put my hands on his hips to steady him so I could enter him.

It was the first time I'd been inside Quinn. He'd admitted earlier tonight that he'd never bottomed for anyone before, not even his husband, but that he was ready to be mine and Beck's in every way. Beck and I had taken our time getting him and each other ready. Just like every night for the past three weeks, our lovemaking was slow and languid. There was no rush to the finish line. Every move, every touch was about exploring each other and showing what we felt for one another when words didn't seem like enough.

It had been nearly three weeks since Beck had run away from us after his fight with Dale.

Three weeks of finally knowing I was going to have everything I'd ever wanted.

Because I was certain Beck wasn't leaving in two weeks. Not

because he'd said so, but because I couldn't fathom any one of us walking away from what we had together.

That wasn't to say things had been easy, because they hadn't been. And that was exactly why I knew what we had was the real deal. Because despite all the challenges we'd faced since Beck had come back to us, we were still us.

One of the biggest obstacles to overcome was our schedules...well, mine actually. My varied shifts at the firehouse meant I sometimes didn't make it to Quinn's little house at the CB Bar until late at night or that I didn't leave until well after Quinn and Beck were working. So I was often climbing into bed with my men after they were already asleep. But they never failed to welcome me home and we nearly always made love, no matter what time it was or how many hours Beck and Quinn had left before they had to get up to work. It would have been easier for me to just stay at my own apartment on the nights I had to work, but I hadn't even once considered it.

Because home was with Beck and Quinn. Even if all we had time for was a few quick words and some rushed kisses or a quickie here and there, it didn't matter. I would always choose them over convenience.

After we'd left Dane and Jax's house that day when we'd told each other how we'd felt for the first time, we'd gone back to the resort and spent most of the remainder of the day talking about the future. We'd agreed that it made sense to stay at Quinn's place since both he and Beck needed to get up early each day to work, though they'd both offered to make the drive to my apartment several times a week to make it easier on me. We hadn't talked about Beck going back to Seattle because there were just too many questions surrounding his future.

Another obstacle had been Beck's fathers. He'd video chatted with them that night to tell them everything that had happened and while Quinn and I had stayed off screen, but still in the room so we could provide moral support, we'd seen every play of emotions across our lover's face as he'd admitted to his parents that he wasn't okay and that he needed help. His fathers had immediately talked about getting on a plane and flying to Montana, but Beck had stood up for himself and told them he wasn't ready to see them. There hadn't been any unkindness in his words, but I could tell by his fathers' silence that they were struggling with not being able to be at their son's side.

But I also knew it was something Beck needed. I'd seen enough from the constant check-ins he did with his fathers to know that the relationship he had with them, though strong and loving, had some unhealthy undertones. Namely, his fathers' constant need to know he was okay and Beck's need to try and regain their trust. I didn't blame any of them for the tight leash around Beck's neck, but I knew it wasn't sustainable. Yes, Beck was young, but he wasn't a child. He needed his independence and his fathers needed to be able to trust him again. At some point, Beck needed to not feel obligated to text them on a pre-set schedule or respond to a text or call within an allotted period of time so as to not cause them to worry, and his fathers needed the freedom that came with knowing their son was okay without needing to hear his voice or see his face.

Beck had come clean about his relationship with me and Quinn too and while I doubted his fathers had a problem with him being with two men instead of just one since Beck's own uncle was in a relationship with two other men, they'd clearly not liked the idea of him staying with us instead of Jax and Dane. I hadn't taken it personally because I suspected it was part of their need to know their son was okay 24/7. Beck hadn't introduced us over the video chat, choosing instead to have us meet his fathers when they came out in a couple of weeks for a visit.

As worrisome as meeting his parents was to me and Quinn, nothing measured up to the anticipation of what Beck would need to share with us when he was ready. He'd been in intensive therapy for three weeks now. Instead of just one session with his therapist each week, he was going three times and the aftermath was always brutal. The sheer exhaustion he seemed to be feeling would roll off of him in waves and there were times he'd come home and crawl into bed and just cry non-stop. Sometimes I was lucky enough to be off on those days, so both Quinn and I could be with him at the same time, keeping him between us until he fell asleep, but the days I had to work while he was in therapy were a unique brand of torture. There was little proof that therapy was helping, but the one sign we clung to that it was doing him good was the fact that his nightmares had started to lessen. Instead of every night, they were only coming once or twice a week now. And they weren't as violent as they'd once been.

Besides the initial aftermath of each therapy visit, Beck seemed to be doing okay. He was enjoying working with Quinn at the ranch and he often made the drive out to the resort to visit with Lilah. The young girl was also faring well, especially after a woman was hired to replace Dale. The new stable hands had also started, two men and two women, and Beck had said that Lilah seemed to get along with all of them. The resort was booked to the hilt on the day it opened and Roman had informed Beck and Quinn that he'd received several comments from customers about how well-behaved and enjoyable the horses were to be around.

Beck's behavior around men continued to be an issue, but we'd seen slight improvements. Being back at the ranch meant he spent a lot more time with Callan. Quinn had told me that Beck had tended to avoid the man early on in the weeks since they'd gotten back from the resort, but this past week Beck had started to interact with him more as he helped Callan with a group of rescue horses that had come in. Callan, for his part, was always careful not to touch Beck or even get too close to him, so he'd definitely picked up on Beck's behavior.

"So tight," I whispered in Quinn's ear as I pressed into him until my balls were brushing his ass. He felt like a vise around me and I knew I wasn't going to last long. Luckily, the way his ass was rippling around my flesh, I doubted he would either. I licked his ear before saying, "Fuck your men, Quinn."

Quinn seemed to understand what I was asking because he pushed into Beck which caused my dick to nearly slide free of his body. I held perfectly still as he pulled out of Beck only to engulf my dick in heat as he pressed back against me.

"Yes," I hissed as electricity fired up my spine.

Within just a few glides, Quinn was eagerly fucking us both. I managed to kiss him on the mouth when he paused long enough to turn his head back and look at me, his eyes bright with lust. But all that did was set me off and I quickly shoved him down so he was lying flat on Beck's back. I took over setting the pace, forcing Quinn's dick deep into Beck's body. Beck's moans and whimpers drove me higher as I set a ruthless pace. I dropped my body so it was flush with Quinn's, forcing Beck to bear most of our weight. But the change in position didn't seem to faze Beck at all because he was eagerly humping the bed, presumably to give his unreachable dick some relief.

"God," I muttered as I rammed into Quinn. "I can't get enough of this."

Since we'd decided to get tested a couple weeks earlier so we could forego condoms, the heat of Quinn's body was magnified around my shaft so any hope I had of lasting was shot to hell. "I'm close," I muttered into his ear.

"Harder," Quinn groaned. "Make us both feel it."

His words caused a guttural growl to spill from my throat as I rammed into him. Both men grunted and groaned with every forward thrust and they were eagerly pushing against me every time I pulled out. Quinn's body was slick with sweat so I was forced to clamp my hand down on his shoulder as I pumped into him.

"Yes," I heard Beck start repeating over and over again, his voice growing higher in pitch the closer he came to finding his pleasure. He lifted his head enough so Quinn could seal their mouths together and the sight of them kissing did me in. I slung into Quinn with jerky, unpracticed moves. I barely heard Beck scream out in relief because the ringing in my own ears had grown so loud.

Quinn and I came at nearly the exact same time. His muscles fisted my shaft, dragging out my orgasm as I filled him with endless streams of hot, sticky cum. The unspeakable pleasure lit up every nerve ending and I found myself biting down on Quinn's shoulder to keep from shouting. Quinn let out a curse and then I felt his hand reach behind him to grab my ass. His fingers flexed into me as I continued to thrust into him. It wasn't until long minutes later as my orgasm released me from its tight grip that a shimmer of worry went through me when I realized how quiet Quinn was beneath me.

Had I been too rough with him?

It had been his first time, after all.

"Are you okay?" I asked him as I placed kisses over the spot where my teeth had left red marks on his skin.

An aftershock ricocheted through Quinn's body causing his ass to massage my spent dick.

"You really need to ask that?" he asked with a chuckle.

I smiled and searched out his mouth.

"I think we killed Beck, though," Quinn said when I released his mouth.

"Beck," I murmured.

Beck said something into the bedding that I couldn't understand.

"I think he said he wants more," Quinn said softly.

Beck turned his face until his cheek was pressed flat against the bed. "I said you guys are fucking heavy."

Quinn and I both laughed. Quinn thrust gently in Beck's body and I bit back a groan at the sensation of my dick pulling out of him. I immediately pushed forward so I could stay sheathed in his tight heat.

"Next time you can be on top," Quinn murmured. "I want that thick cock of yours buried deep inside me."

"Fuck," Beck groaned.

"Would you like that, baby?"

Beck nodded.

"You still want us to get off you?" Quinn asked knowingly.

I smiled when Beck shook his head. "Only when we switch places."

Since my dick was already starting to get hard again, I suspected we'd be able to accommodate our young lover in no time.

"Love you," I murmured to Quinn as I settled against him and began moving my hips in a circular motion.

"Love you too," Quinn said on a moan. My movement had the effect I wanted because within a matter of minutes both of my men were grinding their bodies together. We quickly switched places so I was lying on my back beneath Quinn and Beck was behind him.

Quinn began kissing me as Beck got me ready and then Quinn was sliding deep inside of me. I groaned as his thickness speared through me and he gave me a few hard thrusts. But that only lasted as long as it took Beck to plunge into Quinn's body and I gladly gave up control to my men as they loved me.

CHAPTER 21

BECK

"*How* are you feeling, Beck?"

I glanced at Dr. Emory and nodded. "I'm okay," I said. "Nervous," I added since I knew it was important to use words to actually describe how I was feeling. It was something I'd learned early on in talking with the huge, bald-headed man. When I'd first walked into his office, the tattoos and piercings had thrown me…but that had only lasted as long as it had taken for me to shake the man's hand because my instincts had kicked in and that familiar need had taken over. The humiliation of it all had almost had me walking out then and there, but I'd forced myself to sit down when he'd asked me to. As the psychologist had welcomed me and asked me a few questions about myself before he'd asked that ever-important question, I'd repeated to myself that Hunter trusted the man.

What are your goals not only for this session, but for therapy as a whole, Beck?

I'd studied him for a long time before I'd finally done what I hadn't been able to do for a really long time.

I'd told him the truth.

The raw, brutal truth.

My goal for this session is to not end up with your dick shoved up my ass.

Because even if I act like I want you, I don't. My goal for therapy is to find a way to tell the people I love that I've spent the past year letting men fuck me just so I can pretend I was finally in control of something for the first time in my life and that it was my choice, not theirs.

To his credit, Dr. Emory had barely reacted to the statement. He'd merely said his goal was to help me meet all of mine and then we'd dug into the shitstorm that was my past.

It had been a brutal few weeks and I'd wanted to quit more than once. Had even told Dr. Emory that I was quitting a few times. But then I'd remembered everything I had waiting for me at home and that had been enough to make me cross that threshold each time.

"It's okay to be nervous," he said gently. "Just remember that whenever you need a break, you just let me know. And if there's something you aren't sure you can explain, we'll work through it together."

I nodded.

Dr. Emory and I had already had our normal 45-minute session, but today was different because we were about to embark on my second goal of telling people about my past. I'd debated telling Brody and Quinn at the same time as my fathers, but had quickly disregarded the idea. There were things I needed to say to my lovers that I couldn't say to my parents. Not to mention, I didn't want my fathers to meet the men I was planning to spend my life with that way. So Dr. Emory and I had settled on telling my fathers separately next week when they came out for a visit.

It had been brutal telling my parents not to come when I'd admitted everything that had happened since I'd arrived in Dare. It wasn't often that I stood up to them, but I'd had to put my foot down that day and while I had no doubt it had hurt them, it was something we'd all needed. Because my fathers needed to start seeing me as a grown man. And I needed to be okay with asking that of them.

The last few weeks with Brody and Quinn had had its shares of ups and downs. While I loved every moment I spent with them as we tried to figure out how to build a life together, I held a monstrous amount of guilt for the secrets I'd been, and was still, keeping from them. I knew we couldn't really embark on the next chapter until we got past this one last hurdle. Because I still wasn't the real me with them and I wouldn't feel like I was until they knew everything.

And chose to be with me despite it all.

That was probably the hardest part for me. Knowing that, despite their reassurances to the contrary, I could still lose them when they learned the truth. The unbearable feeling had only grown worse as the days went by and our lives became more entwined with one another's.

On top of that, I was struggling with how the truth would affect my parents. Because unlike Brody and Quinn, I knew without a doubt that the things I told them wouldn't make them love me any less. But they would suffer.

Because they'd blame themselves.

For not seeing things for what they were. It wouldn't matter that they couldn't have known something I'd worked so hard to keep from them; they'd blame themselves no matter what. Dr. Emory had suggested we have a few sessions with my fathers after I told them the truth so that we could talk about how they were reacting to it and I hoped it was something they would go for.

The sound of Dr. Emory's phone buzzing ripped me from my thoughts. My entire body locked up tight as he hit the button to talk to his receptionist.

"Yes?"

"They're here, Dr. Emory."

"Send them in, please, Helen. Thank you."

Dr. Emory stood to head for the door. I wasn't surprised when he dropped a hand on my shoulder. "Deep breaths, Beck," he reminded me.

I nodded. The weight of his hand didn't bother me like it had when he'd started touching me a couple of weeks ago. It was something we'd discussed during our sessions and while I'd known it was an important part of building trust with him, I'd nearly had a panic attack the first time he'd patted me on the hand I'd had resting on my leg. He'd reassured me that my reaction was normal and he hadn't pressed the issue. We'd discussed it at length the following session and when he'd done it again, I'd managed not to jump out of my skin. My reactions had lessened every time he'd done it, but it hadn't been until the previous session that I hadn't felt that familiar rolling in my gut as I'd walked into his office.

I figured it was progress, though I knew it didn't mean I was fixed. My interactions with Callan Bale were proof of that. I'd been working around the man more and more the past few weeks and while I'd nearly vomited the first time he'd given me a gentle pat on the back after telling me I'd done a good job on something, each encounter with him got a little easier. It helped that Callan had taken notice of my reaction and while he hadn't said anything, he'd been sure not to touch me or even get to close to me again after that. It had been humiliating, but he'd also given me what I needed to try and work through my emotions.

Jax and Roman had done the same thing when I'd spent time in their company. While I hadn't come out and told Jax what I'd told Roman, he too seemed to have picked up on things, presumably because I'd admitted the truth about what had set me off the day of Harley's vet visit with Dane. Roman, for his part, hadn't changed his behavior around me much. I'd expected him to look at me with disgust, but like Callan, all he did was make sure not to crowd me. He was as friendly as ever and he'd even invited me, Quinn and Brody to join him and Hunter and their daughter for dinner on several occasions. The entire extended family of men had included me and my men in their weekly family get togethers which was a bittersweet thing for me because it reminded me so much of my own family gatherings. While the crowd wasn't nearly as big, it was just as loving.

I stood as Brody and Quinn walked into the room. They both looked nervous and unsure of themselves as Dr. Emory introduced himself to them. But some of that tension eased when they came over to me and wrapped me in their arms.

"Hi, baby," Brody whispered as he kissed my forehead.

"Hi," I sighed. God, I would never get tired of this feeling. Of being surrounded by them.

Dr. Emory gave us a few moments before he asked Brody and Quinn to sit on the couch opposite the one I was sitting on. He'd chosen that spot specifically so I'd have an easier time making eye contact with both men. It was one of the many things the doctor had asked me to work on outside of our sessions. Part of getting the confidence I needed to stand up for myself came from keeping eye contact with other people. I hadn't ever seen my behavior as an extension of low self-esteem, but the more and more we'd talked, I'd started to see the truth.

I waited until Dr. Emory went over the ground rules with Quinn and Brody. While it was my show, he encouraged my men to ask questions if they needed something clarified. Dr. Emory would make sure we didn't get too far off track.

Before I knew it, Dr. Emory's eyes were on me and he was saying, "Whenever you're ready, Beck."

I nodded and reminded myself to look at the men sitting across from me.

The men who'd promised that they would love me no matter what.

I was about to find out if that was true or not.

CHAPTER 22

QUINN

In so many ways I wasn't ready for this, but in others I was. I didn't want any more walls between the three of us, but I knew how much this would hurt all of us. Nothing Beck told us would change how we felt about him, but I wasn't foolish enough to think his words wouldn't cause me and Brody pain.

For him.

For us.

I found myself reaching for Brody's hand where it was lying between us on the couch. I wanted so badly to be able to hold Beck's hand too, but I suspected there was a reason Brody and I were sitting opposite him, rather than with him. Brody's fingers felt good around mine and I managed to pull some oxygen into my lungs as Beck began speaking.

"My parents both came from good, loving families. They met in college, but when my mom found out she was pregnant with me, they both had to quit school to get jobs because my father's parents disowned him and my mom's mother didn't have enough money to support them while they finished school. That caused a lot of problems between my parents and by the time I was five, they were fighting all the time. By the time my sister and brother came along, my parents were still together, but they'd both started messing around with drugs. I ended up taking care of my brother and sister most of the time. I was ten when my father died. A year later my mother was gone too...overdose."

Beck paused to suck in a breath. I could see a fine tremor in his hands just before he fisted them. He dropped his eyes, but almost immediately raised them again and fastened them on me and Brody.

"We went to live with my grandmother...my mom's mother. It was tough because she didn't have a lot of money and she wasn't the easiest person to deal with. Her memory wasn't great and she wasn't happy about having to take in three kids. But she was really religious and kept saying she was doing God's duty by taking us in. I spent a lot of time watching out for my brother and sister and as a result, my grades started to slip. My grandmother arranged for a tutor for me through her church. His name was Steven. He'd just completed Seminary school and was preparing to join the priesthood."

Beck hesitated and glanced at Dr. Emory. The man nodded his head at him. Whatever silent communication happened between them seemed to help ground Beck because he continued on his own.

"I really liked Steven. He used to meet me at a park near my grandmother's house and we'd toss a ball back and forth. He even took me to a baseball game once. The more time I spent with him, the more I liked him. I'd never been very good at making friends and didn't really have any, so it felt good to have someone to hang out with."

Dread filled my belly as I instinctively knew where Beck was going with his story.

"We used to hang out at his apartment and watch movies after we finished my studies. We'd make popcorn and sit on the couch and he'd put his arm around my shoulders. I liked it...it made me feel safe. Wanted. Like he really liked me," Beck murmured. "One afternoon we started wrestling around after I made a joke about him and something we were watching on the TV. We were both laughing and breathing hard by the time we were done and he was lying on top of me. I didn't even realize things had changed until he got really quiet and just stared at me. Then I felt him rubbing against me. It didn't feel bad exactly…just weird. He whispered my name and then he was touching my face, my lips. I was frozen. He kept grinding against me and I started to feel hot all over. I didn't know what was happening to me. I was scared and I said his name. He told me it was okay and then he was unzipping my pants and his."

Beck dropped his eyes and shook his head.

"I didn't know what to do, so I didn't do anything. He took my hand and put it between us. I was embarrassed, but he kept saying my name and telling me how good it felt…how good *I* felt. And then his hand was on me. I…I started doing to him what he was doing to me. And then it started to feel really good. We both…you know," Beck said awkwardly as his eyes lifted. I managed a nod even though inside I felt like I was going to throw up.

"Steven got off of me and started freaking out. Said what we'd done was a sin and that we would go to hell if we didn't ask for forgiveness. He just…he lost it. He dragged me to my knees on the floor and told me we had to pray together. I was so confused…and ashamed. I repeated everything he told me to say. I was convinced I'd go to hell if I didn't. Steven, he…he started to cry and tell me he was sorry. I didn't know what to do so I told him it was okay. That I'd liked being with him like that…because I did."

Color flooded Beck's cheeks. I knew it had been a hard admission to make and as tempted as I was to tell him I understood, I didn't want to interrupt him. I felt Brody's fingers clench tight around mine, but he too remained quiet.

"Steven took me home and told me we couldn't tell anyone. I agreed because I didn't want to upset him. I was supposed to meet him a few days later for another study session, but he canceled. He canceled a couple more times after that and then he told my grandmother he was too busy to continue them so she started looking for someone else. I was…I was so heartbroken because I thought we'd been friends. I called him, but he said we couldn't talk to each other anymore. I begged and pleaded with him, but he hung up on me. I saw him at church the following Sunday and managed to get him alone after the service. I began crying and telling him how much I missed him. He finally took pity on me and said we could hang out again, but just in the park. I was so happy," Beck whispered, his voice strained.

"But it wasn't the same as before. He didn't laugh or joke with me...didn't touch me at all. It was so...forced. I missed what we had. Everything else in my life was so ugly, but he'd been the one bright spot. I didn't want to lose that. So one day I convinced him to take me back to his house...I lied and told him my grandmother wasn't home and I'd forgotten my key so I couldn't get into the apartment. He agreed. He kept looking at me a certain way and I was sure he wanted things to be like they were..."

Beck wiped at his eyes and I saw the moisture on the back of his hand.

"I asked him if we could watch a movie. He only had the one couch so I knew he'd have to sit with me. During the movie, I kept moving closer to him. When our legs were touching, I looked at him. He looked so...pained. I..."

Beck's voice dropped off and he suddenly looked at Dr. Emory.

"It's okay, Beck, take your time."

Several long seconds passed before Beck continued, but he refused to look at us as he spoke. "I wanted him to like me again...to go back to the way things had been. So I touched him through his pants. He didn't move, didn't speak. I began rubbing him and he grabbed my hand. He told me we couldn't. It was a sin. But he didn't move my hand. I began rubbing him again and told him I wouldn't tell anyone. I thought he'd just touch me back like before." Tears began to fall unchecked down Beck's face. "It happened so fast...He pushed me down on the floor and then he was on top of me...in me. He kept telling me he was sorry. 'I'm sorry my beautiful boy.' He said it over and over again. It hurt so bad, but I didn't make a sound because a part of me didn't want him to stop...I didn't want to lose him. When it was over, he was so quiet. I thought he was going to make me pray with him again, but he didn't. He just kept mumbling something about losing everything and then he got up and went to the bathroom. I pulled up my pants and sat back down on the couch and waited for him, but he didn't come out. It was starting to get dark and I needed to get home so my grandmother wouldn't get mad so I went to look for him."

I could see Beck's breath ratcheting up as he remembered the rest of whatever had happened that day, but before I could say anything, Dr. Emory said, "Beck, look at me."

Beck snapped out his daze and looked at the man.

"Deep breaths, remember?" the man said gently.

Beck nodded and then went through some kind of pattern where he took several different measured breaths. The move seemed to help because he relaxed a little.

"Do you need to take a break?" Dr. Emory asked.

"No," Beck said. "I'd like to continue."

Dr. Emory nodded and then Beck was looking at me and Brody again. Inside I was dying for the little boy he'd been, but I couldn't help but admire the strength in his spine as he continued.

"I found him in the bathroom. He was naked and his hair was wet like he'd showered. There was blood all over him and the floor. His eyes were open and I knew he was dead. He'd slit his wrists with a razor blade. I just stood there, not knowing what to do. I'd done that to him. I'd killed him. I began telling him I was sorry over and over again until my throat hurt so bad I couldn't speak anymore. And then I ran."

The newfound understanding of why he'd said 'I'm sorry' during his nightmares did nothing to ease the bile that was creeping up the back of my throat. I shot Brody a glance and saw how pale he was.

Beck. We needed to hold it together for Beck.

I squeezed Brody's hand hard and was rewarded with a return squeeze. He was still with us.

"I ran the ten blocks home and told my grandmother Steven hadn't shown up in the park to meet me like he'd said he would. When his body was found a couple days later, no one suspected anything and I never told anyone what happened."

Silence fell across the room and I frantically tried to get control of my runaway emotions. I suspected Beck wasn't finished telling us his story, but I wanted so badly to slam my hands over my ears. That and gather Beck into my arms and never let go. I only half-listened as Dr. Emory asked Beck if he wanted to take a break. I didn't miss how Beck's hand shook as he reached for the bottle of water.

"Quinn, Brody, do either of you have questions for Beck or for me?" Dr. Emory asked.

I shook my head because I had no idea what to say. The things I wanted to tell Beck weren't questions. I just wanted to tell him how much I loved him and how fucking brave I thought he was.

Brody remained silent next to me so I could only assume he didn't have any questions either.

Dr. Emory nodded at Beck. "Continue whenever you're ready, Beck."

Beck nodded and put the water down. "Money was tight living with my grandmother and it got worse when she was hospitalized for pneumonia. She recovered, but the bills started piling up. Her memory started to get worse and she'd start to forget simple things like going to the grocery store. I tried to keep my brother and sister fed, but it was tough because there wasn't any money. My grandmother had threatened to let Children's Services take us because we were too much trouble, but I knew what would happen if they did."

"They'd break you up," Brody said softly when Beck didn't continue on his own.

Beck nodded. "I was worried that if my grandmother had to keep spending her money on us, she'd get rid of us like she'd said she would. I tried getting a job at the grocery store near our house, but the guy said 12 years old was too young and no one would hire someone under the age of 14. I didn't know what to do. After Steven...after Steven died, I kept going back to the park we used to meet at. Just for a few minutes each day...I guess I wanted to be close to him. Anyway, there was this guy there one day and he kept looking at me. It made me uncomfortable, but before I could leave, he approached me and offered me fifty dollars if I'd let him see me without my clothes. I said no and ran home, but that night I couldn't stop thinking about that fifty dollars...everything I could have bought for me and my brother and sister with that kind of money. I went back to the park the next day and waited. When he showed up, I was both scared and glad. He made the same offer and this time I said yes. I went with him to the bathroom. I asked for the money first and when he gave it to me, I did what he wanted and took my clothes off. He…he didn't touch me, just himself. He told me if I came back the next day, he'd give me another fifty. So I did."

Beck dropped his eyes again, but then forced them back up. It was something I noticed he'd been doing more of recently…maintaining eye contact.

"I met him a few more times, but then I didn't see him for a while. The money disappeared and I started to panic again. Then he was back in the park. This time he offered me a hundred bucks if I touched him. I wanted to say no, but when I'd had that money, my grandmother hadn't been so angry…I'd told her I'd gotten a job. So I did what the guy wanted. After that, things just spiraled and within a week I was giving him a blowjob. Then I was letting him fuck me. It went on for two months before he suddenly disappeared from the picture completely. I'd saved the money he'd given me, but it didn't last long. I kept going back to the park, but he never came back. I got so desperate, I started looking at some of the other men I'd seen there on more than one occasion. It didn't take me long to find one who looked at me the same way the first guy had."

I wanted to cry for Beck, but I managed to keep it together. I listened as he went on to describe the many ways he sold himself in the few months that followed until he'd inadvertently solicited an undercover cop. I hoped and prayed that was the end of it as he described being adopted by Cade and Rafe Barretti, but when he reached for his water bottle and took another sip before repeating the breathing pattern he'd done before, I knew it wasn't over.

Not by a long shot.

CHAPTER 23

BRODY

Nothing in my life had prepared me for this moment.
Nothing.

It was a unique brand of torture to sit and listen to the man you loved tell you stories about being repeatedly violated.

And to tell them in such a way that it was clear where he placed the blame…not on the adults who'd failed him over and over again, but on himself.

I wanted him to be done.

For me.

For Quinn who was going to end up breaking my hand with how hard he was squeezing it – a notion he surely shared since I was squeezing his just as hard.

But more than anything, I wanted Beck to be done for Beck. Because nothing I'd heard would change anything for me. Nothing I heard going forward would either.

Only, Beck needed to tell his story before he'd finally start to believe that Quinn and I didn't see him any differently. That our love for him was as strong and as endless as it had been from the moment we'd realized he was ours.

So I held back the urge to beg his doctor to stop all this and listened with all I was.

Because that was the least that Beck deserved.

"After my fathers adopted me, things got better for a while. But then I started having trouble in school...it was hard for me to focus. At home, I slept a lot and I struggled to interact with my family the way I had. It took a while, but by the time I was sixteen, I was diagnosed with depression. I was put on medication, but it took a while to stabilize me. Even after they got the dose right, I still had times where I'd struggle, so it was a constant battle. My schoolwork suffered and so did the few friendships I'd managed to establish. I become a loner... the quiet kid who'd rather sit at a lunch table by himself reading instead of hanging out with the cool kids. Things changed when I met Brad. He was a senior, I was a sophomore. I'd noticed him before, because he was really good-looking and popular, but I'd never interacted with him. I ran into him one day in the locker room after school. I'd forgotten something in my gym locker after gym class and he'd just finished working out – he was on the wrestling team. I was surprised when he started talking to me and even more surprised to find out he knew my name. It wasn't really common knowledge that I was gay and I knew he was straight because he had a girlfriend, so I was surprised when he seemed to be flirting with me."

Beck paused only long enough to take a sip of water before he capped the bottle and then began playing with the label. "I wasn't sure that was what he was really doing, but when I started to leave, he asked me if I needed a lift home. My apartment was within walking distance of the school, but I agreed anyway. But instead of taking me home, he asked if I wanted to go to his house to play video games. He said his parents were at work so we'd have the place to ourselves. I was nervous, but he was being so nice that I figured it would be okay. We played for a while and then he started telling me how cute he thought I was. He was touching my leg as he said it. He admitted that he'd had a crush on me for a while, but that because of wrestling, he had to pretend he was straight. I thought he might kiss me, but all he did was touch me and then he asked me to touch him. When he asked me to give him a blow job, all I could think about was the guys I'd sold myself to when I was a kid...but he was so different. He wasn't forcing me or looking at me like I was a piece of property. So I did it...and it wasn't bad. He took me home and asked to see me again. I'd go over to his house whenever his parents weren't around and we'd do the same thing each time. But eventually he wanted more than blow jobs. I liked him a lot and didn't want to lose him, so I let him fuck me."

Beck hesitated before he said, "I don't think he ever even noticed I never came."

I was reminded of our first encounter with Beck. His inexperience with kissing made more sense to me now. My guess was that in addition to not caring about Beck's pleasure, Brad hadn't bothered to kiss Beck either.

"I wasn't sure what to call him since he was still dating his girlfriend. He swore to me he wasn't having sex with her and I believed him. I started telling him stuff about my past...not the part about Steven, but the part about the guy in the park and everything that came after. He told me he was glad I'd gotten out of that situation. But a couple days later..."

My heart clenched as Beck's eyes welled up with tears. I watched helplessly as Dr. Emory handed him a box of tissues since Beck had already used the tissues from the dispenser next to the couch.

"He asked me to meet him in the gym locker room after school. Only he wasn't alone. He wanted me to...to service his friends. I didn't want to, but he told me if I didn't, he'd tell everyone in school I'd sold myself for money. Even though I didn't have any friends, I didn't want people to know about that. I tried to leave, but he wouldn't let me and I knew just by looking at him that it was going to happen whether I wanted it to or not. I was afraid of what they'd do if I didn't do what he wanted, so I did it. In between, he fucked me while his friends watched. Called me names, kept asking me if I liked it. I told him whatever he wanted to hear because I didn't want him to let his friends fuck me. They didn't," Beck added.

"When they were done, they just left me there and I never talked to Brad again. He and his friends graduated a couple months later so luckily I didn't have to see any of them again after that. But I started having trouble at home. I'd lash out at my fathers and my brother and sister, I started drinking. I was failing a few of my classes. My dads finally took me to see a therapist because they thought it was related to the depression. I'd never told them about Brad."

Beck sucked in a breath and he looked at Dr. Emory. "Can I take a break? I need to use the bathroom," he whispered.

Dr. Emory looked at him with sympathy and nodded. "Take your time."

I ached to get up and take Beck in my arms, but I knew if I did that, I wouldn't be able to let him go.

I waited until Beck had left the room before I let out a hiss and covered my eyes with my free hand. "Jesus Christ, I can't take this," I admitted.

Quinn pulled me up against him and I felt his lips skim my temple. I couldn't stop the tears that began to fall.

"He's going to be okay," Quinn murmured as he held on to me. "We're going to get him home and we're going to make sure he knows no one will ever touch him again."

I felt some tissues being placed in my hand and I sat up so I could wipe my eyes. I needed to be strong for Beck. I glanced at Quinn and saw he was dabbing at his eyes too.

To Dr. Emory I said, "Should we be doing anything differently?"

He shook his head. "You guys are doing perfectly. He's worked really hard to get to this point and you're giving him the space he needs to do this."

I wanted to ask how much worse this was going to get, but I didn't need to. My gut was telling me we hadn't even heard the worst of it.

We sat in silence as we waited for Beck to return. When he did, I could tell the hair over his forehead was damp which had me guessing he'd been splashing cold water on his face. He seemed more in control of himself, but I doubted it would last.

When he was seated again, he made a point of making eye contact with me and Quinn. His smile was wobbly, but it made me feel better. As bad as all this was, he was still hanging in there.

He was still with us.

"After I started my junior year, my dads found me a therapist. A man named Victor Colby. It was a long time before I trusted Victor enough to tell him everything. Brad, the prostitution, even Steven, eventually. Talking to him made me feel better, stronger. He was a younger guy and he didn't talk to me like I was a little kid. I actually got to a point where I was looking forward to our appointments. Life finally started to seem…normal. The depression wasn't as bad as it had been and I'd started to work harder in school to get my grades back. My dads were thrilled at the change."

Beck fell silent for so long that I was sure he wasn't going to continue. But he finally whispered "I didn't see it."

I closed my eyes because I knew what was coming. I wanted to scream in denial, but even if I'd been free to do so, I doubted anything would have come out because my throat was so tight it felt like I could barely breathe.

"It was the beginning of March and I was a few minutes late for my appointment because of an accident that had caused a traffic jam. Victor seemed really agitated with me…I apologized a couple of times, but when he started accusing me of doing it on purpose just to get a reaction out of him, I started to get nervous because he was a big guy. I got up to leave, but I didn't make it past the door before he grabbed me. He started saying all this stuff about how I'd been teasing him…that I'd told him the stories about all the guys I'd been with because I wanted him. He said…he said I was trying to do to him what I'd done to Steven."

A harsh sob escaped Beck's throat and it took every ounce of strength I had not to go to him.

"I thought maybe he was right so I told him I was sorry…that I hadn't meant to do that to him." Beck shook his head. "He turned me around and pushed me up against the wall – he was so strong that I couldn't get free. I begged him not to do it." Beck fell silent and wiped at his eyes.

"I trusted him," he whispered. "I told him things I hadn't told anyone else…I thought he cared about me."

Beck paused before saying, "After he was finished, he told me no one would believe me if I told. All he'd have to do was tell my fathers what I'd done to Steven and that would be it. I didn't tell anyone. He called my father that night and told him he couldn't be my therapist anymore because I'd become combative and obstinate and that I'd physically threatened him."

"Did your fathers believe him?" Quinn asked softly.

Beck nodded. "I didn't deny it and since I'd acted out with them a few times, I think they thought it was possible." Beck shook his head. "Everything fell apart after that. I couldn't function. I stopped going to school. I wouldn't eat, wouldn't talk. My fathers were desperately trying to find me a new therapist and the doctor who had been handling my medication upped my meds. Four days after Victor… after what happened in his office, I hung myself from a rafter in my room."

Bile rose in my throat and I dropped Quinn's hand so I could lean forward and cover my face with my hands. I couldn't stop the tears that slid down my face. I felt Quinn's hand on my back, but I knew he wasn't doing much better because I could hear him sniffling.

"I'm sorry," I whispered. I knew I needed to get it together for Beck's sake, but I couldn't get ahold of myself.

"It's okay, Brody," Dr. Emory said. "Why don't we take a break?"

I managed a nod, but couldn't move. I felt Quinn shift next to me until our bodies were touching and then his arm was around my shoulders. I didn't dare look up because I couldn't face Beck. But I didn't have a choice when I felt hands pushing mine away from my face. I looked up to see Beck standing above me, his eyes wet with tears.

"I'm sorry," I said harshly and then I dragged him to me until he was practically straddling my lap. His arms went around my neck and I felt sobs wrack his body as he clung to me. "I love you," I whispered to him. "So fucking much, Beck."

Beck nodded against my neck, but didn't say anything.

Quinn's arms surrounded us both and I heard him whispering in Beck's ear and felt him nodding against my neck some more, but after that, none of us talked for a while. When we'd both calmed down, I released Beck enough so he could put some space between us.

"I need to finish it, okay?"

I managed a nod and reluctantly released him. I wanted him to stay between me and Quinn, but I knew being on the opposite couch made it easier for him to focus on us and get his story out. I used the tissues Quinn handed me to wipe my face as Beck got settled on the other couch again. Several long seconds passed before Dr. Emory urged Beck to continue.

"My dad came home early and found me. He cut me down and got the rope off before I completely stopped breathing. I was taken to the hospital, but luckily there was no permanent damage. I was moved to the pysch floor a couple days later and I was in there for almost a month. I refused to speak to anyone about what had happened, but when I realized that not talking meant I'd spend even more time in there, I started telling everyone what they wanted to hear. When they released me, I went to whatever doctors my fathers wanted me to and said all the right things. I never told anyone about Victor or Steven… they thought I was struggling with the depression and the prostitution."

Beck took a few deep breaths to steady himself. "That spring, the company my father worked for held an open house to celebrate their move to a new building. There were lots of people there including most of my extended family as well as the men my father worked with…he works in security and most of his co-workers are bodyguards and stuff. It was my first real outing after being in the hospital and while I knew I wouldn't enjoy it, I pretended I was having a good time. A few minutes after we got there, I noticed a guy watching me from the other side of the room. I tried to ignore him, but I could feel his eyes on me wherever I was. The longer he watched me, the more panicked I got. I knew what he wanted…it was the same look Brad and his friends had had that day in the locker room. It was the same look Victor had given me. I wanted to scream at him to leave me alone, but in my mind I knew if he wanted me badly enough, he'd take me. I was so angry," Beck whispered, his voice growing harsh. "I wanted to hurt him. I wanted to go up to him and tell him I'd kill him if he touched me."

Beck shook his head. "But I knew I was powerless to stop him. It didn't matter that my parents were there, my family...my brain convinced me that the guy would take what he wanted, when he wanted it. This...this calmness settled over me as I accepted it. And then something changed. I can't really explain it, but I stopped seeing him as a threat. I kept remembering how Victor had accused me of teasing him to get what I wanted. And I started to wonder if I could do the same thing with the guy...turn the tables so I was the one in control. The one with power. Maybe I couldn't stop him from fucking me, but at least in some fucked up way, it would be my choice..."

Beck's eyes shifted to Dr. Emory and I saw the man nod. "It's okay, Beck."

Beck took a deep breath and said, "I approached the guy when he was standing by himself. I told him to meet me in the stairwell two flights up. Most of the party was on that floor so I knew we wouldn't be interrupted. The guy followed me up there. I began touching him, telling him how hot I thought he was. He was a lot bigger than me. He even carried a gun. But in that moment as I touched him, as I told him what I wanted to do to him, what I wanted him to do to me, I was the one with the power. And for the first time in my life, I felt in control of it. I blew him right there in my father's building and then I let him fuck me against the wall. And all I could think while it was happening was how good it felt to not be helpless anymore. To be able to choose what happened to me."

As warped as Beck's logic was, it made perfect sense to me. I risked a glance at Quinn and had no doubt he was thinking about the night Beck had approached him in the club.

"When the guy was finished, I left. He hadn't cared that I hadn't come and neither had I. I hadn't been with him to get off," Beck murmured. "A few weeks later I did the same thing with a guy who worked at a bookstore I used to frequent. Anytime I felt threatened by a guy, I turned the tables on him and became the hunter. It almost became a compulsion after a while. Sometimes I even got it wrong and a guy turned me down, but the humiliation was temporary...the need to stay in control wasn't."

"You said this happened whenever you felt threatened," Quinn said quietly. "That night in the club-"

His words dropped off and he looked at Dr. Emory.

"Dr. Emory knows what I did that night," Beck said. "That night was the first time I actively went looking for someone. I'd met Jax before when he'd come to Seattle to visit my dad. He was exactly the kind of guy I was afraid of so when I found out I would be spending the summer under his roof, I started to feel out of control again. I was afraid of what I'd do when I saw him...in my mind, I knew he loved his husband, but this other part was trying to convince me he would come after me. But I was scared of being found out if I was wrong – if I went after him and he turned me down, he'd tell my fathers."

Beck let out a harsh laugh. "I started all that because it made me feel in control and powerful, but it was all an illusion. Instead of being controlled by strangers, my own mind started playing tricks on me to the point that I couldn't make sense of anything."

He shook his head. "So the more I obsessed about interacting with Jax, the more helpless I began to feel. No man in sight, and I still felt like I had that night at my father's office party. I thought that if I could get my "fix" before I got to Dare, that it would help. And I figured I could go back to that club anytime I started to feel out of control at Dane and Jax's."

Beck smiled sheepishly. "But nothing could have prepared me for you," he said as his eyes settled on Quinn before shifting to me. "Or you." He held my gaze for a moment. "I'd never come with any of the guys I was with...sometimes I'd masturbate, but it wasn't very often because it reminded me of that first time with Steven and everything that had happened afterwards. And then you guys..."

Beck fell silent for a moment and he dropped his eyes. "I didn't know what to think after that night. I was so messed up...being with the two of you felt so good, but I convinced myself it was wrong. All those other guys...it's almost like it wasn't really sex with them, you know? I didn't have to feel anything at all besides the knowledge that what I was doing was my choice. But being with you guys was so much…more."

"So when you saw Dale attacking Lilah," I began.

"I saw myself," Beck whispered. "I saw Victor and Brad and all the guys who'd paid to use me…even the guys I'd pursued…because deep down I hadn't really wanted them. And I saw Lilah just standing there taking it because she knew she was powerless to stop it…"

When Beck's voice dropped off, I nodded in understanding. I didn't need any more explanation.

"I've been talking to Dr. Emory about my compulsion…it's not something that will just go away…he says it's a coping mechanism. He's given me some tools to try and deal with my fear, but it's going to take time."

Beck's eyes connected with me and Quinn as his voice grew firm. "But I won't ever act on it again, no matter what. I love you and I only want to be with you. What we have is worth fighting for and if I have to spend the rest of my life dealing with this thing, I will. As long as it means I'm still yours."

"Always," I said softly and I looked over to see Quinn nodding.

"You're ours, Beck. No matter what," he said firmly.

Tears flooded Beck's eyes and he nodded. We stood at the same time he did and met in the middle of the small office, our arms going around each other as naturally as if we'd been doing it our whole lives.

And I knew in that moment that was exactly what was ahead of us. Our whole lives.

CHAPTER 24

BECK

"Here," I heard Emma say as she approached me from behind and plopped down next to me on the porch step. I smiled at the sight of the kitten she was handing me. The other kitten was pressed against her chest.

They were the same kittens she'd handed me so long ago the morning after I'd arrived in Dare.

It seemed like a lifetime ago considering how much had changed.

"Wow, they're big," I said.

"Yeah, they don't need to be fed with bottles anymore, but Daddy says we need to handle them a lot so they're real used to people when they go to their forever home."

I nodded and cuddled the kitten. "Did you guys find them homes?"

Emma nodded. "Uncle Gray and Uncle Luke are adopting them for Ollie. But don't tell…it's a surprise for his birthday."

"My lips are sealed," I said softly.

I wasn't surprised when Ben appeared a moment later and dropped down next to his sister. I laughed when Ben said, "Cars."

I'd been around the kids enough to know that was Ben's way of asking his sister to play his favorite game with him. Ben had an obsession with Matchbox cars and his favorite thing to do was release them at the top of the bannister along the stairs leading to the second floor and see how far they got before flying off and hitting the wall or floor.

"Swirl," Emma said in exasperation. "I played cars with you this morning."

"Cars," Ben repeated and then he was pressing his head against his sister's arm. I knew she stood no chance against the cute little pout that spread across his chubby face.

"Fine," Emma said dramatically. I chuckled when she handed me the kitten before taking her brother's hand and stomping back into the house. As I nuzzled the kittens, Harley appeared from wherever she'd been off playing with Jax and Dane's dogs and began sniffing the furry bundles in my hands.

"Don't worry, you're not being replaced," I murmured and was rewarded with a sloppy kiss across my mouth. I laughed and used my sleeve to wipe away the line of dog drool. The sound of an engine caught my attention and my gut clenched in excitement.

My fathers had texted that they were on their way from the airport almost an hour ago, so they were due at Dane and Jax's any minute now. But the car that appeared in the driveway turned out to be Jax's police cruiser. I ignored the nervous flutter in my belly as I watched Jax get out of the car.

"Hey," Jax said as he began walking up the stairs. "This scene looks familiar," he said with a chuckle.

It was familiar, but luckily not a complete repeat of that morning when he'd come to my room to take the kittens from me. Back then, I'd been waiting for him to show some sign that would prove he was like all the other guys. Now, I didn't see that at all. No, I wasn't cured because there was still a small part of me that got nervous around the larger man, but it wasn't the same fear that left me feeling sick. I suspected that, over time, my fear of him would disappear altogether, just like it had with the male members of my extended family. And a lot of that had to do with Jax himself, because he'd been earning my trust from day one. Him and Dane both, as well as the other men who were becoming a fixture in my life.

"Your dads on their way?" Jax asked as he dropped down next to me on the step.

"Yeah, they'll be here any minute."

"Is this okay?" Jax asked as he glanced between us. I hadn't told him what I'd admitted to Quinn and Brody during my session, but I had no doubt he'd figured out how uncomfortable he made me. But instead of avoiding me, he was trying to interact with me more often. He never touched me, but he often made sure I was okay if it was just him and me. I hoped there'd come a point where I wanted him to feel free to hug me or pat me on the shoulder, but it was something I wanted to talk to Dr. Emory about first.

"Yeah," I said. "It's good."

Jax smiled and then he was petting Harley who'd stepped to his side so she could sniff him. Like me, my dog was making lots of progress in learning to trust again.

"I heard you talked to Dane about vet tech school."

I nodded. "He got me an appointment with an admissions counselor to see if my grades are good enough to apply."

"Have you told your fathers you're staying yet?"

"No," I admitted. "I wanted them to meet Brody and Quinn first and to see what I do at the CB Bar. I have lots of things I need to tell them."

Jax knew my fathers would be joining me at a therapy session and I had no doubt he knew it was to talk about a lot more than me staying in Montana. But he didn't press the issue. He merely said, "Make sure they see *you*, Beck."

I nodded because I knew what he meant. My fathers would instinctively see the old me...the me who'd decided death was a better option than facing the truth. I needed to show them I wasn't that same person anymore. The person they'd be leaving behind was a man with a future, not a child running from his past.

I was saved from having to say anything when we heard an approaching car. Jax and I stood at the same time. "Here, I'll take them," Jax said softly as he took the kittens from me. I smiled and hurried down the stairs. I couldn't help the tears that welled in my eyes at the sight of both of my fathers climbing out of their rental car.

"Beck," my father, Rafe, said, a smile stretching across his lips as he hurried to me and wrapped his arms around me.

"Dad," I whispered as I gave up on the attempt to keep my tears at bay. I was in my father, Cade's arms next and predictably, he held me just a little bit longer. I drew on his strength and tried not to think about what was coming...not later today when I introduced them to my lovers and not tomorrow when I had my second soul-baring session.

"Glad you're here," I said to him just before he released me.

"Me too," he said softly. He released me back to my other father so he could go greet Jax. An arm went around my shoulder as my father and I watched Cade and his old friend embrace.

It was the calm before the storm, but hopefully it would be one of the last storms I'd ever have to battle.

And if there were any more coming my way, at least now I knew I'd never have to face them alone again.

~

Watching my fathers cry would surely go down as one of the worst moments in my entire life. Being the one who'd put them in that position was right behind it.

My insides felt raw as I used my already damp sleeve to wipe at my face. I'd finished talking more than a minute ago and neither man would look at me. Like when I'd told my story to Brody and Quinn, my fathers were on the couch across from me so I'd gotten to see the play of emotions across their faces as I'd spoken.

Whenever I'd been able to actually look at them, that is.

Most of my story had had the same amount of detail that I'd shared with my lovers, which had been humiliating on multiple levels. Like the fact that I'd never had an orgasm when I'd let all those guys fuck me. But Dr. Emory had said it was important not to keep secrets anymore, so I'd told them everything. And they'd needed to understand what had driven my compulsion...that it hadn't ever been about sex. Which meant telling my fathers everything.

Including the way I'd met Brody and Quinn.

I hoped like hell it wouldn't color their impression of my men because the first meeting between my parents and my boyfriends had gone surprisingly well. After they'd arrived, my fathers and I had sat down with Jax and Dane for coffee as I'd told them about my work and about Brody and Quinn. We hadn't talked about therapy beyond the fact that we'd be meeting with my therapist the following day. After catching up, I'd taken my fathers to the CB Bar where Brody and Quinn had been waiting for us. My fathers had been polite, but reserved. Quinn and Brody had seemed a little nervous at first, but they hadn't changed how they acted around me.

Which meant they'd often touched me or dropped random kisses on my mouth or temple. I wasn't sure if that had helped or hurt their cause at first, but I'd reveled in it. Every time they did it, it was a reminder that all the shit I'd dropped on them a week earlier hadn't changed anything.

Quinn and Brody and I hadn't talked much about the things I'd shared and I suspected it would be a while before we did. I'd mentioned to them both that Dr. Emory had offered to have more joint sessions or even individual ones with them if they were struggling with their feelings. The fact that both men had agreed was yet another sign that they weren't jumping ship.

Although the impending arrival of my fathers had still had me on edge, I'd felt more at ease than I ever had in my entire life. I was…happy.

Such a simple word and yet it was changing everything for me. Colors seemed brighter, food tasted better…the list was endless. I was finally living my life and I no longer cared if I was "normal" or not. Normal was relative. Many would say my relationship with two men at the same time wasn't normal. My thoughts on the matter…so be it. I would choose them over some predefined notion of "normal" any day of the week.

My men and I had spent much of the last week talking about the future, including whether or not it made sense to live at the ranch in Quinn's cottage. In the end, we'd decided we'd need to move at some point. Both to get something bigger and so that Brody could be closer to work and I could be closer to the city in case I did decide to pursue a degree as a vet tech. It would mean a short commute for Quinn, but he was fine with that. I'd talked to Callan about possibly continuing my education and he'd been very supportive and had told me I'd have a job at the CB Bar for as long as I wanted it.

"Mr. and Mr. Barretti, do you have any questions for your son or for me?" Dr. Emory asked when the worst of my fathers' tears had subsided. My father, Cade, had his arms wrapped around my other father. They separated and wiped at their faces with tissues and then Cade was holding out his hand.

I got up and went to him and wasn't surprised when he tugged me down between them. Fresh tears fell as they enveloped me in a tight embrace and told me they loved me and that everything would be okay. We stayed like that for several minutes until we'd calmed.

"What's next for Beck?" Cade asked Dr. Emory. "And us?"

I understood my father's question. He was feeling rudderless and had no idea where to go from here.

"Beck and I have agreed to continue to meet for the foreseeable future so he can work through some of the feelings he still has about everything and to work on finding healthy ways to deal with his stress. As for you and your husband, I'd like to suggest you come see me a couple more times, first without Beck and then with him, to talk about how you're feeling. Hearing news like this…it's a lot to process and many of the emotions you are feeling now will be amplified in the coming days as well as new emotions surfacing."

I felt Cade nod as he kept his arm around my shoulder. "We'd appreciate that," he said. "Will you be able to help us find a therapist in Seattle?"

I stiffened at that and forced myself to pull away from my fathers. I cast a glance at Dr. Emory who nodded.

"Um, I wanted to talk to you about that," I murmured. "I've decided to stay in Dare. I love Brody and Quinn and I want to build a life with them. This…this place…" I stammered as I tried to collect myself. "I fit here," I whispered. "I love you both and I love our family, but here I-"

I could feel the tears starting to build all over again and frustration coursed through me because I'd practiced my little speech over and over again so I wouldn't sound like a blubbering, emotional mess.

"It's okay, Beck," Cade said softly. "I meant could Dr. Emory help me and your father find a therapist in Seattle. We know you're not coming home with us."

Surprise shot through me. "How?" I asked, completely dumbfounded.

Rafe put his arm around me. "We knew the second we saw you with your men. You've come alive, Beck. Your father and I have been dreaming of seeing that for so long…" His voice cracked and I wasn't surprised when Cade's hand found his behind my shoulders.

"We've only ever wanted to protect you, son," Cade said. "But all we ended up doing was drowning you."

"No-" I said, shaking my head, but my father put his hand on my face to stop the motion.

"We made a lot of mistakes, Beck. We thought by knowing where you were every moment of every day…" He paused before saying, "We were doing that for us. But what you needed was freedom to figure things out. You needed to know that we trusted you."

"I broke your trust," I began, but Cade shook his head.

"Not possible. You're our son. We just…" His eyes connected briefly with my father's. "We just felt so helpless…like we'd failed you."

"No," I said, shaking my head again. Tears stung my eyes and then I was being pulled against his chest.

"We'll figure it all out, Beck." I felt him press a kiss against the top of my head. "You, your brothers, your sisters…you're the best thing that's ever happened to me and your father. You know that, right?"

I nodded because that was all I could do.

"I'm glad you were there that day, Dad," I whispered.

My father stiffened slightly and then he was holding me tighter. I had no doubt he knew exactly what day I was talking about. It was the day we'd never talked about because we'd both wanted to forget. But I didn't want to forget anymore. That day had led me here.

"Me too, son," my father murmured against my head. "Me too."

EPILOGUE

BECK

"And Vin is the oldest brother," Brody said as his fingers tightened around mine.

I hid my smile as I said, "Right."

A satisfied grin drifted across his handsome face.

"He was up all night studying," Quinn drawled as his arm around my shoulders drew me even closer to him. We were following my fathers and the rest of my family up the driveway of my Uncle Dom and Uncle Logan's house. With the dozens of cars in the driveway, we'd had to park farther away since we were the last to arrive. And from the looks of how many vehicles were there, I knew it would be a full house.

"Fuck you, Quinn," I heard Brody say, though there was no anger in his voice.

"Maybe later, baby," Quinn said with a laugh. "That is, if Beck can sneak out of his room again…and we can find something to gag you with."

Brody shot him an irritated look, but as soon as he looked away, he smiled. Not to mention the color that flooded his face.

I had no doubt he was thinking of the night before.

We'd arrived at my fathers' apartment earlier in the day after making the journey from Dare to pack up my stuff. It was something I'd discussed with them just before they'd left. They'd offered to pack up my things and bring them out to Dare themselves, but I'd wanted the opportunity to say goodbye to all the members of my family. It was also my way of saying goodbye to the old Beck.

Brody and Quinn had readily agreed to make the journey with me. So two days ago, we'd packed up Quinn's truck, grabbed Harley and hit the road. We'd spent the night in a hotel so we'd be fresh when we arrived in Seattle. My fathers had greeted us with open arms, but as soon as they'd found out we had plans to stay at a nearby hotel, they'd nixed that idea and had informed us we'd be staying with them. I hadn't missed the smirk on my father, Rafe's face as Cade had made that particular announcement. But before I could say anything, Cade had shown us to the guest room and declared it Brody and Quinn's room. And then he'd told them I'd be staying in my room.

When I'd tried to intervene, Cade had pointedly asked my lovers if they had a problem with that. From the looks on their faces, they most certainly had, but both had stood before him like little kids and politely shaken their heads. I'd sworn I'd even heard Brody call my father, "sir."

Once we were alone, I'd asked my father if he was serious. He'd merely smiled, slung his arm around my shoulder, and said, "Welcome home, Beck."

So Quinn, Brody and I had had to resort to sneaking around. I'd gone to their room well after midnight and while Brody had insisted we couldn't make love in my fathers' house, it hadn't taken much to convince him that we most definitely could. Quinn and I had had a lot of fun making Brody see the error of his ways, but by the end just before Quinn had slid into him, he'd had to cover Brody's mouth with his hand to keep him from announcing to the world just exactly what we were up to. We'd taken turns fucking Brody until he'd been an incoherent mess and by the time I'd come, I'd been buried deep inside his body and Quinn had been balls deep inside of me. We'd taken advantage of the huge shower in the guest bathroom before I'd reluctantly snuck back to my own room. I hadn't mentioned to either man that I'd run into my father, Rafe, in the hallway on my way back to my room. Or that he'd merely wrapped his arms around me and wished me a goodnight before he'd returned to his and my father's room.

We'd spent most of today packing up my things. Since I didn't need the furniture from my room, there wasn't a ton of stuff that we needed to get back to Dare. It would all fit in the back of Quinn's truck with no problem.

It had been surreal to start the process of cleaning out my room. In many ways, it had felt like I was cleaning up the remnants of my past. It had been almost a month since my fathers had visited Dare and things had been moving quickly ever since. I'd been accepted into a vet tech course and was set to start in a little over a week. Quinn, Brody and I had found a decent-sized house halfway between Dare and Missoula and were planning to move in when we got back to Dare in a few days.

I'd been talking to my fathers via video chat several times a week, but my daily check-ins were a thing of the past. Now if I texted my fathers, it was because I wanted to, not because I had to. Dr. Emory had helped them find a therapist in Seattle and while they didn't share the details of their visits with me, I'd seen improvement over the weeks as I talked to them. They didn't look as tired and as pained as they had early on when we'd chatted. More importantly, they didn't look at me anymore like they used to so often in the past...like they were wondering how I *really* was when I said I was fine. For my part, I'd learned that I needed to be able to share everything with them. That meant, when I had a bad day, I told them so. It meant not hiding my feelings from Brody and Quinn, either. Fortunately, bad days were the exception these days.

"I wasn't studying," Brody said. "I was just refreshing my memory. We need to make a good impression."

I laughed at that. "Just remember, if you need help with remembering who's who, ask for Matty."

Both men chuckled. I'd told them the night before about the little boy who was best friends with one of our family's youngest members, Leo Devereaux. Matty was the resident expert on who was who in our family and had been tapped on more than one occasion to help newcomers navigate the muddy waters of our unique family tree.

"He's the one who will be hanging out with the half-naked kid, right?" Quinn asked. "Leo."

"Right," I said.

"Looks like I'm not the only one who was doing a little refreshing last night. And here I thought you were in the bathroom last night for a half an hour for a whole other reason," Brody said. The comment earned him a swipe from Quinn's hand, which my man easily dodged.

A moment later, Brody's cell phone rang and all three of us came to a jarring stop as he dug it out of his pocket. I held my breath as I waited for him to answer, but as soon as his face fell, I glanced at Quinn. It had been nearly two months since Brody's brother had shown up in Dare with his cryptic warning that Brody might be in danger. Thankfully, no threat had ever materialized and all three of us were able to relax a bit more, but the fact that he hadn't heard from Nathan was troubling Brody more than he wanted to admit. So much so, that he'd tracked down the number for his brother's campaign headquarters and left a couple of messages asking Nathan to call him. When he hadn't, Brody's disappointment had been a living thing.

Every once in a while, we'd see a story on the news or on the internet about Nathan's campaign and there would be pictures or footage of the man, but while that assured us he was alive, we could also see he wasn't doing well, physically. Even reporters had commented on the candidate looking thinner and run down.

I'd actually talked to my father, Cade, the night before about the situation to get his opinion since it tore me up to know how much Brody was suffering. My father had expressed concern for Brody, Quinn and me, but I'd assured him that Jax was monitoring the situation and that Brody had promised he'd let Jax know if he saw, heard or even felt like something was off. That had appeased my father, but in terms of Nathan, he'd said if the man wasn't willing to seek help either through the authorities or through private means, there wasn't much that could be done.

But that didn't stop Brody from racing to answer his phone every time it rang.

When Brody hung up the phone, he looked at us and just shook his head. He held out his hand to me and I automatically took it, squeezing his fingers. "He's okay," I murmured softly.

Brody nodded and then forced a smile to his lips. "Yeah, I know he is." As we got moving again, Brody seemed to relax and I knew he'd managed to shake off his melancholy.

For now.

As we neared the large house, the familiar sight of the kids out front along with a passel of dogs and a sleek white cat made my heart clench. I hadn't been to a lot of family dinners because I'd often been too down to make the long trip to the San Juan Islands, but I had fond memories of the ones I'd been able to attend. Even though I'd felt like an outsider, I'd still enjoyed watching the people I loved come together and share the goings on in their lives.

"You okay?" Quinn asked me as Brody's fingers tightened on mine.

I nodded, not surprised that they'd both sensed the change in me. "I'm going to miss this," I admitted.

Neither man tried to comfort me with words, but Quinn pulled me to him long enough that he could kiss my temple and Brody could brush his lips over my knuckles as he pulled our joined hands up to his mouth.

But even as I watched first the dogs race towards us, then the kids, I knew as long as I was exactly where I was in this moment, between my two men, I was home.

Cade

Warmth flooded my system as I watched one of my son's men, Quinn, wrap his arm around Beck's waist as soon as he reached him. Beck had been talking to his cousin Tristan, and one of Tristan's boyfriends, Brennan, but he paused long enough to accept the soft kiss Quinn placed on his lips. Within minutes, all four were laughing about something and then Brody was joining them. Seeing my son surrounded by so much love…and seeing him return that love was a balm to my soul.

To say that Rafe and I had fallen apart after Beck had told us the truth about everything that had happened to him was an understatement like no other. We'd managed to keep it together for Beck's sake, but as soon as we'd dropped him off at the ranch after the therapy session, we'd driven around just long enough to find a secluded spot and then we'd held each other as we'd cried.

And raged.

In that moment, I'd never wanted anything more than to hunt down every man who'd ever laid a finger on my son. To know he'd been repeatedly violated even after his father and I had given him what we'd thought would be a better life had ripped a hole in me so wide that I was certain it would never heal. The therapist Rafe and I had begun to see had had lots of suggestions about how to cope with the trauma as well as blanket statements about it not being our fault, but so far none of that had made me feel even remotely better.

What *had* made me feel better was tracking down one of the men who'd used my son like he was nothing more than garbage.

I'd suspected right away who the man had been who Beck had been talking about at my office party. It wasn't because I'd noticed his interaction with Beck that day, but when Beck had mentioned the encounter taking place in the stairwell, I'd been reminded of seeing the man coming out of the stairwell looking flushed. His eyes had connected briefly with mine where I'd been standing at the buffet table and I hadn't missed how he'd quickly looked away. I'd called out to him to ask him if was okay because while we hadn't exactly been friends, we'd worked together often enough that we exchanged friendly conversation whenever we saw one another. He hadn't responded and I hadn't seen him at the party after that. Three days later, I'd been informed that he'd resigned.

With a name to finally go with the faceless man who'd violated my son – and that was exactly what I considered it because no matter what Beck said, he'd been seventeen at the time and that fucker would have known better than to go after my child – I'd finally had a physical source to let all my rage out on. I'd known that if left alone with him, I'd end up killing him, so I'd taken my brother-in-law, Jagger, with me to make sure I didn't do something that would land me in prison. The man, for his part, hadn't even tried to deny it, nor had he fought back when I'd let my fists fly. It had been wholly unsatisfactory and the rage had continued to consume me. I was hiding it well from others, but my husband knew me too well and while he hadn't judged me for my actions, he'd reminded me that everything going forward was about Beck and his future.

I knew he was right, but I'd never been someone to let justice go unserved.

Rafe and I had discussed asking Beck to go to the police about Victor Colby and we'd even talked to Dr. Emory about it, but in the end, it was Beck's doctor who'd been the deciding factor. Beck was finally on the path to recovery. Pressing charges against Victor would mean a trial and exposing Beck's past as well as the men he'd pursued in an effort to maintain his sanity. But just because we couldn't go after Victor the traditional way, it didn't mean all bets were off.

Which was why when Ronan Grisham glanced my way, I held his gaze until he got my silent message and separated from the group of people he'd been talking to.

"Everything okay?" the man asked when he reached me.

"You have a minute to talk?" I asked. Something in my voice must have caught his attention because he merely nodded and then he was nodding at one of the men who worked for him, Memphis Wheland, and then we were all headed toward my brother-in-law, Dom's, study. I'd debated asking Ronan for his help, but I knew the trauma surgeon could accomplish things I couldn't. I'd known both men for more than a year now and while Ronan's group of men were supposedly in the personal security business like me, I'd seen firsthand that they did much more than that. And while I had countless resources at my disposal to go after the worst of the worst, I was forced to work on the right side of the law.

Ronan and his men didn't have that limitation.

Neither man spoke as I shut the door. "I need your help," I said quietly. "You both know my oldest son."

Both nodded. Memphis, who also happened to be in a relationship with Beck's cousin Tristan, and Tristan's best friend Brennan, said, "Tristan's been talking to him on the phone the past few weeks. He said Beck's doing really well and that he's moving to Dare to be with the guys he brought with him today."

I nodded. "Quinn and Brody." I hesitated as I tried to figure out how to say what I needed to say. "Eighteen months ago, my son was being treated for depression by a therapist named Victor Colby. Beck recently told his father and me that Victor raped him and then threatened to reveal some stuff that happened to him in his past if he didn't keep quiet about it."

Ronan and Memphis both stiffened. Anger suffused Memphis's face and Ronan's jaw went tight.

"Victor called me and Rafe that night to tell us that he could no longer have Beck as a patient because Beck threatened him physically. We…we believed him," I admitted as shame curled through me.

"You couldn't have known," Ronan said softly.

I shook my head because it didn't matter. I *should've* known. "I can't ask Beck to consider pressing charges because his past will be exposed. He's just now starting to get better…"

Memphis nodded and then glanced at Ronan who also nodded. "We'll take care of it," Memphis said. "Would you like a temporary or permanent solution?"

I knew what he was asking me and while a part of me wanted to know that Victor Colby would never walk this earth again, it was a line I couldn't cross.

For Beck's sake.

"Temporary," I finally responded. I didn't know what all that entailed, but I had no doubt whatever these men did, Victor would never hurt another innocent kid again. "There's one more thing."

"Shoot," Memphis said.

"One of the men Beck is with, Brody Wilder, has a twin brother who's making a run for senate."

"Nathan Wilder?" Ronan asked.

I nodded. "How did you know?"

"He's made a name for himself. His father was a staunch opponent of gay marriage. Nathan was expected to follow in his footsteps, but he turned the tables on everyone, including some of his most powerful constituents and backed it instead. He's changed positions on other policies too," Ronan explained.

"Well, it sounds like he's pissed someone off who's fighting back with more than just words," I said. "He showed up in Dare to let Brody know that Brody's name came up too…I guess the two have been estranged for some time."

"Has there been any threat against Brody?" Memphis asked.

I shook my head. "My friend Jax is a deputy for the Dare Police Department…he's been keeping an eye on things. But Brody and Nathan aren't in touch and Brody's worried about his brother…which means my son is worried."

"We'll look into it," Ronan said without hesitation.

"I'm getting the impression Nathan doesn't want anything to threaten his senate run. The publicity from hiring any kind of security alone could raise a lot of questions."

Memphis smiled. "We can be…discreet."

Ronan glanced at the man and shook his head. "Consider it taken care of, Cade. Your son will get his perfect future."

I nodded. The idea that my son would never again have to suffer the way he had for so many years had tears threatening to fall, but I managed to keep them at bay. "Thank you," I said softly.

Memphis gave me a light punch on the arm. "That's what family does, right?"

I laughed, finally feeling a little bit lighter than I had in a long time.

"It does." While I hadn't initially been sure about these men being enfolded into our family, after everything we'd been through in the last year, I was beyond grateful that they had.

"One last thing," I said as we headed for the door.

Both men stopped to look at me.

"I could use a little help initiating Quinn and Brody into the family."

Ronan and Memphis chuckled. While Ronan hadn't been put through the ringer when he'd started attending family dinners with his husband, Memphis hadn't been so lucky since he was dating not one, but two members of the Barretti family.

"Leave it to me," Memphis said with a smirk. "And here I thought this evening would be boring."

I laughed and slapped him on the back just before I followed him from the room.

It was time to find my son so I could watch him embark on this next chapter in his life.

The End

Scroll to the next page for a Sneak Peek of Vincent & Nathan's story

SNEAK PEEK

DEFIANCE (THE PROTECTORS, BOOK 9) (M/M)

PROLOGUE

VINCENT

"No," I said without hesitation as I studied the men before me. I'd talked to Ronan Grisham on the phone a couple of times, but Memphis was new. Of course, I already knew as much about him as I needed to though, since I'd done my homework on him as soon as Ronan had asked me to fly to Seattle for a meeting. I could have told them before I'd even left my place in West Virginia that I had no interest in taking on any job they might offer me, but truth be told, the little group Ronan had going on here had intrigued me. I suppose I had Ethan Rhodes to thank, or blame, for that, depending on how you looked at it.

I'd met Ethan Rhodes six months earlier when Ronan had asked me to take a look at a damaged phone in Ethan's possession, which had had evidence of a murder on it. From the moment I'd met the doctor, I'd been transported back to a time in my life that I'd had no wish to return to. It wasn't that Ethan had necessarily looked like David, it was more about the way he'd carried himself. He'd had an air of vulnerability about him, but there'd been a fierceness in him as well. It was the reason I'd helped Ethan go after his lover, Cain Jensen, when he'd feared the man's life was in danger.

For all the struggles David had gone through in our final year together, he'd been unfailingly loyal...and protective. He hadn't always been able to find the strength to fight for himself, but if there'd been even the slimmest chance I was in danger, he'd been ready to stand by my side, guns blazing.

It was that memory that Ethan had stirred in me that'd had me doing something I hadn't done since I'd lost David to his demons.

I'd given a shit.

And that wasn't a good thing.

Not in my line of work.

But I'd done it anyway and I'd started wondering about the kind of work Ronan and his men did. I'd never actually met Ronan - our relationship had been more of a friend-of-a-friend kind of thing. He'd cashed in a favor and I'd paid one off.

It should have been a simple transaction.

I should have held up my end of the deal and been done. But then Cain Jensen had called me and asked me to stay with Ethan while he took care of the man's vengeful ex once and for all. I'd been on the cusp of saying no, but I'd heard that thread of desperation in the young man's voice.

And I'd known what he was feeling.

That need to do anything and everything to protect that one person in your life who completed you...who was your reason for everything you did. Every breath you took, every battle you fought... going on day after endless day, even after you lost them because without you, there was no one left to keep the memory of that person alive.

It was the only reason I'd been able to get up every morning after David had been taken from me.

And despite the bullet he'd put in his own brain, he had been *taken*. The man I'd fallen in love with when I'd still been in my teens had started to disappear before my very eyes the moment he'd gotten that notice from the army that'd said his service to his country was no longer valued.

The same notice I'd gotten.

And all because David and I had made the grievous error of falling in love with each other.

"You're not even going to hear us out?" Memphis asked.

We were sitting in his living room. A white cat had taken up residence on my lap the second I'd sat down. When Memphis had gone to move her, I'd waved him off. I'd take the presence of an animal over a human any day of the week.

I had no interest in hearing him out, though. But I decided to humor him and merely nodded my head at him. I would still be telling him no, since I had absolutely no interest in playing bodyguard to anyone, since that would mean having to spend more than five minutes in another person's company.

Yeah, no thanks.

"His name is Nathan Wilder. His brother is in a relationship with the son of a friend of ours and another man," Ronan said.

I remained quiet, though I was intrigued by the concept of three men in an equal relationship with one another. Memphis, himself, was in the same kind of relationship, though I hadn't met either of his young lovers. The research I'd done on him had just been the basics including financials, employment, and family history, but I could tell from the handful of pictures I'd seen of him and two good-looking young men in their twenties, that what they had between them was the real deal. As someone who was pushing fifty, I'd seen a lot in my time, but a ménage relationship that appeared to be about more than just sex was a new one, even for me.

"He's received some threatening emails and it sounds like there's a chance the assailant has taken it to the next level. Brody, that's Nathan's twin, was mentioned in some of the emails, but we suspect that was more to rattle Nathan than anything else," Memphis explained.

The assailant sounded like a smart individual...psychological warfare made a man an easier target. The stress alone of knowing his twin might be at risk would have had a lasting impact on this Nathan guy. Wear a guy down enough mentally, and he'd be an easy target in the long run.

"We were hoping you could check it out…sit on him for a bit and see what you can find," Memphis continued.

Curiosity got the best of me and I said, "Why me? From what I've seen, your little operation here has plenty of qualified muscle."

Ronan and Memphis exchanged a brief glance. Ronan finally said, "We think your skill-set and contacts would give you unique access and insight."

If Ronan hadn't said the words with a measure of hesitation, I would have thought he was sucking up to me. But the fact that he'd almost seemed reluctant to voice his reasoning had me straightening from where I'd been leaning back against the couch. "How so?"

The men looked at each other again. It was almost comical…like they were afraid to say whatever it was that was on their minds.

"Nathan is running for Senate-"

"No," I said simply and then I gently pushed the cat off my lap.

As I climbed to my feet, Ronan murmured, "He needs help, Vincent."

"Not my problem," I responded as I stepped past him. Irritation went through me as I thought about how hesitant both men had been.

Which meant they knew about my hatred of all things government.

Everett.

Fucking busybody. He'd known exactly what he was sending me into when he'd encouraged me to take the meeting. No, I hadn't made the decision to meet Ronan based solely on him, but between him and my curiosity about what kind of group would go to such lengths to protect a complete stranger like Ethan Rhodes for no other reason than it was the right thing to do, I'd climbed onto the private jet Ronan had sent for me with the expectation that at the very least, I'd get Everett off my back about the whole damn thing.

"Vincent-"

"I don't give a fuck what Everett told you about me," I snapped as I turned to look at both men. "You want to protect this guy, *you* go right ahead. But you sure as shit don't want me doing it because one less politician is a win in my book!"

"Memphis?"

The sound of a man's voice, along with a rhythmic knock on the front door, had me stopping my forward movement.

"In here," Memphis called.

"Sorry, I heard voices, but I figured maybe you didn't hear me knocking," a man said as he rounded the corner from the front hallway. He was heavily built and in his early forties with a bald head. I stilled as I realized I knew him.

"No problem, Dom. We were just finishing up," Memphis said.

"Tristan forgot some sheet music at our apartment..."

The man's voice dropped off as his eyes fell on me.

"Major St. James?"

"Dominic Barretti," I murmured.

I felt my heart constrict painfully in my chest as Dom saluted me. It was something he'd done the few times I'd seen him after my discharge from the army. And it was something he *shouldn't* be doing based on the type of discharge I'd received. While I knew it was a sign of respect on his part, it still cut me to the core.

I couldn't bring myself to salute him back, but luckily, he didn't maintain the position long. He strode forward and held out his hand. As soon as I took it, he leaned in and clapped his hand on my back. I wasn't one for hugs, but Dom wasn't just some guy off the street.

Not even close.

There weren't a lot of people who'd stood by me after the shit that had gone down with the army, but Dom had.

And he'd taken it a step further.

He'd offered me something, both before I'd lost David and after, that I hadn't had after the army had shattered my entire world.

I just wished like hell I'd taken him up on it.

"What are you doing here?" he asked as a wide smile passed over his lips.

I had no idea how to answer him. I knew enough about Dom to know he ran his business legit and I was anything but.

"We asked Vincent to help us out on the Wilder case," Ronan announced without hesitation.

Dom nodded and walked farther into the room, handing Memphis a folder, presumably the sheet music he'd mentioned.

"How do you guys know each other?" I asked, still completely caught off guard that Ronan's group of vigilantes would have ties to Dom's aboveboard security business.

"My husband and I met Ronan last year when one of his men began seeing our oldest son, Eli. And we met Memphis right after that. He's in a relationship with Logan's and my son and our nephew," Dom explained.

"Tristan and Brennan aren't actually related," Memphis clarified. "Brennan's brother and his husband are friends of Dom and Logan's family."

"I'll take your word for it," I said, smiling despite myself.

"Cade will be so glad to know you're helping out Nathan," Dom said. "Beck is worried sick about Brody who's worried about Nathan…"

God, I needed a fucking whiteboard to keep up. "Wait, Cade… Cade Gamble?" I asked.

Dom smiled. "Yep…except it's Barretti now. He's married to my brother."

"Cade Gamble is married?"

I couldn't wrap my head around that. While I'd known Cade was gay when I'd met him and Dom while we were stationed in the Middle East, I'd also known him to be a player…to the extreme. The fact that he was married, and with a kid no less, was blowing my mind.

"Yep. Five kids too," Dom said with a laugh. "You should stop by and say hi."

Part of me actually wanted to take him up on the offer, but the other part…the part that still mourned David even after all the years that had gone by, sent silent warnings to my brain not to get involved. I'd had the chance for a different life, but I'd blown it.

I'd chosen wrong.

And it was too fucking late to do anything about it.

But I couldn't discount what Dom had said. "Tell me about Cade's son," I said.

Dom sobered and then he glanced at Ronan and Memphis. "May I?" he asked as he motioned to the couch. Both men nodded. I went to sit in an armchair because I could tell just by looking at the expression on Dom's face that whatever he had to tell me was not going to be easy.

"Beck is nineteen…almost twenty, actually," Dom began. "Cade and my brother, Rafe, adopted Beck and his brother and sister when Beck was twelve. Beck has struggled with some mental health issues over the years, but we didn't know until this past summer what was driving some of the behavior. He's finally in a good place, but with the threat against Brody's brother, Beck and both his men are feeling the strain. The mention of Brody in some of the emails Nathan received has made things even harder, especially on Beck."

My eyes shifted to Memphis and Ronan briefly before they fell back on Dom. When his eyes met mine, I felt anger settle over me.

But it wasn't directed at him.

It was directed at me.

David and I'd had a chance to have a man like Dom in our corner, but we'd been naïve enough back then to think that the country we'd served would step up and make things right.

Now David was dead and I'd served my country in a different way.

A way that would have shamed David.

I got up and went to Dom and extended my hand. He immediately stood up and shook it, though he looked both confused and surprised.

"You had my back when no one else did," I said. "I've got your nephew's."

As much as the idea of going back to the world that I'd fought so long and hard to escape sickened me, I knew that was no longer a factor in any of this. I didn't give a shit about Nathan Wilder or whatever bullshit he wanted to sell to the American people so they'd give him the power he needed to push his own personal agenda, but I did want to do something that might have David looking down on me with pride instead of shame.

I turned to look at Ronan and Memphis. "If I do this, I'm doing it my way."

Both men nodded. I turned to leave, but then thought better of it and paused long enough to say, "After this, lose my number. It'll be better for all of you that way."

ABOUT THE AUTHOR

Dear Reader,

I hope you enjoyed Beck, Quinn and Brody's story. For those of you wondering if Nathan will get his own story, the answer is yes, but his story will be part of my *Protectors* series.

    As an independent author, I am always grateful for feedback so if you have the time and desire, please leave a review, good or bad, so I can continue to find out what my readers like and don't like. You can also send me feedback via email at sloane@sloanekennedy.com

Join my Facebook Fan Group: Sloane's Secret Sinners

Connect with me:
www.sloanekennedy.com
sloane@sloanekennedy.com

ALSO BY SLOANE KENNEDY

(Note: Not all titles will be available on all retail sites)

The Escort Series
Gabriel's Rule (M/F)
Shane's Fall (M/F)
Logan's Need (M/M)

Barretti Security Series
Loving Vin (M/F)
Redeeming Rafe (M/M)
Saving Ren (M/M/M)
Freeing Zane (M/M)

Finding Series
Finding Home (M/M/M)
Finding Trust (M/M)
Finding Peace (M/M)
Finding Forgiveness (M/M)
Finding Hope (M/M/M)

The Protectors
Absolution (M/M/M)

Salvation (M/M)
Retribution (M/M)
Forsaken (M/M)
Vengeance (M/M/M)
A Protectors Family Christmas
Atonement (M/M)
Revelation (M/M)
Redemption (M/M)

Non-Series
Letting Go (M/F)

Printed in Great
Britain
by Amazon